SANTHA SCREAMED. HANDS QUICKLY COVERED HER MOUTH.

She felt the ripple of an evil so timeless that it transcended itself, thrived in its own universe, abided by its own laws.

Fingers worked at her clothes. Within an instant, Santha was naked. Carried by women who held her arms, her legs, she could see her body extended before her line of vision. Other hands were darting in between those that held her, pouring aromatic oils onto her breasts, her flat abdomen, and her flanks.

They had taken her to the courtyard. The sunlight was dying, shadows converging on everything. Santha was placed on a white and gold fabric. Then she blacked out....

THE RISHI

Leo Giroux, Jr.

IVY BOOKS • NEW YORK

Ivy Books
Published by Ballantine Books
Copyright © 1985 by Leo Giroux, Jr.

Grateful acknowledgment is made for permission to reproduce previously published material:

An excerpt from *The Yellow Scarf* by Lieutenant-General Sir Francis Tuker. Published by J.M. Dent & Sons Ltd., London. Copyright © 1961 held by Cynthia H. Tuker.

A quotation from *The Shorter Oxford English Dictionary*, third edition (revised with addenda, reprinted with corrections, 1959, 1962). Published by the Oxford University Press, Oxford, England.

An excerpt from the song "Celluloid Heroes" by Raymond Douglas Davies. Reproduced by kind permission of Davray Music Limited. Copyright © 1972 by Davray Music Limited.

Library of Congress Catalog Card Number: 85-10314

ISBN-0-8041-0111-6

This edition published by arrangement with M. Evans and Company, Inc.

Manufactured in the United States of America

First International Edition: July 1986
First U.S. Edition: March 1987

ACKNOWLEDGMENTS

I want to thank the following people:

Robert E. Briney, who published some of the better material on Thuggee in *The Rohmer Review*;

Bob Sampson, Chuck Patton, Jan Koltun, and Al Bradford for their helpful suggestions;

Norman Russell, affiliated with Harvard University's Museum of Comparative Zoology;

Phillip Vitti, Head of the Intelligence Division, Boston Police Department;

Joyce D. Shields, R.N., M.S., C.S., Clinical Specialist in Psychiatric Nursing;

and especially the late Eugene S. Dinan, Jr., for the hours of telephone talk that buoyed my spirits.

TO THE READER

The earliest record of the Indian secret society known as Thuggee is dated A.D. 1290. An estimated twelve million victims were prey to the deadly rumel of the Thug assassin.

Not until the 1830s and '40s was the cult discovered, then destroyed, by Sir William Henry ("Thuggee") Sleeman of the Bengal Army under the British Raj.

Sleeman accumulated much of the information known about the cult from various captured Thugs. Among them, the most famous and feared was Feringheea, of Brahmin descent, who bore the title the Prince of Thugs. Afterward he was pardoned and helped Sleeman destroy the Thug network that was widespread throughout India.

Thugs never spilled blood. They used only the rumel. A Thug killing served two purposes: to satisfy the destructive cravings of the Goddess Kali and for robbery. They considered the pickax, used to dig the graves of their victims, to be sacred.

Thugs often held high office in Indian society, continuing their cult practices in absolute secrecy. Thug bands consisted of ten to one hundred men. They were often named after the area they settled in. Thus there were Agureea Thugs (Agra), Arcotee Thugs (Arcot), and so on. Some Thugs used disguises; for example, the Chingurees pretended to be bullock drivers. There were even River Thugs, who strangled only in boats and used rivers for burial places.

Strange, but true, Hindu and Muslim Thugs were united peacefully in their heinous service to the Goddess Kali. The sole difference was that the Muslims preferred to call her Fatima, the sacred daughter of Mohammed, the Prophet.

Sometimes Kali was also called Devi, Bhowani, or Kunkali, depending again on preference and the section of India where the Thugs thrived.

It will be noted that the novel is set in the mid-1970s. This was close to the period of the Emergency, when the late Prime Minister Indira Gandhi incarcerated many of India's intellectuals. I chose the period to help establish the "free thinker" slant in Rama Shastri's nature.

Finallly, the part titles are the elements in a Sanskrit play. A glossary is included at the back of the novel.

Major-General Sleeman:	*Are you afraid of the spirits you murder?*
Nasir:	*Never, they cannot trouble us.*
Major-General Sleeman:	*And how do they not trouble you?*
Nasir:	*Are not the people whom we kill, killed by the orders of [Kali]?*

EXTRACTS FROM INVESTIGATIONS, *1835*,
*by Major-General Sir William Henry ("Thuggee") Sleeman
of the Bengal Army and the Indian Political Service*

Thug.* 1810. [Hindi thag, *Marathi* thag, thak *cheat,
swindler.] (With capital T.) One of an association of
professional robbers and murderers in India, who
strangled their victims.*

Thuggee.* 1837. [Hindi thagi *from* thag *THUG.] The
system of robbery and murder practiced by the Thugs.*

THE SHORTER OXFORD ENGLISH DICTIONARY

*(Pronounced toog *and* toog-ee.)

THE RISHI

PART ONE

VIJA

The Germ

ONE

India, 1975 — the Road to Lucknow

The village was burnished by the descending sun. The chatter of girls collecting offal from a buffalo herd cut into the hush. Doves rose and dotted the saffron sky above the muri paddies. A child wailed somewhere amid the congestion of mud huts. Then the silence returned.

Squatting behind the bullock cart, Chundra Bala whispered in Ramasi, the language of the Thug, to his son Dhan. He stared at the stationary holy man in the village center while he spoke. The tall sadhu, his lean, ash-crusted frame posed like a carved thing, blended into the settling twilight, another silhouette among the smear of village hovels. All the long day he'd stood beneath the relentless sun, swarms of flies settling on his ascetic profile, his closed eyelids. Chundra Bala shuddered.

Holy men were plentiful everywhere, but this sadhu was somehow different, he sensed. If Chundra's wife, who was chosen among many, hadn't dreamed of the coming of the Huzoor of late, he would have ignored the man. But the dreams were sent by the Goddess—dreams that never lied.

"What do you fear, Father?" asked his sixteen-year-old son.

Chundra choked as he suppressed the growl that rose at Dhan's disrespect. He stared back at the campfire, the men huddled around it awaiting his command. His black eyes smarted from the smoking dung cakes used for fuel. "Be still," he warned, "lest I punish you."

Dhan shrank back from the one who was supreme among the Stranglers.

Jadu, the Gravedigger, and his twin, Bidhan, an Arm Holder, joined them. "Is this the night?" they asked, swept away by their enthusiasm.

"Aeeeii—what has happened to our discipline?" chided the

3

Leader. "Yes, this is the night. Kali has granted us seven road-
weary travelers beyond the village rim for this night. Seven
deaths, seven graves, but if you persist in making such a din,
then there will be twenty graves instead—for twenty who wear
the masks of bullock drivers and whom the kotwal will gladly
execute."

Dhan watched the twins sheepishly retreat. He knew his
father was worried: the police were searching for them. After
the recent capture of the Jumaldehee Thugs at Hyderabad, all
India was aware that Thuggee had risen again. Well, at least
his band had buried the victims properly. To think that he,
Dhan, had scouted the forays at Barna, Unnao, and on the
Lucknow road, had found the proper grouping of travelers on
whom the Stranglers could use their deadly rumels.

To follow in Chundra's footsteps, to become a Thug-Guru.
Praise Devi that he had such a father!

Then the thought of Dhan's mother soon blotted out his
reverie, since she was as strange and unfathomable as the old
sadhu.

It was said that Gauri Bala had been different since the
delivery of her first son, Bhima. The ordeal of childbirth had
stirred her to offer herself to the goddess, and from all appear-
ances afterward, Kali had accepted. Gauri had gifts, everyone
said. Unusual gifts—of prophecy, of something called the evil
eye. And an additional power that Dhan was unsure of but that
nevertheless kept him at a respectful distance.

The village headman had been wary at first when Chundra
spoke with him. Was it not true that Thugs often roamed the
roads in disguise?

"Tell me about yourself," the man had urged.

"My drivers and I need rest for the night before we reach
Lucknow," lied Chundra.

Never was the headman direct. "You are from Uttar Pra-
desh?"

"Yes, from Purwa and from Orissa State before that. From
near Cuttack. Surely you did not question the seven travelers
over there as you do me?"

"Oh, but I did. They are doctors, scholars of anthropology

from the University of Lucknow. My nephew did verify to me their answers, since he once attended that place to study commerce." The headman's tone was cynical. "And here he loiters his days away in this village since then, jobless, and too educated to work."

"The seven are doctors, you say? Even the strange one in the robe and cowl?"

"No. He is a pilgrim. An acolyte, no doubt."

Chundra pointed to the holy man in the square. "There seems a likely teacher for any disciple. Did he come with them?"

"He arrived alone from the north somewhere, two weeks past. And there he has remained. A very holy man, indeed, I'm certain. He awaits a sign from some god before he moves on, I suppose. Who knows with these sadhus? They see and hear what we do not. Very well, then. Rest your men and bullocks in the village. You appear a simple man, as most of us are."

Thus did Chundra Bala earn the headman's trust and learn about the seven who had camped at the village boundary.

He then planned with his men that they would attack by moving around the village. Chundra's superstitious nature desired to keep the ancient sadhu at a distance.

To fool any villager looking their way, they stuffed their blanket rolls and left a Thug before the fire as a guardian of the cattle. The rest disappeared gradually into the night shadows, following Chundra among the muri paddies. Forty minutes later, with no moon to betray them, they studied the camp of the seven.

Two of the group were still awake, sitting before the fire on opposite sides. One seemed the eldest of the anthropologists. A huge man with a cloudburst of beard, he resembled a giant Sikh.

The figure opposite, whose back was to Chundra and his band, was in the lotus position, possibly meditating. That he was but a pilgrim and not a guru, whom it would have been ill luck to kill, did little to settle Chundra's nerves. The figure, who wore his cowl even in the daytime heat, was very odd.

Nevertheless, the Thug Leader gave the signal.

Ecstatic, young Dhan trailed behind the band, noting that the procedure was as before. One Strangler and two Arm Holders were assigned to each victim. The killings would be done in stages, since there weren't enough Thugs to do the job at once. Gravediggers were allowed to substitute temporarily as Holders. The boy wished that he, the sole Scout, were also included. But he was to observe—nothing more.

Yet it was an event: to be part of the darting shadows that brought death to others so swiftly, so deftly. They neared those farthest from the fire. The night was warm, and several of the sleepers were scattered over a wide area. Dhan's pulse quickened as the moment neared. He started as the first victim broke into a loud snore. Before him three figures lowered to the ground.

Gently one of the Holders lifted the head while the other Holder covered the mouth. The snore ended, and Dhan saw the victim's eyes open wide. The Strangler eased the rumel around the throat, the slipknot let go, and the still head was lowered. Dhan turned in time to see another sleeper dispatched, but the rapidity of the murders outsped his zeal. Already five of the travelers had been eliminated. Praise Devi, She was truly with them tonight.

The finale was the two by the fire. The Thugs moved forward.

Immediately the aged anthropologist was set upon, he used his massive bulk and strong shoulders to shake off the assassins. He pummeled, kicked, gouged, roaring to his companions, "Robbers! Robbers!" Young Dhan, fearing that the cry would alert the village, leaped into the fray.

Chundra, meanwhile, had chosen the pilgrim. At the exact instant the anthropologist was attacked, Chundra ventured forth. The rumel swung around the neck of the pilgrim, who offered no resistance. The rumel tightened.

Then, eyes agog, Chundra Bala froze.

Someone had seized his arms. He felt fingers digging into his tunic, an awesome grip on his wrists preventing him from using the silk scarf. There was a body, firm, solid, pressing against his back and, with it, the mingled heavy odors of musk and burned flesh. Somewhere, too, was a distant clinking, the sound of anklets.

"Stop him!" he ordered Bidhan, one of his Arm Holders.

"Stop who, Teacher?" Bidhan asked.

"Take him off me!"

Now the two Arm Holders in unison: "Who, Teacher?"

"Fools, can't you see him? He has my wrists. Am I deluded? Is there no one holding me?"

"There is no one, Teacher," replied Bidhan after a pause, and with that he passed one of his hands around Chundra's body, touching even the wrists.

With a growl, the Strangler exerted his muscles, pushing back against whatever held him. Sweat trickled into his eyes. Through the haze he saw that the battle with the anthropologist had ended; but someone was wailing, imploring the Goddess for forgiveness. Fools, the villagers would hear ... Chundra made a final effort to strangle the pilgrim. The force holding him became stronger, the grip painful beyond endurance. Chundra's spine chilled as a command was kneaded into his brain: "Don't!"

Without hesitation he let go and brushed the Arm Holders away.

At the same time a Thug emerged before the fire, wailing, "I have spilled blood! May Devi forgive me, but in fear that the big one would cry again for help, I took this knife from a corpse and struck at his heart."

"And now you would awake the village with your lamentations," chided Chundra. "It is wrong to spill blood but worse still to reveal our presence."

The Thug fell to the ground, sobbing and beating his breast. Chundra ignored him. Although the force no longer held him, he still felt the fingers, long and supple, the nails digging into his wrists. He rubbed them, staring down at the pilgrim, wondering why he had been spared.

"Who are you," he asked in awe, "that even Devi would save you?"

"Teacher," urged Bidhan, interrupting, "let us flee. We are

accursed, since one of us has spilled blood. And your son Dhan—the big one did kill him."

"He speaks the truth," said another voice. "The boy's head was crushed against the tree."

"Let me see who you are," persisted Chundra, approaching the pilgrim, deaf to what the two Thugs were saying. He drew back the pilgrim's cowl.

"Your son Dhan, Teacher—dead..." repeated Bidhan.

"Yes, dead," the other stressed.

Chundra was listening to another voice, remembering that he had heard it tonight in this clearing and that it had spoken to him before of the new Huzoor to come: the Thug among Thugs to lead them all. All.

Gauri's prophecy, uttered in those dark hours, alone in their private chamber...

For a long time Chundra stared into the eyes of the pilgrim while his men pleaded that they leave. Only when the gaze of the pilgrim wavered to a spot behind Chundra did the Strangler rise and turn. There, like part of the smoke, stood the aged sadhu. The firelight snapped at his closed eyes like a ruddy whip. The pilgrim stood then and approached the holy man. The sadhu moved, the pilgrim followed. Watching, Chundra's consciousness burst with understanding.

"Return to your homes," the Thug ordered his second-in-command. "I will join you later."

"But your son Dhan, Teacher? He is dead."

Chundra's eyes focused on the slight lifeless form in Bidhan's arms. "But Dhan was to be safe from danger! He was just a Scout." Chundra's throat made a gargling sound. He finally asked, "Why should he be dead?" He looked at his men as if for guidance, but they were silent. And then, against his will, his gaze returned to the darkness where two men trekked toward what he knew was north.

"You must now become his father," he told the second-in-command, his voice breaking. "Do as is fitting for a son."

Then Chundra breathed deeply, his eyes a mirror of the embers in the fire, and left them.

TWO

Boston, 1975 — Beacon Hill

Santha Wrench opened the casement window and looked out at Lime Street. The morning air was damp from last night's rain. The façade of the stuccoed town house across the narrow street was still rain-streaked. In front, the ornate grillwork of its courtyard gate glistened from one of the continuously lit gaslights of Beacon Hill. Santha shivered in the biting cold, tightened her robe around her, and closed the window.

She sat down at the kitchen table and sipped the rest of her jasmine tea. The strains of Villa-Lobo's *Bachianas Brasileiras* filtered into her thoughts, and, gradually but persistently, George Buchan's face superimposed itself upon the succession of grim memories that had been with her since waking.

Santha brought her teacup and saucer to the sink, went into the living room, and looked at the apartment in frustration. Opened books were strewn about on the lamp table, on the mantelpiece, on a pile of volumes next to her reading chair. The place hadn't been vacuumed in a week, and a bra dangled from the edge of the stereo console. She had left it there the night before while hurrying to bed, exhausted. For months Santha had been working overtime as editor for the new Peabody Museum catalog of Indian artifacts. She had wanted to keep very busy during this especially difficult time, but to end up living in a slovenly way was certainly overdoing it.

Santha resolved to clean house as soon as possible.

Then, noting the time on the wall clock, she headed for the bathroom to shower. As she neared the hallway, Santha's eyes rose to a cotton wall hanging of an Indian girl in a moonlit swale plaiting her hair. A smile was on her face as she sat beneath a teakwood tree. Obviously the girl was expecting the

9

young prince, who watched her from behind a bush. Santha
had purchased the hanging in Madras years ago while traveling
with her parents. Although it had no artistic value, she kept it
for sentimental reasons. During her early teen years, she'd often
substituted herself for the girl.

At the moment the smile seemed to be displaced by a thick
shadow, a smudge that hid the mouth totally. Santha paused,
looked again. The smile was back, the ominous swathe of
darkness gone. Santha shook her head, unbelieving, and after
a few seconds went into the hall.

Later, while dressing, Santha Wrench thought, This isn't
the first time I've seen the Shadow on things around me.

It had started in the last month of summer. As she walked
into Lime Street on a bright, sunny day, the housefronts and
brick sidewalk had been shadowy with a depth that was almost
liquid. Santha had been gripped with an urge to run away, but
the ground shifted suddenly, like a minor quake, and everything
became normal again. Days later, the face of the Peabody
Museum had appeared to be drenched with treacle. That, too,
dissolved immediately.

But the third occurrence was the worst of all: entering the
large museum safe that held shelves of artifacts, Santha Wrench
had felt the Shadow engulf her like a living presence. The
claustrophobic nightness had made her scream, and only then
did it vanish. When other employees had rushed in, concerned,
Santha had lied and said she'd seen a mouse.

And now she was imagining the dark thing to be here in
the apartment! Santha pulled on her pantyhose and wondered
what Dr. George Buchan, psychiatrist, would make of these
hallucinations. She was certain he would consider that they'd
been happening since her mother Kamala's recent death. It was
only logical for George to think that way. In fact, her own view
was in total agreement.

The lamplight fell on the hand prints on the wall that ran
from ceiling to floorboard. Santha felt a sudden deep pain that
momentarily gagged her. Playfully, she had created the column
by staining her hands. Kamala had never accepted the good
humor intended, since Indian village women did the same with

cow dung in their homes. Santha had argued vehemently that she had a right to do what she pleased with her apartment. The dungy facsimiles had now been transformed into a painful jest, however.

Santha's gaze went from her sunburst-yellow bed quilt—imported from Delhi—to the pile of textile samples called chudders on a chest in the corner. Going to the dresser, she touched the vermilion paste for the tikka mark she never allowed herself to use and fingered her two teakwood boxes of jewelry and a purplish stone amulet of Ganesha, the elephant god. The old yearning to go back to India, to wear a sari, to talk Hindi, and to feel like an Indian woman returned.

Santha let her hand dangle limply above the dresser top, and it slowly moved, found its way to the opposite side. There were all the modern toilet articles found in any American drugstore. Among them was a framed magazine photograph of John Lennon and Yoko Ono. Schizoid Santha Wrench, she thought bitterly.

She found her wristwatch among the clutter, put it on, and, noting it was ten-fifteen, hurried her dressing. Her Volkswagen Bug was in the shop for repairs, and she'd have to take the subway to Cambridge. She headed for the hall closet and her winter coat. The darkness of the hall disappeared. Santha blinked in the sudden bright flash.

Men who talked, who laughed without sound were there, waiting for her.

Santha Wrench wondered why she felt no fear. After all, she was in this strange place now, and these strange men were sitting on a mound. Stranger still was the quiet, the great, vast hush.

This was some arid part of the Deccan. In her grandfather's library in Delhi had been a gilt-edged book with a succession of photographs of the Indian peninsula. The same spot, this blistering expanse of scrubland, was in one of them. The same trees, like long necks with tufted heads . . . yes, it was the very same bleak, twilight place, with a smear of rock formations in the distance.

But why here? Why and how and when had she arrived here? And why were the men waiting?

The rocks looked old. They had a weariness about them. Santha thought of erosion. Down. Everything was decreasing, being pulled down. The wind swept across the expanse and the trees nearly doubled over. Santha blinked, shook her head, attempted to scatter the scene somehow, fragment it into the desiccating wind. The glowering purple sky seemed to close in as if it would crash upon her, collide with the turbulent plain.

But there was no sound. No noise where the men sat, no breath from the wind, no rustle in the trees.

Then impressions filtered through Santha Wrench's mind and she understood. To the men she was invisible. And they, the entire landscape, waited. There was something she had to see, learn about.

Heading toward the men now, Santha suddenly felt a silent buffeting, a wind urging, pushing her forward. Her hair fanned out like that of a bird with black plumage into the undertow of a monsoon. She crossed the desolation, reached the long finger of piled earth.

And faced twenty-two men squatting on their haunches on the barely detectable mound. They were talking, laughing, eating from their pouches and fishermen's creels: muscular, nut-brown men, wearing only loincloths and faded yellow turbans. At one end of the mound, separate and, for some unknown reason, meaningful, was a pickax. It was upright, embedded in the loose earth.

The men continued their meal while she watched. The wind poured forth suddenly from the scarps on the horizon, raced across the flatland, and glided in an upward sweep to their faces. Their eyes were restless black specks in the gloom.

Santha circled the long mound. The men and what they were doing here was a mystery; yet she knew that she, too, shared their knowledge.

The wind grew stronger. Bits of earth from the mound spiraled, swirled. The men now concentrated on a tall, gaunt speaker. His sunken eyes glowed with fierce understanding, above cheekbones as eroded as the distant peaks. The encroach-

THE RISHI 13

ing purple discolored his slack jaw as he talked. The backs of
his hands had birthmark mottlings; knobbed, commanding fingers played with the silk of his turban. Unlike those of the rest,
it was free of his head and splayed like a writhing thing before
him, knotted at one end and looping over an imaginary object.
The man was teaching, and the men were very still, tense with
expectation.

The wind buoyed the silk until it began to jerk and snap.
She could almost hear the quick, violent tug of the wind on its
greasy yellow surface. The men stared in hypnotic fascination,
and she with them. Then the wind, ever stronger, tore at the
other turbans. They began to unwind, streamered out like banners, ribboning into the maelstrom . . . like crepe at a festival.

The spiraling dirt had turned into a cloud. Thickening, it
hazed the men into moving silhouettes. Only the part of the
mound with the pickax was clearly delineated. Cracks, a series
of zigzags, were pulling the dirt into holes. The entire crust
was bursting like a powdery shell, spurting soil in geysers of
ocher, spilling into the creels with their remnants of fruit, peppers stuffed with shrimp, and goor sugar.

The side where she stood collapsed in wedges, following
the zigzag pattern as it extended along the mound.

Even in the dim lighting she could see into the crumbling
ground.

Santha saw hair.

Santha saw torsos.

Santha saw hands, legs.

And Santha saw faces. More and more faces.

Santha knew then what the pickax was for.

The mound was a grave, a long depository for dozens of
corpses laid out side by side. Dressed in their clothes from life,
they had been placed evenly, with a concern for order. But the
eyes of the dead were still open! The terror that can come only
from the unexpected was etched there: the telltale sign of an
abrupt end.

She backed in revulsion. Then it quickly left her. A shocked
part of her watched her consciousness accept with eagerness
the battered grave and its contents. It was like watching a

stranger. She heard herself sigh with great relief and bend close
to one of the heads and gasp with excitement, with glee. Santha,
the Santha she had always known, felt she was now fragmenting. Her mind screamed at the ghoul in her body who so
ecstatically breathed in death. The fragment that was herself
hurtled away into a wall of nightness.

Holding the knob of the hallway closet to steady herself, Santha
Wrench took in large gulps of air. Finally her legs steadied and
the sudden faintness she'd felt left her. Santha then groped her
way into the living room and to the couch. Her eyes searched
the space around her, expecting the wild Deccan landscape to
return any second.

The Villa-Lobos music pulled her into the present, and she
knew that only a few minutes had passed. It had all seemed to
happen in a half-breath! In the very arid section of the Deccan,
an area she'd never been in during her former years in India.
Why the Deccan? Why such a bleak, such an alien and turbulent
place?

Her mind cleared more; quickly, wanting to regain command. Her fingers seized and bunched the afghan as waves,
deep, cold tremulations, shocked through her. A final intake
of air that lingered, ended with a tremendous physical release,
and she was restored.

It wasn't a hallucination, Santha Wrench concluded. It was
more like a real event. It was like walking onto a movie set.
For a brief spell she'd been in India again. It was similar to
. . . teleportation.

Santha had heard more than once that yogis and gurus sometimes teleported. She'd never totally believed those stories.
There were so many fantastic accounts of out-of-the-body experiences told in India.

She sensed then that Something within her desired that she
appear normal as quickly as possible. She was becoming calm,
even serene. Santha rose abruptly and went to the closet again,
took out her coat and a white scarf. She combed her hair, put
on the coat and scarf, and shut off the stereo. She moved
automatically, completely engrossed in her actions. For a sec-

ond she lingered at the door, but the strange calmness drove her on and she left.

Walking along Charles Street, Santha became more assured with each step. The brisk day vitalized her; a breeze tugged at her hair and she wished she'd worn the coat with the hood. On the corner of Pinckney Street, Santha stopped and stared down it to the building facing Storrow Drive, the house on the left-hand corner. There, in her parents' apartment, her father, Stephen Wrench, sat alone and depressed in his bedroom. He had been that way ever since Kamala's death in July. Santha urged herself on.

Arriving at Charles Street Station, she managed to cross the overhead walkway in the buffeting wind from the Charles River and descended to the subway platform. Once in the barely filled car, Santha looked through her reflection in the train window and thought of how eager she was to see George.

But I won't tell him about the "event," she decided. George would never accept teleportation as a reality. Never. Then, for a brief instant, she wondered if her decision was entirely her own. But the thought was fleeting. George's face came to the fore again.

They had met seven months ago, when Kamala was alive, when everything was so different. In fact, Kamala had been with her at the concert at the Isabella Stewart Gardner Museum that clear Sunday afternoon, with the scent of lilacs everywhere, full of spring pronouncement.

The concert was a series of string quartets by Mozart, Almeyda, and Debussy. George Buchan sat to her left, with two people between them. Several times during the concert she had noticed his neck craning out among the upright-postured listeners as he stared her way. Once it was over, he approached her and said, "Two weeks from now they'll be starting a Beethoven quartet cycle." He towered above her in a three-piece suit of charcoal gray.

"Well?" he said, waiting.

"Well, what?" she asked, coolly.

"Well, I'm George Buchan . . ." He smiled. It won her.

She smiled back, replied, "Santha Wrench."

Since then they had been seeing each other—lunches, dinners, concerts, movies, plays, sporting events (Santha had discovered baseball), ambles along the Esplanade watching the Harvard boating crews practice, some sailing on the Charles River. All of it very easy and possible, with him living a block away at Otis Place.

The train arrived at Harvard. The station was crowded, mostly with students. Santha moved through the mob, a blur of faces until she saw a woman in a sari accompanied by two men. They chattered freely in Marathi, the language of Maharashtra State. The men had cameras dangling from straps over their shoulders. Santha thought of the many beautiful saris she'd worn in those past days in India.

Yet, once in America, Kamala had felt that Santha, at least, should dress as American as possible. Santha was, after all, an American citizen, Kamala stressed, and Santha should feel that she belonged. "But I've never felt that I don't," Santha told her. "What have clothes to do with it?" But Santha had obeyed.

Had obeyed . . . only to find that in central Boston and Cambridge many Americans dressed as though they came from some other land. Santha thought of it as costuming. And, envying the Hindu woman her sari, Santha thought what a wonderful bit of frivolity costuming was.

Aboveground, Santha Wrench rushed to Grendel's Den. That morning George had seen a patient at the Stillman Infirmary at Harvard's Holyoke Center. He would be finished by now and waiting for her at a table on Grendel's enclosed porch. When she arrived, Santha darted into the rest room.

She studied herself in the mirror, took a comb from her purse, and ran it through her shoulder-length hair. It seemed a separate, black, live thing, tangled and billowing out as if she were again in the Deccan monsoon. Stubbornly it resisted the comb. Santha stopped, stood on tiptoe, and leaned forward to study her reflection more closely.

George mustn't see her strain from witnessing the aftermath of a massacre. The dead in that long grave had been murdered.

Her instincts said so. Amazing, how well she was handling it, though; that her consciousness accepted the fact so easily.

But maybe her eyes . . . Santha stared hard at them. They were wide, and suddenly they liquefied, deep brown floating agates in a still, chalky pool. Santha grabbed and held fast to the basin.

She recovered when the face became just that: the same face she'd always known, narrow, with high cheekbones, the hollows beneath them like small, smudgy bruises. The mouth a suggestion of miniature curved bows, the nose sloping slightly with the nostrils tucked in, the skin almost a Dravidian dark. An overall lean face, with a body much fuller than the face promised.

Santha was dabbing at her eyes with a wet handkerchief when a pounding sounded on the door. "Someone wants to use the rest room," a woman's voice shouted. Santha took a deep breath, then exited with a meek "Excuse me."

When Santha joined George on the restaurant porch for brunch, he was reading a current issue of *American Artist*. Oil painting was his hobby, and it had intrigued Santha greatly that this belied her usual image of a psychiatrist.

Santha bent close to him, kissed him on the cheek, gently stroked his beard, and sat down. She eyed his fruit frappé. "Hmm, looks good. I think I'll have one, too."

Her voice tone was level, natural, and she thought, Incredible, how Something is keeping me so calm. It wants me that way.

"Hungry?" he asked.

"Not very."

He groaned. "Well, I am. What are you going to have?"

"I think a salad."

A waitress came to their table and they ordered.

"Looks like it's going to be another cloudy day," George said, looking out the porch window.

"We could always go to the cinema if it's too dreary."

He shifted in his seat uneasily. "I thought we'd do more productive things. Like get your father out of the house, for example. Take him out for some air. A ride in the car, perhaps."

"He's not your responsibility, George."

"Santha, the man has been hibernating for too long. If it continues..."

"I know he's depressed, but he'll pull out of it soon. Daddy is no ordinary man, George. He's led an adventurous life, has seen death many, many times. He's FBI now, worked for Interpol, was OSS in the Second World War. He's been through much worse."

"Has he? Santha, the sudden death of a spouse is a unique trauma for the survivor. Depression and guilt often follow, and—"

"Guilt? Why should Daddy feel guilt about Mother's dying? He loved her so totally."

The food arrived, and they were silent. When the waitress left, George continued, "Don't you see, Santha? Your father was just about everything a man could be for your mother. He might feel guilty because he couldn't prevent her death. That he missed out on doing something that could've saved her. It's often illogical thinking, but not uncommon."

"He'll be all right. I just know he will. He doesn't need to be hospitalized, George."

"You're angry."

"Yes, it pisses me off when you talk about Daddy that way— as though he were somebody mentally unfit! Give him time, George; give him space to recover, will you!"

A moment later, Santha said softly, "It's just that you never got to know him very well before Mother died.... He was always so together, so well groomed, so confident. And so damn irascible. So wonderfully irascible..."

"I still think we ought to go see him."

Santha nodded. "I'm sorry, George; I didn't mean to be so unfair. You're the psychiatrist, the M.D. If anyone could spot what's wrong with Daddy, it's you."

That's just the problem, she thought—how would he analyze what happened to me this morning? Panic nearly overcame her, and she dropped her fork in the salad plate. *You mustn't ever tell George*, Something warned her. Thoughts alien and like splinters of ice darted through her mind. *Then he'll conclude you're insane and leave you.*

Santha pressed her fingers against her temple. She heard George call her name and stared at him.

"What is it?" he was asking.

"A terrible headache." She reached into her purse, took out a bottle of Tylenol. "My period started today."

Later they drove across the Larz Anderson Bridge into Boston, then circled along Storrow Drive toward Beacon Hill. Despite the lack of sun, the Esplanade was packed with idlers, joggers, and dog walkers. Passing the Hatch Shell, Santha's eyes misted, remembering the many times she and Kamala had attended outdoor concerts there. George Buchan parked his Audi on Otis Place, near his house, and they walked north along Brimmer Street to Pinckney. They entered the massive old apartment building. Santha had bent to unlock the lobby door when she decided to check the mail. She extracted a few advertising brochures and a letter.

"Oh," she exclaimed, "a letter from Uncle Ram. He was Dad's closest friend in India and a very famous official in the Special Service Branch of the Indian police."

In the alcove they passed the old, caged elevator and took the stairs to the second floor. "Daddy," she called, "it's me, Santha," opening the apartment door and peering in. And, "Damn, there isn't a light on." She flicked the switch, and they went along a corridor that led to a living room with an extremely high ceiling. Santha put on a lamp near a couch. There, seated, an overweight, gray-haired man stared at nothing in particular.

"Daddy, there's a letter from Uncle Ram!" Santha cried in a loud voice, plopping herself down next to him.

"It's from Hyderabad, Daddy. Look, I'll open it and read it to you. Isn't it just grand hearing from Uncle Ram again?"

Santha hesitated, watching Stephen Wrench's immobile face. If only he'd flick an eye, she thought, only a little. Finally she sighed and began to read, skipping the part where the writer offered his condolences about "dearest Kamala."

"Listen, Daddy," she urged: " 'I'm afraid, Stephen, old friend, that soon I'll have to leave Mother India. Indira Gandhi has no great love for yours truly, and lately I've been followed everywhere, I'm certain. A babu has been assigned to my office to do our paperwork, and the stupid fellow is obviously a government spy. Of course, I've been outspoken against Indira's current bad manners of locking up anyone with an IQ above 125. Methinks she fears Free Thinkers. I wonder not only about my freedom, but about my safety, too, of late. If I do have to flee, I can think of no place I'd rather be than with you and Santha, old friend. Could you possibly arrange things with the American Government? Remind them of how I helped you in the OSS during the war and of that affair in Calcutta in '62 when your CIA made use of my resources. They just might be grateful.'

"Did you hear that, Daddy! He wants to come here! To us! And he wants you to help him! Daddy, did you hear?"

Softly, then: "I heard, Santha."

"Oh, Daddy—yes, you heard! And listen, there's more: 'Steve, the shame of it, though, is that if I leave now it will be so damnably inappropriate.

"'I am onto something, old comrade, that I'm certain would stir the sleeping adventurer in you, too. Ready? There's been a Thuggee uprising again! After more than a hundred years! The thing seems to be happening everywhere. Through my spy network I've been able to capture fragments of every conceivable Thug band imaginable. Think of it, Steve—Thuggee! Something we used to talk about as having missed. Something from old India, the India of Sleeman.

"'I captured my first band three weeks ago—'"

Santha stopped reading.

George looked at her, puzzled by her silence.

Finally Stephen Wrench said, "Read on, Santha."

And again, "Santha?"

"Yes, Daddy," in almost a whisper. "'. . . three weeks ago in Hyderabad. . . .'"

"Louder, please, Santha."

"Yes, Dad. '. . . Hyderabad. . . . They'd given me a mighty chase from the Ganges Basin to the Deccan. It seems they'd murdered some twenty travelers down there, but when they buried them in that God-awful scrubland, some of the dead wouldn't stay put.'"

Santha stopped and looked up.

"Go on! Please go on," Wrench coached his daughter.

"'The graves . . .'" She stopped again.

"Are you all right?" her father demanded.

Without answering, she continued the letter to the end.

"'The graves weren't deep enough, and the wind uncovered them. Finding that many dead buried together gave us the clue. You remember the Thug practice of burying their victims. It's damned intoxicating, Steve.

"'Can't tarry now. Must go and question the leader of these Jumaldehee Thugs, since that's the group they are. I await your reply concerning my eventual evacuation. My best to what I'm certain is a Santha of great loveliness. Ever your brother in spirit, Rama Shastri.'"

George Buchan, no longer able to tolerate the silence that followed, asked, "What is Thuggee?"

Wrench looked up. He acted as if he'd only realized that George was in the room.

"Thuggee," the big man repeated, half to himself. Then his voice rose. "Thuggee is a secret religious sect in India, handed down from father to son. Their main goal is to murder through strangulation to appease the bloodlust of the goddess Kali. The practitioners are often robbers as well. Also they're called Deceivers, since they could be your next-door neighbor and you'd never be able to detect it."

George became excited. Stephen Wrench had spoken an entire paragraph, not the usual one-word replies, or, worse, no reply whatsoever, that they had got from him since Kamala's death. He looked at Santha, but her head was lowered, staring at the letter. What was wrong with her?

Wrench muttered, "Ram. Good old Ram," excused himself, and went into the bedroom. The door was slightly ajar, and George heard a voice boom, "Operator, I want a Mr. Horace Birch in Washington, D.C."

"Santha," George said, crossing to her, "that woke your father up. Listen to him!"

Santha nodded. She was rereading Rama Shastri's letter as if she hadn't done so correctly the first time. The part about the bodies found in the Deccan. Over and over she read it.

THREE

Rajasthan, near Jaipur

Krishna Rasul. Rama Shastri tried to concentrate on the interrogation reports. Krishna Rasul. The once distant drone of the plane in the bright, cloudless sky had changed to a louder *burr* as it neared. Sometimes the engine coughed, stopped for a second, only to resume *burr*-ing. If only it could just stay stopped, he thought. Plummet straight down out of the shimmering brightness, like a modern, metallic Icarus too close to the sun.

Yes, Krishna Rasul. Come to investigate. Come to meddle, to interfere in this new thing. This new incredible happening that made all the treachery, the omnipresent betrayal around him, somehow tolerable.

Shastri shifted his haunches in the bamboo chair for greater comfort, placed his elbows on the small table before him, and tried again to concentrate.

"'Thuggee? What is Thuggee?'" he read.

And on . . .

Interrogator:	Surely you have heard of Thuggee. All India knows of Thuggee.
Ajit Majumdar:	Sir, you seek to put thoughts in my mind that have never existed before. I am but a poor irrigation farmer and know nothing of this matter you call Thuggee.

Interrogator:	Didn't your father tell you such? One knows of Thuggee in India as one knows of Vishnu or of the Ganges.
Ajit Majumdar:	I have never known of any such Thuggee. Never did my father or my father's father speak of it to me. Or my many uncles. Or my older brothers. Or my mother and my sisters, even.

"We have visitors," Shastri's aide said then, a note of sadness in his voice. He was standing on the veranda steps. "They've sent Rasul again, I wager."

"No one else, Gopal."

"What program will they initiate this time?"

"Sabotage. Always it is sabotage of any progress we might make. Be assured of that."

"Everything has changed so much, Rama. In the old days, even in the time of the British Raj, we were never interfered with like this."

Shastri sighed, pushed the papers away. He could see now the plane's colors, the red fuselage, the rest a flash of yellow. Rasul always made certain his private plane was freshly painted. The psychological strategy was obvious. Even from a distance, as it lowered from the sky, you became aware. Indira's hatchet man was coming, coming to disrupt whatever Shastri was doing. Sweet revenge. Better he had never questioned the woman's rule. Maybe.

"Send Das to me," he directed. "Quickly."

When Das appeared, the plane had finally landed on the makeshift field.

"What have you discovered?" he asked of the dust-stained figure in the shadows. Das, the best police spy in India, could infiltrate anything. Nearly. Too bad he couldn't do so in Indira's coterie. But Rasul knew Das. Rasul had once worked with Shastri. In fact, he was still all policeman in mind.

"They finally trust me. Have I not been in the prisoner's compound for two weeks now?" Das boasted. "They believe my story that I was a Mooltanee Thug somehow separated from my band and captured. The one Ajit Majumdar is still suspicious, but I manage to keep my distance from him."

"I will order that he be placed in isolation. That way he can't possibly interfere with your work. In fact, since"—Shastri pointed to the plane—"Rasul has just arrived, no doubt he will insist that he interrogate Majumdar. He always feels he can do a better job than we have done. That will ensure Ajit's absence for a few hours if my isolation order is countermanded. Das, I must have as much information as possible by tonight."

"They speak with me. But little. They assume that I know more than I do, I'm sure, but still they hesitate. Many times in the past, Thug sects have betrayed each other. What you ask will be extremely difficult."

"Das, this may be my last chance," Shastri hurried his speech. The two specks that had emerged from the plane were now walking toward the police station. "We already know this for certain: all the Thug sects have arisen at once in India—the Agureea Thugs, the Arcotee Thugs, Hindustanee Thugs, Chinguree or Mooltanee Thugs, Jumaldehee Thugs. There must be a reason: a sign, an omen. Perhaps someone claims to have had a vision. Most likely some Leader has sprung up among them with a new plan of service to Kali. He must be very powerful, to have united all these sects who in the past often hated each other. We must find who and what is intended."

"You assume much, Ram. We have no proof yet that—"

"I have to assume. India has not seen this much Thuggee since the 1830s. Get back to the compound and return with something definite for me tonight. Tonight, Das. You are the best among my spies."

Shastri entered the bungalow, determined not to remain on the veranda to be Rasul's official greeter. No; here, Rasul came to him. Shastri was still head of the Special Service Branch of India's police, and as long as he remained in that position, on kotwal ground, Rasul would have to seek him out. He wandered through the spacious, shadowy rooms, looking for Ileana Heng. This kotwalee, the entire prisoners' compound adjacent, the other buildings that housed the police and their families, had once been a cantonment during the British rule. The makeshift airfield had once been a parade ground. With rigorous honesty, now looking back, Shastri asked himself if he preferred those days. Despite the fact that he'd always wanted India to have herself for herself.

No, he didn't, he quickly concluded. He really didn't. Even with the tremendous efficiency the British had had at times. Even with the tendency to be abstract about solutions that he found so common among India's rulers, when an official at a health center would often consider a cholera epidemic God's will rather than do something about a contaminated well. Which was why Shastri had become an agnostic so long ago.

Yet the government of the moment continued, as had the governments of the past, to tell the rest of the world that India's Aggrandizing Programs were working better than ever: that the caste system was dying; that starvation, overpopulation, illiteracy, and sanitation problems were being solved. Shastri accepted such propaganda, even understood why it existed. What he hadn't accepted about the Indira Gandhi rule, however, had been the constant suppression and arrests of whoever questioned it.

Thus he was watched always, of late.

He found Ileana in the west wing. She was playing fan-tan with Sinjar, the handsome young clerk. From the smile on her face and the pile of rupees at her elbow, he saw she'd been winning, probably by cheating, as usual. Pausing at Shastri's emergence, Ileana placed a cigarette in a long holder. Lighting up, she then turned in her chair, the slit of her tight yellow and green-bordered dress exposing a reach of thigh. She was dressed in something very similar, Shastri remembered, when he'd taken her out of an opium den near Lashio—centuries ago, it seemed now. Time enough for love. Time enough, too, to put her pipe aside, which had never quite happened.

Steve Wrench had warned him about that. Steve had been connected with Interpol then, and together they'd gone to Burma. Both were tracing the source of a drug traffic that had spread as far north in India as Uttar. Centuries ago. And someday, too, she'll betray me, Shastri thought.

Already there were little signs. The stupid babu spy, Sinjar, was attracted to her, and Shastri sensed by her covert glances at the boy that she was finally responding. Shastri repressed the rage in himself. He had never felt the twenty-two years' discrepancy between them before.

"Krishna Rasul is here," he announced.

"The Snake to face the Little Mongoose," she replied, with that oriental descriptive flavoring she affected. He wished for the thousandth time he'd never taught her to read, especially since that British tourist had introduced her to Sax Rohmer.

"Tell the women to prepare food. I suppose they'll stay to share a meal. Sinjar."

The young man leaped to his feet. He was afraid of the great Rama Shastri. The older man was unimpressed. Many had feared the great Mahatma Gandhi, too. Still they assassinated him.

"Rasul will interrogate the prisoners, I believe. Have your shorthand notebook ready."

Sinjar excused himself and left.

"Sorry to interrupt your game, my dear." Shastri fingered the fan-tan cards. "How much did you fleece him for?"

"I lost count. Ah, Little Mongoose, you look so weary. Let me hold you and perhaps your Ileana can fill your mind with imaginings"—she kissed him—"of restorative carnal delights when the day is done."

"Restorative carnal delights," he repeated. "You never cease to amaze me."

He cupped her breasts in his hands and bent, kissing them. A long, lingering kiss. There was no helping it. Some things do end, he thought.

He pushed her gently away as a servant entered the room and announced that Krishna Rasul was waiting.

Walking back to the front of the bungalow, Shastri tried to discipline his thoughts, but a sadness had swept over him now. He'd miss her, he admitted that. That he'd miss India he always knew. But India was no balm, no comfort, when aging. Yes, he'd grow older if he left India without her. Ileana had kept him young.

When he met Krishna Rasul he saw that the big man was startled.

"It shocks me that Rama Shastri, whom evildoers fear so greatly, is a man of such slight stature."

"If you measure greatness by girth, Rasul, you must have a high opinion of yourself."

Rasul was skilled enough as a politician to smile; a smile that openly hinted of events to come. "Now, tell me, Rama Shastri. What is this about Thuggee?"

The two walked out on the veranda, which was the coolest spot available.

Shastri told him everything: the discovery in the Deccan of nineteen bodies all in a row, nineteen mounds of decay in hastily dug graves, redolent with the garish colors of death in the glare of a Deccan noon. Shastri was especially vivid here, as he saw Rasul shift in his seat uneasily.

Then of the pursuit and the final capture at Hyderabad, how Shastri had placed his men on alert, how other Thug bands had been seized, his theories about it. In short, everything but of Das. What Das was, hopefully, discovering was for Shastri alone.

Rasul stretched, his white tunic making his massive chest look larger. He placed his hands over his stomach, interlocked his fingers, said, "I've spoken to her about it already. The minute I received your report."

For some reason Rasul always referred to Indira as "her," as if her sex had become hallowed along with her office.

"Oh."

"She and the rest..." Shastri made a mental note of the "rest." They, too, were never named by Rasul, but the word was spoken with some reverence. Ever the peasant, Shastri concluded; this son of a sugarcane grower had never had it so good. Such homage to "her" and "them," the new gods.

"...have a plan."

"Ah, a plan."

"A plan."

Rasul waited. Then, impatient, "You don't even ask what it is!"

"Very well, then. What is it?"

"You are not very respectful, it seems, Shastri. Are you perhaps more respectful toward her opposition?"

"Ah, how direct of you, Rasul."

"Well, are you?"

"One of her opposition, I hear, is an old man who drinks his own waste daily. No, I'm not very respectful of that, either."

"Then be very attentive. It is a good plan."

"A good plan."

"Must you repeat me? It is a good plan. Now I will speak of it."

"Do so."

"The government will make an agreement that if the Thugs give themselves up, no charges will be brought against them."

Shastri was silent.

"Have you nothing to say?"

"Thugs, Rasul, are known for their secrecy. No one can be more secretive than a Thug in India. Sometimes even their own families have no idea that they belong to the sect. I would be very surprised, Rasul, that they would change centuries of tradition merely because the government asked them to."

The big man stared. He raised his hands after a while and slapped his knees. "Well, there it is—settled. Now may I speak to the Leader of these Jumaldehees that you captured?"

"I expected you might want to interrogate him. The clerk that was assigned to me is ready to take shorthand."

"Good. Good. Let us be done with it. I must leave before nightfall. No dinner this time."

Shastri was relieved. Dinner was an important occasion, meant to be enjoyed with Ileana, in full dress, a custom he'd adopted from the British. Rasul would only show his open disapproval of her presence and, of course, of the servants. Ileana because she was who she was to Shastri; Rasul was a stickler on sexual morality. And the servants—well, they were Harijans, the Untouchables. Shastri made a point of hiring only them.

Ajit Majumdar was kept in what was formerly a British officers' club, about twelve yards from the prisoners' compound. As Shastri, Rasul, and Sinjar passed the barbed-wire fence, Rasul stopped to stare at the clusters of Thugs in the yard. Some one hundred and thirty-nine had been captured, and each band had separated itself from the others, mostly standing, a few sitting in the dust. A quiet, surly lot except for a circle of Arcotees who were gambling. They wore checkered pantaloons and short jackets in the old Sepoy style.

Now and then a Thug looked back at the trio with undisguised hatred of his captors. Noting Rasul's shudder, Shastri smiled to himself. "Murderous snakes!" the big man cried.

"Not to their minds," Shastri said. He was searching for Das. Finally he found him in the southwest corner, seated on his haunches, away from Rasul's sight. Das was taking betel nut from his pouch to chew on.

"Not to their minds," Shastri continued, as they neared. Majumdar's prison. He paraphrased in English, "Evil is in the eye of the beholder."

"What did you say, Shastri? My English isn't as good as yours."

"I meant that from their point of view they are doing the right thing. That *we* are the evildoers, thwarting the will of Kali."

"They looked at us as if they wished we were their victims. Did you see that?"

"Yes, because they're fanatics. And you still believe that the government can sway them from their calling?"

Rasul grunted. They passed two sentries and entered the isolation building. An alcove led to a large hall. The bar that had serviced countless British officers was still bolted to the floor, running along the opposite wall. Except for an Indian flag in one corner and a few chairs, the place was empty. The other three walls were broken by long, narrow, uncovered windows. Sunlight burst through the panes, giving the room a bright, hazy look. In the room's center was the prisoner, squatting on the floor. A guard seated in a chair faced him.

"This is Ajit Majumdar," said Shastri.

Rasul blinked again, but this time not from the sunlight.

Majumdar's leathery face was wrinkled into a grimace of such obvious contempt that it shattered the interrogator's confidence.

"Shall we begin, then?" Rasul said, after clearing his throat. "I am Krishna Rasul. You've heard of me?"

"No," lied the other, "but then, there is so much I do not know of."

Rasul took a folder from Sinjar, looked at the interrogation report, and said, "Well then, I see you're not at all cooperative. Do you know what that means? It means prison. Or death. Yes, death. That will happen to you if you don't cooperate."

"Death because I do not know about this thing you call Thuggee? Would that I knew everything about it. Then I might live." This was said with feigned concern.

Rasul pushed his chair back and it screeched. Sinjar jumped.

Rasul bellowed, "You, Ajit, are a Thug. A murderer, a robber, a liar. A Deceiver. You understand that, don't you?"

"The other names—yes. But the name Thug—no. I know nothing of Thug. Never have I known of it."

Rasul sighed, then rose and began to pace.

"Excuse me," said Shastri. "There's work I must do."

Rasul nodded without looking up. Sinjar was still staring at Rasul, his pen poised, waiting. Shastri left. As he passed one of the windows he noticed that Rasul was bent over, whispering in the babu's ear. Shastri turned and descended the porch steps.

At the prisoners' compound he saw that Das was now among the gamblers. Sunlight flashed off the fence wire. The heat was intolerable. Shastri hurried to the welcome shade of his veranda.

Rama Shastri smoked one of the eight Sher Bidi cigarettes he alloted himself per day. Some sixty yards directly east of the veranda, Rasul's pilot stretched beneath a solitary palm. The man had a total view of the kotwalee grounds. Shastri's aide, Gopal, appeared, said, "Does Rasul still play the policeman?"

"Yes. He would show us how to interrogate. But this Ajit Majumdar is no ordinary prisoner. 'Do you know who I am?' asks Rasul. 'No,' replies Majumdar with all his cunning."

Gopal chuckled.

"Such a wonderful irreverence," continued Shastri.

"Much like you, Rama. Yet Rasul won't forget. Do you think he will arrest you?"

"He, alone? Never. No, he will return this time. He will tell them that I don't believe their ideas will work. Perhaps the next time he will have others arrest me. But he alone will never do it. I'm certain of that."

"Will you allow it?"

"I've no desire to experience prison life, Gopal."

"Then, when that time comes, I and your friends will help you escape."

Shastri was about to reply when he saw the pilot stand and begin to walk across the expanse toward the field. Rasul and Sinjar had emerged from the isolation building. Their silhouettes paused for a time, facing each other as they conversed; then the two separated. The pilot stopped and waited until Rasul reached him, and they headed for the plane.

When Sinjar reached the bungalow, he said nothing. Instead, with his head lowered, he passed Gopal and Shastri, clinging to his notebook, and went inside the building.

"You believe he is Rasul's man?" asked Gopal.

"One among many here. I fear we are outnumbered."

"Phah! Children who obey any master who comes along. Fear not, Rama. There are men here, too. Men who know who *you* are and haven't forgotten it."

This was precisely what Shastri didn't want. He was determined that none of his faithful comrades should pay along with him.

The sound of the plane's motor revving turned their thoughts to the field. Silently they watched the speck take off, a blur in the sun-hammered landscape. The plane circled, veered toward the bungalow, and Shastri sensed that Rasul was staring down at him with binoculars. Then the pilot took them up until they became a drone lost in the sky's blinding glare. Shastri settled back in his chair, contented. His world was his again, if only for a little while.

Shastri heard the sound of typing through the screen behind him. Sinjar, ever the dutiful clerk, was transcribing his shorthand notes on the interrogation. To read what had happened after Shastri left should be amusing indeed.

"But first dinner and Das," he told himself and entered the bungalow to dress.

Shastri put on a white tropical suit and a white-and black-painted tie he'd purchased from a student in Bombay. Ileana had changed to a dress of jade green and wore a silver necklace with pendants of small stones that flashed whenever she moved her long, slender neck. She looked more Chinese then ever tonight, Shastri thought, although she was truly a Eurasian. Ileana's father, whom she'd never known, had been a Romanian, a jewelry merchant. One night with her mother, a half-Chinese, half-Burmese entertainer in a Rangoon dive, and he'd returned to the Balkans. Ileana had inherited from both, it seemed: a love of baubles and a dramatic sense.

The latter was in full swing that evening as she fiddled with her cigarette holder, pretending to be a lady of great sophistication, chatting about the latest book she'd just finished.

"*Madame Bovary*," she said. "Really, Rama, I can't understand what all the fuss was about."

"Naturally," he replied.

"What do you mean by that?"

"I don't think, my dear, that you've ever looked at morality quite the same way."

"Will we ever go there someday? France, I mean."

"We might." Shastri looked at Sinjar. There, Shastri thought; retain that in your memory, my boy spy, so that you can tell Rasul that I plan to flee there. No, never France. Stephen Wrench is not in France.

Shastri, cutting into his steak, noted that Sinjar winced. The babu was for the ban on killing cows, and his plate had no beef. The bloom of India's educated youth still fighting for the ban. Even the Harijan cook had outgrown such a superstition. It bored Shastri. His urbane nature resented this sort of thing. A government hatchet man who was prejudiced against Untouchables and a young babu who had his sacred cows. Yet India maintained she was growing up.

Everyone who progresses here seems to leave one foot in

the past for insurance, Shastri pondered. Just in case the new ways backfire and the gods are angry. The old gods never die in India. They never had sense enough to die. Such a stupid lot of gods, useless and decrepit with age but still refusing to die. And now this Thuggee matter, to kill for the myth of a bloodthirsty goddess. Think of that.

He pulled from his reverie as a servant announced there was someone to see him. That would be Das. Damn, he hadn't had his tea. Shastri went.

Das was sprawled in the library, a strange, grimy figure in rags in a plush leather armchair. Shastri gave him a Sher Bidi and lit one up for himself.

"Yes?" he asked.

"Das has done it again," boasted the other, as usual. "You were correct. There is a new voice among them."

"Who?"

"Aha. No one knows."

"No one knows?"

"He is coming. Yet to emerge."

"Well, then, begin at the beginning, that I may comprehend this fully."

"I was gambling with the Arcotees and won their confidence."

"I saw you."

"It was then, in my boundless courage, that I took the great risk. I decided to test your reasoning and said, 'What is the word from the Chosen One? Will he leave us here to rot and die, or will he gather up the rest of Thuggee and free us, one and all?' Whereupon an Arcotee replied, 'We know no more than you, except he is to come, soon.' Whereupon I plunged in further with 'Was it revealed to you as it was to my Mooltanee brothers?'

"Now, what I would've answered had they questioned me, I don't know. But instead they offered, 'By a dream. As we hear, it was sent to each Leader of the Agureeas, the Chingurees, and the rest.' For you see, Rama—and this sets my hackles on end if it be so—each Leader of each band had the same dream. Of black Kali. Who revealed to them that they were to rise again and no longer fight among each other as in the days of old. That a Huzoor was to come who would show the new way. You must admit, Rama, that this is very strange: that such a dream would come to each head of these bands."

"Who knows the truth, Das? One of them may have had the dream and convinced the rest that they, too, had had the same. A kind of mass hypnotism."

"I find that difficult to accept, Rama."

"Why?"

"To so many bands? So many Leaders?"

Shastri sighed. "Well, go on. What else?"

"Rumor has it that the Huzoor is somewhere in the north. That he was discovered by a Thug band near Lucknow and that a most ancient sadhu attended him. That they went even farther north."

"And what lies there?"

"Only the sadhu and the Huzoor know, Rama. Some say they go as far north as Gomukh, the Cow's Mouth of the Himalayas, where the Gangotri Glacier is, where the Bhagirathi Ganga is born."

"But that's two miles high or more."

"True, but there are great gurus there, I have heard, who bathe in the icy waters and know all manner of things. Great sadhus who live in caves and meditate atop glaciers. The rishis who never die are there, even."

Shastri sighed again. "And you couldn't find out why this new Huzoor is headed there?"

"No one knows."

"So what do we have? Supposedly, every major Leader of a Thug band had the same dream in which the Goddess Kali told them that a new Huzoor, Lord, Deliverer—call him what you may—was to come with a new mission. That the bands were to rise again while awaiting the full import of this Deliverer's message. That he was discovered with an ancient sadhu near Lucknow by a Thug group. What Thug group?"

"That, unfortunately, no one knows either."

"As no one knows where the Huzoor and the old ascetic went, except maybe to the top of some Himalayan peak. Or why they went there. Das, I think, as the British say, these Arcotees were pulling your leg. They're masters at that kind of thing. You know that."

"He who told me seemed truthful," Das stated with resentment.

"Das, I don't mean to be harsh. But this business is a bit too—"

From outside the library window came sounds of a struggle and a tremendous howl of pain. Shastri rushed to the blinds and pulled them up. Below the sill, in the lighted rectangle, stood Gopal with Sinjar. The aide held the babu's arms behind his back.

"Well, well," said Shastri. "What have you found here?"

"He was standing beneath the window listening to every word, Rama."

"Indeed." To Das: "We will discuss this matter later. Return to the compound and see what else you can discover. Perhaps more research will disclose different information."

"I doubt it."

"Don't be sullen, Das. You must admit, it's a very unusual tale. Put it to the test again."

The spy left.

Sinjar was in pain, and his face showed it. Gopal still had him in the arm hold. Shastri placed his hands on the desk edge and smiled. "Come, come, Sinjar. Make a clean breast of it. There really is no need for more pain."

The babu was silent. Gopal pulled the arm up higher. The babu howled again.

"Let him go," commanded Shastri.

"But why, Rama?"

"Because I have no stomach for torture. Never have," admitted Shastri. His dark eyes studied Sinjar. He said, "Years ago, my boy, before you were born, I was captured by the Japanese in the heart of the Burmese jungle. I was working hand in hand with the American OSS in those days. Secret work, you understand. There were others captured, too, and all night long as I lay in my hut I heard their cries. In my mind's eye—and that

is always more terrible than anything the actual eye can behold—
I saw then all the torture I'm interested in seeing. So you are
thereby free of such a predicament. But I warn you, Sinjar, I
want answers."

He paused, lit another Sher Bidi, realizing he'd gone beyond
his allotted amount. Damn this fasting.

"Rasul put you up to this, didn't he?"

Sinjar rubbed his arm. "May I sit down?" he gasped.

"Sit."

Sinjar slumped into a bamboo chair, staring at Shastri while
he rubbed.

"About Rasul . . ."

"Yes, about Rasul."

"You are wrong. I was but taking a walk and I happened
to pause beneath the window for a second."

"Untrue," interrupted Gopal. "He was there for a spell,
Rama. I saw him, and Ileana before me."

"Ileana?" repeated Shastri, surprised.

"When he left the dinner early she became suspicious and
followed him. When she noted what he was doing she summoned me. The woman is still with you, Rama."

Shastri caught his breath. "What do you say to that, Sinjar?"

"It is lies."

"Lies?"

Sinjar nodded.

"Gopal and . . . Ileana are liars, you say?"

"Forgive me, I'm flustered. I meant they were mistaken."

"I see. Then you won't admit to anything?"

Something akin to defiance was in Sinjar's "No."

So, Shastri thought, he knows I won't torture him. The fool
thinks of me as weak.

"Then, Sinjar," he said softly, even with sadness, "I must
place you in other hands. Put him in the compound."

The babu leaped to his feet. "The compound!"

"Of course. With the prisoners. Where else?"

"But they . . . they are Thugs."

"Yes, they are. Did you think I would place you somewhere
else? Some nice, soft cell where you could wait with ease for

Rasul to return and free you? And perhaps punish me for it? No, it is the compound for you."

"But they'll know I'm not like them. It would be murder. You wouldn't let them murder me!"

"Murder is one thing, torture another, Sinjar. Murder, depending how it's done, can be quick and merciful. I believe I can sleep well, knowing that merciful murder is being done. Take him, Gopal. I haven't had my tea tonight."

"You mean it. You mean it."

Gopal placed his gun in Sinjar's spine. "Come along."

"No. Please listen. I will tell—everything. Everything."

"Everything?"

"All of it."

"Every detail?"

"Every one."

Shastri rolled his eyes to the ceiling. "Very well. Try it, and if it's truly everything I will change my mind. But hurry. I still haven't had my tea tonight."

The three framed photographs were atop the teakwood cabinet next to his gun case. Shastri moved the tea tray aside, left his desk, went across the library to the photographs, and gently took the one in the center.

He stared at the smiling, attractive Hindu woman, smiling for him alone, since he'd snapped the picture. The smile diffused upward from the thin lip line and tiny, even teeth to the wide, long-lashed eyes. It left a sheen on the dark pupils. A rapt, glowing smile, and for him, even at this moment, wherever she was right now. In that memory space within him, where the dead went to live on, as he saw it, yes, in that special memory space she glowed tonight. Of that he was certain. Glowing with that hint of bantering maiden's laughter that always made his mouth dry.

Kamala. Shastri had loved Kamala once, desired her more than any woman he'd ever known. Maybe he loved that strongly at this moment. Maybe all those years. He wasn't certain. For so long had he willed it otherwise for the sake of friendship that he knew the true feeling wasn't easy to find anymore.

Shastri wanted to believe a metamorphosis had happened, that every centimeter of youthful passion and pain had changed to a totally platonic acceptance that she was Stephen Wrench's wife.

Turning quickly to the other pictures, he addressed them: "Steve, Santha." Just their names, as if addressing them brought them into the room.

Kamala. Well, she was already with him. And smiling about it.

Shastri put the photograph back. It was a silly game, but somehow it had curbed this incredible loneliness he'd suffered during the last fourteen months. Shastri traced his time in India as starting to end then. Placed in a no-man's-land that was no longer his India. So it was when you were considered your country's enemy.

Shastri looked at his chronometer and headed for his bedroom.

"Mongoose," said Ileana from the darkness, "I've lain here so long without you at my side."

"Thank you," he told her as he undressed. "Thank you for reporting Sinjar to Gopal."

"But of course, Mongoose. That silly boy. Did he think he could get away with it? *Enfant bête.*"

Ileana sat up, and the moonlight through the white net captured her flowing shoulders and the hard upthrusts of her breasts.

"A fool, yes. A stupid fool," Shastri agreed and narrated what had happened as he joined her.

"Then it *was* Rasul's doing. Sinjar was indeed his spy. And they want to catch you at something."

"Something to accuse me of. Like withholding information from them."

"Are you, Mongoose?"

"Of course. I always do. Haven't you figured that out by now?"

"They want to arrest you. Put you in prison."

He searched her eyes. But the moonlight gave her the advantage. It made the eyes bright, almost opaque.

"And Rasul told Sinjar he thought the next time would be when..."

"Correct. That next time they'll arrest me."

At that Ileana's small mouth seemed to curl in on itself. Then it twisted, became a snarl. "They can't do that to you, Mongoose."

"Oh yes they can—unless I escape in time."

"Where? Paris, Mongoose?"

Shastri remained silent.

"It's America, isn't it? Where dwells that horrid friend of yours who doesn't like me. I won't go to America!"

He'd thought she would react this way. The back room of the Lashio dive surged into his memory, with Steve's whiskey voice full of warning. "Ferchrissakes, Ram, leave her here. Take her, and you'll have to take her goddamn pipe with her." But Shastri couldn't deal with the words then, but only remain transfixed by the vision before him.

Ileana. Young, lying there, becalmed, isolated from the turmoil of life around her. Lying there, barely breathing. Lying in that God-awful filthy room on a bamboo mat, a tatter of burlap across the lower half of her naked body. A vision asleep in the lap of Morpheus. The fumes encircling her breasts like the translucent, gauzy wisps around those Louvre goddesses.

They were there to find a man, a most wanted, terrible man. But the vision changed that. Shastri clothed Ileana and took her away with him, despite Stephen Wrench's protestations.

Ileana never forgave his friend. The ever active opportunist in her saw him as a threat. And it was somehow worse about Kamala. No matter how kind Kamala would be to her, that sense in Ileana knew, was convinced, that this was the other woman, so completely that Shastri had had to remove the photographs from the bedroom.

They had been at odds about some silly thing. In a rage, his mistress grabbed Kamala's picture, spit at it, while she screamed that Shastri felt she was scum. Well, she'd show him. Maybe she couldn't compare to this "pure lady," this "apotheosis of virtue," who could no more know about loving a man

than would a temple statue. But she was still his Ileana Heng.
And Shastri belonged to her.

That was the only time Shastri hit her. Now, with Kamala
dead, her rage focused back on Steve. No, she wouldn't go to
America with him.

"I won't think of it," Ileana pouted, throwing her arms at
him, pulling him down until he was beneath her. Her fingers
cupped his testicles, darted to his penis and massaged. He
watched the sleek black fall of hair rising, lowering as she
mouthed his erection. He listened to the sucking noises, her
gasps for air as he grew and grew. He felt his loneliness ending,
writhing, moist, throbbing life freeing itself from a cocoon.
Shastri's hands were like things aflame when he seized her in
turn.

Ileana laughed, understanding. She straddled him, now that
he was ready, and eased the penis in. Then she chattered on
and on, pressing forward, then back. "Mongoose, you are too
great to let this happen to you. Too great . . . Oh, so great inside
me now. Oh, Mongoose, what would I ever do without such
a great . . . Oh, great . . . such greatness within me . . . In me!
Mongoose! IN ME! . . . Hold me, then . . . hold . . . HOLD,
HOLD, MONGOOSE . . . HOLD ON . . . and I will protect . . .
you . . . with . . . OH, WITH . . . WITH . . . SUCH GREAT-
NESS IN ME I CAN DO ANY . . . ANYTHING! . . . Yes, more
greatness, Mongoose . . . MORE . . . !"

On and on, while the words became unintelligible sounds,
while the black fall tossed, became sleeker, while her breath
heaved, struggled to continue, and finally died. While the jerking, spasmodic dance that rose suddenly within her flung her
into the night's silence.

Later Shastri dreamed she was still on him. Except they
were enveloped by the stench of Lashio. Above him she glistened, her breasts and arms oiled with sweat as she feverishly
thrust herself upon his hardness. Yet, beautiful in her lust as
she was, the stench remained. And he couldn't understand why.

The loving in a Lashio bordello continued. The bamboo
walls were stained, dripping with the rot of the jungle beyond.

But to Shastri they were made of flesh, stained with love sweat, not jungle.

He couldn't believe he was in Lashio again. There had been a gourd, he recalled, in the corner aside the mat, a misshapen natural thing, suggestive of deformity. Shastri looked. It wasn't there. Then, peering at his stomach, at his penis lost in the mesh of pubic hair, he was relieved that all was still beautiful. Only the stench and his dream that it was Lashio were wrong.

An aberration.

Ileana bent closer, her breath flush against his cheek. The black straight strands of her hair smothered him, and he tried to pull his head away. Again and again the hair coiled, twisted over his eyes, his nostrils, his mouth. Reeking of stench. Of jungle, of rot, of unwashed bodies, of something else. Shastri choked, dug his nails into her neck, yanked at the strands to force her back. Back, distant, away from the pungent wisp of . . .

He finally recognized it, shouted "Goddamn!" in English, and awoke.

Clammy, he remained where he was awhile. The moonlight, still bright, reflected off the walls like a sheet of burnished metal. The atmosphere was cluttered, somehow, and a thread like a medium's ectoplasm moved before his eyes. Shastri sat up. His hand reached to his side. He knew the answer before he groped. Ileana was gone.

Leaving the bed, he crossed the room and, as silent as the trailing wisp, went through the open door into the corridor. Down its length he saw the dark end of the passage, the closed cubicle that was her place of retreat. Shastri whispered, "Goddamn!" again and walked on.

Shastri followed the wisp to the door.

Slowly, hesitantly, he entered the cubicle.

The lamp glow fell the length of a table and onto the divan beyond. It centered on a miniature burner used to set the fragment of opium aglow; distended to Ileana's kimono, loosely tied; then across the lashes closed in sleep and the long pipestem in her hand. Shastri moved to her side. Gently he pried the pipe from her clutching fingers and extinguished it. He stood trembling, watching her immobile face.

Gopal's words ran through his mind, but this time they were veiled in mockery: "The woman is still with you, Rama," Gopal had said.

FOUR

Gangotri Glacier/Uttar Pradesh/Hardwar

"Chundra!"

He heard Gauri calling him. At first her voice was a crashing echo in some hollow canyon within himself. But now, looking through the narrow crevice at the blue ice flank of the Gangotri Glacier, he heard the echo of his name reverberating off its face and marveled. To the northeast, much, much higher, was the famous Cow's Mouth, where the sacred Ganga emerged like a great, moist tongue. Descending, licking most of the long breadth of India.

For many days and many nights he'd heard the cry of Gauri in his sleep, in his awakening. Something was amiss. Very wrong.

He sat up, shivering in the cold Himalayan morning. The sunrise, a sparkling lozenge, blueing the vast whiteness beyond the crevice, gripped him for a moment in its wonder. And the echo stopped, as abrupt in its passing as when it began. Again the trickle of glacial waters and the now and then crack of ice were restored, the sounds at the Roof of the World.

The old sadhu, no more clothed than he'd been in that hot village near Lucknow, left the shadows of the cave and went to the crevice. His lean silhouette faced the bluish glow, and Chundra thought it a nimbus around him. What could go wrong when such a holy man was with them? Chundra had never seen him eat or sleep, even rest. Yet he clearly had the stamina, endured the arduous voyage with the ease of a snow tiger. Never faltering, never lost, never in need, walking, climbing, fearless, abandoned in his energy!

Also, the sadhu had not opened his eyes throughout the trek.

Chundra shivered again and pulled his yak-wool coat tighter around his neck. He heard the pilgrim stir. This new Lord, the new Huzoor, shivered, too. Chundra had seen him wince with pain from the biting winds, had seen him stumble along the climb. Yes, the pilgrim Huzoor was Chosen, true: but human, at least.

The pilgrim was up now, too, breakfasting on his meager rations. Chundra, who hadn't yet eaten, joined him. The meal was shared in total silence. Then, finished, the two men passed through the crevice into the blue dawn. Standing in the very same pose in which Chundra had first seen him was the sadhu, already on the icy expanse.

There were other sadhus present; here, there, mostly in the lotus position, at their meditations. The ones who lived in the caves above the Gangotri waterfall were specks on the high, snow-blanketed ridges. Below, to the west, at the glacier's base, more of them were at their ablutions, some nearly naked.

Was ever a place so full of God? Chundra thought. God was a frozen blue here, a bejeweled blue, a sun like a star made of crystal. Here, it was said, God once uttered the sacred Vedas to the ancient rishis.

The sadhu led, climbed. They climbed in turn. They veered away from the canopied whiteness to a slope, a gray, slated descent cluttered with moraine boulders. Dark holes pocked the surface from the impact of detritus. With the dawn peaking, a distant gorge gradually shifted from purple to a pale green, reflecting the tree belts above it.

On they went, Chundra's breathing labored. The pilgrim, sharing the ordeal, trekked between him and the holy man and gulped at the sky. The crystal sun had diffused with the progressing hours, exposing swirls of clouds around the Shiv Ling peak flanking the Gangotri. The Roof of the World pulsed eerie, pulsed ancient, with ghosts of the great Past in motion. Above them the bearded lammergeiers glided like mythological guardians of forbidden realm.

Chundra's head ached. Would the tireless sadhu ever stop? He and the pilgrim were stumbling, fighting for air at every third or fourth step. He saw the prints of a great cat and knew they were higher than man usually desires to go. As he looked back, the temples, shrines, pilgrim crowds en route to the Gangotri seemed a dream life.

Finally, wild-eyed, Chundra stared at the scarp before them. He couldn't possibly make that steep climb. And he was certain that the pilgrim, now on bended knee, could not either. The scarp reached high into a thread of mist, rimed at its top by more snow. What could possibly be up there but the leopard whose track he'd seen earlier?

The sadhu turned left. A ledge, barely large enough to hold a man of average girth, circuited the base. They started to move along the narrow lip.

How long this lasted was beyond Chundra's ability to estimate. He was too concerned with finding the minimum of handholds the mountain wall provided to think of anything else. Every so often the sadhu and the pilgrim disappeared beyond a turn, leaving him isolated in that high vastness, vulnerable to a wind that rose, howled, plucked at him. Certain he would fall, that the Goddess had changed Her mind about him, that in a moment of caprice he would be cast aside, like so many others, Chundra resigned himself to his karma.

Chundra made it, since the ledge finally widened and the scarp face degenerated into a series of hollows. It was the third such hollow that held their destination: an enormous, sunless, elbow-shaped depression with a faint reedy sound from the air flow.

Chundra spotted a lammergeier perched atop a jutting formation. He shuddered, wondering why the bearded vulture was waiting, why the unblinking gaze was fixed on him. Chundra hurled a pebble its way. A flurry of gray and white as the bird stirred, the plumage settled, and it remained where it was.

The others had already disappeared. Chundra backed from the lammergeier, finally turned and rushed into the hollow.

Like a tenacious, drawn-out note, the reedy sound followed Chundra, as if it seeped from the stone and trailed him.

Unnerved, he rubbed at his rheumy eyes. The darkness was tenebrous. Chundra stumbled, nearly rolled down the slope, somehow picked himself up and continued his search. Where were the others? Where in Mother Kali's name had they gone?

An outline, suddenly discernible, loomed before him. The wall behind it glowed slightly. A hut. It was a hut!

Chundra stepped into the doorless entrance. The walls were of wood up to a certain point, then carved rock. An earthenware bowl and jug were on the floor, next to a mat of woven grass. Chundra walked to the opposite wall and faced a crevice that led deeper into the mountain.

Easing his body into the gap, Chundra found more darkness. He listened intently for the footfalls of the others, heard nothing. Cautiously he slowly extended one foot, then the other, and found, surprisingly, that the ground was level and smooth. Chundra lifted his arms to test the width of the tunnel. It proved wider than his fingertips. He moved sideways, first left, then right, discovering that there was room enough for at least two men to walk side by side.

On Chundra went, noting as he did that the temperature had risen, had become comfortable. He continued to move slowly: the ground might dip unexpectedly. His hand brushed the left wall now—something solid to touch in this dreadful subterrane.

With one of his groping steps Chundra felt he'd finally met a barrier. Stretching his arms about before him, his hands passed through a filmy substance, up to his wrists. But nothing was there, no fabric, no gossamer curtain, even though it was filmy. He held his breath and urged the rest of his body forward.

The barrier clung to his face—his nostrils—for an instant. Then he was beyond it, and his ears popped; a giddiness swept him and quickly settled.

Chundra Bala covered his eyes against the blinding effulgence that, without warning, he'd emerged into. He stood in a place of vivid, startling colors, a mercurial chromatic swirl of a place, massive and full of clamoring hush. The very still-

screamed its presence. He could barely withstand the intense, palpable silence.

Daring to look, he gradually adjusted to the change. Motes of color darted, moved in all directions. He saw the pilgrim and the sadhu, at least ten yards ahead. He headed for them, his spirit buoyant. He felt transformed, a younger Chundra Bala, as young as Dhan. Perhaps the dead boy had united with his soul.

There were no walls, or, if they existed, they were constantly in flux, colors weaving in wavelets. Streaming like festoons, first nearby, then abruptly diminishing in the far distance, then instantaneously near again. Everything shaping, dissolving, reshaping. Concave, then convex spillings of pink, blue, gold, aquamarine, vermilion, lavender, saffron. A semblance of walls that sprang up, dropped, hurtled, meshed into each other; a blending of liquid, sinuous runs of color like dyes spilled and mixed at random. Sometimes a section of vermilion or aquamarine thickened, freed a descending globule from the rest, and trailed like a bloodstain across the lower waves of blue, yellow, and pearl white. Here a streamer imploded, as with that wavelet of gold about shoulder-high that suddenly burst darting points from its core.

The joy was short-lived, however. A pall seemed to descend upon the cavern. Chundra suddenly saw shadow. Like a smear it grayed, wedged into the walls, the air. A gray bar, ever darkening.

The sadhu stirred. His head seemed separated from his waist, since his torso was in the darkness. The shadow dimmed the colors close to its edges, and Chundra was finally able to see what the holy man was facing.

Ahead, each in lotus position, were four rishis, flush against each other, slowly rotating. The shadow hadn't touched them. Ancient, their faces were heavily lined, their heads crowned with long, white tresses that draped their naked shoulders, their beards hoarier still, reaching nearly to their loincloths. Each might have been an identical twin to another.

Endlessly rotating back to back, they chanted in unison, "We are the rishis who experienced shruti. Directly we heard

from Brahma the sounds of timeless finality. Directly we heard
and directly we remembered. *Ātmā devānām, bhuvanasya gar-
bho.*"

And, like a chorus, the speakers from the timeless wind
repeated, and, as before, Chundra understood: "Spirit of all
the gods, seed of all the worlds." Racing through him, a shock
electric along the outer layers of his skin.

Tricklings of the utterance undulating in rising, ebbing tides
of sound.

"Hear the Rishis of the First and the Last. Here, when there
was naught but the mountains of the World," the four continued,
"we did directly receive each akshara. Know ye that a syllable
of the Word of God is the roar of Creation. No man hears the
entire roar at once. No man may withstand its might, its tremor.
Only Brahma hears the mighty, the sound of the terrible Silence.
O Brahma, *TAT TVAM ASI. TAT TVAM ASI. TAT TVAM ASI.*
Thou are that."

And, ending, the shadow bar diffused, thinned, swiftly
changed from its menacing nightness to a translucent gray, like
a cloud that dims a radiant morning with its unexpected presence. This time the four rishis, too, were engulfed, darkened,
for a brief instant . . .

A half-breath . . .

Then a burst, an eruption from their center, and each figure
was hot, made molten by a fire unknown. No more the gray
wash. No longer the ancient rishis. But instead creatures young
and bold, their eyes glowing like fumaroles, their tresses still
long, but now black and sleek. And beardless, with voices firm
and strident.

"We are the Lords of Being-Nonbeing, of Breath and Non-
breath, of Light and its Absence. The Sun gives us Shadow,
the Night gives us the Moon's Glow. All waits for the Balance.
All waits for the Good. All waits for the Evil," they cried out.

Chundra's stare shifted to the Huzoor pilgrim, who was
moving closer.

The rishis continued to rotate, still twins to one another. . . .
But now each of them held something in his left hand.

"Ours is the flowing of history, the mighty illusion that flows as the sacred Ganga, that weaves with the light, that churns in the night, that overflows with purpose, that recedes without meaning."

One of them hurled what he held at the pilgrim's feet.

"Here is the Scroll of the Great Truth. Here is the Scroll of Transcendence. Read, and we shall record it in our hearts."

Chundra's parched throat gurgled as the pilgrim picked up the cylindrical object. The pilgrim unrolled the scroll, read aloud. Strangely, the words were unintelligible, though Chundra was certain the pilgrim's voice was loud enough.

The four Lords spun around even faster, blurred, then slowed once the Scroll of the Great Truth was ended.

"Here," the second of them shouted, while he tossed another cylinder. "Read the Scroll of Events, where Destiny is written. Read to us, that we may record it in our hearts."

Again the pilgrim's words were unintelligible to Chundra, who knew at last that he wasn't meant to hear. His eyes looked for the old sadhu. He was gone!

More blurring. The rufous blaze returned, bit at the eyes, a whirling circle like a pinwheel sun in a spreading twilight. The vermilions, lavenders, pinks, aquamarines, golds—all of the spectrum had dimmed. The wavelets had slowed in their motion, solidified, structured into the walls of an extensive cavern.

Turning back to the Lords, Chundra saw for the first time that they were floating. At least, no dais was discernible.

"Here," bellowed the third of them. "Read the Scroll of the Chosen. Read of the heritage, of the sons of the gods, the avatars who beat the rhythm of the Balance on the Earth, to balance the ways of men. Read, that we may record it in our hearts. For we are Lords and Rishis reborn: Lords of the Present and What is to Come."

Once more a scroll was given to the pilgrim Huzoor.

Chundra's heart swelled. Except for the Huzoor, he was the sole witness now. The aged sadhu now seemed to have disappeared into the heavens. Anything was possible.

And at last the fourth Lord, whose eyes lashed out fire with the fervor of his decree. His mightly arm raised, the scroll sailed. This time the pilgrim, who'd ventured very near, caught it.

"Here," came the final command: "the Scroll of Power. Summon and know thy Mother. Read, that we may record it forever in the timeless heart of the Eternal, that it will forevermore be written on the forehead of Brahma."

This, the most important reading to Chundra, since he was certain it was of Kali, was longer than the others. At its end the yellow-reddish circle whitened. Chundra felt a scream coming from himself. Terror shattered his concentration, spread through his very marrow. The white core was about to implode, he sensed. The ground quaked. He tossed about, barely able to stand. The air ripped a rent in the fabric of the supernal atmosphere. A hissing noise, as of gas escaping, made him convulse.

Chundra was sucked into an invisible vortex, hurtled backward. He hit something that dissolved like a fragile web, and found himself miraculously still on his feet.

But he was like one dead, he thought. His body was ice to his touch. He couldn't shiver. He was numb. Fear, joy, awe— almost all feeling was gone, perhaps because the heart of man could not withstand what he was witnessing.

Chundra stared, transfixed. This was a different cavern, ominous in its murky twilight. Stalactites and stalagmites hung and rose in shapes suggestive of vague, half-formed images, illogical, the ultradimensional shapings of nightmares.

Chundra hesitated as a sickly mist trickled from the countless fumaroles in the ceiling. They gaped down like the sockets of a giant whose eyes had been burned out. He dared not stare at them too long, since they made him dizzy, sure he would rise and fall into the sidereal vastness beyond the threading fumes.

A creature squatted upon a mound covered with bluish algae. Chundra supposed it was algae, as he supposed it was a creature, a something that might have been a bird, an amphibian, a fish, a demon, or even a human being. It constantly shifted out of focus and blurred, re-formed itself into something else, seemingly just born.

There were sounds from what was not yet seen, if ever:

gigglings, gurglings, whispers, sighs, grunts, possible out-
bursts of anger. Possible resentment toward him, the intruder.

Now he was moving with strange, heavy, slow strides. He
passed a wheel—at least as high as a three-story house. Chundra touched it to convince himself, and the porous, rubbery,
massive rim was solid enough, if a bit soft. The pressure of
his fingers left their imprint, and it was then, with a shock that
made him swiftly back away, that he realized he'd touched
flesh.

Flesh.

Chundra shuddered, but it was the shudder of release, a
letting go, and his shock subsided. What he was observing was
suddenly bearable again, and he neared once more. He judged
the width of the wheel's rim at six feet. Though he could barely
see beyond the spokes and hub, he mentally calculated nine or
ten more yards of depth. The imprint of his fingers was rapidly
fading, the pores expanded and contracted, quarter-inch dark
pits mottling a surface that ranged from white to a lustrous
black. The flesh of every race, he concluded—Caucasian, shades
of yellow, red, and brown, the final streaks of the deepest
ebony. And—studying closer—here and there among the variations of flesh tone was a parade of tattoos.

He'd not seen them before, but that was part of the nascent
quality of everything around him. The place heaved with constant birth.

Chundra bent forward, squinting in the milky twilight, fascinated by the progression of tattoos. Reminiscent of a religious
ceremonial train, they told a story. The figures were entirely
in red, and as the dimness eased a bit, he soon saw the markings
were in blood, as raw as the first imprint from the tattoo needle.

The central figure, Chundra thought, was an ordinary bayadere, a temple dancing girl, poised in the dancing style of the
Bharata Natyam. Chundra was aware of the mudras, the tra-
ditional hand and figure gestures. But the bayadere shifted with
a new stance and rearranging of the arms, and the pretty, smiling
woman was replaced. Chundra had no time to question that
the figures were moving.

The woman now lost her beauty. The blood coagulated to

a glutinous black. A hag stared back with fangs and protruding tongue. Two additional arms holding a sword and a strangler's noose emerged into view, moving in unison with the gestures of the arms above to a silent music that jarred Chundra's nerves. A discordant clamor. A paean of strife and disorder, of war and death, unheard and yet picked up by Chundra's nerve endings.

The din was meant to be sensed, not heard, the ultrasound of the terrible Silence.

Recognizing his Goddess, Chundra Bala could barely look upon Her aspect. Naked, except for Her ornaments, a garland of skulls and a girdle of severed hands, She danced down the broad curving rim of flesh . . . danced and glowered and darted and fought.

The other figure, who remained red in color, was the demon Raktavīja. The Thug knew the famous myth and watched it unfold. Each time Kali touched him with Her sword, Raktavīja reproduced himself from the drops of blood. The blur of countless demons made Chundra's head swim, and for a moment the wheel seemed to disappear and he faced an infinity of jeering, monstrous Raktavījas. Then the rim was present again, and now the dancing, thrusting Goddess held the demon high and drank all his blood before it could fall and restructure itself.

Thus it was, it was written, that Kunkali acquired the bloodlust that is insatiable. This it was, and Chundra turned his head away from the now bloated, hideous thing that blared back with the shattering sonic glare of Her triumph.

His body taut, his nerves like wires overloaded with current, Chundra stiffly passed beyond the rim. He tottered for a moment against the spokes, clutching seaweed-like tresses. But his clammy hands dropped the tresses when he realized that they were human hair, woman's hair, long and tangled in the cables of flesh. Somewhere, too, whenever the hair parted sufficiently, there were the faces, lovely faces, weighted with despair, their eyes filled with endless sorrow.

Chundra reached the hub, evading sinuous arms that coiled around the spokes, grabbed at his clothing. There, at the wheel's center, his eyes riveted upon an array of vulvas linked in a quivering ecstatic design. A powerful sexual magnet, it tugged at his instincts, his pubic hairs rising like a bed of dark anemone. He experienced a surge of desire so strong it battered him, even as his strange new defenses bade him leap free of the spot.

Hitting ground again, Chundra slipped, fell on his haunches, and continued to slide down an incline leading to a lateral chamber. He raised himself to his knees and faced the jutting profiles imbedded in the rock at the turn into the room. He blinked until it registered: the profiles were human skulls. He forced himself to stand, wobbling for an instant, and then walked to the column of leering bone on both sides of the entranceway.

His hand brushed the top of his head. It felt bristly.

Otherwise, the fear had left him again, totally. How miraculous, to be able to move on into this world of death!

There was, nevertheless, a seeping into his consciousness of unsurpassed despair like an invisible miasma. But he went on, shielded from the nightmare.

Now, more blackness. A faint luster to everything, a murmur of light. His foot kicked an object, soft, mushy, then another. Chundra bent, strained until the writhing thing was but inches from his nose. A severed hand. Two. No—many severed hands, the fingers extended in hopeless surrender. Maggots glistened, poured forth from the palms. The luster, whiter than flesh, whiter than bone, etched the quivering outlines.

Chundra crossed the space, kicking the hands aside, telling himself it was all so much cosmological refuse. Nothing to concern himself with, really. Nothing, nobody important. All that was important was to follow the alcove to the last nook, to reach that glaucous arc ahead that danced and licked so desperately at the walls. There, he knew, was the finale, the truth he was seeking.

No time to pause, hesitate, even tremble. No time. No time anywhere, anyplace. Yes, this was no Time.

Deeper into the nightness and beyond Chundra went. He stopped, staring at a dais covered by a flickering, translucent membrane. It heaved, pulsed, a living green tissue. Chundra thought of a diseased placenta. Suddenly greatly excited, he knelt at the dais's base.

Detectable through the translucency were two shapes. Chundra recognized the cowl of the Huzoor, who clung to a gigantic figure on a throne of stone. Two black left arms were wrapped around the Huzoor, holding him tight and fast. One right hand stroked his head, the other pressed his face to the sheen-rimmed mound of a naked breast.

The Huzoor was suckling on the hard, dish-sized nipple.

Kunkali!

Kunkali!

Chundra screamed the name in his soul. Her face was hidden in the blackish green mesh above. Only two iridescent points lit the area above Her shoulders. The command came from the points, clawing into Chundra's entrails.

"Chundra! Protect my son!"

After that, he collapsed in a swoon.

FIVE

The Fringes of the Deccan Plateau

It was phenomenal that the old work engine had been able to chug and wheeze its way fourteen miles to the village, pulling two boxcars behind it.

Rama Shastri stood huddled amid the press of sweating bodies. There were twenty policemen, excluding the guide, in this, the forward car, and another twenty-eight in the second one. He shifted his weight for balance as the car tilted back against the couplings. A very small force indeed against an estimated seven hundred and eighty-odd Thugs, he thought again, despite the three dozen UZIs and eleven AK-47s his men carried.

He'd resisted the government's offer to supply his men with

the surplus M16s that had somehow leaked into India from the
Vietnam and Cambodian wars years ago. They were too unreliable, unlike the Israeli and Russian weaponry. The 9mm UZIs
and the AKs were Shastri's pride and joy.

But would they be enough?

They would, if the Thugs heeded their traditions. The legend
stated that, long ago, Thugs witnessing Kali devouring one of
their recent victims were so shocked that from that period on
they never spilled blood to tempt her. Thus they were not apt
to have either knives or guns. But what guarantee had he of
this but the knowledge that in the past these ritualistic murderers
were shackled by their beliefs? And, of course, the word of
the guide.

Murmurs of the coming dawn speckled the disappearing
shadows. A spot at the back of the guide's head showed clearly,
as if it were already daytime. Shastri stared hard at it, wishing
he could bore through the skull to the man's brain . . . to his
many secrets.

Was the guide leading them into a trap? Were those hundreds
of stranglers waiting patiently in that dank cave temple in the
cliff above the village ahead, their rumels dangling?

The car lurched again and Shastri nearly fell backward. It
would never do, that he should land on his haunches before
his men. Enough that the government plotter, Krishna Rasul,
had summoned him to Calcutta in a month. Why Calcutta?
Why not New Delhi? Why that hot, populace-congested blight
of a city? Had Rasul a Black Hole, as had the malevolent Siraj-
ud-Daula of old, to place Shastri in forever? No, Rasul hadn't
the passion for such evil. Rasul was just another petty bureau-
crat who wanted Shastri replaced.

But if so . . . And if Calcutta was to be the moment . . . Then,
to the very end, Shastri's men must know that he stood straight,
unwavering.

The narrow-gauger labored up a slight incline. The antique
served its purpose well. What more harmless-appearing vehicle
to stop at the village? If the Thugs were observing, they might
think it a relic bringing in food supplies, since there was famine
in the area.

Two months had passed since Rasul's visit to the compound, and still Shastri had been unable to learn more about the new Huzoor the Thugs awaited.

Then, one evening, a health official from Varanasi had been overheard in a restaurant bragging that he was a Thug. Opium cakes were found on his person, and he was intoxicated from rice beer besides. Shastri's network of agents had picked him up and delivered him to the kotwalee.

The man, whose name was Chundra Bala, was impressive. His steady, authoritative gaze hinted that he, not they, was in command of the situation. Dressed in a white Nehru tunic, he had hair impeccably parted and sleeked down, a pencil line of moustache well trimmed. Shastri saw that even his fingers had been recently manicured.

When questioned, Bala apologized for his unruly behavior. He couldn't imagine why he'd stated he was a Thug, except that he wasn't by nature a drinking man, and even rice beer was much too much for his usually sober constitution. Now would they be so kind as to release him, since he had a foreign health official from the United Nations visiting him, and he'd promised to take this German on a tiger hunt. Which was the reason for the opium cakes, he explained further, to drug the tiger's drinking hole.

Shastri replied that he knew of the disgusting policy which made addicts of the poor tigers. Why should health officials be involved in this kind of ecological sabotage? Chundra Bala only shrugged. Those were the facts, the shrug seemed to say, and Shastri was to take them or leave them.

Shastri's final reply was a return shrug and an order that Bala was to be placed in the compound.

Later, Shastri had aired his suspicions to Gopal.

"It's irregular," Shastri had said to his aide that bright morning, "that a man with his self-possession should set himself up this way. He wanted to be arrested. Das must watch this man carefully. I'm convinced he has sacrificed his freedom to bring a message to Majumdar and the other captured leaders. And there's nothing we can do about it but wait and see what Das unravels for us."

It took but a matter of hours. Soon after Bala was incarcerated, he approached the fierce Majumdar. Das kept his distance, squatting against the fence, watching, while he pretended to concentrate on filling tough green betel leaves with lime paste and nut.

The two prisoners huddled for a while. Then, suddenly, Majumdar bellowed in rage. Other Thugs gravitated around them, and an instant later a clamor rose that set the guards to open the gate and stand poised with their guns ready. "Disperse," Das heard Majumdar cry out, and the crowd eased away. Majumdar in turn stared at Chundra Bala with a hot look that held a dreadful promise and left him.

Later, Das, approaching one of his gambling companions of the Arcotees, asked, "What news does this new one bring that the Jumaldehee leader is so aroused?"

"Aieee, Ajit Majumdar tells us that this Bala and the rest have betrayed us. We are not to be rescued and must be sacrificed, perhaps executed by the government, for our saintly works. But that is of no consequence, says the noble Majumdar. There is worse yet. Ajit Majumdar will not speak of it, but he tells us openly that all of India has been betrayed. All of India. And that this Bala is one of them behind it." The Arcotee pulled Das closer. "Heed. No one doubts the word of the great Majumdar. He is determined that tonight this Bala will know Kali's embrace." He motioned like one being strangled.

Back at his perch near the gate, Das gave the emergency signal. He passed a filled betel leaf through the wires so that it lay in the dust outside the prison yard. A half-hour later, ten prisoners were picked, apparently at random, for further interrogation. Das was among them.

Once Shastri was notified of Majumdar's plan, he summoned Chundra Bala forth.

Das said, "I think, Rama, that my work here is done. When Bala is kept away from the yard, Majumdar will figure that one of the ten men picked earlier is a spy. Crafty as the devil he is, and it won't take long to ferret me out, I wager."

The other agreed. Thus Das was allowed to be present when Bala was brought into the study.

Shastri studied the man again, offered him a Sher Bidi. Bala politely refused. Then Shastri proceeded to narrate everything Das had told him.

"Now what do you think?" asked Shastri, amazed that Bala hadn't even paled. Damn, but Bala's arrogance and poise irritated him.

"What am I supposed to say? This Majumdar is insane to wish to kill me."

"You should know best; you spoke to him."

"I did?"

"Das here saw you. You went to Majumdar immediately after you entered the yard. Come, let us end this charade. I want to save your life if I can."

It was Das who then offered the theory: "They may not even stop with your death, Bala. They may wish to punish your entire family afterward. Your wife, your children. Even your mother, if she lives. Why don't you work along with us, and we'll guarantee total protection for you and your kin in return."

Bala sighed. "Majumdar did curse my entire line," he admitted, with some trepidation.

"Of course," pounced Das. "You brought him disappointing news, news that affects all of India."

For the first time, Bala was ruffled.

"All of India? Is that what Majumdar is saying to everyone? What else did the liar say?"

"Why are you so concerned?" pressed Shastri. "What is to happen that Majumdar would call it a betrayal of India?"

The man's eyes shifted upward to the ceiling fans. Their shadows rippled across his pinched features. His small, sharp nose sniffed as if there were a bad odor in the room.

"Ajit Majumdar is jealous of my power and position," he replied, the cool ease returning like an old suit that fitted well. "I told him that he and all those men in the yard were expendable. And that I am not."

"You are not. Then you are a Thug."

A pause. A nod.

"At last," whispered Das.

"It is the threat to my family that makes me do this," continued Bala. "Otherwise I would die readily. Majumdar will find some way to destroy my loved ones. He has many followers outside this place. . . . Also, he lies, besmirches my name to the others. I was ordered to tell him that he and the rest can't be rescued. It is impossible."

Bala then revealed that he'd been sent by the new Huzoor, whose name even he didn't know. Sufficient that he was the Chosen One.

Shastri prodded. "Will he, then—this Huzoor, this Guru, this Chosen among all others—will he save your family? Will he think that this Bala, his trusted servant, has been threatened by Ajit Majumdar, and will he prevent the deadly rumel from breaking your neck? Will he do this for you?"

A long, long pause. A convincing pause, signifying a tremendous struggle going on within the man.

But was it so? Shastri, watching every millimeter of Bala, was still far from convinced.

"Two days from tomorrow's dawn. At the same hour. When the sun emerges and illuminates certain cliffs where lies the cave temple of Satī—there the Huzoor will meet with the many leaders. The Arm Holders, Diggers, the others will all be present. . . . At dawn, I repeat, the—"

Another jolt as the locomotive made it over a rise and started its descent. Eight minutes, Shastri estimated, eight minutes before arrival.

Locomotive smoke billowed in. Shastri spoke to Gopal, who in turn ordered the doors opened partially. The air diffused the black onslaught. Some of the men had lifted their neck scarves over their faces.

Shastri, with smarting eyes, scanned the landscape, the extension of gray sandstone and black basalt formations directly to the east. The sun was beginning to climb their backs, splaying the irregular horizon of their summits with ruddy streaks. Somewhere a bit farther south-by-southeast lay the cave temple, somewhere on the fringes of the Deccan close to the Western Ghats.

The couplings screeched their complaint as the landscape

leveled. A succession of weavings, bumps, tiltings, and buckings followed, pressing a half-dozen men against the northern wall; then the car eased into a semblance of balance and control. Shastri doubted they could reach the village without waking it, but he'd allowed for that. When it stopped, only he, Das, and Chundra Bala would get out, appearing to all the world like three bedraggled travelers. The rest were to depart thirty minutes later.

It wasn't the best of plans, considering that the Thugs would have lookouts. Far from it. But that couldn't be helped. There wasn't any other way on such short notice. Gopal had hand-picked the men, hoping they were all faithful, not yet aligned with Rasul and the government. Shastri wanted no interference. This thing was his: his alone.

When they arrived, the scream of the brakes lasted too long for his liking. Finally he dropped into the backlash of steam, facing the small village nestled below the semicircle of the cliffs. Looking about, he saw with satisfaction that no gathering of onlookers hovered at the makeshift depot. Shastri brushed the dust from his clothes, hurried from the belch of steam lashing at his legs, and went behind the ramshackle building. He leaned against the depot wall and lit a Sher Bidi. The wall was between him and the cliffs. Bala, with eyes averted, joined him, Das behind. Shastri dared a peek at the dawn creating shadows in the deep-rutted sides of the cliffs.

"How many sentries do you estimate are up there?" he asked Bala.

"No more than two. From those rocks they can see the world around them for many miles. Only two will be necessary."

"And you say you have the power to command them to leave their posts?" Shastri bore into the man's soul. "You are that highly placed?"

"I am," replied Bala evenly. "I have the power."

"Why pick dawn to gather?" said Das. "Why not the darker hours?"

"It is easier to be trapped during the darker hours."

"This won't be easy, Rama."

"You say, Bala, that there are only three exits from the temple?"

The Thug nodded.

"Then, Das, it may be easier than we think. The openings to the temple are small. Even if they pour forth en masse, they'll be trapped, with our men waiting outside. Not too many could escape. If we miss some, it doesn't matter. Capturing most of them will mean we've broken the backbone of their Cause—especially if we catch the Huzoor."

"Ah," sighed Das, "the King Cobra."

"Let's go, then," commanded Shastri, fighting off Das's skepticism. The moment he stepped from behind the depot, he knew they were being observed, however. His trusted instincts informed him.

Chundra Bala led them along a track that ultimately cut into the cliffs, skirting first an elbowing of village buildings. They passed an enclosure holding a family cow and two noisy goats. The haze before full dawn exposed shuffling figures in half-silhouette leading cattle to the fields or carrying brass lotas for cleaning their private parts after relieving themselves.

They were approaching the rocks from the sandstone side at that moment and had to pause while a man and a woman in a bullock cart crossed their path. The man's head was turned away, but Shastri met the woman's eyes as she bent her head toward them. Her nose ring flashed its sheen blindingly, but when the cart moved out of the sun the dark stare froze him in his tracks. Then, as quickly as the shifting light, the cart was gone, creaking into the fields. Shastri watched her back.

Das said, "Is anything wrong?"

"No," Shastri lied. Gut-level imagery pounded against his reason. Who was this woman, and why had her eyes trodden upon his grave as surely as if they were her very feet? What jeering, dark mockery, what uncalled-for hatred lay in that steady black gaze?

Momentarily unmanned, he paused again.

"Quick, Rama; we don't have much time."

This was true. Soon Gopal would lead the rest of the men forward. Shastri urged himself on.

* * *

Chundra Bala led them to the wide main track to the temple, which proved as easy to scale as he'd promised. The trail wound around a nub of cliff, ending at the northeast entrance, some eighty feet up. It was not only the quickest route but the best, the narrower tracks being much too congested with barriers of shrubbery.

Time was of the essence. They must have the sentries with them in the temple when Gopal and the rest set forth.

Arriving at the halfway mark, they entered the deeper shadows of the cliff lip. Trees and shrubs added to the gloom along the track sides. Passing the hollows in the overthrust of greenery and the niches ahead in the cliff sides, Shastri worried. How easy for a Thuggee rumel to be looped over their heads and tightened. How swift, how simple, and with no cry to reach the others on the trail below.

They finally approached the level where the dirt track merged into a stone walkway, ten or twelve feet wide, depending on the condition. Random detritus marred the descent of lush vegetation beyond, where the walk had crumbled from erosion. They soon encountered the first sign of a religious site. Lying face up on the cliffside was a life-size statue of a temple dancing girl, or Satī herself—Shastri wasn't certain which, at first; upon closer inspection, he discovered she wore a number of necklaces, the longest a trademark of the dancing profession.

Carved in black sandstone, the dancer held a garland that arced across her alluring hips and breasts. Alluring, provocative even in sandstone. Bedecked with flowers in her hair, with pitcher plants strewn at her feet.

Shastri heard the hoot of an owl, tensed, realizing it was man-made. Cupping his hands over his mouth, Chundra Bala replied, repeating the sound. Immediately a leathery, clean-shaven man, dressed only in a loincloth, with a sash around his forehead, emerged from behind a rock to their left. He squinted suspiciously at Shastri and Das and asked in Hindi, "Who are they, Guru?"

"They are who they are," Bala said firmly. "Summon your

brother to join you. The watch is unnecessary. There is no need for it."

The man spit a spray of betel nut over his shoulder. "How can you be certain, Guru?"

"Because I am he who went with the Huzoor to the Mother of us all. To the heart of the Gangotri we went. You've heard it told, Mohan. Now obey."

Mohan shrugged and walked away. When he returned with a man barely free of his boyhood, they all walked on.

Once around the turn, Shastri saw that the cliff poured out onto the landscape as far as the horizon like a cascade of tumbling stone that had been halted in the midst of its fall and held in that state by some freak of impossible gravity. The temple entrance was a few yards ahead.

Once inside, they moved down a narrow corridor with a low ceiling. Columns flanked them on both sides, their rectangular bases surfaced with fading frescoes. The ceiling had a sprawling fresco painting that in the light of the wall torches was little but flickering dabs of color.

The ground gradually lowered, and the corridor, with the same slight degree of change, veered more and more to the right. Shastri decided the builders had dug the incline to lead farther into the greater mass of the cliffs, to end—if he remembered his temple lore of the region correctly—in a huge, multi-tiered central chamber. He became convinced he was right when it proved draftier as they moved on. And there had to be space enough to hold the more than seven hundred Thugs.

He lost count of the number of columns. Above the rectangular bases there bulged vaselike shapes with figurines placed wherever there was a horizontal edge. These dwarfed gods and demons were positioned as if they helped hold the columns erect. Some of them were miniatures of sun deities, breasty earth mothers, even the fierce-visaged buffalo demon with a yoke around his neck.

Now, joining the echo of their stride, were voices, a murmur that reverberated everywhere. Then odors: the cloying scent of many human bodies, spices, incense, and smoking torches. Light flickered from the entrances, a mad dance of crimson on

the corridor walls. The torches misted, smoked in black curlicues between the pillars. Without warning, the place had widened extensively, and they had passed beneath the lintel. Shastri's
eyes rose to the high dome of the new chamber, to the three
tiers of crumbling balconies, then to the apses and dagobas on
the sides leading to hidden altars.

His eyes leaped to the awesome source of the sounds, the
odors. Ahead, Das's outline gave a start, expressing the same
futility that was Shastri's current mood. There were just too
many of them! The look, the noise, the stink of them was
paralyzing. Shastri and Das became as immobile as the temple
statues. Both men had seen their share of crowds. But this!
This was a congestion of death breeders.

Yet Major-General Sleeman dealt with them, and very successfully, he told himself. Thuggee had become a memory for
more than a hundred years. Why, then, couldn't Shastri do the
same?

He studied them. A handful were dressed well. Mostly he
saw limber, glistening torsos between turbans and loincloths
and, here and there, stained white dhotis. A gathering of pan-
talooned Arcotees loistered near a cluster of small naves. New
odors permeated—of ghee, of ashes, of cow's dung, all for
coating parts of the body. Opium fumes wafted slowly to him
and hung like an afterthought to the cumulative stench.

Seven hundred and eighty–odd Thugs! With the mark of
their covenant with Kali emblazoned in their minds. Standing,
sitting on the column bases beside the stone gods, squatting in
the dust and shadows. Waiting and fingering in their dreams
the beloved strangler's cord.

Shastri pulled from his reverie as Chundra Bala barked a
command. Bala shouted again, and the wall of backs turned,
noted who he was, and parted.

In single file they walked into the onslaught of staring eyes,
Bala first, then Das and Shastri at his rear. The two sentries
had blended with the mob. Shastri heard the spreading query:
Who were these strangers? Head averted, he resisted any penetrating examination of himself. Yet nevertheless he sensed
them shredding clothing, flesh, and bone to the man within.

They sought his very being, sought to read if he was one of them.

But Bala's presence subdued their curiosity, and gradually the tension among them eased. The mob returned to its rambling, low-toned chatter. Shastri fixed his gaze on Das's shoulder blades. Das, who walked the gantlet as if he were among brothers. Clammy from toe to crown, Shastri willed himself on.

He neared a ring of statues in the room's center representing various zodiacal beings. The first was a moon god whose name eluded Shastri at the moment. An eight-foot-high black sandstone representation in the lotus position, the god rested on an extremely chipped semblance of a cart. That, in turn, was pulled by a chesty bullock. A dozen or so Thugs leaned against the base, the floor at their feet mottled by bits of chewed betel nut. Farther on, the trio approached a much better preserved statue of the sun deity, Surya, with the legless Arun beneath him on a chariot. The handicapped Arun held the reins to a seven-headed horse.

Bala stopped, pointed to an alter yards away, faintly detectable in the restless light of the tapers. Incense writhed throughout the area in such abundance that Das began to choke. Shastri peered hard at the massive stone figure on the dais and concluded it wasn't Satī. Somehow the Thugs had replaced the temple goddess with another, the black Kali. He couldn't believe they'd been so obvious as to drag it through the village below. There had to be another entrance to the chamber—probably on the opposite cliffside, facing the desert, where there was less chance of being seen.

The figure was higher than any carving present. The lolling tongue and fangs in the bestial mouth showed whenever the flame leaped upward. It ended there, however. Shastri tried to find the rest of the face, but it blurred with the unlighted void, the upper reach of the altar. His eyes dropped to the garland of skulls, the four arms gripping the usual Kali weaponry.

He shuddered.

"What manner of Indian are you," challenged Chundra Bala, "who reject the Mother?"

"There are many mothers in India, Bala. There are Satī, Shakti, Paravati, Uma. None of them demands these repugnant practices."

"If you'd seen the Mother as I have beyond, even beyond the cavern of the Rishi Lords . . ." The exchange had begun in whispers; but now, without warning, Bala's eyes rolled upward and, lifting his arms to the heavens, he screamed shrilly, "Mother Kali. O great Bhowani!" Then he bounded away from them and whirled in a succession of circles in the empty space before the tapers. On and on he screamed Kali's many names and spun about, flecks of foam whiting his lips.

"We are betrayed, Rama," Das said.

"No. Wait. Do nothing unless he exposes us."

Both men turned to the mob, alerted. The rest, however, kept their distance, most of them entranced by Bala's words. Now and then Shastri caught a pair of eyes centered on him; yet even these ultimately swerved back to the solitary Thug whirling in tight circles like a drunken man attempting a dervish dance.

"I have heard. I have seen the Mother!" continued Bala. "Praise be Kunkali! Praise be to the Mother of Us All!"

"He's worked himself into a frenzy, Rama. We're lost!"

About to command that Das be quiet, Shastri checked himself as Chundra Bala suddenly stopped.

Then, rumbling slowly, growing, rising ever steady from the far corners of the chamber and rippling forward like a sonic tide filled with deep bass notes, the reply came: "Kunkali! Kunkali! Praise be to the Mother, Kunkali!"

Chundra Bala's arms reached out, invoking. Shastri, alerted for a prepared signal, braced himself for the expected dramatic response. The presence, on time, on cue, that squelched the din of voices caught the Kunkali chant in mid-stride as it rose again.

Caught like an unfinished breath by the tug of a strangler's cord. Just as abrupt, just as total, thought Shastri.

From behind the altar the measured footsteps descended a stairway. Slowly, from the blackness, a head with shoulder-length hair as gray, as tangled and matted as the flow of his beard. The Huzoor! A white turban was coiled around his high, glistening forehead; and when he drew closer, a white dhoti showed, draped over expansive shoulders. His eyes were lost in the smudges of shadows at the cheek ridges. The exaggeration of those cheekbones was startling to see. They protruded on either side of the aquiline nose as if they, too, were carved, part of the surrounding stone. Below the Huzoor the tapers licked crazily and shielded him from full view.

"He is with us! With us!" screeched Chundra Bala, and his words repeated and rang and dashed into fragments of echo from wall to ceiling.

Shastri's spirit was swallowed by all the dim, impenetrable forces in the beliefs of Mother India he had so long denied. The modern, rational man peeled from his persona like a dead husk, and in its place stood his ancient Hindu soul, cringing in despair. Something invisible, but nevertheless very present, had plucked out his reason. Gopa, who by now must be in the entry hall with his men, was forgotten, Das as well. There was only the Thug Lord speaking to his assassins and the restless lighting playing off the resonance of his voice like visual music.

Disbelieving, Shastri moved slowly forward.

Guttural, the timbre strong even in the echo, the words poured forth from the Huzoor, a rapid staccato in Ramasi. When he paused, a roar greeted him; and then, as quickly, silence. Each Thug lowered himself humbly to the ground in homage. Shastri, stopping his forward motion, somehow followed suit. With his nose pointing to the ground, he dared a look at the dais. The Huzoor hadn't stirred. Still, towering impassively, he watched and waited. Finally, a command, and in one ripple of movement they stood.

This time Chundra Bala translated. Shastri sensed the Thug behind him.

"Hear me, children of Kali," Bala began, as the Huzoor's staccato continued. "I've come to you all, summoned by the Mother to do Her will. She who held me as a child suckling at Her breasts that I might be nourished with the power and zeal of Her great purpose. She who defeated the demon Raktavīja and drank every drop of his hideous blood, thereby blackening Her aspect the more, thereby conjoining Herself with death, with war, with plague, and their meaning in the Eternal Balance of Creation.

"Since that which lives must die. And that which dies, if by the hand of one of you, my children—then indeed Mother Kali is pleased. Then indeed is your reward great. Then indeed have you done what She so long ago decreed."

Someone cried out, "Merciful is Kali. Merciful is She to Her Chosen."

Once the prayers subsided:

"How long ago, my brothers? Think now what your fathers and their fathers passed on. . . ."

It was a condensed history of Thuggee. That as distant in time as the reign of the Persian king Xerxes, his horsemen, the dreaded Sagartii, had skill with the rumel. That the writings of Ziā-ud-Dīn Barnī seven centuries ago recorded the great works of Thuggee. On and on the Ramasi of the River Thugs continued, praising one Thug saint after another.

But—and a somber note mellowed the Huzoor's unrestrained pride—the Thugs had often been humiliated. As he recounted each instance, a groan that increased to a drawn-out wail sounded. What of the thousand Thugs captured in Delhi, grieved the Huzoor, who were branded on their buttocks with a heated copper coin? What of the inglorious day when Nanha, the Rajah of Jalun, executed Budhu and his brother Khumoli, those two wondrous saints of Thuggee?

"But did not Kali avenge them?" implored one, shaking a fist in the air.

"Aye," agreed their Lord. "Nanha, the Rajah, was punished with the affliction of leprosy for his evil-doing. And the very next day!"

A sigh of relief everywhere, a unified suspiration.

"And the final humiliation was at the hand of the British Raj. The Raj has silenced the children of Kali for over a century. The sacred rumel, the blessed pickax have been stifled. Is this to continue forever?"

"No!" came the cry.

"Is the will of the Mother to be forever ignored, even thwarted?"

"No!"

"What then, is to be done?"

"Kill!"

"Yes, kill!"

"Kill, destroy, O Chosen One, for Kali!"

"For Kali, Merciful Mother!"

Then the Huzoor added, "Merciful indeed. Are not the victims guaranteed Paradise through such an end?"

"Merciful Kali! Merciful Mother!"

Mother so Bountiful, the praise rang.

But the thought of murder had brought the policeman in Shastri to the fore. His mind raced to Gopal, determining where he and his men were positioned by now. Undoubtedly they were close to the main chamber. No alarm had come from the Thugs, and so at least they were safe. It was but up to him, Shastri, to fire his automatic . . .

But Shastri's hand kept away from his waistband. Instead, his fingers clawed at the air. His eyes lifted behind the Huzoor to the barely discernible statue. Two slightly arched, burnished discs peered down across the altar space like live things. They seemed perched, ready to spring forth and strike him down.

Raising the clawing hand that he refuted as his own, he tried to cover his face, to deny what he saw. But nevertheless Shastri observed the statue gradually reach forth its lower arms. The ebony fingers grasped two objects, clear now with the taper light flush on their surfaces. The crowd sighed again in awe. They saw it, too! In one hand, a large pickax, the consecrated symbol of Thuggee; in the other, the loop of a rumel. The shapely ebony arms stretched, offering the objects to the Huzoor, who in turn took them and raised them above his head in victory.

The din that followed quaked the world around Shastri.

He tore free from his awe, convinced that he, that they all had been hypnotized by the incredible Huzoor. Defiantly he urged himself to move farther away from the gathering.

But he had to see for certain if it had actually happened, and so he looked again at the statue. The arms were back to their original positions, but the discs, the statue's eyes, still

glowed. Glowed alive! It had to be trickery, some type of
prestidigitation! There had to be another human being behind
the Huzoor, a woman, since Shastri had seen feminine arms
uncoiling from the statue's sides. A woman . . . an actress . . .
playing Kali. Yes, that was it: playing Kali.

He must reveal the truth, prove the Huzoor a charlatan. But
how? He heard someone shout his name. Das! Turning, he saw
the spy succumb and collapse at the feet of Chundra Bala. The
Thug was swiftly releasing his rumel from Das's neck.

Agony, a tremendous agony that he'd betrayed Das, made
Shastri double over. But almost immediately he fired at Bala.
An Arcotee had sacrificially leaped before the Guru; now he
stared down at the increasing dark stain beneath the sash of his
pantaloons. Another shot; the bullet settled into a ruddy blotch
in a forehead behind Bala.

Shastri saw and heard little but a discordant blurring as a
ring of heads and bodies formed around him. Somewhere Bala's
voice was commanding that Shastri must die.

There was a trail of screams near the entranceway. Gunfire
reverberated. Gopal and his men!

Shastri heard the Huzoor thundering above the melee. The
blur of faces stared at the altar. They were shocked. The Lord
had given an order they couldn't assimilate, he sensed. Scarves
hung unused between extended fingers. Growls, a misture of
discontent and rage, sounded. Some fell to their knees, appealing to heaven. Again and again the Huzoor repeated his demand;
and Shastri, too, faltered in confusion.

They were being told to surrender, he decided. It made no
sense, but it had to be so. Why else were so many dropping
their rumels, wailing, and beating their breasts?

Ajit Majumdar had warned that the moment of betrayal
would come. As soon as the Thug revival in India was revived,
it was to be betrayed. Why? Why?

For a moment, Shastri thought himself safe. An overwhelming urge to turn and study the giant's face, to pierce the meaning
behind his strange command grew in Shastri, but he willed
himself stationary. Beads of sweat dotted his forehead as he
strained to face the altar.

A slithering noise. A Thug nearly as large as the Huzoor was at Shastri's left. Nails dug into his gun arm, raked down toward the weapon. Shastri kneed the man, but with little effect. He pulled the trigger, and the Thug recoiled with a cry, the bullet whizzing past a muscular shoulder. Shastri regained his balance, aimed, and shot again. The Thug stood transfixed, his one remaining eye wide, as if it could still see, and finally toppled.

Shastri's gun was a Mab Autoloading Pistol with a fifteen-shot magazine. He waved it at the handful of approaching Thugs called forth by Chundra Bala. He searched for the man, but he was being protected by the group. They were under orders to surrender to the kotwal but first ease their frustration by killing Rama Shastri. This was what Bala told them now in the Hindi that Shastri could understand. This was the famed kotwal leader, Bala ranted, who'd led his men here and thus interfered with Kali's will.

The scattered gunfire from Gopal's people was closer. It rang louder, since the Thug resistance had ebbed. The Huzoor's voice in turn was still. They were obeying him almost to the man, and there was no need for his commands. Distraction grappled suddenly with Shastri's concentration. Was the Huzoor's quiet due to his escape?

The handful shuffled toward him, their legs apart, their rumels ready. Shastri backed. He caught a glimpse of Bala's tunic as he left his hideaway and darted past Shastri's right toward the dais. Shastri spun, but quickly saw it was futile. Bala had disappeared behind the ring of tapers.

Too late he realized that the diversion had worked. The Thugs, five in number, were on him. One, a grizzled, wiry man, was swinging his rumel.

The scarf raised, spread, a yellow bat's wing, and fluttered down. A roar accompanied the listless motion, and the Thug, while completing his hurl, jerked. He was dead before the scarf touched ground.

Another Thug fell after a second roar. As the crowd behind them parted, Shastri saw Gopal's smoking gun shining in the

flame light. The other three stranglers stopped when they saw
the bodies, and rewound their scarfs into turbans and sashes.

Breathless, Shastri tottered to the sun deity's platform. One
of the three glanced in his direction, and the wisp of a smile
formed. Alerted suddenly, Shastri threw himself onto his face
and heard the snapping silk above him. He rolled and, from
his back, saw his near-assassin. The man was a young Arcotee
crouched behind the wheel in the shadow of the legless Arun.
Gopal's gun flashed, and the youth fell and hung across the
wheel rim.

"The Huzoor, Chundra Bala—stop them!" Shastri cried,
jumping to his feet and heading into the altar area. As he rushed
between the tapers, he heard a low chanting. With a bound he
was on the basalt dais, his fingers gripping the Huzoor's dhoti.
Nails dug into Shastri's face and pushed his head back with
brutal force. Shastri released his hold.

Shastri tried again. His hand groped, slid along the fabric
of the dhoti, and then seized something from the Huzoor's hand
that felt like parchment. Shastri pulled and the parchment gave,
tore, and Shastri toppled backward. When he rose again the
dais was empty.

Gopal reached him then, found Shastri standing mouth agape,
his body trembling. Before them, in her radiant splendor, was
a statue of Satī, not the black Kali.

Shastri barely glanced at the fragment of parchment as he
shoved it beneath his achkan. Then he followed Gopal and his
men into the dark concavity. A wall partition was slightly ajar;
with the aid of a light, they discovered that it led into a narrow
tunnel. The group moved in between dank walls, deeper and
deeper into the hillside, until Shastri stopped them by announcing, "There must be another passage we missed along the route.
This tunnel goes on too far. Have some of your men follow it
to its end, but I am sure they escaped by a shorter route and
are by now far from here."

"How can you be so certain, Rama?"

"Because I have witnessed the skill at deceiving of this
Huzoor. Have some of the men pound the walls of the route

we just passed until they find the secret exit. That will at least make us feel that we've done our best."

Returning to the temple chamber, Shastri viewed the hundreds of squatting prisoners. He felt no elation, was as empty as any Thug present, despite the fact that in less than an hour and a half the new Day of Thuggee had ended. Or had it?

The man Bala who had killed Das was free somewhere. Bala and the towering Huzoor. And with those two, the spirit of Thuggee was still alive.

Shastri bent close to Das's body, wishing he believed in prayer at this moment.

The woman sat in the cart next to Bidhan, the Arm Holder, and watched the brush along the cliffside. At last the foliage stirred and two figures rushed down the slope and through the tall grass toward them.

The prophecy had come true, she pondered. First, the bad omen of the hare that had crossed their path weeks ago, then the vision that followed. But the Huzoor, Chosen as he was, knew well how to deal with defeat. And perhaps Rama Shastri had been destroyed. If so, then this was victory, in a fashion.

But when the two climbed into the cart, Gauri learned that the defeat had been total.

Shastri has survived. Worse still, he now had a piece of the fourth rishi scroll. The Huzoor had been invoking Kali's power when Rama Shastri tore a fragment from his grasp. At the moment, no one wished to speak of the implications of that. The shock was too great to think . . .

Gauri Bala brooded on the little man she'd seen earlier trailing behind her Chundra. Shastri had made her think of a scholar more than a policeman. But in her vision he'd been an avatar, a warrior; diminutive, yes, but armed with a bow, poised and ready to aim at Kali's breast. There were others with him, too, vague, undelineated figures, armed the same way, each placing an arrow to his bowstring. All prepared, determined to strike the dark Mother. . . .

Chundra Bala was wroth with himself. He'd failed, he moaned. Rama Shastri was his to kill.

"The man was charmed," he ranted. "Again and again I directed a brother to end his days. Like an agile cat he defied the hunter and slipped free of the beaters. What cursed, unknown deity protects him, O Lord? The man believes in nothing. Rumor has it he is an agnostic, that he quotes the Western philosophers. He isn't even a true son of India but a product of the British Raj, trained, educated by that cursed regime. Why, then, should he be charmed? Why is he our major enemy when he is so unworthy of the role?"

The Huzoor replied, "He but thinks he has won. Fear not, loyal Chundra. Whatever protects his being isn't as strong as She Whom we serve."

Bidhan urged the bullock on. The cart left the field, turned onto a road leading south. Dawn, long gone, was replaced with an almost supernal brightness that made Gauri's head ache. Though scholar he'd appeared, she had felt in Shastri's stare the force of a formidable will, a will as disconcerting as this terrible sun, full of merciless light. Gauri stooped and picked up a strip of black fabric that was piled at her feet. She wrapped it around her head, covering her eyes. The cart moved on, jolting on its axle.

SIX

Cambridge/Beacon Hill, Boston

She couldn't get it out of her mind. No matter how hard Santha concentrated on her catalog, she couldn't forget the object in her safe.

She tried again. She lifted one of the figurines on her desk and checked her sheaf of computer printouts. It was a naked torso of a man carved in red sandstone, found at the Harappā site in the Indus Valley. Its realism was amazing, considering its approximate dating of 2000 B.C.

She compared the figurine to one of the glossies on her desk, decided the photograph was good enough for the catalog. She turned the glossy over and marked it with a pencil: *PLATE VIc*.

The next figurine was a terra-cotta hen from the same period and area. It had a hole in its back at the base of the tail and was believed to have been a child's whistle. The thought of a small boy ambling through the streets of Harappā blowing his hen-shaped whistle was so charming that she settled back in her chair, relaxed for the first time that day, as she compared the artifact with a glossy and annotated it.

She was reaching for the third figurine when her eyes fell on a small envelope. The letter should be in her drawer, she thought, not on the desk top where anyone could see it. Still, Santha left the letter where it was.

The third figurine was bronze, from Mohenjo-Daro, and one of her favorites. It was of a girl dancing, caught just as she swiveled her naked hips. Santha had wondered more than once whether this was the beginning or the end of the dance, whether the girl had shed clothing while dancing or performed as naked as she was from the very first step. Santha liked to think that the dancer had started with only her necklace and bangles, as the figurine showed. Somehow it seemed more proper than if she'd stripped gradually.

Santha thought of George Buchan. What would he think if she danced for him that way?

She searched for the glossy that fitted the bronze, and, in doing so, her hand brushed the letter to the desk edge. Santha snatched it up before it fell to the floor. Now, holding it, her fingertips dug into the envelope. The action shocked her. The fingers had acted without her volition. Or had they?

Santha finally succumbed. It was, after all, only a letter from Uncle Ram to her father. She took it from the envelope, fighting off a surge of guilt.

But this was a letter she hadn't read to her father. He had recovered sufficiently to want to read it himself. All she knew was that the letter packet contained a cylinder, and her father had asked if she could arrange to have some of the Indologists of the Peabody study what was in it. Stephen Wrench had explained that it was a fragment of an ancient document but still hadn't let her look at the letter.

So Santha had pilfered it. She intended to return it to its place when she visited her father again. She still couldn't believe she was capable of such deceit. But she had to know what was in the letter.

She unfolded it, read:

Steve,

This is for you alone. Call it typical policeman's uneasiness, but I prefer that none of this leaks out except to the proper authorities. The world is much too small today and what happens on the banks of the Brahmaputra is media news in New York by nightfall. But let me explain further.

Exactly twenty-two days ago, those members of my force still aligned with me and I raided a Thug gathering in a Temple of Satī near the Western Ghats. We captured over seven hundred of them, but unfortunately the Huzoor and his second-in-command, Chundra Bala, escaped. And Das, one of my best men, was killed. You remember him, Steve. We used his expertise at undercover work in the Anatole Dupleix counterfeit ring at Cal. His death is a tremendous loss to me. He saved my life at Pondicherry when a group of irate disciples attacked me for arresting a bloodthirsty guru who was preaching the murder of local Harijans. I grieve that I couldn't repay my debt to him in kind in the temple.

I will save the full account of the raid until we are together in America. The matter at hand is that during a skirmish with the Huzoor I tore a fragment of a scroll from his grasp. It is a scroll reputed to have been given him by a group of ancient rishis in a cave in the Himalayas. Obviously, this is the ruse through which he has kept every Thug band in India in his power. They see him as a twentieth-century avatar, an incarnation under Kali destined to revive Thuggee. I have seen him only in the unsteady light of tapers, but it was enough to stir one's hackles. His face is a garish memory, his body huge and formidable. Of course, that may have all been so much disguise. Theatrics have always been a part of the Thug's weaponry. Still, I must confess that the Huzoor's rolling bass haunts my sleep to this moment.

I am sending the fragment of scroll parchment to you, old friend. Perhaps Santha can recruit one of the Peabody Museum's Indologists to analyze it. The thing is about as old as time, I wager. Tell Santha to hide it. The scroll is the lifeblood of these Thugs, I believe.

Again, I must repeat, Steve, that from now on, Santha and anyone else are to know as little about this as possible. I have no doubt that the survivors of the raid will go to any length to retrieve this fragment. I am trusting you to keep the cylinder safe.

I have left unsaid the other reason for sending you the cylinder. There is a small possibility that I may not escape India. I have been summoned by the government to Cal, and I expect the worst there. Nevertheless, I have also made my own plans, so be assured that shortly I will phone you from Hong Kong, a free man.

Sincerely,
Rama Shastri

Santha rested her head against the chair back and closed her eyes. Thuggee again. She had never heard of it until Uncle Ram's first letter. Since then she'd become convinced that the men sitting on the Deccan mound in her vision were Thugs and that the dead in the grave were their victims. Why, she asked herself, why should she be linked with the reawakening of Thuggee?

Santha froze—a flicker of motion in the dark room corner near the windows. Her chair screeched as she rose quickly and stared. Straining to see through the haze of sunlight filtering into the room, Santha found nothing in the corner.

She thought for a moment. Maybe her teleporting to India was due to a beneficent power. Perhaps she had been given a great and unusual gift to help Uncle Ram and her father. Santha breathed deeply; the tension left her. That was it, of course. Whatever was behind this had to be beneficent. What else could it possibly be?

Santha Wrench left her desk and went to the office door. She opened it slightly, peered into the hallway. At the corridor turn into the wing with the Mayan exhibit, her supervisor, Dr. Angela Kim, was talking with a staff member. Dr. Kim was one of the best Asian Studies people at the museum, Indologist enough to examine the scroll fragment. Santha had seen and spoken to her three times that day, and yet never once had broached the subject.

Santha closed her door softly, locked it, and approached the huge walk-in safe. She paused, looking back as if she expected someone to break down the door and demand to know what she was doing.

It was a silly image. Why was she acting like a criminal? She only wanted to look at the fragment alone, uninterrupted. Santha felt entitled to that much. She was a scholar specializing in ancient Indian artifacts. Wasn't that a suitable reason?

Santha walked into the steel-lined interior. On either side of her were padded shelves and drawers filled with museum pieces. Santha slid back a glass panel. Among a statuette, an eleventh-century bronze Siva, and a stone-carved Buddha bodhi tree was the cylinder. Santha took it, closed the panel, turned to leave, and stopped in mid-motion.

She thought she had heard a clinking noise beyond the safe's door. She waited. The safe felt suddenly hot. Brushing her hand across her forehead, she discovered it was wet. She stared about and wondered if the shadows would darken as before. But the interior didn't change. The overhead lighting flashed from the steel lining and hurt her eyes, but that was all.

The clinking noise didn't repeat itself. Clutching the cylinder, Santha left the safe and braced her body against the metal door while her eyes searched the office. Finally convinced she was still alone, she rushed to the desk.

Clearing the blotter, she sat again and took the contents from the cylinder. The fragment was wrapped in layers of rice paper. Santha unrolled the rice paper, then studied the parchment. A few times she adjusted the desk lamp for better lighting and, using a large magnifying glass, scanned the fibers of the fragment and then the script on its surface.

Using a small plastic ruler, Santha measured the piece. At its highest point, on the left, it measured approximately seven inches high, and, on the lowest side, to the right, two and a quarter inches. Only two lines of script at the bottom were unbroken.

The material suggested the Himalayan districts, since it was the inner bark of the birch tree, well pared and smooth. Southern India had used the leaf of the talipot palm. The script was very early Brahmi, since it read from right to left. The language was Vedic Sanskrit.

As Santha Wrench touched it, the room became vast, a spacious dank place with the distant sound of a tread and a clinking.

Santha quickly withdrew her fingers from the scroll. She now recognized the clinking noise: the sound of many armlets and anklets, a sound common to the women of India.

She ventured to touch the scroll again. This time nothing happened. Using the magnifying glass, Santha began to translate it. She discovered inflections complicated beyond her knowledge. This was ancient Sanskrit, all right, probably the original language of the *Rig Veda*, the earliest of Indian writings.

On and on she worked. Santha translated the words for "mother" and "anger"—or was it "wrath" or, worse still, "dark wrath"? The afternoon passed.

That evening, Santha and George Buchan ate at a small Italian restaurant on Charles Street. She had been preoccupied, and now, noticing that George was looking at her, said, "Damn, but I'm still working on the exhibit catalog. I can't seem to shut it off. Sorry, George."

He shrugged amiably.

"As I was leaving the Peabody this afternoon, I spotted a

poster on the lobby bulletin board. Nirmal Kapur will be giving a concert here on the Hill a week from Friday. Care to go?"

"Nirmal Kapur?"

"The Indian rock star. That doesn't really fit him, though. His music isn't just rock. I'd really like to go, George. Interested?"

"Why not?"

"Good. I'll get the tickets at the Harvard Square kiosk. And maybe we can even talk Daddy into going."

"I saw him today."

"You did? But I thought you'd spend your day off sketching."

"I did. I went to see him in the morning. I stayed for two hours."

"George, you didn't have to. He's not your responsibility."

"I told you. I don't think of it that way. He and I are finally getting to know each other. He was pleased to see me. . . . Besides, he's an uncommonly interesting man. He did most of the talking, and that's certainly progress."

"Knowing Daddy, it must've been a never-ending treatise on India."

"Yes, he spoke of India most of the time. I think he misses the country."

Afterward they walked to Otis Place. There had been little conversation during the rest of the meal, and now the silence continued as they ambled past the pools of light from the gas lamps.

Entering the Otis Place courtyard, Santha could barely wait for them to be alone. The short distance past his parked Audi, the climb up the few stairs to his door, the seconds that George fumbled with the door key—the time felt stretched out beyond endurance.

Inside, George turned on a lamp in the alcove. They went by the doors of his office and into the living room. It was a large room with well-preserved old furniture inherited from generations of Buchans. The place had always fascinated Santha, since it told her much about George's childhood. He had known a similar living room in his parents' Concord home as a boy. Santha felt she shared a bit of his past whenever she entered it.

George was at the fireplace. "Maybe I ought to start a fire," he said.

"Don't," Santha told him, and, taking off her coat, scarf, and gloves, placed them in the Morris chair. She approached him, unbuttoned his topcoat, started to slip it from his shoulders. "Making a fire takes too much time." He responded with a kiss, at first a brushing of her lips with his, and then a long, lingering kiss, as her hands slid over his back gently, over and over again.

George's mouth moved to her neck and the lobe of her ear. Santha whispered his name softly, as if the sound of it was a caress. He returned to her lips, his mouth open, and she opened hers with total abandon to the moment.

George's hand moved to her breasts, cupped one, then the other, remaining just long enough to arouse her hunger for him more. Then his fingers started to unbutton her blouse. Never once did he take his mouth from hers.

When he did pull free, it was only to lower the blouse from her shoulders. George's fingertips barely touched her skin above the slope of her slip. They grazed the surface of her neckline, expressed what his eyes told her.

While they embraced, he bent to her lips again. His hand lowered, unzipped her skirt. It fell past her hips, her knees, to the floor.

George's face burrowed into her slip, into the space between her breasts. His mouth moved to her nipples, hard and taut against the silk. Santha's palms brushed up and down through his hair.

George took her head and nestled it against his shoulder. His hand stroked her hair, and he said, "You're so beautiful, Santha. So incredibly beautiful."

Santha had closed her eyes. She felt herself lifted from the floor and, when she reopened her eyes, found herself in his arms as he walked across the room to the doorway. He carried her into the hall to the staircase. She placed her lips to his chest and closed her eyes again, lost in the comfort of him.

Once in the bedroom, he put her down on the bed gently and bent over her. Santha groped with the buttons of his shirt, and he smiled and helped her by unfastening his other clothes. Naked now, George eased himself onto her, kissing her breasts again. He raised her a little, undid her bra, and pulled down the slip.

Santha watched as George's mouth worked its way to her nipple. Once the mouth found it, Santha arched her back and thrust up her breast until the nipple touched his teeth. The slight pain made her giddy, and when he turned to the other breast, the teeth left their imprint.

O my beloved kesari, she thought, as his face lowered. He pulled her slip down farther, kissing, kissing. My dearest beloved, you're so good to me! The thoughts suddenly became audible: "George, beloved. Darling, oh, that's so loving, my dear heart."

Santha's eyes widened as he burrowed between her legs. The sound of his lovemaking added to the surging fire she felt. Her fingers gripped his hair, and she held him between her thighs, wanting him there forever. Santha moved her hips in rhythm with the motions of his face. Her fire grew and enveloped her.

George moved to enter her, and she wrapped her arms around him. Even when he was in her, it didn't seem to be enough. She wished she could dissolve somehow, be so much a part of him that nothing would be left but the ecstasy of their merging. The feel of him in her, each motion and thrust, spoke so directly of their love. No words could ever say it as well.

Their bodies spoke and sang on until Santha finally fragmented and the ecstasy flung her away. An instant later, George cried out. She felt his hot flow in her, pulled him to her, and held his head against her breast for a long time afterward.

Later, George rose, stretched, and looked down at her. Her dusky body curled, her head resting on a bent arm. "My handsome kesari," she said. "So handsome, everywhere."

"What's a kesari?" George asked. But the question went unanswered.

For Santha Wrench suddenly sat bolt upright, staring across the room.

The scarlet hibiscus. It vied with the pink roses, the white bhant, the lumpy pilings of jasmine, champas, marigolds, and the droppings from a kadamba tree that were floating yellow puffs. The flowers were fresh, alive, covering the crumbling yard and walls; the house a finite, decaying memory and little else. The late day grayed the air, and still the hibiscus throbbed red like a floral pulse. It was an afternoon without breeze, another sultry Indian hour heavy with fragrance, mingled with the trailing scent of sweat and ghee.

A festival, that's what it is, she thought, a festival in some lost, abandoned place. But what kind of festival? And why was she present? Had she been invited or had she stumbled into this desolate courtyard surrounded by shattered, isolated walls and a banyan grove with trunks and branches embracing each other?

She kept away from the grove. Santha walked, then suddenly danced, and walked and danced again past the onetime garden, past festoons of living things, past unclear, shadowy groupings. The fall of hibiscus, ever steady from the roof or the sky—she couldn't see which, look up as she did—pronounced the festivity time, and its buoyancy again stirred her sandaled feet to a dancing beat. Now four steps of beat, now six, now nine, or was it more? She was dancing the nautch, although she'd not known it before. She danced without music, without anklets, danced through the increasing hibiscus, shuffling, crushing the scarlet petals, leaving a flat winding design behind her like a tail made of flecks of blood.

Her cadence quickened. Stomping, beating time on the pavement, Santha accepted her abandonment fully. She was meant to do this thing. Spinning, moving forward and back and forward again, she felt that the festival was for her: hers and hers alone that day. The sky, the earth, all nature were celebrating her. The reason why became as blurred, as obliterated as the descending flowers. She whirled, cried out . . .

And a mocking challenge answered her.

Perched on the rooftop brim, Santha saw four squatting

monkeys. Two were sacred hanuman langurs smashing mango rinds against the stone. The largest, about thirty inches long, ruffled his white fur at her, his black proboscis jutting out as he screeched. He was the leader of the quartet; the rest only noised when he began. One of them, a small rhesus to the left of the langurs, leaped up and down and threw clutches of shoots at her. The last, a lion-tailed macaque, shook his head until the hair of his wide mane bristled out. They were upset at her joy, she knew, and, stopping her dance, she darted through a narrow doorway.

Inside, in a room that ran the breadth of the main house, Santha stood quietly while the monkey protest subsided. Remnants of sunlight eased across the threshold, thinning into a pinpoint that ended in the dark beyond of the place. Her concentration fell on the slow seeping of hibiscus through the doorway. Santha stepped forth and let the scarlet flow pile around her feet.

Beyond was an uncompromising gloom. The tip of the sun streak was lost in her shadow, but nevertheless she still waded with the stream of flowers. But one final step and it was over. The festival spell was gone. Santha could dance no longer. The room was too abandoned, too vacant, like the sorrow of death. The place was a lingering shell of a tragic yesterday.

There was a stirring against the distant wall. Santha ran to it. A filmy blue in the wall had appeared through the gloom, and in that haze was a figure. No, two! Santha reached the recumbent woman and the child she held in her arms. The woman was dressed in a bright saffron sari.

Pain, deeper than life, more than reason allowed, filled Santha. She had recognized the woman's face! It was her mother, Kamala, and the little girl was none other than herself!

Then she heard the clink of anklets and quickly turned again to the blue haze, thinking the woman had awakened. A new shape, blued in the light, was holding something heavy and round above its head. The round object descended with a crash, as dust and debris floated to Santha.

Rising, Santha passed through the dust before it settled. Reaching the woman again, she froze at the open eyes. Part of the woman's forehead had been crushed beneath the stone. The lovely face was speckled with blood and bits of flesh and brain. The baby was still alive, still asleep.

Santha could only stare as she drifted within herself and waited for what she was certain must happen next.

The clinking, a summons. Santha obeyed, looked at the wall and at the second woman standing there. That woman smiled, beckoned. She had hibiscus in her ghee-scented hair, and a sliver of scarlet glided down, gently touched her nose ring, and continued its graceful course to the ground.

"Santha!"

She closed her eyes.

"Santha!"

She didn't want to go to the wall. She opened her eyes, saw that her arms were outstretched to push the woman away.

"Santha . . . my darling!"

George had grabbed her wrists. He was talking, desperately trying to get her attention. Santha's eyes were still fixed on where the woman had stood, but now it was another wall, with a Currier and Ives print of ice skaters on the pond of the Boston Public Gardens.

Santha pulled her arms free, staggered, and hit a gateleg table. The abstract sculpture in Steuben crystal on its top tottered and nearly fell. Santha moved on, examining George's room. Once convinced she was no longer in India, she turned to him.

"What happened?" George persisted in a calmer voice.

She shuddered, placing her arms over her sweat-streaked breasts. She could feel her heart thumping against her palms.

"Santha, you were in a trance. You seemed to see something across the room. Something repelled you terribly. What in hell did you see?" George searched her face. His hand slid to her wrist again, and he felt her pulse. His other hand touched her forehead, stayed there awhile.

"George," she said firmly, "I'm all right. I must've been dreaming."

"You weren't asleep, Santha. We were talking when it happened. What was it, darling?"

"I don't know. I . . . can't remember. And I don't want to discuss it now, Dr. Buchan."

"It's nothing to be ashamed of. You've been under a lot of strain lately."

Santha pushed at him until he released her. She started to pick up her clothes. "Turn it off, George," she said. "I'm not one of your clients. You're prying."

"Prying! For Christsake, Santha, I'm in love with you! We no sooner finish making love than you go into a trance state, pointing and gasping at something in the room, something that only you could see! Why wouldn't I be concerned?"

She was dressing hurriedly. "I need some space for myself. Some time to think . . ."

"Santha, has this happened before? Are you ashamed? Don't be. Hallucinations can happen to anybody under certain conditions."

"Hallucinations!" Santha seized her topcoat. "I'd better go."

George stood in her path. "Santha, can't you stop for a moment and explain what you saw?"

"I'm tired. I want to go home. I need . . . to be alone. . . ."

"I don't feel right about your leaving now."

"Oh, you don't! How will you stop me, George? Put me into an institution for observation, as you once wanted to do with Daddy?"

"That's damn unfair!"

Santha gripped his arm. "George, try to understand," she begged, her voice muffled as she placed her face against his chest. "Maybe I am ashamed. . . . I need some time to myself, George, to think things out. I'll phone you before I go to sleep. Let you know I'm okay. I promise, love."

She heard, "This has happened before, hasn't it, Santha? When did it start?"

There, he's at it again, Santha thought. She looked at him coolly. He'll never understand, she concluded. She had to leave now, before he probed further. The event, even though terrifying, a nightmare, was still hers alone: her private journey to the East.

"I'll phone," she promised, kissed him lightly, and hurried from the room.

SEVEN

Alipore, near Calcutta

Krishna Rasul hulked forward above his food, glared across the table.

"Then you agree, Rama Shastri, the Thuggee matter has ended at last?"

Shastri paused and shrugged.

"There you go again, Rama. What exactly are you saying?"

Shastri cut off a piece from his tandoori chicken. He gazed down the table as if someone else had made the query. Sixteen men, all officials, sat on both sides of the long, marble surface. Most were Rasul's staff, the others government men who knew Ved Addy.

The hall was one of the larger ones at the Addy family mansion in Alipore, south of Calcutta. Its lush, carefully nurtured lawns and gardens held statues and fountains reminiscent of any European city. A courtyard opened into spacious rooms with floors designed from marble bits. And then along the maze of apartments and galleries more statues, busts, oil paintings, priceless urns filled with varieties of aspidistra—and very little of the art Indian. Walls with last-century British wainscoting, walls of white and red marble, layers of satin drapes bordering towering windows, crystal chandeliers in the center of every major room. Farther in, and almost the complete area of the southwest wing, was the ballroom. Swathes of shadow from the huge, drawn wooden blinds hid oils ranging from a few early Turners to modern abstracts by Bengali artists.

Such was the wealth of Ved Addy, who was only a landlord and not part of the royalty that still resided in Calcutta.

"Well?" asked Rasul. "What are you thinking of, Rama Shastri? Don't you believe the matter finished? Come. Come. Are we to be burdened once again by your unnecessary detective games? Is this another one of your assaults on the government?"

Shastri checked his chronometer. Now, among the crew of white-tuniced and -turbaned servants poised against the wall, the floor cleaner's cue should come any second. Every five minutes so far, the man had set about his task. Suddenly, as if by an innate sense, since there was no clock in the hall and he did not wear a timepiece, it happened: the cleaner bent, seized his basin and a damp cloth, and proceeded to mop the floor around the chairs of the eaters.

"They did agree to the government's terms," persisted Rasul. "They have surrendered fully, these Thugs. Have vowed by Kali, their Mother, to cease their murderous practices. What more do you want? The government has won, don't you see?"

"The government has done nothing," replied Shastri finally. "It was the Huzoor who demanded their surrender. I was there, present in that temple, remember?"

"Are you certain he gave that command? You say you don't understand Ramasi."

"Admit it, Rasul: your reports state that the Thug prisoners say it was so."

"I ask you again, Rama. What more do you want?"

Shastri eased his chair back to allow room for the floor cleaner, squatting and mopping between his feet. He looked back at Rasul and noted the open, angry focus on him, the big clenched fist on the tabletop. Ah, he's more aggressive, more expressive of his wrath, Shastri thought; the time is near.

"Well?"

"Rasul, I want that Huzoor. I want this Chundra Bala, who killed my man, Das. I've said that to you these past five days. Need I repeat myself?"

"What can they do, those two? Where can they go without being sooner or later captured? You act as if they can grow

wings and fly to Peru. We will find them. The case is closed.
The mass of the Thugs have been arrested, and that is sufficient."

"Sufficient, yes. Sufficient that the press will have no more
news of it, if you have your wish. Then the government will
continue to appear progressive. Sufficient that they have put
an end to the old embarrassing ways like Thuggee."

Despite Rasul's cutting stare, Shastri lit a Sher Bidi with a
steady hand. Rich baritone laughter sounded at the table's head,
and the hand faltered. Ved Addy had just exuberantly responded
to one of Ileana's remarks. Sprinkled with naughtiness, it had
carried. Shastri spotted Rasul's smile of mocking triumph. This
was one time Rasul hadn't minded Ileana's presence. Shastri
should never have brought her with him, but the old habits
lingered again. She hated being alone at the kotwalee, and
besides, he'd sensed these were their very last days together. . . .

No doubt of it. The time was at hand. Soon—today, tomorrow, the next day—they would try to imprison him. They
would easily create some charge against him, especially now
that "the Thug matter" was over, now that they had him here
in the state of West Bengal. And why not? He was needed no
longer, feared less and less as his strength as the kotwal was
gradually depleted. Those still loyal to him, like Gopal, could
do little to help because of their minor positions in the official
hierarchy, while those high enough who might sympathize
feared, justifiably, for their own freedom.

Feeling Ileana's eyes on him, Shastri returned to his best
detached mask. She understood it for what it was, so there was
no gain there; but at least Ved Addy wouldn't know the truth
about him: that, whatever Ileana's defects, she'd been to him
as much as most women could be to a man.

Whether Ileana's new plans had evolved before their arrival
four days ago or when she first met Ved Addy was unimportant;
but it was certain now that she had set her course. Once Addy
and his surroundings were present, the opportunist in her seized
the hour. Her motives, though, were primarily emotional, not
mercenary. To his credit, Shastri had arranged an annuity for
his mistress of so many years, a sizable sum, so the need for

money was secondary. That Shastri intended going, if he had to flee, to America without her instead of to Paris with her was the breaking point.

Thus she had focused on Ved Addy.

Shastri recalled how the relationship had developed.

Huge, like Rasul, Addy had a far superior body tone; has boot-black hair was streaked white in waves, his face jaggedly handsome, with much thick eyebrow and a jaw millimeters less than undershot. A sportsman skilled at polo, he had bragged garrulously about his game at the Royal Calcutta Turf Club, and Ileana had gushed. Adding, of course, how wonderful it must be to see him "at it." Amazing to the observing Shastri, since she'd never gone with him in the past to watch the sport, claiming it was all "blustering male games," a method of "proving one's manhood"—something her Mongoose didn't need to do.

Smitten, Ved Addy had showed her his treasures: his grounds, his house, his pieces of art. The only possession he had wisely omitted was his wife, whom he'd left in the women's quarters throughout the entire visit.

Fifteen years younger than Shastri, as educated, as Westernized, Ved Addy considered himself cultured. He owned priceless objects, quoted the great authors freely, played a reasonably good piano. But he lacked the soul of a philosopher or poet and fell very short of his lofty opinion of himself. It was perhaps a family trait, since from the earliest days of the British Raj the name Addy was synonymous with "frightful bores."

Nevertheless, he and Ileana had freely discussed books, theater, music, paintings, in short, all of the interests Shastri had taught or told her about, and including, needless to say, Paris, which Addy, picking up her enthusiasm, had claimed to visit every five years or so. And, come to think of it, he was due to see it again. *Due*, he had stressed, with a look of firm conviction, as if it had been weighed, truly planned for, and meant to be adhered to, like that other Five-Year Plan.

Shastri was brooding on how quickly he'd been replaced, when a uniformed man came up to Rasul's chair carrying a dispatch. Rasul read it, dismissed the man.

"I have here," he then told Shastri, "a communication that will interest you. The government has seen fit to take control of those Thug prisoners at the kotwalee compound. It is felt, since there are so many of them, it is best that your men have assistance in guarding the place. We've sent troops, you see. . . ."

Shastri made a flickering motion, as if he'd been distracted by some small flying thing. "I expected as much," he replied calmly.

Surprise. "You did?"

Another nod.

"Then you won't contest our actions?"

"I won't."

Rasul was disappointed. "Why? I don't understand. I mean . . . you usually do. . . . Are you saying that you finally agree with our policies?"

"Oh no, Rasul," Shastri assured him. "Not that. Consider it common sense, Rasul. I don't intend to fight the government on this matter. The prisoners are all yours with my blessing. I've done my job by capturing them in the first place, and therein my job is finished."

The usual slap on the massive thigh. "Good. I'm glad that you've finally seen reason, Rama. The dispatch goes on to say that we've communicated with their leaders already, and they are more than willing to cooperate. They will return to their homes, vowing first to cease their practices, of course. Didn't I tell you it was all very possible, months ago?"

"That you did."

A long silence ensued. Rasul began again. "There is a mystery, however, that must be solved. . . . This dispatch also states that one of the Thugs is missing. He seems to have escaped. No doubt he bribed one of your guards, Rama Shastri, and we are determined to get to the root of it. This Jumaldehee leader— the one Ajit Majumdar. You know that he is missing?"

"Yes. He escaped, somehow, shortly after we returned with the prisoners. We searched and searched for him everywhere, Rasul. To no avail. I don't think he can do much damage, however. He stands alone now."

"As I recall, he was a very dangerous fellow. The same one that I interviewed, you remember."

"I remember. And he was especially dangerous, I agree. But I can't fathom where he is or how he ever escaped."

"You're certain of that, Rama Shastri?"

"You don't think I helped him, do you, Rasul?"

"Of course not!"

"Then how could I possibly know? And why are you disconcerted about the loss of this Thug? You have most of them, don't you? Except the Huzoor and Bala. It seems to me, Rasul, that your concerns are misplaced. Concern yourself about those two instead. They are deadlier than an army of Ajit Majumdars. And yet you show no worry about them. Now, excuse me, Rasul; I must go to my room."

Rasul smiled as Ved Addy's laughter rang out again. "Of course. But I didn't realize our little banquet would weary you so soon."

Shastri barely heard him. He had already crossed the hall to the exit.

Now he moved silently over the grounds toward the Addy House extension in the rear.

Shastri stopped, waited for a domesticated peafowl to fly to the branches of a tree ahead, lest its cries alert the many sentries Rasul had positioned everywhere. Once the fowl settled, he ventured on, rapped finally on a door placed deep in a wall. It was opened by Gopal.

"Tonight. It must be tonight," Shastri said as soon as the door closed behind him.

He didn't hear Gopal's response as he turned to face the figure seated on the edge of a charpoy. Although he was dressed as a fellow policeman, Ajit Majumdar's grim face with its blazing eyes and grotesque cheekbones was recognizable. How they had been able to delude others that the Thug was one of them was nothing short of miraculous, considering the look of him, Shastri thought.

"He's been a model prisoner," Gopal informed him. "He

lets me tie him when we sleep. He never tries to escape. Not once."

"Of course not," Shastri agreed. "His curiosity is too aroused. Isn't that so, Majumdar? Curiosity and a desire for revenge keep you to this spot, am I not correct? You wonder if I truly mean what I say, that I will trail the Huzoor and this Chundra Bala to the ends of the earth, if necessary. You are rooted here in confusion, quarreling within yourself if you should betray them. Again, I impress on you: Why hesitate? Did they not betray you and hundreds of your brother Thugs to the authorities?"

When there was no reply, Shastri pulled up a chair and began to smoke. For minutes he smoked and thought and stared at the Thug and was quiet. He'd discovered that Majumdar held him in some awe when Shastri had returned from the cave temple to the kotwalee with his many captives.

With this in mind, Shastri had commanded Gopal to smuggle Majumdar from the prisoners' compound, nourishing the lie that the Thug leader had escaped. Again and again Shastri had questioned the Thug about the private conversation Majumdar had had with Bala weeks earlier. Shastri was certain that Bala had revealed something important that day, something which had driven Majumdar into a murderous rage. That much Das had discovered. And, determined that the dead infiltrator's effort would not be in vain, Shastri had pressed on and on.

"Majumdar, you are so obviously wise in the ways of God— tell me this: Why have the Huzoor and Bala fled? Why didn't they surrender with the rest? What other scheme, what new plan have they? Have they, too, completely forsaken the teachings of Kali? Have they, too, sworn never to use the rumel again? Answer me that, Majumdar."

The Thug rubbed his gnarled hands, with their birthmark discolorations. But he had kept silent, and Shastri had had to let the interrogation rest for a while.

This night, the night of his leaving India—everything— behind, Shastri went at it with full confidence. Given his last chance to discover the secret, he was like a man possessed.

The policeman in him screamed to know. This, his most important case, wasn't finished; he must at least find the truth of it.

"Listen, Ajit Majumdar," he ventured in mild tones, "I no longer have anything against you. You have been a faithful Thug, faithful to your beliefs. Beliefs, practices which, I admit to you freely, I abhor. But you are powerless, helpless to pursue them any further. Your brother Thugs have surrendered to the government. They have sworn by Kali, their Mother, to forsake the ways of Thuggee forever. They wouldn't listen to you if you were to beg them to rise again. Do you trust what I say? Or do you think that I lie?"

Surly: "I know you do not lie, Rama Shastri. You are my enemy, but you do not lie."

"Then let me say that this is the last night that I am with you. I must flee, since the government would arrest me as surely as they would arrest a thief or murderer, although I am neither of these. Now, when I leave, I can free you as well. You are no longer my responsibility, and I don't desire to leave you a prisoner here, perhaps forever, bound and gagged, with no one to know that you are in this place. To die in time, you understand, from hunger or thirst. It serves no purpose. But I warn you, I am determined to learn what Bala told you."

Shastri poured water from a pitcher and rinsed his mouth. Then he swallowed, waited until his throat was clear, and continued. "Has it ever occurred to you that you were a victim of a ruse?"

"A ruse? But all the Leaders of the various bands had the same dream! . . . That a Huzoor was to come, appointed by the Godess."

"Yes, I know of that. Was it ever proved that this man— this one whom Bala claimed to be the Huzoor—was it ever proved that he was really so?"

Shastri tested the silence, but it remained unbroken. He charged in again. "Would the real Huzoor, the real Chosen One, would he have suggested something that would affect all India so badly?"

Still nothing.

"Would he? What was it, Majumdar? Answer me. You are

protecting a charlatan, a false Lord. Tell me, and save yourself from a horrible end."

Success came. It eased forward slowly, hesitantly. Majumdar blurted, "Yes. It is possible. Very possible. We had only Chundra Bala's word for it, the word of a man who by rank and age should have served me instead of my obeying him."

"Then you will tell me."

A nod.

"Then please do, and swiftly, if we are all to escape in safety."

Another nod.

"I urge you, Majumdar . . ."

The Thug's eyes searched the room, hoping that at the last moment Kali would rescue him. He paused, sighed, writhed with inner pain, and surrendered. "Bala confided this and this only: he said . . . first, that we in the compound wouldn't be rescued. That he himself would leave, though. He had a plan to—"

"Yes," interrupted Shastri. "Knowing that I must have a spy in the compound, he took the risk that I'd save him from you. But that's another story. Go on. . . ."

"We, all of us, I was still inspired by how the Huzoor had gone to the Roof of the World and received the great scrolls from the ancient rishis. These scrolls granted other powers as well, the dreadful gifts of Kali Mother. It was this tale that Bala told, of how the three of them—an ancient sadhu, the Huzoor, and he, Bala—went into a cave at the Ganga Gangotri and therein saw the four rishis, who proclaimed themselves and hurled the scrolls to this Huzoor, our Leader. . . ."

"Remember, now, it was from this Bala you heard this. No one else."

"Aye. But such a tale he told. He spoke of seeing the Goddess Herself give suck to the new Lord. He spoke of a place like no place ever, where creatures reside that no man has ever seen . . . until then. He spoke like a man who'd seen the end of Time itself. . . ."

"Think now, Majumdar. There are those who can weave great falsehoods, can create from their fertile imaginations epics of falsity. Perhaps you've met such before. Perhaps this Bala

is of such a breed. Think more of what he told you later that
made you want to kill him. Think, fasten on that, and you will
see a Prince of Deceivers indeed."

"Aye, we had a villager, Kashi, who told marvelous fab-
rications concerning Vishnu. The god had appeared to him as
a young man near a stream and offered him riches beyond
measure. The god manifested as Mahadeva, the matted-hair
ascetic. This time Kashi claimed the god promised him his
treasures in a fortnight. That was when Kashi was thirty-five.
He is now close to fifty, as poor as ever. But he embellishes
so well that the villagers listen with much attention. When I
last heard him, lovely devas were sharing his bed. You see,
his wife died and—"

Shastri raised his hand. He'd found himself smiling, as if
Ajit Majumdar were just any Indian giving a friendly account
of life in his neighborhood. This man with his whimsical story
was a murderer, he reminded himself, one who'd strangle that
same Kashi with guiltless ease if he felt Kali desired that particular victim.

"Then you do know of what I speak," he pressed. "Think,
then, of Bala as a man with this genius for fabrication, although
much more devious than your villager friend. How else could
it be? Would a true Huzoor threaten the very soul of India?
Now tell me of this thing that made you wroth."

Rage snapped from Majumdar's stare. "Bala's wife has
visions, dreams. So he stated, and this Huzoor—if he be so—
trusts her every word. Bala said that two nights before he
arrived, she dreamed that you might stop us."

"Me? How is that?"

"How is that? Haven't you done so? The woman communes
with the Goddess. Chundra Bala says that his wife, Gauri, has
long communed with the Mother. And in the dream there lurked
a strong possibility that you might succeed. If so, the Huzoor
had made arrangements to go someplace else. First they would
seek to destroy you. But if that failed, then they would flee to
another land."

"Where? Burma? Thailand? Malaysia, Indonesia?"

Ajit Majumdar stood, his lean, muscular body trembling as

he cried out, "No! That was it, Rama Shastri! A nearby land meant hope. Ultimately, if you succeeded in stopping us, we could rise again, recross the border unseen, and perhaps even assassinate you someday. I would've gladly done it. Gladly invaded your quarters and used the rumel on you. Gladly sacrificed myself to keep the Cause of the Mother alive. . . . But this land was far away! A land without belief in Kali or Vishnu or any other of our gods!"

"What land? Tell me, man. Did Bala say what land?"

"Yes. Bala said America. Even now, I cannot believe he said America."

Shastri moved to the table near the door and took a flask of whiskey from a drawer. He drank long before he sat down again.

"You are certain? You are telling the truth?"

"It was as I've said. Why else would I have been so incensed? Every Thug brother in India they have betrayed. What business have we in America?" He spit and repeated, "America. It is uncommon strange, Rama Shastri, that a Thug Huzoor would pick this land. I have not seen his face, but he cannot be the true one who was foretold in our dreams would come. A true Huzoor would never have chosen this America."

Shastri did not believe in coincidences. But Gauri Bala's dream, his importance in it, and now Majumdar's revelation that both he and the residue of the Thug uprising were heading for the same hemisphere! The continent, the country on the other side of the globe, the United States! It reeked of concepts Shastri had long considered part of somebody else's deluded cosmology. The vocabulary of the Great Unwashed. A vocabulary of license, of words that only strengthened ignorance and stagnation. Predestination, destiny, God's Design—all the verbal ingredients that made up the people's opiate. No, he refused to succumb to any religious explanation. It was nothing but sheer coincidence. A mind-boggling coincidence, true, but little else.

He decided. "Gopal, fetch our rags. We'll leave now."

His aide returned with stained dhotis and turbans, and, while they took off their uniforms, Gopal whispered so the Thug wouldn't hear, "So the trail leads on. Even over there it continues. You were meant to thwart their evil ways, Rama. Someone smiles on you."

"No one smiles," Shastri growled. "And perhaps Bala lied about their destination as well."

"I think not, old friend. I think you are greatly smiled upon. God loves whom He wills, whether He is loved in return or not. Any aspect of His Goodness may be smiling. Krishna, maybe, or Lord Vishnu. Or that Prince of Sagacity, Ganesha. Yes, I think the stars have already planned this thing, and it is you who have been chosen to follow this Huzoor's trail to America."

"You are getting old, Gopal, and it's fitting that you're due for retirement. Perhaps in your old age you can sit cross-legged and quote from *The Panjika*. As if there weren't enough foolish astrologers in India reading from their almanacs." Shastri noted the pain in the other's eyes. "Here," he offered in a warmer tone. "Drink from my flask. There's a chill tonight. Drink to me and my journey and that you are the wiser of us two. Drink that you're right, for if indeed I'm meant to grapple with this son of Kali again, I will need all the smiles and the power of the stars that you talk about."

Shastri turned quickly from the tears in Gopal's eyes. "I drink instead," he heard, "to perhaps the last of India's great men that I will ever meet."

Once on the grounds, the trio kept to the shadowy blotches beneath the trees. They reached an open space before a long, colonnaded porch splaying out intervals of lighting from the mansion's high windows. Doubled over, they darted past. Each time a bar of window glow touched them, Shastri held his breath, but they were never once spotted by the guards. As they scurried by the northeast corner near a flank of more trees, Shastri saw a woman peering out at them. He wondered if it was Ileana.

Their destination was an old gate once used for delivering food supplies. It had been sealed with plaster, but Gopal, the previous night, had dug the plaster loose from its place between door and wall. Beyond the wall, hidden well among shrubbery, was a battered 1969 Renault R-10.

As they neared the gate, they listened to the stirring of peafowls above. Again they had been spared detection. But only a few minutes later, a hand grabbed Shastri's wrist. Gopal cocked his gun, but soon lowered it as he recognized Ileana.

Shastri scanned her eyes, then turned his gaze swiftly into the sepia night. She said nothing, but her nails raked gently across his arm. He wished she'd stayed within the mansion with that ridiculous Ved Addy. It was unfair—unjust—for her to have flaunted her affections as she did with such a man and then to come to him at this moment. Why hadn't she come to him before, if she cared?

Coldly, wanting to hurt her, he finally said, "I won't be in Paris."

Ileana nodded. Her fingers never stopped the raking, and he knew she was experiencing sorrow.

He wanted to say, "So now you know what you have lost!" but he wouldn't play that game. He'd leave it all behind. Not a sign, not a flicker of affection would he show, but give her nothing but a bitter memory for her troubles.

Ved Addy's voice rang in the bush: "Ileana, where are you? Ileana!"

"I didn't . . . !" she began, and Shastri covered her mouth while Gopal stood prepared with his weapon.

It was then that Ajit Majumdar moved. Falling back, he blended into the shadows and was soon crawling toward the voice that persisted in calling Ileana's name. Each time the Thug heard the call, it pounded through him. The sentries might hear and come. The three of them would be caught and, as he saw it, he would be imprisoned once again. And that couldn't be. Ajit Majumdar had reasoned throughout the interrogation, had weighed, evaluated every one of Rama Shastri's suggestions; and the answer that had evaded him these many months had exploded in his mind like a quick dawn. Crawling on, he unraveled his turban, found the proper-sized pebble, and tied it to one end of the fabric.

Ajit Majumdar thanked the strategy of Kali Mother that She

had blinded Shastri so well. Marvelous was Her web of deceit, to have ensnared Her greatest threat in this manner. Now the hunter Shastri must leave India, and the false Huzoor with him. Now the government—indeed as blind—would release his brothers, thinking the hour of the Thug ended.

Now it was he, Ajit Majumdar, to whom these things had been revealed. And now, in time, the Mother would fulfill the prophetic dream and show to all, to every band, how they had been mistaken in their choice. Now she would embrace him, the same Majumdar who had been ever faithful, he who had been sorely tested and proven true. It was he who was to be the One.

But the voice must be stilled first. Majumdar edged beneath the trees on his haunches, staring up at the fluttering, colorful array of peafowl wings. He slowly stretched himself along the trunk of a palm, holding the scarf in a loop. The hugh body stood before him. Majumdar waited until Ved Addy had finished a sentence and then lowered his rumel.

"Where have you been?" Gopal asked fiercely when Majumdar stood in their midst a moment later.

"I hid. I was afraid."

"Well, he's stopped calling. Rama, shall we go?"

"I didn't tell him. I would never betray you," Ileana said, and Shastri surrendered and held her close."

"I know," he replied.

"I will go to Ved and lead him away from here," she volunteered, breaking free.

Shastri watched her turn and dissolve into the grove.

They had found the Renault and were slowly leaving the grounds when Shastri noted Majumdar adjusting his turban. For a second a thought nibbled at Shastri's consciousness, but the bumpy road gripped his concentration. He would be relieved when they let Majumdar go at the outskirts of Calcutta. It was hard enough fleeing India minus Ileana, without having to worry if the strangler's hands of Majumdar were forever stilled.

EIGHT

Beacon Hill, Boston

Parking her Volkswagen on Brimmer Street, Santha Wrench took out her compact and freshened her face. She wanted to look her best. George and Stephen Wrench were waiting for her at the Pinckney Street apartment, and she sought to hide any telltale signs of stress. Since the night of the second "event," at George's place, Santha had managed to ward off his questions successfully. Sometimes her responses had been very aggressive. Now she worried that in time she would alienate him from her, that she'd lose him totally.

After all, to his thinking, Santha was mentally disturbed. George had never said so outright, but how else would a trained psychiatrist diagnose her? Putting herself in his shoes, she found it very understandable.

But limited, she felt. The Indian in her saw reality, saw what was normal in much broader terms. Western psychiatry didn't include metaphysics or mysticism in its study of man. Unless, of course, one included the theories of people like Carl Jung and R. D. Laing, thinkers who weren't especially popular with Dr. George Buchan. That much he'd told her once, and it didn't bother her in the least then. Now it did, strongly. Santha admitted that her attitude about psychiatrists had always been unfairly prejudicial; that it was only a defense mechanism she refused to accept. It was because of her Indianness, plain and simple.

Her experiences weren't psychologically rooted. Despite Kamala's presence in the last one, Santha was convinced she was in touch with Something beyond clinical analyses.

Santha closed her compact, then prepared to leave the car, to step into the downpour. The storm had intensified during

the last hour, and the drive from Cambridge to Boston had
been very difficult. One could barely see beyond a few yards
ahead. She had left work later than usual, still attempting to
translate the fragment of the mystery scroll.

It wasn't easy. The verbs of Vedic Sanskrit were especially
demanding, the mood or sense of them extremely complicated.
Santha had searched Harvard's Widener Library for any material on the early language. She hadn't dared to speak to anyone
about it, since she now felt possessive about the scroll. The
reference to the Wrathful Mother Santha had concluded meant
Kali, sometimes called Devi, Bhowani, and Durga. Or, worse
still, Kunkali, the Man-Eater. Any of the names conjured up
the memory of the Indian woman who had crushed her mother,
Kamala, in the last psychic event.

That thought made her pause, and Santha wondered why
she wasn't terrified. Instead, she felt comforted that things
ancient and Far Eastern were so close to her again, that India
had reached across time and space to her. And, yes, even
Kunkali was part of it, dreadful as she was.

Santha had come to believe more and more that she was
being prepared for some great new work. The psychic happenings, the changes in her recently were a part of a training,
of her soul, orchestrated by some unknown force. It was mystical, personal, private. She must wait, meanwhile, for the
outcome and follow her strongest instincts.

Santha left the car. Opening her umbrella, she headed for
the Pinckney Street corner. Beastly night for a concert, she
thought; if the feature weren't the fabulous Nirmal Kapur, she'd
have preferred not to go.

Santha reached Pinckney Street and rushed into the corner
building. She closed her umbrella and looked out at the street.
The wind had risen along the Charles River, and it pressed the
storm back across Storrow Drive and under the building's awn-
ing. The onslaught hammered the door with a clatter nearly as
loud as a surge of hail. Santha had never adjusted to New
England winters after her early years in India. Now, even in
the warmth of the hallway, she shivered.

A man was exiting. Santha turned, cried, "Hold the door,

please," and rushed up the stairs and passed him, then darted into the lobby. As she pulled open the elevator's steel grating, Santha realized that her father and George didn't know she'd finally arrived. Because the man had let her in, she didn't have to buzz her father's apartment.

The elevator stopped at the next floor. Santha started to head for the apartment. Suddenly she stood still. George and Daddy don't know I'm here, she thought again. I wonder what they're talking about. Santha tiptoed the rest of the way to the door. She hadn't yet returned the spare apartment key she'd used when checking her father's condition weeks ago. She took it now from her purse and fitted it in the lock. Slowly she turned the key, and the lock clicked. She grabbed the knob and gradually eased the door open.

The hall leading to the living room was unlit. She heard voices, muffled. Santha resorted to tiptoe again and went halfway down the hall. Now she could hear every word, clearly, distinctly.

"... has no medical history like that," Stephen Wrench was saying. "No seizures as an infant, no epilepsy, no amnesia, and definitely Santha has never been susceptible to anything resembling hallucinations."

George coughed. "I understand that this is difficult to accept, but she acted as though she saw something in the room. She froze—literally froze—made motions as I described."

"Brief me, George. You're the expert. Could this possibly be connected with Kamala's death?"

"It's very possible. Especially since there were no such incidents prior to the death of your wife."

"Christ! And my condition didn't help any, I suppose. Poor Santha, trying like hell to keep herself together, since someone had to. She had no time to grieve properly." Wrench's voice broke. Then: "You don't think it's anything worse than that, do you?"

"I can't answer that."

"Of course—insufficient data. Ferchrissakes, man, you handle schizophrenic types, people who hallucinate all the time, don't you? Can't you tell whether it's the same thing or not?

Couldn't it be a simple reaction to death? It seems to be a reasonable explanation."

"A trance or some facsimile in which a person thinks she sees something that isn't there isn't exactly a simple reaction."

"Okay. Okay. . . . But Santha didn't admit she saw any-thing."

"She didn't have to. Her gestures, her motions said it all."

"Holy shit! And she's been defensive whenever you bring it up, heh? Well, Santha has always been very protective of her privacy, George, especially her inner privacy. In India the inner world of a person is a pretty sacred place. Santha might've been baptized by an Episcopal minister, but she still has Indian roots, remember. It's in her genes. My point is that Santha's resistance stems from the fact that she interprets what you call hallucinations differently."

A pause. "Could you clarify?"

"Sure. In India they believe in visions, an awakening. I don't know if you believe in that sort of thing."

"Yes, I do. But I don't believe what happened to Santha was like that."

"You called it a trancelike state. I saw a sadhu in Benares go into a meditative trance that lasted three days. His disciples had to feed him the best they could. You've never seen anything like that here, I bet."

"I've read about it, though. Enough to be able to differentiate between that and a catatonic state. So trust me—what happened to Santha was different. Her eyes never left my living room wall. In the beginning she seemed happy, even made an attempt at dancing. But later she cringed, was repulsed, it seemed. Her hands made gestures. She was trying to push something away. It lasted only about three minutes. And it began so abruptly. . . ."

"That's very significant, I gather."

George was silent for a while. Santha became impatient, started to ease away, when he said, "Her abrupt stupor and the abruptness of her reentry to normal behavior was similar to some cases I've seen. If it is schizophrenia, Santha's age cer-tainly fits the statistics. Women have a high incidence between twenty-five and thirty-four. But it would be premature to conclude so at this point. Besides, she has none of the other symptoms so far. No change in her affects, no delusions or marked depression; she doesn't seem unconcerned about her appearance. These are the characteristics common among schizophrenic patients. And I've seen no sign whatsoever that she hears voices. . . . Nevertheless, whatever it is, it's damn serious. A trance state like that might occur anywhere, at any time. Suppose she were driving when . . ."

Santha crept back into the hallway without a sound. She closed the door slowly, heard the soft click again. Her head throbbed. George seemed so brutal, so cold, talking clinically about her that way. She thought of their intimate moments together. But he was also a doctor of psychiatry, Santha reminded herself. How else could he interpret what happened?

The sonovabitch could give me the benefit of the doubt, she argued, and almost decided to go home to Lime Street.

Instead, though, Santha chose to make her appearance. With more noise than usual, she replaced the key in the lock. Entering the apartment again, she cried out, "Here I am, everybody. Sorry I'm late." Then she rushed into the bathroom to discard her raincoat and overshoes. Moments later she was facing them in the living room.

Stephen Wrench was lighting his pipe before the fireplace. "There're shrimp scampi on the stove," he said, eyeing the clock. "Better get at it. We haven't much time."

In the kitchen, the scent of Wrench's cooking picked up her spirits. His scampi were a little bit of heaven. Santha smiled broadly at his culinary skill and even more broadly as her father's voice rumbled on about the New England Patriots. Daddy, the international policeman, was always a good actor, she mused. Now let's see how good at it George is.

Again in the living room, Santha looked at both of them squarely for the first time since she entered. She sat, set the plate of scampi on the coffee table, poured tea from the china pot on a trivet at her side, and concentrated on Stephen Wrench first.

The unshaven, ashen figure huddled in his bathrobe in some unlighted corner was gone from the place. That alone mattered.

Stephen Wrench was present again, standing in a swirl of pipe smoke, his vest tight and flush with his massive torso, his white shirt laundered, starched where it counted most, while his pale gray bow tie blended with the sharply creased black suit, with the gleam of his best cuff links and the black sheen of his shoes. Why, it was like dressing for dinner, colonial style, the way they always did back there, back then.

It was wonderful when he came home in those days, she recalled. He was away so often on those mysterious journeys with Uncle Ram and the others. Wonderful when he'd return and stand, as now, before the fireplace, smoking, full of his own secret thoughts. She was so small then and he so large and impressive with that special magic of who he was and what he did. He seemed to have breathed in danger, adventure, all those wonderful things, only to exhale it everywhere when he returned, so that the very air was somehow more thrilling. And always he dressed, as he did tonight, for the dinners, more exciting, more wonderfully awesome than all the maharajahs with their jeweled turbans and gilded howdahs, or the vulture-faced Afghans who filtered through the gateway at Peshawar, or even those marvelous gigantic Sikhs, whom she thought of as India's jinn. But most of all, the greatest thrill, greater than every one of her imaginings, was that he was her daddy and no one else's.

"Working overtime on your catalog?" he asked.

Santha nodded. "It's nearly finished." She turned casually now to George, who started. Good, Santha concluded; my doctor-lover just lost his poker face. "It'll be a simply grand exhibit, with artifacts from the Mohenjo-Daro site, chiefly. It's the first time they've been shown here. Then the drive here slowed me down considerably. It's almost monsoon weather outside, Daddy."

With that, Santha blew George a kiss and watched him flush. She reached for him, squeezed his hand. "Everything all right, darling?"

"Fine," George replied. "Mr. Wrench and I were discussing Indian music and . . ."

"Football." She almost giggled. George hated football. "And call Daddy Steve, George. He doesn't mind."

"Correct," Wrench added, squinting down at his watch. "As soon as you've finished the scampi, Santha, we ought to get going."

Santha could scarcely believe he was eager to leave—daddy, who growled in the beginning that he'd "heard about enough sitar music to last ten lifetimes," who also usually loathed rock and only shrugged when Santha explained that Nirmal's compositions were synthesizations of various kinds and periods of music, some Eastern, some modern, even some Bach. "It's the most extraordinary stuff you've ever heard," she'd explained and put on the album *Kapur Nights* that he might understand.

Santha had suspected then that he'd liked it more than he showed. Later, when she learned that the concert was for a benefit, the starving in Bangladesh, he'd agreed to go. The old phony, she mused. Stephen Wrench had an image of the unwavering conservative to maintain, and it was her conviction he wasn't that made her treat it as a game. True, when he'd returned to America in the sixties, her father quickly rejected the new wave of liberalism, but that had only been because of a nature that rankled at what the English of the Raj called bad form. He suffered, as she saw it, from an old British code of behavior mixed with Yankee Puritanism. But it never successfully disguised the hidden liberal lurking behind the persona bush—the one that sprang forth when necessary, and then only. The unseen, unsuspected liberal in Stephen Wrench that broke all boundaries between men.

Thus the great binding love in him for Rama Shastri. Thus this fierce hunger in him to be with his friend once again.

Parking space being as scarce as a pearl in a polluted oyster bed, they had chosen to walk to the performance hall on Beacon Hill. So they set forth in the heavy rain, the wind from the Charles River buffeting them. By the time they reached the place, which stood off Cambridge Street, they were drenched from crown to sole. But to Santha's joy, none of this seemed to bother her father. He never grumbled once, but walked into the hall explaining to George what a saptak was in Indian music.

"I love you," George said to her when Wrench disappeared into the men's room.

It was so unexpected, Santha stammered back, "Ditto, George."

He hesitated. Then, "Is everything okay?"

"Now, don't spoil this," she warned.

"I had to ask, Santha," he told her firmly. "I had to."

"Don't spoil it, sweet. Please don't do that tonight."

George took her arm when they went to their seats, and it brought her concentration back to the people and the stage. The typical Boston-Cambridge student types were present, dressed in dungarees, but there were others dressed like first nighters. Also, a smattering of the elderly were represented, from generations ahead of her father. That ought to put him at ease, she thought; the sedate roaring twenties are attending.

Santha's eyes settled on a small, turbaned Hindu then, seated three rows behind her to her left. He was looking her way, and she decided after a while that it was she he was concerned with. It wasn't exactly apparent, since he held his head to the side, which suggested the idea that he was concentrating on the ceiling. But every so often the barely visible eyes deep in the monkeylike face would dart to her. It was unsettling; she turned away.

The lights dimmed. Wrench lapsed into silence at the tail end of a dissertation to George on how the compositions of Holst and Roussel were heavily influenced by Eastern music. Before the hall became totally dark, Santha looked once more at the little Hindu and thought, while the stage curtains separated, What a wise old face that is, whatever its ugliness. And such a memorable turban of satiny blue with gold trim.

The small stage burst suddenly into strobe life. Flicker, flicker, flicker it flashed hard, even painful on the watching eyes. The *chock* and flat *thud* of drums sounded, and, as the strobe lessened with the rise of the main lights, a tall black in an open calypso shirt and cord pants, cross-legged at stage center, moved his fingers and palms on two tabla drums, left and right. Behind him sat Nirmal with his sitar. And behind the two players a young girl no older than ten sat on a stool before a gigantic synthesizer.

The audience applauded at the sight of Nirmal. He bowed a head of lank, black hair, to them or to some unknown god of music, and the sitar notes droned out, subtle, repetitious, all simultaneously complementing whatever the drumbeats evoked. Casually, unexpectedly, as the drone rose and rose and the drums quickened their pulse, the child yanked a knob aside the lower keyboard of the synthesizer, and a *blaam*, half echo, half bass fiddle, reverberated in discord against the walls. Again and again the child yanked and yanked, until the discord amplified and smote the ears while the sitar droned frantically.

Then silence, hush, the lights dimming, and Nirmal stood, a guitar in his hands. The drumming continued, the child was still. Nirmal, lean, his profile effeminate and smooth, produced the rock beat. The strobes stirred, were reawakened, the child pulled more knobs, pressed pedals, and a mixture of organ and electronic bleepings filled each musical pause. The timing was superb, uncanny, and the audience applauded the child now with all they had.

For an hour and forty minutes they played without interruption. The flyer gave the concert a name, "Nirmal Awakening," and the clashing of East and West was everywhere in the sounds. At one point it was especially strong. Both Nirmal and the black, named Billy Dangerfield, stood before the strobes and played a succession of chords to sitar music recorded earlier by Kapur. It was like a conversation among the three instruments, first the sitar, then the guitars, and it grew more and more hectic, a great, amplified tonal argument. Nirmal spoke, his embroidered vest of many colors swaying, his intense smile gleaming on his olive, young-girl face, his hairless chest taut and lean as he bounded around the stage, tossing his black, shoulder-length tresses. Dangerfield replied, sometimes in competition, sometimes with improvs that stirred every viewer. It was still rock, the rock that all knew, and yet the fierce, personal inner voice of each player somehow transformed the chords to fresher, unexpected heights.

Santha turned, watched the strobe flicker, dance off her

father and George. Features were unclear, just light bouncing off instants of profile, but she thought Wrench looked amused. Then she thought of the Hindu and, slanting her head, caught again the small eyes on her. She beamed: Enjoy, strange monkey man, whatever you are studying in me. Nothing, not him, not anything could destroy the spirit of the thing, and she dared to conclude that order was restored, that no longer would the events return. She was free. This Now was too vibrant, too alive to be overtaken by anything else.

The concert finale was the child's moment, nearly every second. She stood to reach the higher keyboards, and a composition with Bach interludes like filtering images of a rich and pensive musical past ruled this world of sound. Finally the organ became a murmur and Nirmal's inspired fingers plucked the sitar. Tones dropped, the twelve chief notes of the saptak fell delicately, a string of melodious petals.

Quiet. A darkening stage, three heads bowed. The hall exploded as the viewers stood, clapping, clapping. Except the Hindu. Santha saw his back shuffling toward the lobby, the blue, gilded turban seeming a heavy weight for such a small head.

Later, in the lobby, she flowed with her newfound freedom, waiting with folded program for Nirmal Kapur and company to autograph it.

Backstage, Nirmal was explaining to Billy Dangerfield and the child that he was about to exit via a back door that the janitor had left unlocked for him.

"Not again, man," howled Billy Dangerfield. "Here you go, doing it again. What the hell's wrong with you, man? Me and Esmeralda's always stuck with the mob out there. It's one thing if they were just groupies, but Jeesus, man, that's Public. I mean, they know Brahms from The Who. Dig?"

"Yeah, I dig. But Baba's my godsend. He's kept me off coke, off everything—you know that. Would you like it to be like the old days, when I was so spaced out I couldn't tell a sharp from a flat?" Nirmal bent and embraced Esmeralda.

"Besides, she don't mind facing them. Do you, honey? Just leave it to her like you usually do."

"Well, that's for certain. She takes a bath in it. Just scrubs herself all over with that praise and adoration."

Billy lifted Esmeralda and placed her on his shoulders, piggyback. She pulled his hair and then kissed the top of his head. "Shush, Jealous. Move your black ass on. Our public's waiting."

Nirmal found Baba Hanuman waiting for him on the alley stairs, peering at something among the garbage cans. Investigating, he saw a rat emerge for a second into the overhead light.

"Baba Master," he said, "what does that creature tell you?"

The little man adjusted his turban and stood. "Simply that he is a hungry rat," was the reply.

Nirmal laughed. "Did you enjoy the concert, beloved Baba?"

"Yours is a dashing soul, my son. All hopes of your achieving serenity are dashed by the first strains of the sitar."

Nirmal, downcast, placed his hands in his raincoat pockets. "I only compose what I feel. I can't do better."

The old man laughed. "You seek too hard," he said gently. "You come to me seeking a path. Master, you cry, as a boy in India I scoffed at the parades of sadhus I saw everywhere, but now I see the greatness of their ways. Teach me, that I, too, may know peace. Then, when I try, you linger, balk at any change, and fight for this right to feel. Those emotions, you tell me, are the stuff of which your compositions are made, this civil strife within you. Then, I ask you, why desire a teacher? Can a teacher, like a god, hold back a tidal wave, an avalanche?"

Nirmal wished that Baba Hanuman would move on, but he didn't. The rain had stopped, and the alley was dank, unpleasant, poorly lit. Nirmal waited with respect. Waited for this swami, who was father, mother, even destiny to him. It was Hanuman who had taken him in, two years ago, and gradually weaned him off drugs. Hanuman who had, in a sense, resurrected Nirmal from a living death. And the ease, the lack of self-consciousness had been the key. To Swami Hanuman the way to God was neither ascetic nor rigid. No ashen-faced guru he. The Way, the Path, was a discipline, true, but only when it came easily, naturally, each step a logical progression from the other. One grew a trunk as did a tree, and then the branches, but solely in the time and through the method one's willingness designed.

"Now," the Swami stated, his flat nose squinching as if the alley odor offended him. It was actually an affectation, Nirmal knew; it was what the Monkey God would do, and Hanuman had taken on his name. "Learn, indeed, this lesson for you and me. Life is only sweet, exciting, memorable when we are faced either with total Light and the Radiance of things that cradles our spirit or—and mark this particularly—when the *Darkness* comes and broods around and about this world, clouds everything. Then Life has been touched by the Frown of Evil. Thus, with either Light or the Darkness at their greatest extremes, do we feel truly awakened."

"You're heavy tonight, Baba." Nirmal noticed with relief that Hanuman was walking toward the street at last. Anything could happen in an alley this poorly lit. He dipped his chin into his coat collar. Besides, the night was quirky. Right now it was goddamn cold, and only a minute or so ago he'd been enjoying the temperature rise from the passing rain. Nirmal moved at a fast clip, hoping Hanuman would hurry, too. Something was brushing against his back, and he was forced to pause and brace himself. Krishna, it was like a small hurricane! He nearly toppled onto a discarded box with a piling of newspapers. Then he felt another kind of coldness working up his spine. The papers weren't stirring. Not a goddamn fraction, not even a corner turned up!

"Let's hurry to my car, Baba," he said, turning and facing the alley tunnel. The wind blast increased, and he danced backward while it buffeted him.

But he found the Swami had stopped, was staring back, too. "Did you see the pretty Indian girl in the audience?"

"I never look beyond the strobes," Nirmal answered, shivering and dancing the more. "This wind is terrible, Baba. Aren't you cold?"

"She was Indian. I know that," said Hanuman with conviction.

"Can't . . . can't we move on?" implored his disciple, stomping his feet. "This wind's going right through me, Baba."

"The Zen masters speak of listening to the wind, my son. Indeed, what a wind has come to America. And what, indeed, do we hear?"

"By the Mother of all Things, let's get to the car, Baba!"

"Yes . . . a Mother . . . Then, come, Nirmal."

Nirmal nodded with zest. He took a step, heard a sound, turned again. The alley was darker. The overhead light above the exit back there had weakened. Rain poured from roof gutters, splattering on the ground, on garbage covers. A crash. One of those covers pushed by the rat, no doubt. It rattled and clanked. No! That was something else, thought Nirmal. That was what he'd heard. Like a sound he had been familiar with years ago. Like . . . like footsteps. Just as Nirmal spun to the alley exit, Hanuman uttered a long, sustained, "Aaaaaaaaaah."

At first Nirmal thought the Swami was ill. However, another drawn-out sound, as if from an emptying air tunnel, caught in the hurtling *whoosh* of atmospheric release, came from the alley depths. Nirmal perhaps shouted. He couldn't tell, except that his lips were moving up and down. When his breath returned, he found himself flat against a wall he'd been picked up and thrown to.

Some force! Some power, some explosion, some what? . . . And the rooming house sign across the way blinked and reddened the more, a rectangular neon keeping time with his thoughts. It was getting brighter, hurting his eyes, smarting them, expanding bursts of yellow, orange, then a blinding red; an encroaching stain across the structure. Across the face of one of these old places that nestled almost atop one another in this poorer area of Beacon Hill. These firetraps . . . trap . . . FIRE! FIRE! The idea took hold. Nirmal couldn't believe it. The wood was already an ashen shadow; smoke billowed out like an angry cough.

"Baba!" Nirmal screamed. "Baba! Where are you?"

In his ear: "Move slowly, my son. Hold my sleeve." Which

Nirmal did, desperately, trying to pierce the gloom. Smoke shrouded them both as they edged along the wall opposite the blaze. Had a boiler or stove exploded in the old house? Nirmal asked himself. What caused the force that had seized him bodily? Though he tried to think rationally, the memory of the something that had followed behind haunted him, drove home its unimaginable cold that lingered still in his marrow. Nirmal felt a hard tug and fell forward out of the alley into the street.

Hanuman was hanging on, pulling him farther. The flames licked, taunting red and black banners reaching over the sidewalk. Nirmal, still clinging to the Swami's sleeve, stumbled across the street. He settled finally on his haunches on a curb in the darkness between a pair of cars. Sirens, shattering and detached, broke the spell. The fire engines hulked, their monstrous shapes blotting most of the blaze from view. Nirmal stood, tottering from the ordeal. He searched the street corner below, praying the concert viewers were safe. They were, he soon saw, and heard Billy Dangerfield and the child Esmeralda calling his name.

"Baba," he said in gasps, "my mind rebels, but my instincts say we were attacked. What was in the alley?"

"Be assured it was Indian." Hanuman's voice was soft, soothing like that of a parent with a child.

"Does that make it any better, Baba?" Nirmal cried, with some impatience.

"No, my son. Perhaps worse. But at least it is familiar."

PART TWO

DIMA

Gloomy and Calamitous Events

NINE

Pisgah Tract, New Hampshire/Boston

The long sedan moved slowly through the brisk New Hampshire night. The old dirt road was rarely used anymore, and the encroaching growth at the roadsides forced the driver to move carefully. They were on the border of what once had been the famous Pisgah Tract, almost totally destroyed during the hurricane of 1938. Remnants of the virgin timber still lingered, and Duane Longstreet recognized original hemlocks and hardwood trees in the headlights like towering primeval phantoms. Ahead, at about a forty-yard distance, the road eased into a gradient that sloped, a steep cup, into the clearing where Toby, the old recluse, lived. Duane knew this area very well.

"Toby used to be a forester," he explained from behind the steering wheel. "When he retired he settled here near the base of Mount Pisgah. You'll find he keeps a few sheep here, pigs, chickens, a goat." He nearly strangled on the next sentence. "Even two dogs."

"The dogs will warn him," Chundra Bala said.

From the rear of the car the Huzoor soothed. "Duane will approach him first. The man and the dogs know Duane. Once the man is sufficiently distracted, Makunda will seize him from the rear. Bidhan, I expect you are strong and forceful enough to kill the dogs. Don't use the rumel but the knife on them. It is quick and efficient, and the spilling of animal blood is not denied us."

Duane swallowed. He was a veterinarian, and the thought of what he must do was very upsetting. Tranquilizing, then killing animals and draining their blood into Indian water jars aroused his conscience. But the Huzoor had promised him a spiritual reward, a release from the torment within himself.

A sigh from behind him broke into his thoughts. Chundra, by his side, looked back with concern. Seated among the three men in the rear seat was the woman. Duane detected that the road opened at the next turn, and pressed down on the accelerator. The blood was for her and he must hurry!

With a bound the sedan roared into the clearing, swept into the land cup, and pulled out with a loud metallic shudder. Then it crossed between the long scrub grass to the cabin nestled against a white pine ridge that fingered from the mountain. Two dogs darted out of the darkness. Their growls cut through the hollow silence.

When Duane stopped the car before the well near the livestock area, the dogs leaped again and again at the windows.

A light went on in the cabin. A door slammed.

"Remember to serve the woman well," the Huzoor said. "You have all seen what she must endure to serve us. Through her you have seen the Mother. Now do not fail."

A voice called gruffly, "Who's there?" In the headlights stood an elderly, bearded man holding a shotgun.

Duane lowered the window slightly and shouted above the attacking dogs. "It's me, Mr. Toby—Duane Longstreet, the vet that used to work in Winchester."

"Duane, that you? This your boat? Com'on out and talk with me."

"The dogs, Mr. Toby."

"Sure. Charlie, Bruno—stop it, ferchrissakes!"

The dogs, a Doberman and a collie-shepherd, moved away into the shadows. At the same time Duane heard the back door click, on his side. Duane got out. Behind him, squatting on his haunches, was Makunda. Duane closed the door, moved in front of the car. Somewhere beyond the circle of light, Makunda was moving stealthily, he knew.

"Thought I'd come to see you, Mr. Toby." Duane extended a hand toward the old man. "I brought friends with me."

Warily the man replied, "I dunno. You know I don't entertain much."

"I thought we'd talk about the wildlife," Duane continued in a level voice. He wished Makunda would get it over with, dammit! "Remember, we used to talk about the wildlife in these parts? You had some funny raccoon stories, I recall."

Toby chuckled. "Those sneaky bastards." Then he checked himself. "No, sorry, Duane. I ain't up to entertaining folks tonight."

Duane saw an arm arc forward from the dark fringe. At the same time Bruno, the Doberman, saw it. The other sedan doors flew open. Duane backed in terror, sensing Bruno's pending leap. The arm snaked in its arc. Duane saw the rumel lower, saw the black lightning of Bruno cleave the air. Then something flashed in the headlamps near the dog's neck. Bruno whined once, shot even higher in a convulsive heave, and fell to the ground. Bidhan's knife throw had been on target.

But now Bidhan had to reckon with Charlie. The collie-shepherd was already onto Bidhan's wrist. The giant Thug's free hand held a second knife, however. With a growl that blended with Charlie's, he thrust upward. Still the noble-hearted dog lunged, the blade imbedded in his chest to the hilt. Bidhan leaped aside, dug his wrist deeper into the dog's mouth, and placed his other arm around the furry neck. With one mighty heave, Bidhan pulled the neck backward. It broke.

Duane looked down at the dead old man. His eyes veered to the two dead animals and tears trickled from him. Poor beautiful, dumb creatures. He had liked those dogs.

"Now make haste," the Huzoor commanded. "Bring the woman forward that she may be replenished." Duane ran to the sedan's rear compartment and unlocked it. He gathered up his equipment—the syringes, the surgical knives, the siphoning tubes for the blood. The tears fell steadily now. It was all Janet Beth Voss's fault. He had fallen in love with her and she'd rejected his proposal of marriage. Instead, she'd walked to the altar with Winchester's leading jock.

He'd lost his job because of Janet. He just couldn't concentrate. He'd prescribed an overdose of Cardoxin for a cat with heart trouble.

"Bring the equipment," a voice bellowed. Stunned, Duane looked up. The Huzoor was carrying Gauri toward the livestock barn. Her face showed in the lights, ghostly to see. Her eyes were closed and the lids and mouth trembled. "Hurry!" the Huzoor commanded. Duane scurried after him, his arms filled with paraphernalia. Gauri Bala needed to drink blood to survive because she'd been used too many times as a vessel of Kali, always seeking desperately to find the missing fragment of the Scroll of Power. The fragment must be restored even if the cost was that the original bloodlust of the Goddess was taking her over.

Duane fought back the tears. He must keep in mind that the killing of these animals was a way of helping the Thug cause. He must remember that when his college friend Deborah Klaus brought him to the Huzoor, he saw things he'd never believed possible.

He must not forget this. And most of all, he mustn't forget that he would soon be avenged. The Huzoor had promised that Janet Beth Voss and her husband would be his first victims when he finally learned to wield the rumel.

Three days later, at the Mai Yogini Yoga Center off Kenmore Square, Boston, the Yogini herself hurried to her dressing room. She had just finished addressing her pupils in the Beneficence Chamber, and it had lasted longer than usual. Her "darling little chelas" had more questions than expected this evening, and she promised herself that next time she'd make her address much shorter to allow for them.

She opened the door. In a mad rush she went to the dressing mirror, slipping off her bangles. Her beauty reflected back at her, sheathed in a rustling blue and roseate robe. Mai Yogini smiled at herself and began to loosen the sash at her waist. Then her gaze centered beyond the reflection's shoulders, and what she saw made the shoulders slump.

A flicker of anger nearly demanded that the man staring at her in the mirror stop smoking. Smoking wasn't allowed at the center, her thoughts trailed, drifted weakly.

Next to the big Indian with the cigarette, she saw a smaller man with a pencil-thin moustache and, finally, seated in a wingback chair, a woman.

Ordinarily it would have been just an unexpected annoyance. An intrusion by three strangers, former countrymen, was a matter the Yogini could deal with easily, but the sight of the woman with the eyes of a mad dream changed that.

"You are aware of who I am?" the something like a voice demanded.

Mai Yogini nodded. Her breath was a wedge in her throat. Saliva accumulated in her mouth, weighted, strangely heavy. She wanted to choke, spit it out, but couldn't. She slumped further into herself, still on the seat before the mirror. Her legs felt like stalks, an ungainly child's limbs, and her arms covered her breasts as if they were naked, vulnerable.

Chundra Bala introduced himself. His tone was harsh, filled with unrestrained disgust. He was the smaller man and was to be the spokesman. He knew every moment of Mai Yogini's life, every well-kept secret. He mercilessly revealed it all.

She was born Claudine de Brisson Jaiswal in Lahore, India. Her mother was French. Her Indian father had been handsome, reckless, a reprobate who was a suicide because of his gambling debts. The great family house in Lahore had been lost to others, and Claudine's mother had soon died, brokenhearted.

Bala's accusations droned around her like the fierce humming of threatening insects; yet none of it was as bad as the presence of the woman. The woman, the look of her, her eyes, her voice—it couldn't be possible. The Yogini had never believed in such things.

Claudine de Brisson Jaiswal had found survival difficult afterward, Bala continued. She'd turned to opium selling in Bombay, to prostitution. Finally it was arranged with the assistance of a few affluent lovers that she come to America. Here she became a citizen.

However, life in America soon proved difficult, too. Claudine turned to prostitution again. Then, in a moment of desperation, hoping to improve her lot, she started a small yoga school in Cambridge. Yogini knew only fragments of the teaching learned from Sri Bhagabati, the household yogi who lived in the once great mansion at Lahore. But in America even a little bit of the knowledge proved lucrative.

"You soon learned the extent of human gullibility here. That your followers listened and believed merely because you are

Indian." Bala snarled his open contempt. "You have succeeded in a manner that grieves any true Indian's heart. You've made a mockery of God's knowledge and India's unequaled divine heritage. Profiting from false wisdom, false prophecies, you have also sexually indulged with men in secrecy, like a common dassis. All this you have done and more, and now we are here to demand tribute. You will be taught to serve in our ways. Through the center, you will aid in the recruiting of suitable disciples for our cause. You will be given a new Path with a new Realization. You will even learn the art of the scarf that whispers Kali's kiss."

"But my nature would never permit me to take human life!" Mai Yogini replied.

The woman lunged. Fingers like cryogenic clamps sank into Yogini's stomach. Through her sari they squeezed and squeezed. Mai Yogini opened her mouth to protest but instead, vomit rose and streamed down her lips and chin. The woman freed her, her alien eyes rippling black laughter. Mai Yogini stood, wanting to run, to flee, to scream, and again the vomit rose.

Gasping, she fell against the makeup table, and jars of facial cream, eye shadow, and scents scattered from her groping touch. Yogini faced herself in the mirror, her mouth grotesque and ugly. She gulped over and over like a fish on land, only to convulse, as more vomit cascaded onto the glass. She tried to speak, beg, implore, but again and again the seizures came, and now the result had ceased to be undigested food but was a greenish bile that seemed to coat everything. Again more spurted from her.

When it ended, they left her semiconscious in her wingback chair. The walls, floor, her expensive sari-robe seemed covered with her viscera. Mai Yogini was convinced she was hollow, scraped clean. The three left without a word, but Mai Yogini knew that, if she survived, they would return. She was forever lost. She was like a miniature doll held in the palm of Kali. The Goddess's gigantic fingers could caress or crush her at whim.

* * *

That night the Huzoor stood on the balcony of his ashram. Below, the regulars of the Thug band were teaching the new American recruits, those willing acolytes whose prior lives had been so empty. The disillusioned, society's losers. Those who had a burning rage, a touch of madness, a bitter disenchantment that they'd go to any lengths to dispel—these were the Chosen. And once they'd seen the Mother through Gauri, the pact was sealed.

The Power they saw and linked with was dark, the Power of destruction and chaos, but it held within its confines the structure of its own meaning. And, dark as it was, this was preferable to the emptiness they'd once known.

Below, Makunda lay prone, while Ayub, the Muslim and Strangler, placed the rumel around his neck. Bidhan held Makunda's arms, his brother Jadu the legs. They were demonstrating the best position and circumstances in which to strangle someone: when the victim was asleep on the ground. In barely passable English, Ayub was stating that, preferable as it was, having three Thugs to one victim wasn't always possible. The surrounding disciples listened attentively.

The Huzoor turned away. Behind him followed Yoni-Elvira Moniz. A tall, rangy woman with hair the color of a blackbird's wing reaching the base of her spine, she was dressed in a white sari.

Yoni-Elvira Moniz had risen rapidly to the head of the women's faction of the Kali Akali, the name of the newly formed Thuggee cult.

Leaving the balcony, the two moved through the halls of the ashram and stopped before an open door.

Inside, Gauri Bala sat on cushions behind two lighted tapers and a brazier of burning sandalwood. Gauri was at the moment teaching her secret knowledge to the group of women squatting before her. The Huzoor was the only male who could enter the room at a time like this.

The female acolytes began to fall on their faces at the sight of him. The Huzoor motioned that they were not to do so. He acknowledged Gauri with a nod and stood in their midst, bathing in their adoration. "Ah," he began, "our great work is at hand."

He focused on one of them. "Tell me, now, Deborah, have you unburdened yourself to Gauri Mother? Have you freed yourself of all past yearnings, desires, emotional ties that would hamper what you must do in time?"

"Not all, my Lord," Deborah replied, with her eyes downcast. "Not everything yet."

"But you must, my child. You are no longer the Deborah Klaus of yesterday. There must be no hidden thing between us. Faithful Yoni, step to my side. Speak to them of whence you came and what you endured. Tell all and demonstrate how naked we must be to each other." His voice lowered, became firm. "Especially the lot of you, my children, since never before have women been allowed to use the rumel."

Yoni-Elvira Moniz passed her tongue over her lips and looked nervously at Gauri for strength. The radiant face was inspiring. She told her story.

Years ago she had left a Poor Clare convent in the middle of the night. An apparition had come to her cell, a robed man resembling Christ. "Are you He?" Elvira asked, near-faint from the rapture of the sight. He replied, "You must leave this place forever."

Elvira obeyed immediately. But she soon found she had no further direction, that the nameless apparition never came again. Embittered, in time she denied Christianity altogether and soon met Norman Taurog, a Vietnam veteran deep into Tantric Buddhism and drugs. Always the disciple looking for the Master, Elvira found momentary solace in esoteric addiction and sex.

They both took on new names. His was Kaula, a form of Tantra, and Kundalini, the Serpent and sometimes sex power in yoga. Elvira, in turn, chose only one cognomen, Yoni, which in yoga is the female sex organ. They bought a small piece of farmland near Laconia, New Hampshire, where they could live happy and anchoritic ever after.

Kaula knew Yoni's nature well, her need to be immolated. Holding his erection in his hand like that two-edged sword of divine power, Kaula screamed her adopted name in the street English that both defiled her and stirred her blood. "You're my Yoni," Kaula cried. "You're my Cunt! Cunt! Cunt! My precious ever fucking Cunt!" Yoni-Elvira, the deflowered virgin and martyr, surrendered easily to the assault that followed.

But afterward there was the guilt, the strong conviction that she was recrucifying her forsaken Savior again and again. Kaula Kundalini tortured her with the crazed pleasure of his Tantric practices and hyper sex drive, while later the pure, bodiless Christ of childhood weighted her with the heavy, dark habit of despair. Yoni could no longer live with either one. Both lovers in her great Passion Play must die.

So one night, during the love act, Yoni-Elvira Moniz murdered Kaula Kundalini, once Norman Taurog.

Elvira had let her hair grow as long as possible, a reaction to her days when a Poor Clare. Her hair was braided into two thick, black ropes. Often Elvira wound them around his thin frail chest while they loved. This evening Elvira chose his neck instead. Norman was screaming that he was coming when she tugged forcefully on both ends of the braids. The noose of hair tightened. Shutting her eyes while Norman uttered a succession of choking and gagging noises, Elvira flowed into her own sexual release.

For three hours and forty-five minutes the wonderful, passionless time, the samadhi-like void lasted. Norman's watch, resting on his pile of unwashed clothes, registered exactly 10:50 P.M. when the fear swept her. Thoughts crashed in, clawing, shredding her bliss. Suppose she was caught by the authorities! She could be incarcerated! Elvira rushed into the bedroom, picked up an unwashed sheet from the cot in the corner, and, returning, wrapped it around Norman's small, naked body. Then she dressed, lifted the bundle, left the house, and placed the body in the back of Norman's battered '67 Chevy pickup.

At first Elvira traveled on the main roads northwestward, with a minimal sense of direction. Somehow she managed to control her speed despite surges of panic. Every passing car light made her cringe. Now and then, when a patrol car showed, her hands glued to the wheel. Ergs of willpower were summoned later to release their hold. Convinced she'd be stopped, Elvira was stunned when she arrived at the country road she wanted. Ahead, in a small clearing, was the hollow stump of a massive dead oak. She raced the shuddering pickup to the wedge of gray among the darker sheltering trees.

Once she parked, Elvira dashed to the truck's rear, lowered the gate, and pulled at the corpse. Her fingers gripped and dug into Norman's exposed toes. Elvira yelped at the feel. Like frozen putty! Then, without warning, the sheet rose, fell from Norman, as his corpse sat upright. It sighed when the excess gases left the body. Sweat dripping from her nose and chin, Elvira watched the sheet lower again. The interior of the pickup blammed from Norman's impact, and it echoed and shuddered the metal more.

Elvira held on to the truck fender and sweated with dread. The wood sounds had returned, the crickets stirred, the night creatures chirped, whistled, growled, and hooted. Elvira recognized them, relaxed, then strained in the starless density. Her sandals shushed through the heavy piling of autumn leaves everywhere. She stared at the stump, the surrounding trees. And at the trees again. And her heart skipped. A murmur of an outline, a figure in a robe, the sloping of long hair!

Was it really Him?

Elvira rubbed her eyes. When she looked at the spot next time, the upthrust of what seemed a silver beech elbowing to the sky was all she saw.

Her Yoni self chided, "Still the stupid dreamer! Remember, *you have killed Christ*!" Yes, yes, repeated Elvira; yes, I killed Him. And in anger she seized Norman, slung him over her shoulder, and headed for the stump. She circled it, found the lowest lip of its hollow mouth. Even then she had to stand on her toes to hoist and lower the body and its makeshift shroud into the natural bowl. But alas, to her grief, his head and shoulders jutted above the rim. She could see his tangled, unkempt beard spiking from the hollow. Elvira leaned her elbow on the edge and with her free hand pressed and pressed on Norman's face until the body wedged completely, thoroughly between the stump's knot-ridden sides.

Exhausted, Elvira slid down against the outside bark, her dank braids catching on the rough surface. She lay breathing heavily, listening for the night creatures, for solace.

Instead, the leaves swished, and the night air clinked as though the buzzing life had suddenly turned metallic. "Oh, my Jesus," her lips formed but were unable to utter. A bright circle of light blinded her. Elvira knew it came from the electric lanterns that campers often used. When she adjusted to its beam, Elvira saw two slender, feminine arms extended to her. Her trembling hands reached to the long fingers, an instinctual act. Hammered gold bracelets flashed in the light, and the arms, strong yet somehow tender, lifted Elvira to her feet. Elvira stared at the face. And then the eyes.

Thus Elvira Moniz, or Yoni, met Gauri and the Huzoor and a handful of the Brotherhood. Gauri urged her closer that night, placed her mouth on Elvira's, and therein sealed their meeting. It was the special kiss, a spirit communion never to be broken. That night, too, Elvira fell prone before the Huzoor and confessed all. He assured her she was safe, and Jadu, reverting to his former station, took Norman from the stump cavity and dug a grave with the skill and penchant for a hidden burial place that marked the best of Thugs.

Elvira rejoiced at these memories. How miraculous that it was the very night when the Huzoor chose to visit the clearing. He wished to purchase land there in the future. The deep New Hampshire woods were a fitting place to build a new ashram.

The Huzoor studied the women after the story's end. He saw they had grasped its hint of predestination. They sensed the Power behind events, even. He smiled, and thought himself the most fortunate man in all creation.

Three weeks later, the Huzoor was to experience his first setback. He was on his throne, conversing with Chundra Bala, Makunda, and Sahib Khan, the most intelligent of the three Muslim Thugs. They were speaking of the old traditions, especially Sahib Khan, who knew more of Thug history than anyone, when Trande Gautam, the Arcotee, begged an audience.

"Yes?" the Huzoor urged, impatient with the interruption.

The Arcotee was prone, wailing like a man mortally wounded. "My Lord, I have discovered a terrible thing. And I believe it is my chela who is responsible."

"What has this chela done, my brother? And rise. We are all brothers together this night."

"After the chelas left," the Arcotee began slowly, "I counted our rumels, as I always do before I put them away."

The Huzoor frowned. He thought he felt a tremor beneath his feet. Except the tremor was far, far away, in another place that served as a foundation to this plane. What God, what Force was at work against him?

"Continue," he growled.

"My Lord, one of the chelas has taken a rumel."

There was silence. The rumels were sacred, handed down through many generations. Many a Thug saint had wielded them.

"And why do you think the chela was yours, Trande Gautam?"

"He lingered long at the table where each chela leaves them when he goes. Oh, this indeed is a great burden for me to bear, if it is so."

The Huzoor stood. "If it is so, then it is the chela who must bear the weight of Mother Kali's wrath. And that is a burden which will crush him. But let us not accuse until we have proof." Then he paused. "But why should he do so?" he wondered aloud.

The Huzoor never answered his own question that night. He tossed fitfully in his sleep, and by dawn the belief that the thief desired the rumel as a souvenir had died. Another thought supplanted the first, and the Huzoor felt the tremor again.

The chela intended to experiment with the stolen rumel.

TEN

The shuttle arrived in Boston from New York on schedule, despite the persistent storm warnings. Now the adventure truly begins, Rama Shastri thought when he first saw Stephen Wrench. Once he was settled in the airport cocktail lounge with a mild vermouth, other things finally landed. A solid, three-point landing, at that. He hadn't really failed Das and Ileana. More important, he hadn't failed Mother India.

From the moment of his escape, Shastri had heard a distant, silent thunder, accusatory. Though intellectually he knew he was innocent, predatory guilt pursued him, a vulture hovering above him, waiting.

No matter how he chided himself for being puerile, the feeling came with him to Hong Kong. There, before his flight on Japan Air Lines, he searched a kiosk for reading matter . . . and first saw the news of Ved Addy's murder. The headline from *The Bengal Herald* boldly challenged his mock ease. Other announcements were widely spread across the faces of *The Bengalee*, *The Amrita Bazaar Patrika*, *The Sandhya*, *The Hindustan Times*, *The Times of India*, and *The India Gazette*.

Thus, en route to Tokyo, he read of the Thuggee-style killing of Ved Addy, recalling then Ajit Majumdar's short disappearance in the gardens. Shastri's palms sweated as he quickly scoured the *Bengalee*'s pages, prepared that Rasul had seized this opportunity to blame him for the crime. The follow-up account shocked him, however. For a quarter-hour he sat with a hand shielding his eyes.

Ileana had discovered the body, the column continued. She'd stated to the police that she'd seen a furtive shadow scale the grounds' wall. Then, since she was a close friend to the indom-

129

itable Rama Shastri, she immediately told him of what she'd witnessed, and he and a faithful lieutenant had taken up the pursuit. Shastri paused over his vermouth. Ileana had again proven the infamous axiom: the greater the lie, the more quickly it will be believed. He could cynically observe that Ileana had fabricated solely to save herself. But no one could possibly think her capable of a Thuggee strangling. Women weren't allowed in the sect. Besides, she'd then revealed to the press "the great Shastri's recent case" involving a current Thuggee uprising. The rest of the article was a long, detailed history of the cult until its former suppression by Major-General Sleeman.

He knew well she'd lied to protect him. Somehow she'd got to the news people before Rasul and leaked everything she could that would make Shastri appear more and more the hero. She dreamed, perhaps, that now the government wouldn't dare arrest him; that he would return to India, perhaps, and then to her. . . .

Perhaps. Yet the purple prose that surrounded his name in the Indian press, the myth that journalists delighted in developing had finally touched even him. He was always a hero to the public; the one, if not only, personification of justice. Something their thousand and one sadhus couldn't be, since what had they to do with justice? But he—he was Rama Shastri, who was pursuing Thuggee wherever it flourished.

And that was no longer in India. The Huzoor was here. In America. Here.

"Are you still with us, Ram?" Steve asked.

"Yes. But I was thinking of Ileana. She may have saved my reputation, maybe even my hide. I'm certain she did. To the very end."

He checked himself, realizing that Santha had brought a male companion with her. He studied the pair without appearing obvious. He was allowing full rein to his envy of George Buchan when Santha said, "Uncle Ram."

Shastri turned to her, noting again that she was so much the best of her mother and something additional. He wondered simultaneously what callous Prime Mover had so afflicted him twice, casting him both as best man and adopted uncle in this lifetime.

"Yes," he replied, trapped in the past-present as if he'd arrived by a time machine instad of a DC-10, as if the chronological designator had been defective. It was a terrible burden to speak to mother and daughter in the same host body.

"Jet lag," he whispered to himself.

"What, Uncle?"

"I believe I have jet lag."

She nodded sympathetically, then remembered what she was going to say originally.

"Do you still eat beef as much as ever? I've told George about your feelings concerning the beef ban."

"Yes, I do." Her English sounded the way they spoke it in India. But that was where she was originally schooled, he reminded himself, and Kamala had spoken that way. He welcomed it as opposed to the harsher, less crisp American sounds. Yes, it was the Queen's English, and wasn't that the way every good little Indian boy and girl learned it? He laughed at that, told them why.

"I hated the old Raj so much," he admitted. "Still, I'm tied to its euphonious diction."

The others rambled on, then, about various American dialects, including the broad Boston *a*. Shastri lit a Sher Bidi— he was back to his quota—and pressed the soles of his feet on the tile floor. Aha, he'd landed at last. He was here, and the guilt vulture had left.

Behind him. That was where it was. Still up in the air with the DC-10 or the 747 used for the Hong Kong—Tokyo leg.

Some enemy of Rasul's had got Ileana to the newspapers. It had to be, he concluded. Probably one of the political people at the banquet desirous to fill Rasul's shoes. The murder was a scandal, and this was stressed again and again in print. Ved Addy had been important enough to stir inquiry as to why the government had been unable to protect him from such a death. And on his own grounds! *The Sandhya* asked: Why hadn't Krishna Rasul foreseen the possibility of a Thug entering the area? Rasul had been a former policeman. Wasn't he trained to think in that fashion? And why hadn't the government warned the press about the extent of the uprising, where it would reach a large slice of the population immediately? But then, what could one expect when a government official like Krishna Rasul couldn't protect another public figure like Ved Addy? At least Rama Shastri had had the temerity to disappear underground, so to speak, to capture the perpetrators. . . .

"Ram, did you hear me?"

Shastri's lips automatically mouthed a "Yes," and Wrench's head was replaced by a billowing bluish gray veil like a moment of Magic Realism. Shastri caught the pungency of the pipe's tobacco mix as Wrench puffed hard and tried lighting it a third time. It had been ages since Shastri endured that constant pipe.

"I'm sorry. It's the lag." But Shastri knew Wrench thought otherwise. In fact, everyone had been extremely untalkative, considering. A brief embrace when they first met, then this interlude over drinks before they left for the city. Very little conversation about anything. He'd expected more questions from Steve. But George Buchan was here—tall, with an impressive beard, good manners, and a worried look whenever he doted on Santha. Yes, "doted" was the word. George had helped her with her coat in the overly heated lounge, had quickly handed her what Shastri just knew was bad pâté for her crackers. Nothing extraordinary. Except an urgency in the fingers holding the pâté dish, Shastri gauged; the young man didn't seem to be the fidgety, nervous type that can't differentiate between a woman and fragile porcelain. And Santha would never tolerate it, he further concluded.

Wrench's face again, clear beyond the dying smoke screen. Shastri queried, "What is it, Steve? You've had that look since I arrived. That cat-with-the-mouse grin."

"Oh, do I?"

"Yes, you do. Is there some sort of surprise ahead?"

"Well, no welcome-to-America party, rest assured. I know you don't like them very much, Ram. This is the closest thing we'll have to that."

"Then what is it?"

"Daddy," Santha interrupted. "See, I told you he'd see

through your playacting. Tell him." Then she added, almost defiantly, "We—George and I—are letting you and Daddy off somewhere this afternoon."

Wrench scowled. "Dammit, save some of it for me, Santha."

Wearing a false apologetic face: "Pardon, Daddy."

"Well," Shastri persisted, "you'll drive me to another Sher Bidi if you don't tell me soon, Steve."

Wrench didn't hesitate. A brief scowl at his daughter, and he said, "They're in Boston, Ram."

Shastri was suddenly cold. He broke a cracker between his fingers, stunned that he was so frightened. In Boston! Here in America, most certainly, but not in Boston, the one city he'd flown to! The guilt vulture was replaced by an anonymous shadow flapping its wings. Again the peculiar sensation of a life beyond chance and random happening ushered out any balanced rationalizations he might have.

Wrench explained, "Three nights ago a body was discovered in an alley off Symphony Road. A man strangled. And with a rumel."

"How can they be certain of that?" Shastri demanded, piqued both at these new "coincidences"—the fear of control sifting from his fingers like so much sand—and the openness before Santha and her boyfriend, lover, whatever he was.

"They found a rumel. Next to the body, Ram."

Shastri blinked. Impossible. Next to the body! No Thug in a million years would lose his rumel. Doubts surfaced, began to crush the web of supernatural design, and he relaxed. Wrench, the police were wrong. It wasn't a Thug rumel. Only an ordinary scarf. Nevertheless, he groped for a Sher Bidi. Now his eyes were cast meaningfully on the young pair.

"They know," Wrench replied to the unspoken question. "Santha read your letter aloud to me when I was ill. George was there. He's expressed an interest in Thuggee."

"How intellectually stimulating," Shastri remarked.

"Oh, come off it, Ram. They were trying to be helpful, that's all. I was damn out of it, what with Kamala's ... I've discussed Thuggee like any old subject, true, but what else could I do while I sat here on my butt wondering if you'd even be able to make it over here? Talking about it kept me going."

"It kept him alive, Uncle Ram." It was Santha with that habit of interrupting he'd have to adjust to. She smiled afterward, and Shastri melted despite himself. The bits of colored glass in the ceiling meshed with the tousled blackness of her hair. Shastri wished to think of it as Indian hair. It was black, beautiful hair, thick and full of feminine suggestion and promise. God, she was a sight. He thought of the charm of that toppled statue, the dancing girl bedecked with garlands, near the temple cave off the Deccan ghats. And he thought of the seven hundred and eighty-odd men with the calling of death-giving who had been within that cave.

"I'm sorry," Shastri told them. "Of course, it's all been much more a detached matter for you, Steve." He paused. He'd expressed it awkwardly. Well, it would have to do. This wasn't the time or place for more details.

Stephen Wrench was saying, "I've arranged with the police for us to see the body and the scarf. George will drop us off at the morgue when we leave here."

"Yes, of course," Shastri agreed, watching Santha rise to go to the powder room. He still wished she were ignorant of all this. What damage could it do? he asked himself. Or, rather, what danger could come of it? Nothing seemed likely, but the cold sensation continued to ripple along his ganglia.

And Santha, meanwhile, left in a daze, excited that the two men were together at last. That fact offered a freedom she hadn't known for months. Now she could finally concentrate on George alone. She walked buoyant, restored, and it showed in the eyes of onlookers. Santha noticed and felt the prettier for it, accepted the spell she could cast, even on this gray afternoon. She reveled in its power. It was wonderful to be young, to be a woman, to be in love.

Entering the powder room, Santha crossed to the larger room beyond, opened a stall door, lowered her clothing, and sat on the seat. She'd been softly humming,

> There are stars in every city,
> In every house and on every street.
> And if you walk down Hollywood Boulevard,
> Their names are written in concrete,

one of The Kinks' ballads, stopping on the Rudolph Valentino line, when her mindless calm was shattered.

Santha heard . . .

Heard!

. . . anklets sounding against each other. She identified them immediately: the same clinking as within the abandoned building in her "event." The same tread, the same noise, the familiar clatter of a heavily ornamented Indian woman.

She sat, frozen, shocked in her vulnerability.

But she'd been alone in the place only a minute ago! Santha hadn't checked, but one usually knew these things in a ladies' room.

Again! There it was again! The tread, the dead fall of metal against metal and . . . louder!

Holding her breath, Santha waited. She dared not even think.

Or hear, dammit!

And then another sound. The farthest stall door at her left was opening. Then, a silence. The worst kind of distilled silence, filtered through expectancy. Thin, reedy.

The door finally closed.

Santha's body flowed with a sudden surge of giddiness. It was only another woman who, after all, happened to be wearing a lot of jewelry. In this age of bizarre fashions, why shouldn't a woman wear imitation Indian anklet baubles? So relax, you hysterical ninny, she chided.

Santha started to hum *Celluloid Heroes* again. She stopped at "on every street." There! Yes, she was hearing correctly. The goddamn clatter. It . . . she . . . wasn't in the stall . . . ?

A new door opened. Santha's breath wheezed from her as if she'd been stricken. What was . . . the woman doing? Was she looking into every stall? Santha eased from her seat. Her flanks were clammy. Tension. Silly, hysterical thing, that the sound of a handful of baubles can do this to you . . . The door clicked shut. The tread . . . CLUNK. CLINK. CLUNK . . . The next door.

Santha asked hoarsely, "Can I help you? Are you searching for . . . somebody?"

CLUNK. CLUNK. CLANK. The drop bar being pulled back. It was the stall adjacent to Santha's.

"Is everything all right?" she cried out, and it echoed slightly in her cubicle. Then, like a contemptuous reply, her sphincter muscle let go.

"Christalmighty! Christalmighty!" She collapsed back on the seat in embarrassment. Simultaneously: CLICK. It seemed very, very loud. Then, just as simultaneously, the barrier evaporated. Envisioning now, Santha watched a shapely bare-footed leg rise, remain bent and stationary for a second, finally descend slowly, cautiously. Toes, ebony soles flat on the tile, anklets slipping onto one another. A dance stride. A god or goddess stride, much as she'd seen in Hindu theater. Sambuka, the demon of Bhavabhuti's play, walked that way. Why think of demons? Or the Kathakali dancers transforming themselves into supernatural beings by effort of will, their eyes bloodshot from the application of vegetable seed.

The barrier returned, the light gray metal surface. "Ohmigod," Santha wailed in dismay at the bursting noise of her sphincter relaxing more. Her hand slapped her mouth and clung there while she stared.

The silence. The same brittle silence. Now, that's enough of that! Santha bellowed in her mind. She forced herself forward, gritted her small teeth edge to edge. Pressing her palms against the stall sides, she demanded, "Answer me, damn you! I know you're out there!"

Her vulnerability was horrible. Her stall door was locked, but all security was gone. She was trapped, netted. She felt already victimized.

CLUNK!

She watched for a shadow, for the sliver of light between the door and the floor to be blotted out.

CLUNK!

The handle moved. Jiggled back and forth.

"Keep the fuck away!" Pounding the door, Santha fell to her knees and elbows. Her pantyhose began to run as they stretched between her knees, but she didn't care. Peering under the door, she surveyed the area beyond, anxiously. She had to see it! Seeing her threat would at least make it finite, and she desperately needed that, whatever the outcome.

But, focusing on the area before the stall as she had never focused on anything in her twenty-five years of life, she found . . .

. . . no legs, no anklets, no shadow.

Nothing.

Santha rubbed her eyes. She discovered the fingers of her other hand interlocked in her hair. The tresses were stuck to each other. The curl in them had straightened, and they hung like black strips of treacle, dripping wet with perspiration . . . wet, down her forehead, down her neck. Santha lowered her cheek to the tile again and searched once more. Still nothing. Was she insane? Had it all been in her mind?

Lying with her back to the stall corner, she thought, Am I responsible? Do I make these "events" occur? But she couldn't fathom this as a thing she did alone. Something linked with her mind, some unknown force. That was far more feasible. Deep in that place called the "gut level," it felt right. Whatever . . . Please, God, Santha prayed without hesitation, please, God, no more. The spontaneity of the appeal shocked her momentarily, but she continued, Please make it go away.

Eyes closed, she remained where she was. Her heavy breathing subsided, and when calm returned, so did the embarrassment. Quickly Santha rose and regained her balance. Standing on putty legs, she leaned against the cubicle and waited longer. A door whished in the powder room, and a pair of heels clacked on the tiles. The woman hurried into a stall.

Santha stirred, cleaned herself, flushed the toilet, and left. Her actions rushed, automatic, she went to a sink, washed, and then worked on her face. The dim lounge lighting would temporarily hide any revealing marks, she concluded upon investigation, peering into the mirror. My mind, her thoughts raced, I know it's partially responsible. Maybe I ought to talk to somebody about it, after all. Maybe Uncle Ram.

NO!

Santha dropped her comb. Looking around, she noted the room was still empty except for the rustle of fabric from the occupied stall. But the voice had been nearer.

NO!

It jolted her to view her reflection. A whining noise caught in her throat. The reflection was her, all right, but she was different, in dress (a saffron sari and necklaces and bracelets on her wrists), and eyes thick with kohl on the lids. The face stared, and Santha listened to the third

NO!

Strong, emphatic. The lips hadn't moved, though full of snarl and fury. It was the eyes that threw out the word.

NO!

And Santha surrendered to the understanding that this thing was private. Quickly and unnaturally. All hers; the "events" were totally hers. Totally. Not Uncle Ram's or her father's or George's or anyone else's. They belonged to Santha Wrench. She backed then, erect, self-possessed, while the woman left the stall and crossed to another sink, the high heels shattering whatever presence lingered in the mirror. Now Santha saw only herself, the same person who had entered.

The same who should be back in the lounge, she decided. Then, with a serenity that belied what she'd endured but minutes ago, she set forth.

ELEVEN

"It's certainly a Thug's rumel," Rama Shastri announced, fingering the old scarf. Its faded yellow surface was mottled with flecks of dried mud. He stared briefly at the clothes on the table and the knapsack nestled up to a small stack of pamphlets. The top pamphlet had part of the cover turned up, and all he could read was "LIVE LONGER" in large print. The irony was as cold as the Boston day outside.

He ambled away from the other three men, still holding the scarf, and watched the slow snowfall from the window. Below, someone scurried across a parking lot to a cherry-colored car, leaving a narrow black snake's curve on the thin white glaze. Shastri had never felt snow before, and it was a new fascination.

Captain Adair said, "You're sure?"

He asked it the way he puffed cigars, with his teeth gritted and his mouth lines askew. He must always have a bad taste in his mouth, Shastri concluded.

Shastri left the window, returned to the desk, repeated, "Yes, it's an Indian rumel. This was made by Indian hands." He displayed one end. "This is a rumel knot. And this coin placed in the rumel is a rupee from the time of the British Raj. This is often a Thug custom."

Lieutenant Terranova decided to join in. He had been Stephen Wrench's link with the Boston police in the past, a case in which the FBI confiscated drugs from the Golden Triangle when they arrived in Boston Harbor. "You mean they actually strangle a man as easy as one, two, three with a scarf like that?"

"As easy as four, five, six," Shastri replied glibly.

From their arrival, Adair had made them feel unwelcome. Wrench had pulled strings to see the victim of the strangling off Symphony Road, and the captain resented the intrusion on his case. Especially from an FBI consultant who'd spent two thirds of his lifetime in another country and—he'd mouthed the words as if he were suddenly dyspeptic—from "India's greatest hot-shot detective."

Perhaps none of this would have affected Shastri if he hadn't already been distracted by an earlier matter. In the airport lounge, Santha had returned from a long stay in the powder room, different, ruffled.

The matter openly agitated George Buchan, who nervously questioned her. "An upset tummy," she told them. But neither Shastri nor George was convinced.

It was more than that, Shastri deduced. Santha had left them vibrant, as wholesome a beauty as he could imagine. She'd returned strained, aloof, with a cool and almost mocking undercurrent transmitting from her like a subliminal wave.

So when he met Captain Charles Adair and Lieutenant Dan Terranova, the Santha transformation was nagging him, and the attitude he encountered at the morgue was just as the old Raj lads used to put it: "A bit too much."

First Shastri and Wrench had been ushered downstairs to the morgue proper, where the body awaited viewing, long, thin beneath a sheet on the medical examiner's table. Shastri, all business, immediately went over and proceeded to investigate. Somewhere in the background, Adair, in a sonorous voice, read from a series of sheets on a clipboard: Victim's name, Abel Joseph Fairley; residence, 19 Symphony Road, Boston; age 30; height, 6'1"; weight, 170 pounds. Fairley was noted for handing out pamphlets that he published himself. They dealt with everything from politics to everyday social issues. He was familiarly known around Boston as Abel, the Mad Pamphleteer. But Shastri's concentration deterred him from hearing much.

He'd seen it before, of course, but this time the markings from the scarf, actually lacerations from digging in so deep, were extremely apparent. Sometimes Thugs were so swift with their rumels that barely any telltale signs were left on the neck. Apparently there had been a struggle; Fairley's death had been slow, painful.

"No skilled Thug did this," he murmured to Wrench.

Adair continued that at 9:48 P.M. Wednesday (date given above), two students at Northeastern University, Philip Grunberg and Edward Nyes, had turned onto Symphony Road from St. Stephen Street when they heard sounds "of a fight." There in the dim lighting they saw the victim fall while a man and a woman hovered over him. The woman, seeing the students, shouted, "Let's get the fuck out of here!" while the male (both were Caucasians) seemed to panic and dropped what is believed to be the murder weapon (see Exhibit marked A). The pair then turned and ran down the alley in the opposite direction, leading to Gainsborough Street.

Adair's voice faded. Shastri's index finger touched the laceration and followed it around the neck. It certainly hadn't been a quick or merciful death. Nothing about it was Thuggee. He raised the head for a moment, noted the loose drop to it due to the break.

"I'm not convincned so far," he told Wrench. "Women aren't allowed to be Thugs."

"Wait till you see the scarf."

Admittedly, that changed things. Holding the scarf beneath a Tensor lamp upstairs, Shastri trembled. He held it to his nostrils and caught the faint scent of betel nut. The scarf was old, the rupee older, with most of its inscriptions faded. Probably handed down, father to son. The usual way they did things. But how did it ever get into the hands of the two murderers who barely knew how to wield it? And a woman? A young Caucasian woman, the witnesses thought, if their account could be taken seriously. The lighting was very dim in that alley, the report said.

He returned to the window. There was snow in the Himalayas, of course. But he, Shastri, had never been there. Never once to see the ashrams, shrines at the Ganga Gangotri. The snow burst against the pane, became an asterisk or some such thing, and stuck. Below, a woman nearly fell on the thin ice glazing that was forming everywhere. She looked attractive.

Whatever was wrong with Santha?

Adair's theory: the killing was the work of crank thieves who had nothing better than a scarf to kill with. He was offering it again.

Fine, thought Shastri. But why this scarf? this rumel?

Stephen Wrench said, "Fairley still had his wallet."

"Sure," the captain agreed. "Maybe the punks didn't have the time to take it."

A point. Stretching it like hell, but a point. The snowfall increased suddenly, and all the asterisks became a thick smudge that spoiled the view. No, the kind of scarf. The rumel and rupee changed everything, trampled on Adair's logic.

What had happened in the powder room? He must talk with George Buchan.

"I feel a chill," Shastri stated aloud. Yet he was next to the radiator, which was sizzling and pounding like a recurring theme.

No one replied. Wrench, who'd been mopping his brow at intervals, stared at him.

Terranova broke the silence. "Can you tell us more about Thuggee?" he asked.

Shastri proceeded to at last, convinced that with Terranova he had an interested listener. He told him of the Goddess Kali and how the Thugs believed they served her best by robbing and killing. "And it's done with a scarf like this so they won't spill blood. It appears that the people who killed Abel Fairley were attempting to perform a Thuggee-style killing. They were obviously not very good at it, or Fairley wouldn't have had a chance to fight back."

"It's a surprise he didn't get wasted before now," Adair cut in. "Real pain in the ass to the neighborhood with his pamphlets."

Shastri picked up one of the photographs taken at the murder site: a close-up of Abel Fairley, his head turned at a right angle, facing a brick wall. The eyes were open, filled with shock, the mouth was agape. Another photo beneath showed a trail of pamphlets strewn up to the back lots by the wind and the scuffle.

"Was he breaking the law distributing them?" he inquired.

"Naw. But he was always bothering people. Full of ideas. Listen, fellers," he told Shastri and Wrench, "it's getting late and I've got other work to do. If you're finished, I'd like to close shop."

"Charlie, ferchrissakes," Terranova said. "The man might have something to teach us."

"Okay, teach." Adair placed his feet on the desk. "Go ahead."

"Well, to begin with . . . Fairley's killers had to get this Indian scarf someplace. From someone."

"Sure. From a novelty shop that sells Eastern junk. Everything from turbans to hookahs or whatever they're called. There's a few of those places off Harvard Square. Look, fellas—face it: around this town and in Cambridge we get a thousand and one weirdos who are into all sorts of cult stuff. Witchcraft, devil worship, Hari Krishna, free love—anything. So maybe two of these freaks read up on Thugs and decide to try it out on some poor bastard. It could've been worse—they could've tried it out on a more respectable citizen. I mean, Abel Fairley was almost as weird as they are. Look, I know you guys mean well, but I tell you, nothing shocks me anymore. This new breed of kid'll try anything once."

"Bullshit!" roared Wrench. He hovered over the desk. "Adair, if this turns out to be more than you think, your ass'll be—"

Shastri took his arm. "Steve, that won't work."

"You bet it won't work," Adair shouted, standing up. "Just who the hell do you think you are, Wrench? I'm getting god-damn sick of feds like you messing up my act. I didn't want to be here in the first place."

"That's apparent."

"Sure it is. I've got better things to do than to discuss this 'Gunga Din' shit."

Shastri motioned to Wrench to cool down. "It wasn't a pleasant death," he stressed. "A brutal murder conducted by amateurs at using this." He held up the scarf by its weighted corner. "Whether these murderers are connected with a Thug-gee movement or not, Captain, they are certainly dangerous. Capable of inflicting prolonged torture—"

"Fairley couldn't fight his way out of a paper bag, anyway. I guess I ain't very impressed. Over here in America things are a lot rougher. It's guns and knives and muscle. No goddamn piece of silk . . ."

What possessed Shastri he'd probably never know. His small hands flicked the scarf, and the weighted end that held the rupee arced around Adair's neck. Shastri held on while the knot on the other end pressed under the opposite ear.

Trying to cry out, the captain's lips opened and closed like those of a goggle-eyed fish. The pressure was extraordinary, and his throat began to constrict on itself as Shastri lightly tugged at the scarf's tails.

Then, just as quickly, as easily, Shastri let go. "See," he said.

"You bastard," choked Adair, holding his neck. "You"—he

uttered something that was unclear—"bastard!" Shastri thought the strangled word was "black" but wasn't certain.

"You see," Shastri stated, "the rumel is as formidable a weapon as a gun or a knife."

Adair's rage was boundless. It mottled his face while he choked and screamed that Shastri had tried to murder him.

"That," the other assured him, "is not true. And you know it."

Adair's free hand groped for his holster. Terranova leaped quickly and shoved Adair against the wall, urging, "Easy, Charlie; easy." Then, over his shoulder, "You two better scram."

Wrench, who up to now had stood aside stunned, found his wits and pulled Shastri to the door. "Ferchrissakes, Ram, what the hell got into you?" he bellowed as they exited. Behind the closed door Adair was still screaming.

They rushed down the corridor to the front entrance and left the building. Wrench saw a taxi passing an intersection and hailed it successfully. Once seated, he said, "Goddamn it, Ram. You made an enemy there!"

"He already was, Steve."

"Where you gents going?" asked the cabbie.

Wrench gave him the Pinckney Street address. "Now Adair will never cooperate with us."

"He wouldn't have anyway. His mind was already made up, and we were only confusing him with facts."

Wrench fumbled for his pipe. "You should've left it to me. Christ, only a minute earlier you were chiding me for losing my temper. And then you give him a rumel demonstration! Hell, Ram, he's captain of detectives. He's got some clout. A stunt like that is enough to get you deported. I better make a phone call right away."

Shastri studied the design of the flakes on his side window. The fall had lessened slightly, and he felt disappointed. He wanted a blizzard, wanted to know, experience, the full extent of snow.

He agreed. "I'm sorry, Steve. You're correct. I just couldn't resist doing it. Adair had absolutely no pity for that poor chap Fairley. Can you imagine how much Fairley suffered? The more he struggled, the more he choked. Those amateurs prolonged what should've been a swift and painless death—chilling as any Thug strangling can be."

"You sound as if Thuggee is a kind of mercy killing."

"I had enough of that with Adair, Steve. Of course I don't condone even the best of Thug work. But an adept with a rumel dispatches his victim in seconds. Fairley's death was slow torture. And what frustrates me is that I can't connect it with what we're searching for. . . . Two unskilled assassins, one a woman, both Caucasian."

"The scarf, the rupee . . ."

"I know. I know. Nevertheless, maybe Adair was right. Maybe they did pick up the rumel at some novelty store or something like that."

Wrench settled back, puffed on his briar. "Well, I'll get Washington to cover you; but for Christ's sake, Ram, we've got to be careful. We'll end up looking like old fools fallen into senility if we don't become a damn sight more tolerant. We have plenty more lunkheads in authority in this country, some far worse than Adair, and you've got to learn to turn the other cheek a little. Otherwise, I'll be seeing you off to India before we've even begun. Aw, hell—I'm talking about me, too, Ram. I was too quick on the draw back there."

Shastri nodded. Women on exposed street corners were fighting to keep their skirts down. "God, I hate barbarians," he admitted, and when Wrench didn't answer, it was just as well. The women preoccupied him suddenly, looking so distinct and separate from the world of men, full of their own special concerns and motions in the whirl of flurries. Alien women's thoughts and body curves and odors. Like Ileana . . . who'd lied for him, protected him even from a distance. He missed Ileana terribly, and the sight of the women heightened the pain, the loss. Perhaps, unconsciously, he was sabotaging everything here to ensure his immediate return to her.

Shastri confessed it later in Wrench's apartment.

"I miss India, everything about her, good or bad, and it's baffled me," Shastri continued. "I'll have to learn to handle that. I've never been such a patriot."

"Why not?" Wrench added sympathetically.

"There was an old Chinese gentleman on the flight from Tokyo. Really a very pleasant, appealing man, but I'm afraid I was unable to appreciate him. He had, you see, a miniature pagoda, a toy, with little Mandarin figurines that went in and out of the doorways." Shastri paused, peered at Wrench a minute to check if he was bored. The subject wasn't Thuggee, but much more personal then usual. The big man, however, sensing his doubts, gave Shastri the wisp of a smile. They were old friends, remember, it seemed to say.

"The figurines," Shastri ventured again, "were a delight: both hoary, bearded Mandarins, one in yellow, one in red, with those quaint hats with the little knobs on top. They each had a doorway, and at intervals, hands tucked in sleeves, they exited from the pagoda, bowed slightly, and returned. An incredible toy. A collector's item.

"Now, I traveled first class, and we were all up there, the impeccably dressed old Chinese, myself, and a woman with a rather bratty eight-year-old boy. The pagoda toy finally caught the boy's gaze, and the wise Chinese placed the child on his knee, fiddled with a mechanism in the pagoda's bottom, and the two miniature Mandarins proceeded to exit, bow, and reenter over and over."

Shastri left his chair. Below, from the window height, he marveled at the Esplanade, whitening, whitening. "The Chinese gentleman, who never did tell me his name, noticed my newspapers and asked me if I came from India. I said yes, and without hesitation he then revealed that, although he was an American citizen these many years, he'd been born originally in Hong Kong. 'I used to resent Indians,' he told me in precise English. In those days the British imported Sikhs to act as policemen in Hong Kong, and all the Chinese resented them, considering them to be drunken, violent men. While the Chinese were developing mathematics, the Sikhs were no doubt carving each other for breakfast. That was the consensus among the Chinese population. Later, when he moved to New York, he met a group of Indian exchange students and soon discovered that not all Indians were like the Sikh policemen."

Silence.

"And?" asked Stephen Wrench.

"And I sat, listened, and found myself a raging patriot. A Sikh is as much a part of India as Dravidian peasants, who were probably our first indigenous peoples. Also—and this is what hurts, Steve—I'm positive that these Sikhs were over-zealous at their job then; that the old man was more than justified. Yet I resented his criticism of anything Indian. It's been unsettling to discover that I'm becoming, as I travel, a variation on the 'ugly American.'"

"I doubt that, Ram. Look, most of us become defensive about our homeland once we leave it. Over here you're a stranger in a stranger land. It'll pass." He laughed. "Consider how quickly that will change when you return to India some-day."

Shastri's thoughts raced from Ileana's arms to Krishna Rasul pounding his fat thighs and constantly referring to "she" and "they." Yes, he could use a reprieve from that awhile. He let himself enjoy the feathery white veil descending on the world. "Make your phone call," he said. "You've more than convinced me I'm exactly where I belong."

TWELVE

"I love you, kesari," Santha Wrench said. She watched George Buchan brake in time to miss colliding with a station wagon turning onto Berkeley Street. He gritted his teeth while the Audi bucked and skidded slightly to the left. She listened to him damn the narrow New England streets, built originally for horse carts, not automobiles. Santha knew he was upset with far more than the difficult driving, though.

A moment later, George asked, "Now you're calling me 'kesari' again. What's it mean?"

"Kesari," Santha repeated. "Lion . . . My noble kesari."

George shook his head. "I don't feel much like a . . . like that. Lion? Hell, right now I feel about as ferocious as those two big pussy cats in Rousseau's *Yardwiga's Dream*."

He was referring to one of Santha's favorite paintings, his tone bitter.

"Why would you want to be ferocious, George?"

He didn't answer, and she was relieved. Santha looked at the city beyond the white barrier. The heavy traffic and snow seemed linked together. The storm was in control, the cars did what it dictated.

The hurtling flurries made Santha think of herself; she, too, was being tossed about by Something. She wished now she could tell George everything, but the memory of the face in the mirror in the ladies' room at the airport prevented her. George must never see that face. Never.

Santha could tell he was angry with himself, at his hesitancy in questioning her. Sooner or later, the doctor in George would probe again, or his other side, the artist, would discover the truth. In time there would be no escaping George's insight.

Santha feared the artist the most. George had been drawing her lately, with the intention of ultimately painting her on canvas. Would his work show, for all to see, that she had two sides also? Or was it more like something superimposed?

The face in the mirror. She must have had traces of that face still with her when she returned to the lounge, and George had spotted them.

The face Santha had seen had been twisted. Why did she think "twisted"? Why not another word? "Askew." Like in the novels. "Her makeup was askew." Or "her lipstick was smeared." That was worse. Was it her lipstick, after all? Santha used makeup sparingly: no extreme eye shadow.

Where had that twisted look been? In her eyes? In her mouth? In her voice? Puzzling present, puzzling someplace. But where? And who, what Santha was there?

George tooted his horn. The driver ahead didn't understand you could turn right on a red light.

George left the city center, arrived on Charles Street. The hazy outlines of Beacon Hill appeared.

"Let's go to DeLuca's and buy food and eat at your place," Santha prompted. "I feel like cooking." George agreed. The idea seemed to relax him. They needed to be together again, close. She read it in his eyes when he looked at her. The other Santha couldn't still be with her, then. It was as if nothing had happened.

They found DeLuca's crowded. People were stocking up for the storm. Pleased with George's change of mood, Santha shopped with gusto. They would have lamb curry, she announced, her voice crisp above the shopping din, with artichokes and good dinner wine. She managed to reach the butcher's counter and ordered her lamb strips to be cut. Excited to do some real cooking again. Someday now, with Daddy well, she'd go whole hog (a funny Americanism) and cook true Bengali fish curry. That and kofta meatballs or an Indian fish dish like macher mauli or even make kulfi, Indian ice cream.

Her eyes darted to the others before the glass-encased meats. An elderly lady with an ornate walking stick ordered with all the posture of a grande dame commanding her household staff. I bet she's somebody, Santha thought, playing her favorite Beacon Hill game, a place where "somebodies" dwell. I bet, she continued, she's a writer or something like that. She just sounds so literary, has the vibes of a Boston Athenaeum browser. Perpetually invading the Athenaeum's magnificent old library, that stuff. And has to speak three to five languages fluently. Has read the entire *Comédie Humaine* of Balzac. It has to be Balzac. Proust would bore her. She's elderly enough to prefer the classic novel form.

Farther on, a plump young woman shifted her knapsack while peering at an array of veal cutlets. Obviously a student, Santha decided, given the notebook-congested knapsack. But what's her major? Can't possibly be humanities. Too well organized, clothes with that purposefully weathered and worn look but freshly laundered. Slips of paper sticking from books in sack. Squinched but controlled script on the papers. Then: yes, a psychology major or maybe social studies. Santha nodded at her reflection in the glass case. There. Wouldn't Uncle Ram be pleased with that piece of deduction?

Santha's investigative gaze leaped free of the room to the liquor section adjoining. We'll need an apéritif and a dinner wine this evening. . . .

She suddenly mused, I wonder what *he* does?

He, to begin with, was very tall. An inch more, at least, than George Buchan. Santha turned to check where George was, saw him at the vegetable stand a yard away, and allowed herself the luxury of looking at the stranger again. He wasn't the sort of man women stared at while their lovers were present. She estimated his age around mid-thirties. A woolly Michael Caine type, Santha thought, with hair prematurely gray. If there was such a color as mellow gray, the term fitted him. The brows, too, were light, his face so boyish that she marveled at his curled white-gold beard. That he had one at all.

At that point he moved toward a rack of bottles, and his eyes fixed on her. He was too distant for his eyes to be distinct, but she guessed them to be as blue as the iced sheen of blue agate. He turned his back, and the camel's-hair topcoat bent over the bottles.

George ambled to her side. "The artichokes look fine," he said.

So they went to the vegetable counter, adding Spanish onion for the curry, and joked that if they kissed afterward, it'd be okay since they'd both have onion breath. And odors led to more odors. Santha sniffed, startled. And Santha listened. She spun about and immediately joined two men at the tomato section.

They were Indians. Santha talked freely with them for a while. When she returned, George looked relieved.

Santha told him, "They're from Varanasi. But they were speaking Bihari, since the big, bearded one, Makunda, is originally from there. My Hindi is better, so I got them speaking it and directed them in the bagging of tomatoes and peppers and how to understand the insufferable Massachusetts tax. Funny, though—Makunda has attar in his beard, which is a custom of some of the northern Muslim tribesmen. He'd been north for a time in his youth, he said, and he'd adopted the habit while there. Attar is a perfume from rose petals."

"What's so funny about it?"

"How memories return after many years. When I was a little girl in India, we had a Muslim servant who often held me in his arms. He always put attar in his beard."

"That Makunda was certainly staring at you. He held your hand a little too long in the end."

"He said . . . I was lovely."

"You are, but he looked as though he'd just as soon abduct you here and now."

"So what harm is there in that? He can't abduct me here, can he?"

"No. But I didn't like it. He looked at you as if you were some of the food—available for plucking and eating."

Santha laughed. "Just package me, put me on the scales, and ring up my price per pound."

That made him laugh, too, a snicker. "Com'on," she urged, pushing the food cart to the liquor room. "Now, why don't we stick to wines? How is Campari for an apéritif?"

"And Chablis with the meal."

"Agreed," she chirped and nearly bumped into the tall wine browser with the eyes of agate-sheen blue. She saw in a second that she'd been right about them. The eyes met hers, twinkling at some private thought. Santha stammered, "Excuse me," but ended looking at his pink shirt and solid black tie while he stared over her shoulder and said, "George. George Buchan! It's great seeing you!"

Shocked, Santha watched George shake the other's hand energetically. "Kurt Leinster! Jesus, I haven't seen you in years! I thought you were in Rome!"

He had been, the man called Kurt told George, but he'd returned to the Boston area about six months ago. Did George ever continue in medicine at Harvard? Yes, George replied; he was now a psychiatrist. Great, and how were George's folks? They were in Arizona vacationing at George's uncle's ranch near Phoenix. What about your people, Kurt? Well, rats in mazes, rats in mazes. Skinner is God and they are his prophets. Nothing new. Say, whatever happened to . . . and they reminisced about classmates, these two very tall men with Santha between them, and never once a notice or an introduction.

Santha suddenly felt like an outsider. She pushed the cart toward the wine section.

George called, "Oh, Santha, I'm sorry."

She turned, grinning ear to ear. "That's all right, George. I understand when old friends meet . . ."

"You see, Kurt and I were at Harvard together."

"Reeeally."

George ruffled at the sarcasm, but Kurt didn't seem to notice. "Santha Wrench, Kurt Leinster," George began the introduction. "We met via collision," Santha heard, and tightened at the way his eyes were fixed on her body. "'Lo," she replied coolly and prepared to steer her cart back to the wine aisles.

George offered, "Let's get together soon."

"How about tomorrow, George? I'll phone you tomorrow. And we'll all go out for dinner on me."

"Fine. But phone. Don't wait years again before . . ."

"Don't worry. I will."

Fiddling with the purchases in the cart, Santha kept her head lowered. But when she heard, "Meeting you has been an event, Santha," she quickly raised it. Event? Why did he say "event"?

"The same," she replied in her best offhand voice. But she couldn't refrain from looking at him as he headed for the other section of the store.

"Imagine meeting Kurt." George beamed. "He's really a different kind of person, an anomaly in our time. He's very cultured. Speaks about seven languages fluently, including Russian. And he's a better-than-average musician. Plays the psaltery."

"That's impressive."

"He also sketches well, has written and published two books of poems . . . is an expert on Florentine, Flemish art, all sorts of Russian and Greek icon work, can give you a blow-by-blow description of every major battle of the Peloponnesian Wars, recites both Homeric Greek and 'Jabberwocky'—"

"He's already over my head. Except for the 'Jabberwocky.'"

She frowned. "So you mean Kurt's an anomaly since he's about as contemporary as Prince Albert's gaiters."

"Something like that. Yes, he's a Miniver Cheevy. He'd have been happier had he been born in an earlier age, before jazz or rock, films—even automobiles. He doesn't even drive, as I recall."

"Why, that's plumb un-American," she joked, but quickly tensed again. "At least we've got the rest of today to ourselves," she growled, once outside.

"What are you upset about?"

"Oh, George, let's go back in time!" Santha cried, while they turned onto Mount Vernon Street. She grabbed his arm and led him into the little alley between the Charles Street Church and the firehouse. Somehow the alley was insulated from the rest of the world when the snow was thick and draped the backs of the old Beacon Hill town houses. Somehow she knew this was exactly the way it was before the turn of the century, a New England village in the heart of the city, priding itself on its security and importance. She could almost pause at this very spot, say "amen" to it all, and not feel silly.

"I love this spot so much." Santha almost added that the place made her feel in some way protected. Instead, she shuddered and thought of the rest room at the airport. "I need a bath."

"A bath!" repeated George.

"Yes, a bath," she said defiantly. "What's wrong with that?"

"Nothing. Nothing. But why so edgy?"

"I guess I had too much of your reminiscences with your anomalous Harvard buddy."

"So you felt a little snubbed?"

"For a moment." Santha laughed despite herself.

She knew George wished his arms were free of groceries, that he wanted to kiss her. She laughed again, enjoying the brief moment of power. Snow shook free from her hair, and everything scintillated like a mantle of jewels.

"Your hair makes me horny as hell," George admitted.

"Good," she told him. "Now you can suffer for a while

longer. It's good for the masculine soul—if there is such a thing." Santha laughed again.

"Then take a bath at my place," he grumbled.

Santha agreed. They went to Lime Street first. The shades were up, the curtains parted. Whatever light existed on this stormy afternoon barely filtered into the living room.

Santha rushed to the bedroom closet. She chose some fresh clothes and packed them in a tote bag with a few toilet articles. She poked George's stomach with a finger. "Let's go!"

Santha buttoned her coat and swaddled the lower part of her face with a long white knitted scarf. Then she eased close to George, her black eyes enticing above the half veil, as she'd seen Calcutta street women do, and grabbed his hand to usher him out. He needed no urging.

When they arrived at Otis Place, George said, "I'll cook. Take that bath you need so damn much. I guarantee, when you return, dinner will be as satisfying as a night at Joseph's."

"I see—that saves time, doesn't it? You really are a horny fellow."

"That I am, my dear. Very."

Santha placed the scarf below her face, gave him the street-walker tease with her eyes again, and bounded out of the room before he could touch her. In the bathroom, Santha hummed Joni Mitchell's "I Had a King" while she fiddled with the taps.

She thought then of Kurt Leinster and became quiet. If only George hadn't accepted Kurt's dinner invitation for tomorrow.

She hadn't liked Kurt's eyes pawing her when they were introduced.

Santha climbed into the tub, nestled to her chin among the bath suds and aromatic oils. Kurt's look had been more than lustful, she concluded; it was goddamn possessive. "I belong to George Buchan," she said aloud.

The word "belong" suddenly felt like an assault. She belonged to nobody. Yet. *Nobody*, she stressed, while she toweled herself dry and wrapped herself in her kimono-style robe with its meek Bengal tiger faces. Her reaction was so strong and unexpected it frightened her. Santha went into the hall and opened a small window overlooking the courtyard below.

The storm burst in. Santha's skin sparkled with stinging droplets of moisture, her hair, momentarily fanned, lost its bunched kinkiness, and a gradual white web of flakes covered its blue-black surface. Santha's eyes widened, her lips parted sensually, waiting. She loosened the kimono and her breasts rose to the storm.

And then she stared at the vague glow beyond the haze where the streetlight broke the turbulence.

Santha Wrench jerked, backed painfully, and slammed the window shut. Flush against the wall, she dug her nails into the wallpaper and pulled the kimono fast around her breasts.

No one could possibly be there in this weather, on this night. No . . .

Santha had seen someone. A figure, barely distinct, standing, facing the Buchan town house.

Despite the whirl of flurries graying the lamplight glow, the faint outline had left a blurred impression of a bearded man and the shadowy bulk of a turban atop his head. The beard was curled and the snow clung to it like white shavings. Beyond doubt it was perfumed with attar. Beyond reason or explanation, it was the man called Makunda.

THIRTEEN

The storm had diminished considerably, with the wind no more than a throb at the window. Rama Shastri's hand brushed the pane, thrilling at the sharp bite of the cold through the glass. The snow patterns fascinated him. Snow had always been just beyond his reach, beyond the horizon, in a sense. During his brief stays in England, Shastri had seen bits of it but only on Oxford roofs and steeples. Somehow he'd always been away in India when the snow season came to the British Isles; and when he'd returned, the snow had already evaporated from the ground.

The upper Ganga, among the glaciers and snow-capped peaks—he'd never desired to go there. The ascetic brunt of it discouraged him. Shastri preferred philosophy to mysticism. His logic demanded that he live one world at a time, and from this he never wavered.

But he had glimpsed in the distance the peaks with their white crowns during those days he had spent at Peshawar when the British had opened the gates, allowing caravans of Afghans, Bokharans, Turkomans, and Middle Asian Christians into the south. He'd spied for the Raj then, a job he'd not enjoyed. He'd dressed either in Afghan white, Bokharan green, or a tawny Turkoman tunic and mixed with the horde, sifting information about uprisings in the north. How the British worried about the north! Constantly, always, the tribes beyond the gates concerned them. And Shastri's heart hadn't sung at playing the spy, as it had later during the war years against the Japanese. No, to work for the Raj against Hindu, Muslim, Buddhist, or Christian wasn't the same. The Japanese had been like a plague to be cleared from Southeast Asia. The Raj—well, it was a pest in the house, a roach, a rodent, a fly one needn't tolerate but for some inane reason did. Now, upon looking back, it seemed dotty that one had tolerated silly John Bull with his swagger stick for so long.

But even from Peshawar he had seen no snowstorm. Perhaps someday, here in Boston, he'd experience a blizzard.

It was his progression of thoughts about snow that made Shastri decide to go outside. He had to touch it, to walk through the drifts. He went to the closet that Stephen Wrench had given him. It was filled with winter clothing, including what Americans called rubbers. He extracted an expensive-looking beige coat complete with hood, fur-lined interior, and belt. Shastri's physical dimensions hadn't changed much over the years, and Wrench and Santha had found the shopping an easy task. Shastri also found a black pair of furred leather gloves, a thick light-blue turtleneck. Shastri proceeded to dress.

Shastri pondered for a moment whether he should leave Steve an explanatory note. Wrench had told him to rest from his jet lag while he went to the shopping plaza to buy more food. Since Shastri planned only to walk along Charles Street for a while, he decided against the note and left.

By the time he reached Charles Street, however, his intensions had changed. He hailed a cab but, before entering it, bent over a snow mound at the curb and stood up, both gloved hands fashioning a snowball. "Symphony Road where it runs into St. Stephen Street," he told the driver, remembering Captain Adair's report. The cab took off, and Shastri studied the snow in his palms as if it were a fortune-teller's crystal.

This was unwise, he warned himself, wandering at night in a strange city, alone and unarmed. It wasn't the largest or the most unruly of cities that he'd seen, but he knew it had its share of dangers.

The snowball felt marvelous between his fingers. He pressed it harder, reshaping whenever he could; concentrating on it, and thus forgetting about the surrounding streets.

Yes, Shastri weighed, he'd been more reckless than usual lately. His recent adventure at the temple near the Western Ghats, where the Thugs had gathered and Das had died, reeked of the pluck of storybook heroes. He had lived a fantasia, felt reborn with a zest and pulse attributed to youth. But he knew that was so much myth. Youth was often queasy, unable to perform with autonomy, unable to take the risk. Youth was represented as courageous, daring, imaginative. But, in truth, most times youth worried much too much. Youth believed too greatly in the future, while those who were older could already hear the final beat of the drummer, the final chord that was soon to be played. So, *voilà*—sometimes age shrugged and became the champion.

"This is it, mister," the cabbie said. Shastri placed his snowball on the backseat and reached for his billfold to pay the man. After the cab left, he suddenly discovered he'd forgotten the snowball. He started to pick up a new handful of the wonderful whitish mystery, refrained, and instead managed to light a Sher Bidi. Then he clapped his hands, stomped his feet. Shastri was cold. He was dressed warmly, but the snow bit at his nose and eyes, and he imagined it seeped down to his toes. Then he chuckled at the unscientific thought.

Shastri looked around. He was on a corner in the nimbus glow of a streetlamp. The street he faced was at a right angle to the street behind him. This, then, must be Symphony Road: a street so short that he could see its end through the gradually dying storm. Yet, short as it was, it had a blurred and thus suggestive desolation.

Stephen Wrench had told him that within a few hundred yards' radius of this spot were a handful of famous Boston landmarks: Symphony Hall, the New England Conservatory of Music, the Museum of Fine Arts, and the famous Isabella Stewart Gardner Museum. But the street at this hour, with the white smear of the dying storm, separated Shastri from any sense of surrounding civilization.

He walked on, listening to the snow crunching beneath his tread. Shortly he stood at the fringe of the alley.

Rama Shastri had seen his share of murder sites and, indeed, of corpses; stabbings, shootings, decapitations, even worse. Yet this murder had haunted his thoughts, because of the unnecessary, prolonged brutality of it. Even torture frequently had its purpose, serving as the means to the acquisition of information. But a Thuggee killing by amateurs was a starvation, the absence of something vital, in this case air. That prolonged struggle for air unnerved him. The policeman in him foresaw no end to evil on this planet; but at least, if it must exist, then let it be done swiftly and with precision. That much the innocent of this world were entitled to.

Shastri waded through the drifts to where—and it was only guesswork at most—the murder had supposedly occurred. The alley was being bombarded as layers of snow dislodged from roofs split off and crashed below. The faint whimper of a wind scurried along the tenement backs. The snow in the streetlight glow looked blue, glazed and sparkling like a dream landscape. The unreality of the place chilled him more. Shastri wondered why he had come. What possible clue would there be in this spot, now so cleaned of everything by the storm.

Or was it?

Shastri threw his Sher Bidi into a lumpy pile against a sooted brick wall. Of course there were no telltale clues, police manual style. But Rama Shastri had come here to sense, not to think. To sense like a psychic searching for emanations in an abandoned house where ghosts were rumored to dwell. He was trying to extend feelers, psychic antennae for . . .

The temple. Looking, probing for what he thought he saw in that Deccan temple. What had been behind the Huzoor?

"You've become a fool," he cried aloud and trudged up the incline and back to the corner. He urged himself along St. Stephen. At the corner of Gainsborough, he detected the fluorescent-lighted glass side of a McDonald's and admitted he was hungry. He hadn't eaten since the airport, had told Wrench he wanted nothing. Maybe his lack of food accounted for his mental balance being disturbed.

In the restaurant, the thought of meat became an obsession. He picked a Quarter Pounder. Unlike something called a Big Mac, that was at least decipherable.

When he saw a uniformed man with the stitched word "Manager" above his pocket, Shastri asked, "Could you please tell me exactly where I am?"

"Yes, sir. This is the corner of Huntington Avenue and Gainsborough Street. You're in Back Bay."

"And where is Symphony Hall? You see, I came by taxi but I was . . . preoccupied. I didn't notice."

The man pointed to the left. "At the end of the block." He paused and offered besides, "If you're interested in music, the New England Conservatory's right across the street."

"No, it's not that. It was a matter of getting my bearings. . . ." The Quarter Pounder was ready. Shastri paid the counter girl, thanked the manager, and went to a table next to the huge window facing Gainsborough. He tried the hot chocolate he'd ordered with the sandwich and found that good. Aaaah, Shastri sighed, now the beef!

Shastri hadn't considered that the hamburger might have something on it. He bit in and felt that his palate had been assaulted. Shocked that anyone would do this to his prize viand, glorious and sacrilegious beef.

Shastri pushed the Quarter Pounder across the table as if an imaginary companion were seated there. He drank the hot chocolate instead and then returned to the counter for another cup. Then, once again before the large window, he looked at the slow descent of the last snow. Reflected off the glass he saw a customer stand, and her narrow hips sheathed in her jeans were superimposed and blended onto the graceful ease of the snowfall. Shastri smiled, recalling that Steve Wrench had often accused him of being a lecherous old man, and he wearily supposed that it was true. But hadn't the gods designed such young and nubile beauty to be admired, stared at, even hungered for?

The gods? Yes, the gods that never were and somehow had always been. The same gods he'd scorned, denied, condemned as the only true enemies of India. Those imaginary, bungling Prime Movers that fitted any unknown. The created answers for the inexplicable. Why, if things went askew, was it their will or their blame?

Why else did Jaipur suffer from floods that claimed up to four hundred lives when it really needed drought? Why did the monsoons last as long as three months and sometimes produce up to thirty-nine inches of rain? Why, when water was needed, did deluge come? And why, in areas like Maharashtra, Tamil Nadu, and Karnataka, where rain was sorely needed, did drought hold sway? What quirk of fate, what mad Creator's sound and fury gave India too much water where it shouldn't be and none whatsoever somewhere else?

Wasn't it said to be the will of those forces beyond? How easy, how simple to believe and settle for that. Since the gods were the sum and substance behind all life, all events, all being—the breath, the body, the decreeing voice, the Shiva fist . . .

The eyes!

The dying storm, the glass, its reflections rushed by like a nightmare blur that was the dissolution of reality.

The eyes! Shastri could not accept the eyes!

Lurking throughout his reverie were the three standing outside on the Huntington Avenue corner. They registered now in his consciousness: two men and a woman. The snow had ended,

and the hollow quiet of its aftermath carried through the pane
of glass.

The first man became a hint, as he passed Shastri's right,
of Chundra Bala. As softly as the snow, the fact glided into
Shastri's preoccupied mind, and still he remained dulled by his
reverie of gods, of their fickle and unreliable will, of their
bodies, dancing with the Destiny of the Shiva's fist . . .

of their . . . EYES!

Her eyes shattered. Completely, as though the glass were
suddenly pounded, fragmented before Shastri. Shattered his
final link with reality.

Gauri Bala paused in her stride. Her head was covered with
a part of her sari. Over the garment she wore a fur-collared
gray coat. She had not removed her nose ring when she'd come
to America, and this sped along Shastri's memory of the woman
in the cart before the temple at the cliffside.

Gauri, recognizing Shastri, plucked at Chundra's sleeve.
Bidhan, the Arm Holder, stopped behind her. Shastri watched
her lips form his name. Light from the restaurant beveled from
the window to the nose ring, and it became a ring of fire
spreading to the oiled black pitch of her hair.

The three of them stared, but still it was the woman's eyes
that rooted Shastri. Gauri held the sari high over most of her
face, with the eyes ablaze and taunting above the ring. Black,
ancient of days, with the collapse of contemporary time, they
mocked him.

Shastri compelled himself to dart for the exit. The three
moved, too. He saw them travel the distance of the huge window, their gazes fixed on him with every stride.

Before the door he froze. He had no weapon, no power of
arrest in this country. Nevertheless, he meant to follow them,
stalk them, until they were captured and the faithful Das avenged.

Dry-mouthed, Rama Shastri ventured into the night again.
He heard their voices sifting into the windless solitude of Gainsborough Street. The mantle of snow seemed to hold the breath
of the world within itself. The voices continued, seeped back
to him in a low, indecipherable murmur. Shastri saw that they

were crossing St. Stephen Street, Bidhan's tall and massive back trailing behind Chundra Bala and the woman.

The crunching snow beneath Shastri's feet meshed with his rage. The woman's challenge lured, tugged at his vitals, dried his mouth until his palate felt brittle, almost powdery. Somehow she clawed into his being until he screamed within himself for vengeance.

Vengeance on *this*—that now profaned so much, he shouted with some silent echo of his psyche. *This* that had stepped forth from the wings into life, beyond his comprehension, behond the logic of causality.

How that rankled him, tore at the fabric of what Shastri cherished. When she looked back, the streetlamp brightening her saffron sari for an instant, he stumbled in his agony.

The street was otherwise deserted. It ended a block away at another street running perpendicular to it. Shastri chose to walk down the center of the street, plodding through the heavy snow, dragging through it at times. He didn't question any action, any throbbing heated thought. He moved and watched the three, ahead, beyond the parked automobiles to his left on the sidewalk. Shadows, the hulks of cars covered them from view at intervals, and then the three appeared again. Over and over, their voices trickling back, the darkness increasing, the disappearance, the reemergence, and closer, ever nearer. Until a reemergence, and there were two.

Two. The number popped in and out of his consciousness like an agate on a Chinese checkerboard. The saffron sari looked ruddier now in the shadows, brownish and bloody. Another disappearance, and then one.

One.

Again the agate rejected the hole.

But in the next stride he was arrested by a lighted bay window and amplified sound that swept the white hush of the street away. To the left of him, slightly ahead of the waiting woman draped in blood, a party was in progress in a first-floor apartment. The building jutted out like a round lump, and, from its bright window, figures danced to rock music so ampli-

fied it replaced his inward scream with another that rang down
the expanse.

One, *one*! thought Shastri. *One*! And he panicked. Instinc-
tively he fell to his knees in the drifts, and the honed training
of years of exposure to danger came to the fore. He rose as
quickly, his two hands alive again, while they pressed and
kneaded. His peripheral vision restored, he sensed the two
missing Thugs lurking. *One* to seize him from behind, *one* to
work the rumel. . . .

Two in all, to kill with precision, unity. . . .

Rama Shastri hurled the snowball.

· As a youth, when he was first reading English, he'd found
in a primer the account of a snow fight between children. In
that story fragment, one of the hurled snowballs had . . .

Glass cracked the night. The amplified music amplified
more and, with it, a progression of screams, bellows, and
curses.

He heard another voice, in what he concluded was Ramasi,
a command, and the stir of men moving through snow hurriedly.
Shastri neared the spot where Gauri had been. The party people
were already out on the walk searching for the vandals, but he
didn't care. The woman, he must find her again, he urged.

And, as if conjured by his need, she leaped from shadows
he hadn't seen before. Nails raked his cheek, two specks of
black lightning fused into his eyes for a second, and Shastri
knew his dreams would not be peaceful again. Falling from
the blow, he heard the rasp: "You I shall destroy soon." When
Shastri raised his head a second later, she was gone.

FOURTEEN

Rama Shastri leaned on the button and buzzed and buzzed. Wrench's voice came over the intercom: "Ram, that you?"

"Yes. Let me in."

Wrench did, and they met on the stairs beside the old elevator cage. Shastri's face was blue from cold, but a pallor underlaid even that. And his right cheek showed scratch marks.

"Suffering Christ!" Wrench bellowed. "Where the hell have you been? I've been alone, sitting on my hands and listening to music to calm me down. Besides, Dan Terranova phoned. He wants us to meet somebody who might have a lead."

"We must talk first," Shastri insisted and passed him into the apartment. The Trumpet Voluntary of Jeremiah Clarke's Suite in D Major came to him from the living room. Wrench took his arm and led him into the bathroom. He began to doctor the scratches. "One pass too many," Wrench jibed.

"Yes, with the Queen of Death and Despair," whispered the other harshly.

"She must be a bundle of charms."

Shastri pulled away from the dabbing. "Those charms left me breathless. Literally almost without breath, Steve. It was the Thuggee Queen."

Wrench spilled the iodine. "What?"

"Or Thuggee Mother. Who knows? She certainly wasn't a woman. . . ."

"Not a woman. What the hell was she, then?"

"Not a woman."

"Not? Ram, let's have some tea to warm you up."

Angrily: "I'm very familiar with what a woman is, Steve."

"I know that, old fellow."

"Not a woman. Female, but not a woman. A woman's body, a woman's face, but not . . . The eyes!"

164

"Where the hell were you? Why did you go out?"

"I went to Back Bay. to the murder site."

"Oh, ferchrissakes, Ram!"

"She isn't a woman. A force, maybe. An elemental . . . something inhuman."

Wrench turned into the hall, announcing over his shoulder, "I'll put on tea."

Rama Shastri asked for some scotch instead and sipped while he narrated his night's adventure. Backgrounding at a lower volume were the final four movements of the suite.

Stephen Wrench stopped pacing before the fireplace, set the phonograph on replay, and, when Shastri ended, flung at him, "There's no excuse, Ram! You had no right to go out there! We just might've lost you, goddammit." And, in a murmur that Shastri had to strain to hear, "Then where the hell would I be?"

"Maybe I had no choice, Steve."

"Bull. That possession business is out of character for you. Call it jet lag or misspent emotion over Das, but not that bull about possession."

Shastri ventured again, "Steve, something happened to me when I looked into those eyes. You know I've always been disinclined to believe in anything . . . inexplicable. But those eyes . . ." Shastri put down his drink, his brow furrowed from intense concentration. "During the cab ride here, I searched and searched my imagination to discover analogies that fit those eyes. They are eyes that set the very self to shiver, Steve. Not just the body, but the very self."

Wrench fumbled with a match, blew the flame out before he burned himself. "Now listen to me, Ram," he urged in softer tones as he neared. "You once told me about an incident at a Calcutta movie house. That incident has always represented Rama Shastri to me. From his early youth, he stood liberated, untouched by the centuries-old Great Lie."

"I'm still that way." With some resentment: "You're just not listening to me."

"All right, then; I'll make a deal with you. Tell me the story of the movie house, and I'll try to keep an open mind about those eyes. I just want you to weigh your thinking then against your thinking now. That's all."

Rama Shastri sighed, but began. "My father was a doctor, as you know, and with his scientific bent, had little use for the myths, superstitions—well, the entire Indian cosmology. He recognized neither the gods nor caste nor—most of all—suttee. Father was so repulsed by suttee that once, when we passed such a pyre on the outskirts of Delhi, he blocked my eyes so that I wouldn't see the horror of a widow walking into the flames." Shastri extinguished his Sher Bidi. "Need I continue?" he demanded, with a burst of indignation.

"Suffer me this one thing, Ram. And think hard of what you vowed then."

"What I vowed then," the little man repeated. He took a deep breath and narrated in the tone of a schoolboy reciting a list of boring facts: "I was seventeen when I attended the cinema in Calcutta. The film was titled *Shiva Rastri*, a very popular entertainment at the time. The story was mythological. The protagonist, a bully and a drunkard, treated his family without honor. He left them to starve, often returned home to beat his wife, and once, in a rage, killed his son. But then Parvati, the goddess, brought about a change of heart, and the hero arrived home one day repentant and died in his wife's arms. The final scene of this saccharine tale showed the wife with her husband's head in her lap, sitting on the funeral pyre, smiling in ecstasy while the flames engulfed them."

After a pause, "Go on, Ram. You became damn angry, didn't you?"

"Yes, the film was maudlin enough to my mind. . . . Steve, I'll finish this, since you're so confounded insistent. But I flatly refuse to discuss anything further until you feed me. Promise you'll feed me."

"I'll feed you, but get to the point, man."

"What ired me the most was the audience reaction. They seemed totally apathetic through the entire picture until the very end. The suttee, the funeral pyre with the widow sacrificing herself, stirred their hearts to an outcry of praise and applause. I could tolerate it no longer. I stood and shouted at the din, shaking my fist at the screen. 'I vow,' I stormed, 'that I shall never acknowledge a belief that condones such barbarity. I vow that I will dedicate my life to the destruction of such a merciless credo. This obscene ritual must end.'"

"At the risk of your skin you said this, didn't you?"

"Yes. I had to be escorted from the cinema by the police. The audience would've killed me on the spot otherwise." Shastri stood, waving Wrench, the entire episode away. "Now feed me before I collapse. It's been a taxing night, Steve."

His host quickly supplied a half-dozen thin slices of roast beef, a small bowl of cold green beans, toast with marmalade, and Russian Caravan tea. But even replenished, Shastri was furious with Wrench's explanation that the woman with Chundra Bala was obviously a master hypnotist and nothing more.

"No!" He gulped the last of the tea, settled back in the chair, and stressed, "I appreciate that you're trying to save me from the Indian compulsion to see life in supernatural terms. I know what I vowed back there when I was seventeen, and I've abided by it ever since."

Shastri left his chair, went to the big windows, pulled the drapes back, and stared at the automobiles working their way along Storrow Drive below. The snowfall's end seemed the demise of a newfound friend. It saddened him, made him feel helpless. After all, it was snow that saved him but a few hours earlier. . . .

The eyes!

"Eyes!" he repeated aloud. "The mirror of the soul, someone once said. But what if the soul were subdued, buried beneath a greater identity? Suppose man does walk with a foot in two worlds, Steve? Suppose, despite foul, despicable beliefs like suttee, caste, the uncleanliness of the Untouchable's shadow, and Thuggee, despite false interpretations, imaginings, mythologies, and creeds, something does exist. Someplace beyond our usual ken, beyond our overrated five senses."

"Fine," came the reply. "I don't find that unpalatable. I'd like to believe, for example, that"—Wrench's voice lowered— "Kamala is in that someplace, that maybe she waits for me, for Santha, for all of her dear friends. . . . But that's not the issue, Ram. When you talk about that woman, you talk as if she's Kali herself."

Shastri, turned. "Precisely."

"Precisely, my ass. Kali, Ram, is a myth, a figment of some raving Hindu's imagination. Kali, the Bloodsucker, is as much fiction as Bram Stoker's Dracula, and you know it."

"You must listen to me, Steve. You promised you would. Suffer me, old friend, as I had to suffer you. And while we're both enduring so much, put on more tea."

While Wrench brewed the tea, the Indian walked back and forth over the kitchen threshold. "Steve, we are both intelligent enough to accept the paranormal with some ease. I won't go into all the research that's been developed in this area the last decade or so. But allowing a certain percentage of probability to some of the accounts, a reasonable man is, at the least, impressed. Correct?"

"If you're speaking of the Duke University findings, a handful of UFO reports, people like Uri Geller, Hans Holtzer, and the like, I agree. So?"

"So consider that perhaps there are physical and psychical laws that haven't yet been discovered. That a few yogis, a few mediums have perhaps tapped those unknown sources. Accept that much, and we have a beginning." Wrench nodded. "What, then," Shastri continued, "would you say to the avatar or incarnation idea? That there have been human beings who were incarnations of God? Jesus comes to mind. 'My Father does these works through me,' or some such thing. Isn't that what he said, more or less?"

"More or less."

"Then why can't the Goddess Kali—if she truly exists, of course, in that nether zone—enter this world, as did the Christian Father through Jesus? Through a medium or through possession, if you will. Yes, a kind of higher form of demonic possession."

"Now, there's a movie I saw," quipped Wrench. "All about a little girl named Regan who swallowed too much pea soup."

Shastri frowned.

"Sorry, Ram. That was a private joke I couldn't resist. I'll tell you its meaning sometime."

"I'd like to feel you're really listening, Steve."

"I am. But I'm embarrassed. That's all."

"About me?"

"No, myself, Ram. I've never seen you so convinced about a thing, and so it damn well has to be true. You're nobody's dupe. I know that for certain. I guess I feel like an ass for doubting you."

"I would be disappointed in you if you didn't doubt me. We've been policemen all of our lives, not metaphysicians. But the eyes did it for me—try to understand. Those eyes are alive within themselves, separated from the human shell they inhabit. Don't ask me how that's possible or whether it's illusion. My reaction wasn't in the least illusory, I'm certain. It was a revulsion, taut, gripping like seizures. A sense that suddenly something was very, very wrong in this world. That something new was present and that this something left the fabric of existence, as we cherish it, fragile, vulnerable as it's never been before."

Rama Shastri closed his eyes. He kept them closed so long that Wrench wondered if he was asleep. Wrench coughed once, twice, and finally his eyes reopened. Of course, the big man thought; it's been so long; I forgot about the discipline.

"We must return there tomorrow," Shastri said then, his vigor momentarily restored from his brief meditation. "They live somewhere in that neighborhood, perhaps, and we must find them."

"And if so—then what?"

"Steve, one step at a time."

"Excuse me," the big man said, and went into his bedroom. He returned with two semiautomatics, a Browning .38 and a Walther .32. He said, "We've got to get ready to go with Dan, Ram. But from now on, wherever we go, we'll be armed." Wrench picked up the phone and dialed. Looking at Shastri, he added with feeling, "Please, Ram—don't go off like that again, ever."

Rama Shastri suddenly realized the full extent of Wrench's

loneliness. With Kamala gone and Santha surely likely to marry soon, Shastri was all that Steve had left in the world. And Shastri needed his old friend every bit as much. "I did a stupid, unthinking thing," he admitted.

When Lieutenant Terranova picked them up, it was past midnight. His handsome face flashed a smile as they climbed into the car. "We're going to see Bernie Thurnauer," he said. "He's one of our best undercover men. He just happens to be at home tonight. He expects us, although he probably thought we'd show up earlier than this."

Terranova drove to North Cambridge until they reached a side street that branched into Somerville. A few more blocks, and they parked before a two-story house. All the lights were out except for one on the porch. Terranova rang the bell and another light on the first floor went on.

The undercover man was in his bathrobe. He let them in and they followed him to the kitchen. Somewhere a baby was crying.

"The bell woke Gary up," Bernie said after introductions. He looked like a stand-in for a Jesus Christ role.

"Sorry we're late, Bernie. But we need some information, and you're a hard man to find," Dan replied. "Undercover cops just don't hang around the precincts very much."

"Agreed. But aren't you off duty?"

"This is strictly off duty. Adair would have a fit if he knew."

"That prick. Now you know why I'm undercover. The job keeps me distant from guys like him."

Dan said, "He makes me ashamed of being a cop. He's . . . aw, to hell with him." Dan told Bernie about Abel Fairley's killing, of Rama Shastri and Wrench. "We need information about Eastern-oriented cults in Greater Boston. You might have something we could get to work on."

Bernie Thurnauer took a pen and a piece of paper. When he finished writing: "Here's a list of centers, meeting halls, and ashrams. But to save you time, I'd suggest you concentrate on the top one. They have open house every so often, and sooner or later members of other groups show up there."

He pushed the paper to Terranova, who left it flat on the kitchen table for all to read.

The first place on the list was the biggest and reputedly the most Westernized. "Mai Yogini's Yoga Center offers strictly watered-down mysticism," the undercover man explained. "Nothing too heavy, too demanding. Her clientele is mostly straight and very affluent. You know—executives who are worrier types and want to slow down the beta waves and replace them with alphas. Or middle-aged women fighting the bulge and hoping to trim down by learning the proper breathing and a handful of asanas. She comes high. I mean, you pay top dollar for a mantra, even."

"You mean the suckers buy prayers?" Terranova said.

"Hold on. A mantra isn't just a prayer. It moves events, turns the cosmos inside out." Bernie looked at Shastri. "Am I correct?" Shastri nodded. "Depends on the kind of mantra, understand," Bernie continued. "Some are more costly than others. Mai Yogini claims she's had a pipeline with this source that provides the mantras. Anyway, it's all scam, but they believe her. She also does some fortune-telling, but that's only for certain special clients. Big-bucks people is my guess."

"What's she like?"

"Ever see Hedy Lamarr in that *Pépé le Moko* flick?"

"That pretty?"

"Uhuh. And she's part French, besides. Her real name's . . ." Bernie rose, went to a nearby alcove, unlocked a desk drawer, pored over a dozen file cards, and finally read, "Claudine de Brisson Jaiswal. Anyway, get your asses over there, you three; it might be worth your while. I mean, on some nights, the center is jumping with wall-to-wall navel lovers."

Bernie described further: "The place is pretty big. A meeting hall, some offices, and classrooms. They teach a lot of legitimate stuff, too: readings from Vivekananda, the Nagas monk." Again, to Shastri, "You know, the sect that wore no clothes. Then they're into Tota Puri, a Nondualistic Vedantist, who taught the great Ramakrishna. And someone usually recites from the *Rig Veda*. Mostly 'Hymn of the Supreme Person.' A real eclectic package of Indian mystical thought. But wait until you see the mural, though, on the wall outside the place. There's a smaller version of it in the big hall, too. Behind the podium." Bernie shook his head. "The Yogini's sure an original."

Wrench finally spoke. "It sounds different from what we're looking for. These people seem pretty harmless."

"Maybe. But there's a sort of grapevine among these cult people. Someone may have heard about the group you're looking for. Never can tell."

Wrench agreed. He turned to Shastri. "What do you think, Ram?"

"We should check out something else first," the Indian reminded him. "The neighborhood I suggested to you earlier tonight."

"Where's that?" asked Terranova.

Rama Shastri sighed wearily. He wasn't about to tell his story to another skeptical policeman. Not at this hour, anyway. He could hear the baby still crying and a female voice singing softly to it. The baby's wail backgrounded the silence that followed.

Terranova ventured, "Was it the same neighborhood where you got those scratches, sir? If so, you might need police help next time."

Steve came to the rescue. "Dan, the minute the Thugs know that the local police are involved, they'll disappear from sight so thoroughly we'll be lucky if we find them again in a lifetime. Let Ram and me handle this alone for now. I promise you if it gets too hot for us, we'll contact you immediately." He then added, "And we won't ignore Mai Yogini's Yoga Center, either. Phone me by 6 P.M. tomorrow, and maybe we'll go there later."

Terranova was satisfied. He gave the two men his winning smile and the meeting was over.

FIFTEEN

When the storm was still peaking, Gauri had emerged from a trance, demanding that they leave their small apartment. Obediently Chundra Bala and Bidhan had faced the onslaught with her.

Sometimes her demands seemed beyond human endurance.

Still, the glorious transformation in Chundra Bala's wife lately had touched him deeply. It made even her current dependency on animal blood bearable. He reminded himself that that wasn't Gauri but the Goddess present in her, stronger each time, filled with blood thirst. The blood was the only way to calm Kali Mother these days, to send Her back. Chundra remembered the cavern beyond the Place of the Ancient Rishis and shuddered.

And hadn't the Huzoor promised that soon the American recruits would be ready and that Kali's bloodlust would then be satiated in the usual way? By the sacred rumel's kiss?

Disgusting as was the sight of Kali-in-Gauri draining bowl after bowl of animal sustenance, the aftermath—a new, fresh, radiant Gauri—made it worthwhile for him. She seemed newer than when they'd met as children, when their marriage was arranged, more beautiful, more serene. These days she was a sadvi-like Gauri, with a splendor that was beatific. No longer did she suffer physically or seem on the verge of death.

So, whatever her commands, Chundra always obeyed.

He, too, was something new. The experience in the Place of the Rishis gave him stature among his fellow Thugs. Ah, the things, the great truths that he had seen up there! By his side was the beloved Huzoor, now complete. He whom Chundra was directed by the Mother Herself to serve and protect. Among the men, he was second in command, the Thug guru who had been present at his Lord's initiation!

173

After the attempt on Shastri's life, the Huzoor's sedan had come to take them to the ashram. In the backseat the rasping voice demanded, "His skull must be attached to my girdle! Among the greatest of the dead that I carry with me, Rama Shastri's skull shall rattle."

They had known failure that night. They had roamed the Back Bay streets, the cold and snow like an alien breath. This certainly was an uncomfortable land. The grating tones of Kali emergent had commanded, exhorted, raged that Rama Shastri was nearby. Then they'd seen him in the restaurant window . . . and had failed . . .

She continued, "He will die! He must die! Rama Shastri, defiler of all holy and enduring mysteries! Dung pile of unbelief! Slave of the laws of the filth-minded Raj! Betrayer of all things Indian, of gods and saints! Scion of logic and science and the maggot-ridden West! Indian most un-Indian! Cursed fly speck that dares to seek to destroy the Mother! Aye, like the spirit of the once-favored Feringheea, who, too, did betray and pursue his own brothers! How I weep for my sons destroyed by the dogs of lowly man's law!"

Chundra dared a look back at the figure clawing her hair, her breasts, the upholstery. The rest in the car——himself, Bidhan, the American Duane Longstreet——cringed at her roupy sounds. Nails of ice fire scraping up one's spine, Chundra thought.

Then the figure sank into the seat, breathed in the shadows, and was silent. Bidhan, next to her, sat pressed against the door, intimidated.

Through the narrow New England streets, past the sooty redstones the sedan sped. It turned onto Massachusetts Avenue, crossed the bridge into Cambridge, reached M.I.T. The huddled outline in the back remained silent. Someone cleared his throat. Someone else followed suit. Gauri Bala was spent, asleep. The three men relaxed.

Gauri slept until they reached the ashram. When her eyes opened, the wide mercurial pools had settled into the still black depths Chundra cherished so much. She smiled and the men smiled. They were filled with the serene magic projected by this renewed, gentle sadvi.

Shortly, walking along the cinnabar carpet between the darkly draped walls toward the Huzoor's throne, Chundra's excitement grew. The Huzoor had summoned them to this late meeting for no small purpose.

The Lord entered, sat, grim and thoughtful, for a while. The throne, too, was draped with cinnabar. The Huzoor explained that things occidental had been added to appeal to recruits unacquainted with Indian thought and customs.

Tension lingered in the air like the reverberations of a stricken gong. The large room had twelve rows of pews in its center. Seated there, separated from each other to meditate the easier, were twenty-three acolytes. Standing, their backs to the pews, were the twelve of the Thug Brotherhood, the regulars from India. Each was a guru to two of the acolytes. But tonight one guru was missing a disciple.

Wisps of sandalwood incense angled from the braziers, full of old-country scent. To the right of the Huzoor's sandaled feet, Gauri sat in lotus position, her eyes closed, her smile ecstatic, her right hand resting in her left, which in turn rested on her upturned left calf.

Above the Huzoor, on a stand, danced the ebony and gold statue of Kali, nearly as tall as a full-grown boy. Flames licked at her carved limbs in motion. Her anklets, bracelets, miniature cymbals, girdle, skulls, pickax, noose, weapons, lolling tongue, and eyes were gold. As the flames flickered redder, so did the gold.

Within the base of the stand was a hidden door and a hidden compartment, and within that were the rishi scrolls, but only the Huzoor and Gauri knew that.

The sense of urgency, of expectation was like a hot wind.

Ayub, the second-oldest Muslim Thug, posed his question. "Why, my Lord, are there now female Thugs? Tell us the logic of that again," and he looked at the five women behind him suspiciously.

A titter of laughter came from the Brotherhood.

"Thick-headed fool!" scolded Sahib Khan. "Thou shamest

Mohammed himself with thy refusal to accept what our Lord and his Mother have decreed! Has he not said before the reasons why? Is thy matted beard of ewe's wool or of hair, tell us."

"Hair, of course."

"Then, as that is plain as the nose on thy worthless-dog visage, so is the command of our Lord, this Prince among Stranglers."

"Hush," the Huzoor said gently. "Never before has woman been of Thuggee. No mention of such comes from your fathers before you. But the plight of the centuries has changed. Here is a land alien to all we believe in. Here women are of great importance. My Mother, All-Wise, knows well that the hands of a woman can be strong and her spirit of the killing as heady. Question this no more, brave Ayub, since I will not answer you again. Do not tempt my great beneficence."

Chundra Bala, having awaited his turn, began, "My Lord Huzoor of the Sacred Scrolls of the Eternal Rishis, I would inform you of this night's adventure with Rama Shastri, he who . . ."

Each of the chosen twelve tensed, eager to concentrate on the kotwal chief who had captured their brothers. Shastri, who had trailed them to the ends of the earth. Well, let him. Somewhere a rumel was waiting. . . .

"You have seen Rama Shastri?" the Huzoor demanded.

Chundra moved closer to the throne and gave his report of the incident on Gainsborough Street. Bidhan growled when Chundra told of the snowball.

When Chundra Bala finished, the Thug Lord stared at the floor, his chin in his hand.

Chundra pointed to his wife. His voice was frantic. "She still dreams of Rama Shastri, poised with his bow, his arrow aimed at our Mother, our Kali Mother!"

Ayub, the Muslim, spit at the invisible threat. "What can we do, O Lord?" he cried. "Surely these dreams are omens, portents of doom for the Way of Thuggee."

"Aye," agreed Sahib Khan. "The breast of Fatima must never be pierced, or our days are over. Praise Allah, this cannot be!"

Makunda stepped forth and waited for the agreeing "ayes" to end. "I say this is but a warning that we must heed, a threat that we must prepare for."

Ramanuja, who had accompanied Makunda to DeLuca's store on Charles Street, moved forward, inspired by his imaginings, and cried, "Lo, my Lord, has not the radiant Satī been seen? Radiant as the darkening hour when the lingering fingers of the day caress the marigold petal. True flame of the night, Her black tresses the spun shadows of the moon." He spoke in Hindi, for his English was insufficient.

"Say more," urged the Huzoor in the Thug tongue, Ramasi.

"Aye, more, my Lord of Deception. She is the one, indeed. The one we seek."

The Huzoor's eyes momentarily fell on Gauri. "The other one. The other woman. The other vessel."

"Indeed, the other. Perhaps, indeed, the greater. Such beauty stirs the pulse. A goddess's beauty. Beauty that compels. That overcomes and rules. Beauty suitable." His gaze fell to the sitting woman, and he added in a whisper, "Beauty more fitting than even that of this first of Kali's daughters."

Gauri's eyelids twitched.

"You cunning dog," the Huzoor replied, with the wisp of a smile.

"Ah, my Lord of the Rumel, I have given thee a light heart."

"You have, Ramanuja. Well are you named, you with your poet's soul. What think you of what he says, Makunda?"

"This woman Santha is all he says of her, Great Huzoor. And more so."

Gauri's eyes began to open and her mouth lines tightened. Chundra sorrowed for her. Fool woman, didn't she realize that this meant possible release at last from the constant control by Mother Kali? Release from drinking that foul . . .

"What think you?" the Huzoor asked of Sahib Khan, eldest of the three Muslim Thugs and of the line of the same Sahib Khan who was captured and interrogated by the dreaded Major-General Sleeman in his day. "Tell us your wisdom in this."

"My Lord of All Deceivers from the Four Corners of the Earth, I say, if she is that radiant, then she is Fatima, daughter of the Prophet Mohammed. For it is written that none can be as fair as she, ever, in time or in eternity."

"She is Satī incarnate, I say," insisted Ramanuja. "And how wouldst thou know, Unbeliever? Were Bhowani and Kali and Fatima not one also, I would forget we are brothers of the Pickax!"

"Aha," chuckled their Leader. "The old debates continue, I see. Therein lies the great miracle of Thuggee, that the Hindus and the children of the Prophet are one in this service. It pleases the Goddess much. Does it not, Gauri, Chosen One?"

"It pleases." In a low tone.

"I hear thee not, Vessel of Night."

"It pleases."

"There." The Huzoor turned to the Brotherhood. "Who would know better than she?"

Then he settled back, stared at the acolytes in their pews, glowered, and raged, "Still our missing chela hasn't arrived. Will his Teacher declare himself?"

"I am that Teacher," announced Trande Gautam, the Arcotee.

"Then tell us, my brother. Who is this chela who no longer presents himself?"

"He is a Robert . . ." Gautam struggled with the last name. He turned to a shaking figure in the pew below. A motion, and the figure jumped up and managed to step into the aisle. "Explain," commanded Gautam.

"Bob Fevre, Robert Fevre," replied the woman's hoarse voice from her cowl.

From the Huzoor: "Let us see your face."

The cowl fell back.

"What is your name?"

"Deb . . . Deborah Klaus."

"Louder when you speak to the Lord Huzoor!" snapped Makunda.

"Deborah Klaus, my Lord."

The Huzoor smiled amiably. "You are not on trial, my child. We are your brothers, your sisters. Now come to us, child."

It was all said in warm, soft tones, and Deborah felt giddy

with relief. She had never known such terror, for a rumel was a sacred object to a Thug.

"Come, child," the Huzoor urged again.

Deborah left the pew, moved forward, and stopped near the Brotherhood.

The Brotherhood stared as one pair of eyes. Her terror rose again. Gauri chided, "Let her speak. Child, please, how can we help you if you do not tell us?"

"Yes, Mother," Deborah agreed quickly and, when the calm returned, "Bob stole the rumel."

"You are certain?"

"Yes. Yes, my Lord—I saw it."

A din. Voices crying out simultaneously: "She saw him with it! Kill the blasphemous chela!"

"Cease!" The din ended. "Would you frighten our sister? Come, child; make an effort. What happened then?"

"You didn't know Bob. He's crazy. He wanted to experiment with the rumel on his own. Bob never liked authority. He told me no one could regiment him. The army hadn't been able to, so why should any of you?" Deborah covered her face with her hands and suddenly wailed, "We got high on cocaine and he talked me into it." A deep breath. "He said we had to break the Akali rules right away before we were sucked in by the group. That's why he stole the rumel. The more coke we took, the more he felt we ought to experiment. He thought it would be a great thrill to strangle somebody. Sort of play Thug on our own. So we . . . we did it."

"Did what?" snapped the Huzoor.

"Killed him."

"Did you say 'kill'? Speak louder!"

"*Killed him. Killed Abel.*" Something was going wrong. She was shouting hysterically. The terror had returned and she could barely control her bowels. "*I met this guy Abel. He peddled these pamphlets all the time. Wanted to help people. The ones he had that night said: 'Live longer with love.' I remember that. I got him to come into an alley with me. Bob jumped him with the rumel.*"

Their silence was a judgment, she could tell. Still she couldn't stop shouting. "*But Bob knew Abel. He couldn't do it right when he saw Abel's face. It was awful. He almost dropped the scarf. 'Jesus, I know him,' he kept saying. He would've let Abel go, maybe, and I knew it was too late for that. So I helped Bob do it . . .*

"*Abel gripped the rumel with his fingers, you see. He was putting them between his skin and the cloth. And he kept ramming both Bob and me against the sides of this building. Strong. He was suddenly so strong for such a thin guy. Anyway, I noticed that his knapsack full of pamphlets was in the way. Bob, who was behind him, had to reach beyond the sack, and . . . Well, I pulled down the sack's straps around Abel's arms, and, with the arms pinioned, we finally had a chance. Still, it took so long. For a long time I saw Abel's eyes bulging and bulging, until finally . . .*"

Deborah collapsed.

The Huzoor moved, grabbed her shoulders. "The rumel? What happened to it?"

"Someone saw us. We had to run. . . ."

"*The rumel!*"

In a whisper: "We left it there."

A silence that ate up the air. Deborah felt faint. In her daze, she barely felt the hands lifting, leading her forward. Fingers dug into her arm. The fingers were in a hurry, determined. Then they yanked back her cowl sleeves, and the smell of betel nut and sweat she'd come to associate with Trande Gautam awoke her from her stupor. What were they doing?

Deborah blinked, stared at her naked wrists placed over Gauri's drinking bowl. Gauri's hands flickered in a blur of motion, and Deborah felt two sharp pricks. She watched the miniature knife rise from the two thin red lines along the wrists. They grew into ever wider red tributaries, flowing steadily along the arms and into the bowl. Deborah closed her eyes, accepting, prepared, even glad, to die.

But an instant later she screamed as hot fire shot through her consciousness.

Gauri held the bowl steady before her until it was heavy and the liquid lapped precariously near its edge.

"And what," stormed Gauri then at the poetical Ramanuja, "has the beauteous Satī to do with the House of Kali?"

The Thug backed, fell to his knees. Elvira rushed to the end of the dais. Gauri closed her eyes. The corners of her mouth moved with her outthrust jaw. Her neck began to sway to a rhythm within her. Slowly at first, her head turned, left, right, and then the pace increased. Faster and faster, in abrupt starts, her neck and head swayed, thrust. Fierce, powerful motions, yet never once did she spill the contents of the bowl.

Beneath the sari Gauri's legs splayed, her naked feet at right angles to each other, her knees bent. The free hand, the left one, talked, with its supple fingers, the thumb fluttering to the silent beat.

Then Gauri drank the blood, her face hidden behind the small bowl.

Murmurs sounded—elation, awe, disgust, repulsion. Gorging noises soon silenced them.

Finally the bowl lowered. Fingers fluttered again, baubles clinked persistently. Dark tributaries descended from the corners of Gauri's mouth to her chin. Her eyes were swollen, the neck expanded, the cheeks ballooned. The bloodied lips parted, and her lolling tongue fell, long and lifeless, like a mottled petal. Slowly drops of blood bubbled from its tip. Then, unexpectedly, there came a maddening, drawn-out cackling that brought even the Huzoor erect on his throne.

"My Lord, no more!" Chundra supplicated. "This is beyond endurance!" He wanted to say that Gauri was endangered. But her name stuck to his palate. His words transformed into viscous, gummy things, sticking to his mouth. He gurgled, started to strangle. The swollen eyes were fixed on him. Chundra's arms grappled with the air, trying to push the merciless stare away. Then the eyes closed an instant, and he rediscovered his breath.

"It will end soon, faithful Chundra," promised the Huzoor sympathetically.

Gauri had slumped. Her body eased to the floor, the distended tongue withdrawing back into her mouth as if it were a lair. Her heavy breathing diminished. The spirit was leaving her. In time she would sit once more in repose, beatific.

"Soon. Soon her ordeal is over. The new vessel had been found at last."

SIXTEEN

She was following the stream of the Ganges along the side of the Beni Madhav Temple in Varanasi. Santha had visited here before, and everything was familiar, just as it was then. She passed the congestion of pilgrims everywhere. Women, men, children, cows jostled one another. Men in saffron, blue, and red stood on the yellow sandstone stairs to the waters. The domes of the ghat shrines flashed vermilion in the sun.

People chanted, "*Bivo viswanath*, O Lord, O Master of the Universe," while some prayed, "*Pahi, pahi*, protect, oh, protect us."

Santha felt estranged from them, repelled by their chanting.

Backing from the scene, she entered a narrow street with overhanging godowns that blotted out the sunlight. The surrounding darkness was threatening, and, turning at the sound of footsteps, Santha discovered that the woman with the nose ring was walking by her side. Who is she? Santha wondered. She walked faster and then started to run, suddenly gripped by terror.

The street led to a marketplace. The hammering heat was almost unbearable. Santha looked back. The woman was gone. When she looked ahead again, the view of the marketplace appeared warped, as if something had happened to her perspective.

A nearby elephant with a farmer astride its back bulged in her mind's eye. She thought its breadth was expanding and she darted away, veering to its left.

Santha barely missed a fakir on his bed of nails. A strong

desire to jump on him until the points penetrated almost over-came her. A street woman oiling her coarse black hair stared. For a moment Santha thought it was the strange woman with the ring. Santha went closer, peered into the doorway where the woman sat, and saw that it wasn't.

The marketplace blurred more; only a few things here and there were distinct: a booth with stacks of woven tapestries, beggars scurrying and fighting for coins in the dusty street, a pink-turbaned ear cleaner with his tiny spoon and vial of oil.

A Brahman in a white dhoti emerged as if out of the heat waves in the air. The need for violence surged through Santha again. She wanted to grab the Brahman and hurl him into the group of beggars. Instead, she spun and frantically rushed toward a holy man behind a prayer wheel.

As she stood before the wheel, the sadhu rose and, pointing a finger at a spot behind her, cried, "Kunkali! Kunkali!" Santha turned. There, but a few yards away, was the woman with the nose ring, lips parted in a smile, arms extended, ready to embrace.

Santha Wrench awoke and for a long time saw nothing but the woman's eyes.

She finally realized where she was. She looked at George asleep beside her, burrowed her face in the pillow, and wept. What an insane dream, she thought, yet so real at times, just as in the psychic "events" of the past. Kunkali! Why should she dream of Kunkali, and was the strange woman She? Was that what the sadhu in the dream meant?

Santha leaned on her elbows and studied George's face. It was so untroubled, so content. Her memory resurrected their lovemaking hours ago. It had been better, more beautiful than at any time before. How could she have dreamed such a terrible dream after that?

Looking at the clock, Santha saw there was still about an hour before the alarm would ring. She eased out of bed, went to the bathroom. When she washed her face, she searched for the other Santha and found no traces of her. Why should I? she asked. But somehow, now, she felt there was a strong

possibility the self she saw in the mirror of the airport ladies'
room might show itself soon.

The thought disturbed her so much that Santha desperately
tried to blank it out. She left the bathroom and hurried downstairs to the kitchen. There she prepared coffee, tightened her
kimono, and opened the front door. The sun was beginning to
crawl across Otis Place, and the surface of the snow was already
hard. It gave the small court a plush and satiny look. Santha
picked up the *Boston Globe* at the doorstep, paused again,
listened to the drip of the gutters. A car passed along Mount
Vernon Street to her left, and the thud of its snow tires reverberated. Santha closed the door.

Santha rushed back to the kitchen, placed the *Globe* on the
counter, and took an English muffin from the refrigerator. She
shoved it into the toaster, set down butter and marmalade on
the kitchen table, and waited. Scanning the *Globe*'s headlines,
she sighed, since they bored her, and moved about seeking a
task to do.

Santha's movements were quick, jerking. Her hands touched
the sink, the cabinets, the bread box, and refrigerator. She had
never felt so nervous. The muffin popped up in the toaster but
she left it alone. Her hands had finally touched her breasts.

A fierce, raging fire was in her suddenly, rising from her
bosom. It rose like a flush up her neck, into her face. She bent
to the toaster's side, and the lips in her reflection seemed redder,
the eyes even darker. Santha giggled.

George was on his back, still sleeping. Standing on the bed,
her legs straddling his body, her hands holding up the kimono
to her waist, Santha moved forward until she was above his
face. She giggled again, spread her legs wider, and began to
descend, slowly bending her knees. George stirred as if he
sensed something was happening. As her vulva neared his face,
he opened his eyes.

"My God!" he said, and then the rest was muffled. Santha
moved herself back and forth against him. She felt George's
hands grab her thighs and then felt their force as he pushed
her away.

"What the hell are you doing, Santha?" he demanded, sitting bolt upright.

"Waking you up with my cunt," she replied and burrowed under the sheet toward his penis. George flung the blankets back and tried to lift her head away. But Santha's mouth was already around the penis's tip.

"Santha . . . okay . . . hey, let me wake up a little."

Santha's lips moved down his penis, trying again and again to induce an erection. George stared at her, unbelieving.

When she pulled free, her fists clenched, and she pounded his flanks. "Get big, George," Santha screamed. "I want you like a lion. Big as a kesari's prick."

George pushed her away. He looked very sad and shook his head. "No, Santha." His big hands cupped her face, and he stared into her eyes.

"What's wrong with you, George?" she asked as she rubbed her breasts against his chest. "George," she pleaded. "I need it now. I want to be fucked right now."

He was silent.

Santha's hand worked toward his crotch again.

"Please . . ." Her fingers dug in his arms, and with a shove she pressed him down on the sheets. George looked stunned at her tremendous strength. He stared at the trickle of blood on his biceps, where her nails had punctured his skin.

Santha laughed. "Don't be so stodgy, darling. This is 1976. A woman can be the aggressor nowadays."

He turned his eyes away.

"Why do you do that?" she cried, hitting his rib cage. George winced. "Don't you like the way I look? Don't I look like me anymore?" She straddled him again. "Nothing's changed, hon. This is the same pussy you fucked last night. Feel it. Doesn't it feel the same?"

"I don't want to," he told her.

Santha giggled again. "Georgie's getting mad at little Santha. What's the matter, Dr. George? Something you can't control? Is that bothering you, Georgie? You can't control Santha."

"I'm sorry . . ." His tone became softer. "Santha, let's talk."

"Don't want to. Fuck me, George. I need to be fucked, don't you understand?"

"I can't. Not when you're acting like this."

"Like what? Like an animal in heat? Why not? What's wrong with being an animal?"

"This isn't you, Santha."

"Is that what you see in my face? What's wrong with my face, George?"

She was feeling him getting hard despite himself. She took his penis and stroked it. "There," she said and seized his buttocks and tried to roll him over. "Please, George," she said.

George did what she wanted. Santha lay beneath him and wrapped her legs around him. For a second her voice became soft, gentle. "There, kesari."

Her legs tightened. He groaned. "Did I hurt you, kesari? That's right—keep doing it. Oh, what a nice fuck you give a girl. . . . Oh, come on, come on, go farther in. In, George. I want it in. . . ." She slapped him. "Com'on, com'on." She slapped his buttocks again.

But Santha suddenly knew he was having trouble keeping his erection. "Don't do that to me, George!" she screamed. "You've no right to be repulsed by me. I've got a right to want a fuck when I need it. Goddammit, George!"

He was rising from her. He was almost in tears as he stood.

"George," she begged, her fingers moving along the lips of her vulva. "Don't do this to me."

George slumped in a chair by the window. He ran a hand through his hair. "I can't," he told her. "We've got to talk."

"Talk!"

"Santha, you're acting strangely."

"All I wanted was to be made love to. What's wrong about that?"

"Then try to calm down," he was saying. "Try to be softer."

"Of course, darling," she urged.

When he stood before her, Santha lowered her head between his legs and licked his testicles. She pressed her lips around one of them and then the other. Her hand groped, found his penis, and felt that it was hard again.

"Now," Santha whispered.

George entered her. They began to move together. Santha knew he was convinced this time it was right. She had been very careful to act as he wanted her to; but still she noticed he didn't look at her. Not once. He must be afraid to, she thought, and that bothered her tremendously. The rage was rapidly becoming as overwhelming as the orgasm would be. The two were meshing, becoming one; anger and ecstasy coupled like lovers.

The momentum built. Except for their moans, they were silent. Santha's orgasm was finally about to start. Her hands raised, and she cupped his face again before he could stop her and kissed his mouth fiercely. Her eyes grew wider and wider as she came, and he flung her back simultaneously, horrified. Santha screamed out her ecstasy while George feverishly pulled free, his erection still alive.

Santha waited for George to speak. Wearing just slacks, he stood before the window. His back had been turned to her for a long time. Whatever he'd seen in her eyes at the end of their lovemaking was responsible, she was certain. She had even gone to the bathroom mirror to check, had found nothing there.

But George had definitely seen something, something that had repelled him so deeply that he hadn't spoken to her since.

She heard, "Are you going to work?"

It was such an unexpectedly normal question that she started.

"Of course I'm going. Why do you ask?"

He didn't reply but faced her instead. Santha was taking underwear from her tote bag. George neared her slowly. She looked up. He stared at her face, then seemed relieved.

"Santha, what happened?"

Unable to answer him, Santha pulled back the sliding door of the bedroom closet. She took out a beige pants suit, placed it on the bed.

"Santha, we've got to talk. You've got to see a therapist soon. I wish I could sugar-coat the pill, but I have no choice but to be as direct as I can. Too many unnatural things have been happening. Lately you've hallucinated, and just a short

time ago you underwent a personality change that was so extreme
I can barely discuss it."

Santha nodded. "I hurt you, didn't I? I was pretty disgusting,
I guess."

"Do you remember it?"

"Enough. But only the way you remember a dream. Sort
of hazy, with some gaps."

She was dressing. George took her hands in his. "Darling,
I can't just shrug this off. As your lover and as a doctor, I
can't let you run from this."

"I'm not running. I'm confused, George. . . . I . . ."

The phone rang.

"I know a very good therapist, dear. I think . . ."

The phone rang again.

". . . you'd like her, I'm sure. She . . ."

Again.

Santha pointed at the phone. "George . . ."

He picked up the receiver. "Yes? Oh, hello, Steve. Yes,
she's here."

He gave Santha the receiver.

"Yes, Daddy."

"I called Lime Street first and when you weren't home"—
Her father cleared his throat—"thought I'd try George's."

"That was reasonable," she told him, smiling to herself.

"Er . . . Uncle Ram and I were just discussing that scroll
fragment I gave you. Do you think Dr. Kim is finished with
it by now? It was Dr. Kim you said you were going to give it
to, wasn't it?"

"Yes. But she returned it. She hasn't looked at it. You see,
she's been so busy with the upcoming India exhibit. We'll just
have to wait until afterward."

"Santha, it's been over a month."

"Yes. I'm sorry."

"Wait a minute, Santha. What's that, Ram?" Then, "Is the
scroll fragment in the safe, Santha?"

"Of course."

"Santha, Uncle Ram and I want you to bring it back. Today.
Bring it over tonight. Don't forget, now, dear."

"I won't."

Another pause. "How are you feeling, Santha?"

"Fine, Daddy, fine. Got to set off for work now. I love you, and Uncle Ram, too."

"We love you, too, dear."

The office felt like the loneliest place in the world. Unable to work, Santha sat behind the desk, her face in her hands. Tricklings of memory of her squatting above George while he slept now haunted her. Santha no longer rationalized that her strange "events" were caused by a beneficent force. How could she, when the unknown Something was rapidly destroying her relationship with George?

George had reassured her otherwise before he drove her to work. He had left his Audi at the Brimmer Street Garage so it wouldn't have to be shoveled out of snowdrifts in the morning. Once en route, though, Santha had noted that he was very quiet.

But, she reminded herself, he did kiss me warmly when we parted and told me he'd phone later. Those certainly weren't the acts of a man who'd lost interest in her.

The phone rang. Santha picked it up, and as she listened, her face showed disappointment. The publisher of the exhibit catalog was on the line, not George Buchan. For ten minutes she discussed layouts with the man. When she hung up, she found she was still depressed.

Kunkali, she remembered. The name Kunkali had been in her dream, and then later she'd changed into a wild thing. Even demonic, maybe.

What had George seen in her face, what had repelled him so much? I'm insane, that's what I am, she concluded. I'm bloody hallucinating, as George says. Santha tried to recall what she'd learned in the only psychology course she'd taken in college. Silvano Arieti had outlined four stages of schizophrenia. She was at least in the third stage, in which psychotic insight emerges and the schizophrenic understands the world through a new system of autistic thinking. Santha hoped she remembered it correctly.

Santha laughed—loud, harsh. Well, goddamn, if that definition didn't also fit some of the mystical awakenings she had read about. What a joke on old Silvano.

Nevertheless, none of that made her feel any better. Com'on, Santha, she rallied; you're a bright girl. Figure it out. You've got a Bachelor of Arts from Boston University and an M.A. from Harvard. That should be enough to decide whether you suffer from multiple personality or demonic possession.

Possession? I've got to work, she urged, rising from her seat. Got to work and not think.

Opening the safe, Santha walked in. It made her feel secure again, sheltered from the unknown. The surrounding artifacts were familiar things, friends, in a sense. Each had a story of its own; each had a solid, earthbound past. She reached for the panel covering the shelf with the cylinder.

Someone came into the office. Santha heard the door click shut. Santha turned to see who it was.

The person standing at the safe entrance wasn't one of the staff. Santha backed, slightly alarmed.

The woman before her was tall, lean, with two long braids that reached her hips. She wore a buckled canvas coat with a fur-lined collar turned up to the lobes of her ears. She was olive-skinned but definitely not Indian.

"May I help you?" Santha managed.

"My name is Elvira Moniz," the woman replied in a deep, mannish voice. "Are you Santha Wrench?"

Santha asked, "How do you know my name?" She started to move forward. She had suddenly realized she was inside the safe and the woman was close to its door.

"You've been studying Vedic Sanskrit, haven't you?"

"Please answer my question: How do you know me?" Santha was inches away from the woman now.

"Someone from the Widener Library told me."

"Who?" demanded Santha.

"I don't remember his name."

"That's odd. Let's discuss it in my office, please."

The woman didn't move.

"Ms. Moniz," Santha said, fighting the panic she felt, "please let me by."

"Are you trying to translate something from Vedic Sanskrit?" The woman's eyes were darting over her shoulder to the shelves. "Perhaps I could help you."

"Allow me to pass, Ms.—"

"Could I see what you're working on? Is it in there?" Santha ducked. The pair of hands that reached to move Santha met only air. Santha kicked at the woman's shin. The woman sidestepped the kick, and this time, before Santha could rush out of the safe, the pair of hands pushed her back into its aisle.

"I'll scream for help," Santha threatened.

"Do that and I'll close the door. Nobody will hear you then." A smile, unpleasant, teeth ill cared for and broken at the mouth corners. "Can't we come to an understanding? I came here to help you. I could help you translate if I could see . . . whatever it is."

Santha needed a moment to think, to plan. The panic was terrible. "Go on. . . ."

"Could I see the fragment?"

"Fragment?" Santha repeated. "Fragment of what?"

"It's a scroll, isn't it?" The intruder placed a foot beyond the safe's threshold. Then another foot and she was inside, looking through the glass, searching.

Santha lowered her head, clenched her fist, and charged. Her head butted the woman's chest, and both hurtled into the office. The desk chair stopped Santha, but Elvira Moniz hit the wall instead. Santha jumped to her feet, closed the safe's door, and locked it.

"Get out!" She rushed to the phone. "I'm going to call Security!"

Elvira Moniz rubbed her scalp. There was a smear of blood there from her collision with the wall. "I'll go," she said. "But you're being very foolish. The scroll is rightfully ours, Santha Wrench. It might even be rightfully yours, too, someday, if you accept your karma." She went to the door, looked back briefly, and said softly, "The left-handed Path," as she went out.

Shaking, Santha leaned against the desk. Left-handed Path? What did she mean? Was it the esoteric Path of Evil Santha had heard spoken of in India? The Path through which one found release from the karmic wheel through dreadful acts? That would be something like Thuggee.

And the scroll? How did this Elvira Moniz know about the fragment? Or, more baffling still, how did she know it was in the safe here at the Peabody?

As if in reply, an answer came to hear, the thoughts like splinters of ice again. *The Spirit of the Scroll is alive even in its fragment and calls to those who hear, that it be restored to its whole.*

"What was that? Who are you?" Santha cried out and waited. But there was no reply.

Riiiing!

Who? What was it that could speak in her mind like that? Riiiing! Riiiing!

So cold. So cold and gripping in her mind.

Riiiing. . . . Santha Wrench put the receiver to her ear.

"Santha?"

"George. Oh, George." She began to cry.

"Santha."

"Please come and pick me up, George. I know I'm a pest, but I want to go home. I'll tell my boss I'm sick. It's the truth, anyway. I am sick, aren't I, George?"

"I have one more patient to see. Then I'll come right over," he promised.

"I'd call a cab, but I'd rather be with you, George. You don't mind, do you?"

"Of course I don't, darling. Are you certain you'll be okay meanwhile?"

"Yes. Don't worry. I love you, George."

"I love you, Santha. I'll be there in a short hour and a half."

Hanging up, Santha thought of Elvira Moniz and started to shake again. She rushed from the office, wanting to be around people she trusted. She went to tell Dr. Kim she'd be leaving early.

SEVENTEEN

The following morning it snowed full force. By 10 A.M., the Greater Boston highways were jammed. Automobiles churned their snow tires through the new layer of snow filtering obliquely in the forefront of a nor'easter. That most insidious of New England winds was rapidly undoing the good work achieved by the all-night snow plows. The wind-swept haze, the snow piles drifting back into the streets, the increased wind chill factor seemed to be an excess of punishment upon an already climatically oppressed population.

A short time before noon, Mai Yogini's limo crawled along Massachusetts Avenue in Cambridge.

"We're nearing the Monkey House," her chauffeur announced.

The Yogini straightened her stockings. Then she studied her makeup in her compact, the one with ruby inserts. She had to look her best, since Nirmal Kapur would be there. Without him her scheme was nothing. It was through Nirmal she would get to Hanuman.

Mai Yogini, feeling chill, tugged at her leopard-skin coat.

"Fredrico, is the heater on?"

"It is," the chauffeur reassured.

So much has happened to me here, she concluded. America corrupts. Everything happens, happens, over and over, aimlessly, without meaning. *"L'homme est une passion inutile,"* she mused. It was exciting to quote Jean Paul Sartre instead of the Wisdom. So much was always expected from her and the Wisdom. Those worshipful, upturned faces, so completely devoted to every word she uttered . . .

At least with Nirmal, she could relax, be offhand in her remarks, witty, cosmopolitan. How relieving to be openly petty, to speak with calumny. Gone the soft voice mouthing beneficence to all creatures, to all things, big and small. With Nirmal she needn't believe in anything—anything whatsoever!

She fiddled with the sari she'd designed for herself. Mai Yogini also wore stockings with a garter belt, but that was a secret only her lovers knew—her lovers who gave her the baubles she craved. With everything they demanded, the Huzoor and that Bala woman, at least they left alone the money she'd hoarded and the jewelry stored in her bank vault, Mai Yogini thought suddenly.

The snow hammered fiercely, as if attempting to break through the window glass and rush at her. Suppose the Brotherhood hurt Nirmal while trying to destroy Hanuman? Mai Yogini yelped.

"Is anything wrong, Yogini?" asked Fredrico.

"I stabbed my finger on a brooch."

Fredrico said nothing. He knew more about her than anybody, had driven her to many a rendezvous. Totally trustworthy, his tongue never loosened. He protected her always, carried a switchblade and brass knuckles on his person, a .45 in the glove compartment.

That he loved, hungered for her was obvious to the Yogini. She knew Fredrico would even die for her if necessary. And she cherished her power over him.

Mai Yogini stood hesitant before what she had dubbed the Monkey House. It was the one of a triptych of buildings fronted by a courtyard. Each building had a stone porch broken by steps, and the entire design ran together in a half-circle of brick. Over each alcove were arches cluttered with scrollwork. During the milder seasons, well-nurtured rose bushes bordered the wings of the court.

Fredrico had stopped a few yards from the place at a cleared driveway. She told him to return in approximately an hour and a half. Then, easing her expensive Pappagallo boots onto the snowy walk, she managed to reach the courtyard.

And hesitated. Mai Yogini had met Swami Hanuman only once, when it was clear that he saw through her. For he was legitimate, a true Master; the rumor was strong, Swami Hanuman had powers.

A flicker, a shadow to the right, in the drifts before the barren bushes. Mai Yogini jumped, startled, and almost slipped and fell. Forcing herself to look at the spot, she saw nothing. But that's not so, she thought; there was a shape, a draping thing, waving its arms! And it struck her like ice slivers in her breast: is She here, then?

She rang the bell to the door on the left. The strange two-dimensional shadow wraith blended with the drifts. She must be here, the Yogini shuddered, watching me. I wonder, can She enter this place?

It was said that Swami Hanuman had retired one day into samadhi, that Vishnu and King Rama had visited him and proclaimed him to be the famed Monkey God. "Oh, come!" Mai Yogini scolded herself. "If this be true, what has Hanuman to do with me? I'm not his to save now."

Still, Yogini concluded that Kali could not enter, that the Thug Huzoor's power ended at this door, too.

The door swung open. Yogini looked at the young woman in the white T-shirt and dungarees. PRIVATE PROPERTY was printed across the shirt.

"Oh, hi, Yogini."

"Hello, Molly. Is Nirmal in?"

"Sure. But he's meditating. Com'on in and wait."

Inside, Yogini sat on the couch, moved suddenly when a spring popped. She moved to the other end.

"It always does that," explained Molly Doyle after she made a bubble-gum bubble and pulled it in again. "We never seem to get it reupholstered. Want some tea? Got some good herb tea."

"No, thank you, Molly."

The girl went to the window, stared out at the day, and scratched under her arm. The noise from the gum was the only sound besides the loud ticking of an ugly bronze clock with seminaked Pucks that rested in the center of an otherwise barren mantelpiece.

Mai Yogini ran a finger along the coffee table and frowned at the circle of dust on her skin. Molly sneezed, wiped her nose on the T-shirt, turned, said, "See ya," and left. The upper layer of the shirt bounced. Molly had a lot of property.

Why does the Monkey Man surround himself with a filthy creature like that? Mai Yogini asked herself. Molly Doyle, Nirmal had told her, was thirty-two (Yogini's age) but looked and acted like thirteen because she suffered from arrested development. "Her parents, who are both alcoholics, never bothered with her, and she's so angry she refuses to grow up. She told Swami Hanuman she wants to reach samadhi to have power over others and maybe even get back at her folks."

"But that's not a proper motivation for acceptance. . . ."

"The Swami says there is no such thing as proper motivation at this level."

"Well, I don't know if I'd accept . . ."

"Yogini, please stop this hypocrisy. I can't imagine you rejecting a student if she'd pay. In fact, you'd even think up a demonic mantra for Molly then. There are demonic mantras, you know."

"Yes, but only the asuras, the demons, can chant them effectively."

Nirmal had mumbled something about her pat answers and she had laughed.

Mai Yogini sighed. Those were the days. She and Nirmal would often converse like that between lovemaking. But then he had decided one morning to leave her and move here. She rechecked her face with her compact and set about to break the Monkey House rules.

There was a door behind her. Making certain that no one was around to see her, she went to it and, placing her hand on the knob, turned it slowly to muffle its opening. Crossing the threshold, Mai Yogini then tiptoed down a long corridor. Small, high windows to her right lighted the corridor's darkness, revealing a progression of doors. Yogini stopped at the third door and again turned the knob slowly. On cat feet she entered Nirmal Kapur's quarters.

There was only one light on, with a bluish tinge. Nirmal sat in a lotus position on a cushion at its side. Against the farther wall were the shadowy outlines of his cot and musical instruments. Yogini moved nearer, softly.

Nirmal was totally naked. His body limned by the bluish cast made her pause in awe, as if she were truly before a young Krishna. His closed eyes added more delicacy to the already effeminate features. The sleek, lank hair was still. Not a part of him stirred, and Yogini fell to her knees and watched. And trembled.

Why had he ended their affair? Why?

Yogini's eyes wandered over his hairless chest, the tight mold of his torso.

Why?

Her abdomen ached.

"Mai Yogini," he said, without opening his eyes.

"How did you know?"

"Your perfume!" Nirmal cried and bounded to his feet. Yogini stared at his flanks, his testicles, his penis, and a terrible sadness gripped her.

"This is a private place," she heard him say. "You don't respect a fucking thing, do you?"

"I doubt very much you were about to enter an astral world," she replied, suddenly irritated.

"Not with you around, that's certain."

Mai Yogini swallowed her pride. "I didn't mean that. Nirmal, I had to come. I need you."

When he didn't reply, she pleaded with all the actress in her. "Nirmal, they've finally caught on to me. I'm ... in trouble. Real trouble this time."

Nirmal still remained standing, looking down at her. A scowl. "This isn't one of your little games to get me back?"

Yogini shook her head. Her hands shook, fingers hungry to reach out and touch him.

But she lowered her head, working to appear repentant. "You always warned me, Nirmal. I should've listened to you. My chelas, my followers, are beginning to doubt me. They see the expensive furniture, the materialism at the center."

"Hell, you can get out of that. Tell them there's nothing wrong with nice furniture if your attitude about it is right. Tell them they can have a lot of fine things. As long as they remain detached, as long as they're filled with bhakti. Detachment and devotion—that's the way."

"Is it?"

"That's always been your message, hasn't it?"

Yogini nodded. Tears flowed down her cheeks. They were authentic this time. Looking at him, she missed his body so.

She continued, "They know about Irish Jack."

"Yogini, are you all right?" Nirmal bent, supported her with his arms. She was nearly faint.

Eyes wide, she gasped, "Nirmal, you must play at the center. You must bring the Swami with you. For me. My chelas will think then I am still pure. They know that the Swami is the best. Besides, they believe in us."

It spilled from her, a torrent of words, as she sobbed fiercely in his arms.

For a moment Nirmal held her close, stroked her hair. Suddenly he eased her to the floor, rose, and disappeared. When he reappeared, he wore his jeans.

"I know," he told her cynically. "They want to believe that every Hindu is enlightened, brimful of godliness." He took a pink silk shirt from a chair, put it on. "What are you really afraid of, Yogini?"

"I need to survive. . . . You know how hard it was for me, father's suicide, mother's death, alone here in America."

"Now, don't pull that again. I'm booked solid for the next two weeks. Sorry, Yogini. Tonight's the only time I've got free, and—"

Quickly: "Tonight would be fine. I could phone all my chelas and tell them. They know the Swami wouldn't be there unless he was convinced I was a true—"

"I can't expect Billy Dangerfield and little Esmeralda to play on such short notice. And I don't think Swami Hanuman will be interested in going—"

"Oh, you must bring him. Please make him come, Nirmal!"

He paused. He had never seen Yogini so frantic. Something was very wrong here, something hidden. The Swami of late had been directing him to be more aware, more perceptive, if possible. The Swami was worried about something that he wouldn't reveal, but he kept saying to expect a very great danger and that it might come in any form. Probably from an unexpected direction. Nirmal knew his Master never exaggerated. "Let's go ask him, then," he said.

Yogini followed Nirmal to the corridor end. Another door, and they were in a sizable room; six people were present, including the Swami. A tall, extremely thin man wearing bifocals was speaking. The others were two young women; an older woman, obese and in pedal pushers; and a middle-aged gentleman with a Lucite cane. The Swami's gaze settled on Yogini, and she squirmed.

"What is it?" whispered Nirmal.

"Nothing." But she felt as if her persona had been shredded. Nervously Yogini tried to concentrate on the series of miniature paintings on the wall, of the Monkey God Hanuman helping King Rama win back his beloved Sitā, leaping over the ocean and setting fire to the city of Lankā.

"Now, if we accept the premise that all levels are in synchrosimilarity and Wheeler's theory of superspace, we know then that the singularities of space-time are points of entry or exit and that added to the Kantean idea that space-time is a construct of the human intellect, it might well be that . . ."

"My God," Yogini said aloud, "what's that all about? Why does Hanuman allow such gibberish?"

"Shh. He believes people must begin as they are. He's not exactly wild about blind faith, you know. He differentiates between belief with understanding and forced faith, when people are forced to believe or agree upon faith, as in church congregations, where a belief is agreed to and accepted by a group. He says such faith works, but only for a while."

The speaker was silent. The other man, with the Lucite cane, told him, "That sure is something, Bill, except it did go on and on, didn't it, and I'm more befuddled than ever. The question, as I recall, was: How can we believe that anything is possible? Well, then how can we believe it?"

"Who is he?" she asked.

Bill replied with anger, "If you'd really listened, it wouldn't be confusing."

Nirmal, frowning: "He's a writer. A novelist."

"Oh."

"Well, Bill," quipped the man with the cane, "I beg to differ. I did listen."

"You just want everything pat and literary."

"Well, it helps to edit a little. Or condense somewhat, for us humanities morons."

"I was bored," said the woman in the pedal pushers.

"You were born bored," Bill said.

"This isn't very spiritual," complained Yogini.

"It's not meant to be. It's a discussion."

"Oh. But why? I just teach, they listen."

"That's exactly the problem."

"Life isn't a piece of fiction," Bill announced. "You're all caught up in words."

"Funny, your talk made me think it was you," said the man with the cane. "You reminded me of the man who learned to spell banana and didn't know when to stop."

"B-A-N-A-N-A-N-A," chirped one of the younger women, and they both giggled.

From the fat woman: "I don't get it."

"Me neither," Yogini agreed.

Bill was flushed. "You're just talking so much bullshit, do you know that?"

Hanuman finally spoke. He wasn't wearing his garish blue turban with gold trim, and so his small dome glistened in the overhead light. He squinched his flat nose in that monkey affectation he had. He lacked the air of tolerant condescension one would expect from a Master, seemed amused, and his tone said as much. "We have been exploring doubt today, and yet we are obsessed with convictions. If logic were enough, we'd all be so instantly enlightened and wise. But to think out matters as basic as: Is anything possible? is never sufficient. Things are what we're concerned with. And object, event, imagining, apparition, even any thought—they are all things. And doubt and faith are no different. All of us have experienced doubt or lived it. But let us concentrate on faith, the faith that moves things, the makes *anything* possible. The basic faith that meets reality head on, changes its substructure, transforms, transmutes it into something new. Something that we might consider impossible.

"Man, if he is to see truly, must go beyond the optical illusion of his ideas, of the misshapen reality that most settle for. Through the inner eye, my chelas, is the only way to see without blurring, to go beyond the impediment of illusion. But this inner eye must be freed first, nurtured, developed to its fullest capacity by meditation, contemplation, and, most of all, understanding. In understanding lies the faith that moves, changes things, and never dies. Instead of blind faith, understanding is the way to see what truly exists, what is truly happening."

Hanuman sat in his chair. The session was over.

Nirmāl said, "I'll ask him before the chelas surround him with their questions." He rushed to the Swami's chair. Mai Yogini watched them huddle. When they broke, Hanuman nodded and smiled at her. Nirmal said, as they went back down the hall, "We'll be there tonight."

"Eight-thirty?"

"Right."

"Oh, thank you, Nirmal. I could kiss you."

"Don't."

A pause. "Then I'd better leave now." She checked her Longines. "I'm late. Fredrico has probably circled around a thousand times by now. What did he say?"

"Who?"

"The Swami."

"That it was fitting you came to this particular symposium today."

"He said that?"

"Yes."

"Why? What did he mean?"

"I don't know. That nothing is impossible, I suppose."

Briefly, she felt, there is hope. Anything can be, can happen. Even freedom from Her, from the Huzoor and the rest.

Outside, the flickering among the drifts was waiting. The flat, wafer-thin shadow seemed more distinct, and, somewhere above the traffic noises, was the steady, paced flapping of wings. Mai Yogini rushed to the limo, away from the darkening drifts.

EIGHTEEN

Rama Shastri was cold. The cab's heater seemed to be faulty. Wrench was by his side, holding a clipboard with papers attached. He drew on his pipe.

"You're right about that piece of scroll, Ram," he commented between puffs of smoke that hazed the closed-in section. "It shouldn't be anywhere near Santha. We've put a priority on the wrong thing—the mysterious death of Abel Fairley."

"I took it from the Huzoor, Steve. It has to be important to them." Shastri tried to sink farther into his coat for warmth. "It's my fault. I can't even use jet lag as an excuse. We don't want Santha involved in this."

"I would have thought she'd have shown it to one of the Indologists by now, though. Hell, Harvard has enough of them, I should think. . . . She's been badly affected by Kamala's death, Ram. George Buchan told me she went into a kind of trance a few weeks ago, even hallucinated, he claims. . . . Holy Christ! and I was too caught up in my own grief to help her. . . ."

"Santha has all the help she needs, Steve. Buchan looks like a solid chap. She'll heal in time. She's got pluck. I could see that immediately."

"Trauma, hallucinations are nothing to be so casual about."

"I agree. But, still, you mustn't be overprotective. Remember, George Buchan is a doctor of the mind. If something is wrong with Santha's mind, then I can't think of her being in more capable hands. But it's up to us to protect her from Thuggee."

Wrench shuddered, fumbled with his pipe. The windshield wipers worked overtime, scraping chunks of white aside. Flakes kept hurtling at them, and it was so dark the cab's high beams were on. He felt as though they were bounding down a tunnel made of fragmenting air. Somewhere, unseen but nevertheless in his life, a momentum was building after all, faster and faster, nearer and nearer. . . . Like Destiny, he and Ram and the things with them moved. Wrench passed a hand over his eyes, wondering if he was losing touch again.

Shastri pointed at the table behind the McDonald's window. "It was right there." Then he fingered the long white woolen scarf that Wrench had wrapped around his neck that morning. Santha had knitted it one Christmas for her father. The shorter Shastri had to wind it around him until he was certain his head would disappear behind its folds. "I'm sorry, I can't help staring. They stood here. Right before me, over there. Damn, but seeing her disrupts the psyche, destroys the false, smug security of logic."

The snow seemed to bustle, busy, busy. Up ahead, a man was desperately working an automobile engine, demanding it come alive. A few seconds of roar and thick smoke from the exhaust, and then the car would die again. Busy. A female student did an unexpected dance as she crossed the slippery avenue to the Conservatory. She kept her balance, the rind of caked snow on her coat crumbling and falling at her feet.

"Makes a man doubt," Shastri concluded. "Are we doing right? Are we defeated before we begin? Assuming I was neither hypnotized nor deluded in some way, we are definitely dealing with the supernatural. Now, at this exact moment, I sense that She knows . . . She knows we're coming. She can tell without having seen us. How can we contend with that?"

Wrench argued back, "Ram, let's find out, anyway. If you're deluded, or I was instead, in this, that's possible. But both of us aren't apt to be wrong. That's pretty nearly impossible and, frankly, at the risk of appearing conceited, improbable. So let's find out for certain, okay?" Wrench patted his coat pocket, adding softly, "Besides, we're armed. Maybe She's invulnerable to bullets, but Thugs, never! Thugs die, Ram. That's a matter of record."

While they trudged along, using the street for better mobility, the sun emerged from the gray cloud cover. Wrench saw their grotesque shadows: he, a long, broad, dark splash; Shastri smaller, with the thick scarf bulge where his head should be. He had a fleeting thought that they were but two old, quixotic men trying hard to believe they were needed in this.

"See, they haven't replaced the window," Shastri told him then.

Wrench stared. A board had been placed before the break in the corner. Cracks in the glass radiated around the board, and one crack marred the entire lower surface of what had once been an impressive bay window.

Nothing seemed foolish anymore, suddenly. Wrench wondered if they should've shoveled his Volks Rabbit free of the drifts that morning. At least, then, poor Ram could've hugged the heater whenever the cold got too tough. It would've made amends for his doubts, since lately Wrench hadn't been able to suppress the idea that they were just attacking the most convenient windmill. Two overaged little boys trying to renew a lease, that yesteryear when they were young and alive with India, that time when adventurers fitted, were feasible.

Unlike these last few decades, when everything questioned itself. Good, bad, morality, its opposite—the whole goddamn philosophical structure of mankind was on trial. The complications made him reel. Please, Wrench almost prayed, let it be the way it once was. Let the earth be solid, finite, like yesterday. Send a plethora of Thug scoundrels my way, an army of murderous bastards with evil sweating out of every pore. Please have some mercy. The world's become much too flimsy and elusive for a man like me.

Reaching Hemenway Street, Wrench pulled the clipboard and paper from inside his topcoat. "Hopefully, your theory is right, Ram," he said. "They live nearby." He paused.

Rama Shastri was touching the scratches on his face and squinting at the spot on Gainsborough where it happened . . . reliving it. . . .

Wrench tried again. "We'll take this side of the street first, until we reach Huntington Avenue, then we'll take the other side. I'll check the lobby registers for Indian names. But I'll also ring every bell, in case they're using somebody else's place. I'll say I represent the Mayor's Office and that I'm conducting a survey to check if everybody's satisfied with the cleanup after the storm. Heard it on the radio, there's been some complaining this year. . . . Rama, are you listening?"

"I am, Steve."

"Anyway, that'll smoke them out to the door. Looking just for Indians makes it simple. How many Indians do you figure are living on this street, if any? A statistical probability is just about one family at the most, the way I calculate it. It might just be them."

"It might. But, Steve, this is an academic area. Exchange students are everywhere. You might encounter another group of Indians, even someone who resembles Chundra Bala or, although I doubt this greatly, an Indian woman with such a ring as I described to you. So we must be absolutely certain that they're the ones. Accusing an innocent countryman of mine of Thuggee is like accusing any Italian-American of belonging to the Mafia."

Resentfully: "I'll be restrained. You ought to know that."

Shastri stamped his feet, rubbed his gloves, blew into them with desperation. "I sense . . ."

"Sense?"

"Call it a policeman's nose. Frozen as it is, it's still functioning. Felt it last night, too. That's what disturbs me. It's too easy, too convenient again. If they're here, it's too obvious to be a coincidence. Like at the temple cave . . ."

"Not another trap! That other time, Ram, Chundra Bala sucked you in. This time, it's just you and me. . . ."

"Nevertheless. Be careful. God, let's leave this corner. Geographically, they're wrong—the North Pole is right here!"

"Where will you be while I'm gone? They'll recognize you, if you trail me."

"Fear not, I'll find a warm hole somewhere. And remember, Steve, check them out, whether they're living here or not. No more than that. Once we know for certain, we'll contact the proper authorities to stake out their building."

Exasperated, Wrench barked, "We agreed to this before! Ferchrissakes, stop fussing, will you." He hated sharing with the authorities. They'll take it away from us, he thought. That's if they can manage to stretch their small imaginations a bit to believe what we're telling them. Adair's face flashed before him, and he suddenly grinned. No chance, he decided; no chance they'll believe that quick. With that, he and Shastri moved on.

NINETEEN

It was breathtaking to feel the sleek black palace walls. They felt like neither stone nor any other building material, and Gauri pulled her hand away, perplexed. She was on a wall overlooking what resembled the Gangetic Plain. She concluded immediately, however, that it was an imitation and, with that, knew she was in the place where Kali dwelt.

She was standing above the great gate; behind her was a massive courtyard and a kind of inner palace with sculptured arms on columns extending at angles that lacked balance, symmetry. All was black, even the woman's face on the towering edifice beyond. The face was nearly indistinguishable in the mist and steam that rose from the ground everywhere. Despite the height of her perch, the steam reached Gauri. Sweating, she tried fanning herself with her hands.

Something—not the breeze—tugged at her sari. It wasn't breeze, wind, but a susurrant voice. "As Surya rides in his chariot over the many lands, I lurk in the Night, where the whispers of adulterous lovers hover in the jasmine gardens, where even darker deeds ripen and burst their husk like melons too long on the vine."

Then it was quiet again. The moon lapped the sleek surfaces

and left a long train across the plain, as if something were to emerge from its distant end. A ridge of highlands, mountains, perhaps, Gauri thought, although it was too dark to see them.

Footsteps sounded along the surrounding walk that followed the inner side of the wall. Gauri saw the Huzoor. He paused at her side. His eyes glowed as he showed the silver medallion that hung from his neck. The silver flowed and yet was solid. It quivered, alive, and had a compartment within the medallion's center. The Huzoor flicked his nail across the mercurial surface, and the compartment door opened. The moisture of the night air filled Gauri's lungs, and her breathing became labored. But she couldn't stop gaping.

Within the compartment was a heart: black as the palace, except for the red traceries of veins. The tributaries expanded and then contracted to the pulse. Gauri placed her ear to the small compartment and heard its beat.

The Huzoor closed the door, said, "There, I've hidden Her heart where they cannot find it. This time it will not be pierced by their shafts."

Gauri knew of whom he spoke. She knew now why her eyes constantly darted to the sliver of moonlight that needled across the Plain. It was to happen again, the group of usurpers were to come this very night, to try once more to send their shafts at Mother Kali's breast.

But not only the ever throbbing heart was hidden, but the Mother also! Gauri rejoiced. What cunning, what wiles. The Queen of Deceivers was indeed prepared this time.

And then, like a taunt, the plain trembled. Gauri Bala stared at the onrush of brightness, a bluish cloud with flashing light within it. She had to turn her face from it at intervals, it was so blinding.

The cloud neared. The walls again susurrated. "Think of me. The foul and decaying sweetness is everywhere. The dead and the dying are my bounty. I am a monsoon that rises unexpectedly, to ravage the time of Man with a merciless flood of war and pestilence. I am Kali. Think only of Me!"

But the bluish thunder was too compelling. Gauri watched it take form. A massive, bejeweled elephant, with a canopy and a howdah of gold, rushed at the palace. Within the howdah were the determined, silent men. Leaping between the animal's flapping ears was the Taunting Monkey. The howdah's curtain parted, and she saw the Archer Leader direct the charge. A name unuttered formed on her lips: Rama Shastri.

The Huzoor shouted at the din. "Open the gates! Let them see the hostage!"

The courtyard echoed with a loud clanging. Gauri looked below. Tied to a black pole was the girl . . . the Chosen Vessel to come. She was asleep, and her tangled hair covered most of her face.

And another voice now plucked at Gauri, a bass that came from the elephant's thunder: "Santha, Santha, Santha." It was their war cry.

The animal stopped yards from the open gate. Its trunk lifted and it roared its challenge. The turbaned monkey darted from its great head to the howdah and back. Gauri saw the other Archers—the big one, the one like a young Arjuna, and another, less distinct.

Gauri heard a command from Rama Shastri, and the blue beast lumbered into the yard.

The ebony walls shrieked, and Gauri covered her ears. The arms on the columns moved, applauded, shook their armlets. A loud whooshing noise, and the walls began to crack, to crumble. The cracks glowed red and resembled the black heart's tributaries. A flood of blood, Kali's blood, swept the courtyard, built into a gigantic wave that headed for the elephant.

In one bound, the monkey leaped from the beast's head to the top of the black pole. It chattered its wrath at the wave, shook a fist, and lowered the other paw toward the girl. Then, in obedience to the monkey's waving directions, the elephant seized the pole with its trunk and, uprooting it, turned and sped toward the gates. They were nearly closed when the elephant butted them, and, with a rending screech, they gave. They clanged and clamored with metallic protest, but in it Gauri sensed much pain.

That was when she discovered that Kali had shaped Herself into the palace.

Now the elephant was moving along the plain, the moon scintillating off its golden headdress. The blood wave curled up against the palace walls, went through the gate before it broke into pools. The elephant was too far away. The big Archer had descended, was freeing the girl. Once that was done, the elephant lifted the black pole and flung it with its trunk at the gate. When it landed again, Gauri once more sensed Kali's agony.

The blood pools edged back to the palace confines. The pools burbled redly. From the distant ridges, out of the shadows, the elephant trumpeted his glory.

Gauri started to topple, and the entire Kali-palace folded in on itself. She found herself suddenly seated in a large silver box. The Huzoor was by her side. Beaded curtains stirred next to her shoulder, and she parted the silvery, alive things with her hand. Looking down, she saw they were in a howdah, atop Kali, who was now a black elephant. The howdah and the great beast's back swayed as the Goddess thudded through the night.

Kali was fleeing. Fleeing!

The howdah lurched, and Gauri felt dizzy from the tremendous speed. The thudding was deafening. Suddenly it seemed to double in force. Gauri looked from the curtain again. She saw the blue flank of the other elephant. It was already ahead of Kali. The big Archer was coolly aiming his bow. A shaft like a beam of fire left the hide string. Kali lurched, and Gauri nearly fell from the howdah.

She held to its sides and felt another lurch, and then another. Pain, rage bellowed from the elephant form. Now it was the Arjuna-like boy's turn. Another shaft plummeted into the black mass. Kali had halted, her elephant lungs working hard, breathing in the humid, tepid night in massive gulps.

The boy shook his long tresses and shouted his joy and, whispering into the monkey's ear, hurled him at the howdah. The monkey somersaulted through the bead curtain, bounced off Gauri's knees, and attacked the Huzoor. With shocking ease, he snatched the medallion's chain, yanked it until it broke free. Before the Huzoor could react, the monkey leaped back through the curtain.

The Huzoor's grief mingled with Kali's agony, and Gauri thought she could bear it no longer. Wide-eyed, she watched the monkey fling the medallion up, up, the compartment door open.

Rama Shastri, braced on the blue beast's flank, fired his arrow. The tip neared the compartment's space. The very atmosphere throbbed with the heart's hurried beat. The tip penetrated, imbedded into the black quick—

"Husband!" Gauri sat up, her back rigid, her body drenched from the horror of her dream. "Husband!" she called again.

But Chundra Bala was away, about the Huzoor's business.

This had been the worst dream of all. Gauri could still imagine the speeding arrow tip plunging hard into the throbbing pitch. She knew it boded death: not for the Goddess, who was immortal, but for someone who was part of Kali's heart. Perhaps even herself. Perhaps . . . Her cry rose shrilly in the darkened room, "My husband!" The midmorning glare hurt her eyes then, and she fell back, burrowing her face in the pillows.

When Chundra Bala finally returned home, he found Gauri still weak from her dream. She told him about it while he stroked her sleek hair. Then they made love.

Now Chundra Bala raised his head from his wife's breast. It was as it should be, Chundra told himself as he dressed; lovemaking had never been so blissful before.

Chundra whispered to the figure asleep in the bed, "Are you truly Gauri?" The exposed, pendulous breasts heaved for a second, like a reply. As they swelled, they radiated, glowed ripe and beckoning, and he hungered to return to them. But he stood and watched her as her head faced the lavender wallpaper with its petals tumbling down the wall in long, curving arcs. Gauri's hair hid most of her face. Only the ring held some of the hair back, and he moved a step, aroused to kiss her neck again and then . . . descend . . .

Sensing his erection, Chundra laughed harshly into the room's shadows. Lately he couldn't have enough of Gauri. Not ever. Not when she was his wife, herself and serene, rather than that monstrous, blood-lusting entity he'd seen last night at the Huzoor's ashram.

Never had Chundra loved her more . . . or dreaded her more. Chundra had talked long with her, once they'd returned to Elvira Moniz's apartment that morning. Talked and talked about the new vessel that Makunda and Ramanuja had seen and followed yesterday. How she, Gauri, should willingly accept this new woman, should be glad to share her great power.

Gauri had been a child when they married. Chundra had observed every stage of her early womanhood. Different and appealing as she was then, nothing saintly, nothing transcendent thrived in her face, as it did now.

During their talk, Gauri had smiled at him patiently. Her steady gaze focused on him, yet simultaneously turned inward. He had managed to stress that, as pleasing as the attention she'd received of late had been, she should delight in the release to be provided by this new vessel. The Huzoor Lord would become dependent on the new Chosen One, and the burden placed on Gauri's shoulders would lessen considerably.

For a moment, Gauri's serenity had dissolved. Frowning: "But then what will become of me?"

"You are the first. Surely he won't forget."

"This new vessel. Makunda, Ramanuja both say that she is very beautiful. Have you not heard them? As blessed as Satī is she in that fashion."

"Is this a bad thing, my wife?"

"It is different with me. I am yours, your Gauri in marriage. She is lovely, and she is unmarried, they say."

"What has that to do with our discussion? The Huzoor seeks no woman, only the Mother."

"Granted. But if this new one is given more power than I, she will have the greater influence. I know this in my heart. The Huzoor will seek her more than me. I will be forgotten."

"The Lord is not so cruel, so lacking in depth. I repeat, you are the first of the vessels of Kali."

Gauri patted Chundra's hand gently, sadly. "My husband, no one knows the Huzoor as I do. No one on this earth."

Uneasy. "What does that mean, my flower?"

"I have at times been a surrogate mother to him here on earth, as is decreed and fitting. When the Goddess comes to me, we serve the Huzoor, even direct him at times in what he must do. When the Goddess comes, I am still aware. It's much like that time before sleep, a dozing observance of what occurs. I know, I see, I hear, I feel with all my senses; yet I'm as one helpless, paralyzed. I experience then Her thoughts, feel Her heart beat with mine. Thus I know the Huzoor well, I say to you."

Gauri wet her lips, seemed adrift somewhere in her mind. Then she bent closer, until her nose nearly touched his. Her black eyes merged into his for a spell, until he felt her peace. "I cannot stop that which is decreed," she admitted further, "nor would I if I could. But oh, my husband, sometimes I grieve that perhaps an end to me will come too soon."

"Don't speak that way."

"I have surrendered to it. No turmoil seethes in my breast. I accept readily anything that may come someday. It is, I believe, a kind of death already."

Chundra wondered that he, too, had no pain from her words.

Gauri seemed to read his thoughts. "We are already there— both of us."

"Where, my wife, where?"

"Wherever Kali wills, Chundra. Who knows? The joy is with us, my husband, but I suspect it is only the joy that is here now, in the present, and that alone She gives us. When She comes to me, I witness Her enshrouding darkness. Kali gives and grants frugally to most of us who serve Her. None of us mean to Her what the Huzoor means."

"Which is proper. He is Her Chosen Son." His eyes searched the room, the corner shadows.

"Yes. But Kali grants and takes at random always. She has whims, dark unfathomable desires, secret purposes that override any consideration for Her followers. Kali is not of us or like us, my husband, rest assured."

Chundra Bala's memory leaped to the final cavern, beyond the whirling rishis and their scrolls, the place of countless nascent things. He nodded, understanding, and his palms were sticky.

Gauri continued, "Kali neither loves nor knows hatred in the same fashion we do. Her thoughts, Her desires spring from a different source, have grown from that which is beyond our limited ken." It was a summary of all Gauri had experienced. She had never revealed so much before. The truth startled Chundra, but, he quickly reasoned, there was no alternative to this. Suppose Gauri's suspicions were valid and she might someday be discarded as no longer serving a purpose—what of it? There was no escape. They were not free, nor had they ever been. To be free was unimaginable.

"We have been given a Path," Chundra told her with a flat finality that surprised him. The statement came from beyond his reasoning or logic. "We're still more blessed than most in this."

Gauri quickly agreed. She had stared at the chiaroscuro pattern the blinds cast on the wall. The window quaked from the wind. The blinds trembled, and the patterns with them. "Yes, for that let us be grateful. For this moment, this present." And, with a meditative smile frozen on her face, Gauri had disrobed, and they had made love as never before.

Chundra Bala entered the living room. The snow-crusted windows reminded him of those days at the Ganga Gangotri. He wondered where the old sadhu had disappeared to in the Cave of the Rishis—no doubt to some hidden place to rest, to sleep the centuries away, until reawakened. Fool, he jeered, why need he sleep? Does the Mother or Vishnu or Brahma himself sleep? Does Eternity need rest? No—the sadhu, the whirling rishis forever watch, tending to the order of Creation. Chundra sighed wearily—only Time and Man rest: Man, since he is weak and mortal, while Time is but the myth that fatigues itself in the constant retelling. Chundra had learned that much from his Gangotri adventure.

He saw that Bidhan's door was open. The man wasn't in his bedroom, or anywhere in the apartment. Chundra cursed, kicking the ashtray on the floor near Bidhan's bed. Bidhan was probably heading toward a store to buy cigarettes. The ashtray was crowded with filter stubs. The Thug loved the American brands. Well, Chundra would teach Bidhan not to leave him and Gauri alone again. It was unsafe. It threatened...

A shriek sounded. Then a second. And a third.

Chundra Bala rushed back into his bedroom.

"They're below! In the street!" The rasp worked up Chundra's spine like an ascending trail of ice. Then he staggered into the living room again. The force of Gauri's hand against his chest had sent him reeling, and he collided with the table. A pepper shaker toppled, rolled across the rug.

"They're coming! They've come, as I wished!"

Chundra stared at the woman, speechless. The black flecks danced with malevolent energy. The tongue drooped, started to loll again. She was half dragging, half dressed in her roseate and yellow sari. "They're here! On the street below, as I desired! Below! Below!" She pointed out the window.

"What do you want me to do?" he asked. "Bidhan is out! I'm the only one with you!"

"Below!" she persisted and flung him aside. Her strength was awesome. Chundra Bala spun into a shelf, freeing a small kettle from its hook. It clattered between his feet. The clatter was like the indignation he felt but couldn't express. Then a glass fell, shattered, then another.

"Mother Kali," Chundra implored.

She urged him to join her at the window. With her sari she was frantically rubbing moisture from the pane. Stunned as he was by her violence, Chundra nevertheless picked himself up and went to her.

"Look!" The roupy sounds gurgled from her lips. Foam bubbled, speeped from her mouth corners, and Chundra smelled a burning, musky odor mingled with heavy sweat. He stared at her profile, saw how her eyes, nose, mouth, chin seemed to stretch as she searched the street below. The flesh had blackened considerably, and the strange elasticity cracked the skin. Chundra panicked. Where, where was Gauri?

Her fingers wandered up his arm and kneaded his shoulder

in her excitement. Her nails cut through Chundra's shirt, tore skin, and he winced. "As I wished! As I wished!"

"Did you will them to come, Mother?" He asked more out of a need to say something than curiosity. He kept his head turned, away from the stench. Try as he did, he saw no one in the street.

Rage. "Would that I could will Rama Shastri to do my bidding!"

So it was Shastri, as he expected. Who else would incite such rage?

Her breath wafted to him, and he averted his head even more. "Rama Shastri came, as I wished him to. After last night, he must investigate. . . . I know it's him! I see it's him!"

But how? Chundra questioned. How could she see Rama Shastri? Searching the street, left and right, he saw no pedestrian, only a passing car or two laboring the final tricklings of storm.

"Rama Shastri, the stalker. The policeman's mind designed by destiny. He had to come," she gloated. His shoulder was numb, chilled.

"There, there is Shastri's companion!" The fingers released Chundra. He slumped against the pane, saw a big man dressed in a brown mackinaw and wearing a trapper's hat directly below the building. The man, carrying what looked like a board with paper attached, headed toward the building entrance.

But where was Shastri? How could she know, be so certain?

The goddess seized Her hair, pulled at it in ecstasy, and the black strands flared out and held there, emitting soft, crackling noises like static.

"He hides!" She announced. "Shastri hides, the fool! But we will make him come to us, Chundra Bala."

He remained searching at the window, until the bedroom door closed behind him. Then Chundra collapsed in a chair, bleary from strain. For minutes he couldn't think or feel. The deep, repetitive throb in his shoulder finally stirred him to a question: Was Gauri gone forever? Had what she'd foreseen

already happened? Was she burned away in an invisible cremation? Was this the end...

The door opened. Chundra's heart bounded when he saw
the blissful smile. "After the man knocks, open the door, my
husband," she told him.

TWENTY

Stephen Wrench rested for a minute in the building lobby, and
he looked back to the entrance—two doors down across the
street—where he'd left Rama Shastri. How many buildings
had Wrench entered, how many people had he already spoken
to? He counted them off the sheets of his clipboard. Six buildings, eleven people. Below the names were notes, scribblings
from the answers he'd received.

For example, next to elderly Mrs. Phyllis Taylor Wright
was a congestion of singular word, incomplete phrases. She
owned the corner building, had lived there since 1919. And
with this "so-called age of progress," you'd think the plows
would arrive faster than they do. They didn't, she maintained,
with a stamp of her Hush Puppies. But that was only one
of the many things wrong in "this age of the New Boston!"
The city was being destroyed by that very same progress.
Too many schools, too many insurance companies. Where
were the old buildings, the old landmarks? All torn down for
"progress."

Wrench pressed the bell ring to Apartment 1A.

A woman's voice. "Who is it?"

Wrench told her his spiel. Into the voice box.

A pause. Then a buzzing sound, and the main door to
the building unlocked automatically. Stephen Wrench went
in.

He walked along a wall cluttered with graffiti and peeling
wallpaper and found the door. It was registered under a Mr.

John Barrows. A cleaner patch of wood showed where the decal numbers had once been. The door opened before he could knock. Wrench stared at a dungareed teenager with her hair in curlers. A mixture of blaring hard rock and the odor of deep-fried meat followed her. She stared back suspiciously. "Who didja say you were?"

Wrench patiently told her the spiel again.

"Oh well, my mother ain't home."

"Who else lives here? In this building?"

She puckered her nose. "Why do ya wanna know?"

"I just wondered if you'd know if they're in or not," Wrench replied, with a slight edge in his voice. He kept raising his voice as she strained to hear over a pair of amplified guitars. "If they're out working or not. Saves me the trouble of climbing the stairs."

"Oh." She stood in silence, thinking over what he'd said. Finally, abruptly, "Don't feel like it."

"Why not?"

"'Cause I ain't no snitch. How do I know you ain't no cop looking for dopeys."

"I work for the city, but I'm not a cop."

"Uh-uh. I ain't taking no chances. Cal told me to watch out for undercover narcs." And with that she slammed the door. Wrench growled, turned, faced 1B, saw the odd cognomen, Umerzurike, and knocked. No answer. He headed for the stairs.

The second floor had three apartments. Voss at 2A was out and so were the Kellys at 2B.

The next door had four different names. There was no reply to his knock, but Wrench heard someone moving on the other side. He knocked again. Still the door remained closed.

Wrench read one of the four names and had an inspiration. "Cal?" he asked. "That you? The kid downstairs said you were in."

A minute or so passed. Wrench sensed that whoever was in was directly behind the barrier.

"Cal?" he ventured again.

The door opened slightly. A pimply, twentyish youth peered at him. "Ginny sent you up?"

"Yeah, Cal, I talked with her. She said, 'See Cal, upstairs.'"

Eagerly: "Why? You got—stuff?"

"Stuff? Oh no, not that. You see, I'm conducting a survey, and—"

"A survey? What kind of survey?"

Wrench told him.

"I'm just a student. I don't live permanently in Boston. I don't know from nothing about snowplows."

Wrench placed his broad shoulders before the door. Cal Nugent tried to close it but couldn't. He blinked at the door-knob. When it registered why the door didn't close, he glared. His pupils were dilated, and the glare only made them larger.

Wrench kept his voice just above a whisper. "Look," he soothed, "I know you're worried about narcs. Ginny told me. Well, I'm not one. I'm trying to do my job, that's all. A survey for the city, nothing more than that. Okay?"

He endured Cal Nugent's intense scrutiny. "What about your roommates?" Wrench said, in his best inoffensive tone. "Are they transient, too?"

"Marty isn't. She's always lived in Back Bay, I think. She isn't here." Cal had mellowed. Wrench had passed the test. "Too bad. She might have a thing or two to say. She's real big on social reform."

"Well then, I'll leave. . . . Anyone home on the third floor, do you know?"

"Dunno. But I warn you, nobody knows from nothing about snowplows. I mean, how many people think about goddamn snowplows? You only see the fucking things once or twice a year. I mean, if it was cars, they're always around. Everybody thinks about cars. I mean, they fuckin' think and think about them all the time. A helluva lot more than they think about people, even. It's cars, it's chassis, it's carburetors, it's mileage and front-wheel drive. It's mufflers and radial tires. Mother-fuckin' radial tires. Freaks me out, man! All those thoughts about auto parts crowding everything—"

"Be seeing you," Wrench said then, hurrying away. And I hope not, he thought, puffing while he climbed; I hope I never, ever. Sure as God gave lady platypuses a pair of teats, he paraphrased, this has become a hard, cruel world. At the third landing, he leaned against a newel post to catch his breath. The walls were in worse condition than below. The wallpaper hung in strips, and between them a muddy yellow showed. It was stuffy, and he loosened his tie slightly. He sniffed at tricklings of aromatic cooking everywhere. Wrench approached a door, read "Elvira Moniz." There wasn't a "Ms." or "Mrs." before the name. Stephen Wrench knocked.

A man who fitted exactly Ram's description of Chundra Bala stood in the doorway.

Wrench's thick fingers dug into the ersatz survey sheets and nearly tore them from the clipboard.

"Yes?" asked Bala, with that touch of clipped English from the Raj years.

"My name's Stephen Wrench," replied a voice that slurred like a man a bit drunk. Wrench coughed for time, muttered an "Excuse me," released the air from his lungs, and prayed that the constriction around his stomach would ease. "I represent the Mayor's Office, and I'm making inquiries about the cleanup during the storm. . . ." There, that was better. More normal, convincing.

Bala's eyes told him nothing. He just looked at Wrench, and that was the fatal flaw. People didn't just look at a stranger at their door. There was usually wonder, suspicion, fear, big-city paranoia. Wrench was certain he had his man. He shifted his bulk, trying to see over Bala's left shoulder. But Bala stood with his hand on the doorknob, and only the apartment ceiling was visible beyond the Hindu's head.

"A survey?" Chundra Bala repeated, as if attempting to understand. Then he smiled. Warmly.

Wrench let his right hand drop near his coat pocket. Bala's eyes flickered quickly to the hand. Now Chundra Bala knew that Wrench was armed, which was exactly what the policeman wanted.

Chundra Bala said, "I'm afraid we can't help you. We aren't

citizens, you see. We only use this apartment temporarily. It belongs . . ."

"What is it, husband?" a woman asked in Hindi.

Wrench saw a bejeweled hand grasp the door edge and push it totally back. Bracelets clinked down her wrist like punctuation. Wrench dropped his hand to his side under the pleasant and steady gaze of the woman.

Bala resorted to English. "This man is a representative of the city government."

"Aaah," she said, nodding. The sari lowered from her face, the nose ring pulled the thick, black hair strand taut. He'd seen such large rings before, in India, mostly at weddings, and he knew the hair eased the ring's weight.

The woman said "Aaah" again and queried, this time in Muslim Urdu, "This man understands us?"

"I believe so."

But Wrench never wavered. He played dumb, poker-faced. He recognized the cool mockery in changing languages this way. They already knew he wasn't what he pretended to be. He'd sensed this, somehow, from the beginning, and when he groped as to how he'd known so quickly, his blood turned to ice. Wrench couldn't explain it.

Then, in English, she said, "Why have you come, Mr. . . . ? I'm sorry, my husband didn't tell me your name."

"Stephen Wrench. I'm making inquiries, a survey about whether the streets were sufficiently cleared of snow."

"I see." In Bengali now to Bala: "He knows Hindi, Urdu. He knows much."

To Wrench: "You have been to India."

"Never," Wrench lied.

"You have not been there?"

"No."

Gauri Bala tilted her head and smiled. Her teeth were very small and very white. "We know nothing whatsoever about this clearing of the streets. I have watched the snow fall and seen the large vehicles push it to the sides. Do I describe that correctly?"

"Very well."

"It has appeared sufficient to me, then. You may write down, if you wish, that Mr. Chundra Bala and his wife, Mrs. Gauri Bala, of Varanasi, approve of the clearing of the snow that has been done."

Wrench scribbled something. "Thank you."

Gauri placed her fingers and palms together before her chest—the namaskar, the Indian greeting, or acknowledgment of an equal.

"I'm sorry we can offer little else," came from her husband.

Wrench thanked them. The door closed. He waited, his ear pressed to the panel. Wrench heard nothing, grunted, and turned toward the stairs. He had to find Rama Shastri. It was them, all right, at least, two of the three Ram had described; and although the woman was unusual enough, he couldn't grasp what all the flutter was about. Wrench had seen thousands of such Indian women in his lifetime. At the most, this one, this Gauri Bala, exuded a bizarre sort of charm, almost saintly, considering she was a Thug's wife. Where the hell was Ram . . . ?

Blam! He spun around. The apartment door had been wrenched open and hurtled against an inner wall. Wrench's hand was in his pocket, ready, but instead of Chundra Bala showing in the doorway, something like a wind rushed out onto the landing. The force hit him below the abdomen like a gigantic fist, and he spun back and collided with the newel post. Wrench's vision blurred, and when his eyes rolled to the skylight above the stairs, it became doubled. Wrench rose from his knees, listening to his brain urging, urging. . . . He must get away. He must . . .

The blurring, the double vision stopped. Now she'll come, he suddenly knew, and grasped, too, that it wasn't solely his thought. She wants me to see her, to know . . .

He was right. In the doorway, her arms extended, the sari draped out, a fragile, colorful wing it seemed. Stephen Wrench saw the face and shouted, "Holy Christ!"

"*Tamakhu Kha-lo!*" rasped back at him, the Thug death call that meant no more than "Smoke-tobacco!" but to them were the code words for the final thrust. Wrench groped again for his gun. The woman leaped.

Impossible momentum and power flung him against the wall. He forced his right shoulder to take most of the impact and bounced. His arms were quickly yanked back until his wrists were flush with the base of his spine. He'd not guessed Chundra Bala to be so strong and cursed aloud when he saw the Thug before him, swinging the rumel.

It was the woman who was holding him!

"*Sanp! Sanp!*" came the guttural cry behind him. "Snake! Snake!"—commanding the best position to place Wrench in for death. She was wheezing, her rancid breath putrescent. Wrench managed a quick glance as she climbed on him with her legs. Terror, a rage to live revived him, made him fight.

Her body reacting like a contortionist's, the woman squeezed her arms between her extended legs and still held him pinioned. Her legs meanwhile coiled, squeezed. Wrench expanded the muscles of his neck, arms, and back until he heard them crack with strain.

It was a strange, quiet struggle, despite its ferocity, a staccato of grunts and raspings. Somewhere nearby, Chundra Bala shuffled, his hands caressing the scarf, awaiting the right moment.

But Wrench kept turning. Every time Chundra was about to lunge, Wrench moved, and the woman became a barrier. "*Sanp! Sanp!*" it continued, a frustrated, rasping demand. Wrench sank his teeth into the dangling strand that held the ring, tasting the disgusting mixture of ghee and sweat that oiled the hair. He tugged with his teeth, tugged hard, until she screamed and the powerful fingers let go. Still she straddled him on his right side. Her legs were around his waist now, and where the sari fell free of the thighs, he could see them bulging as they squeezed tighter. Wrench's freed arms pounded the thighs again and again. He whirled his bulk until he was faint with dizziness, and she hung from him, her body straight out in a terrifying parody of an acrobatic act. The woman screeched now in guttural semi-words, her hands flailing at the air, the lolling tongue quivering like the pistil of a dark, fetid flower.

Finally Wrench began to succumb. The dizziness was unbearable. The roaring in his head threatened oblivion. His rotations slowed, try as he did to continue. Chundra Bala immediately stepped forward. Then Chundra Bala suddenly stepped back, and the woman released her legs, rolled over, and sprang to her feet. Wrench tottered as he tried to understand why it had ended. Then he heard someone racing up the stairs, calling "Steve! Steve!" The woman gave a command, then a scurrying and the door slammed.

When Rama Shastri reached Wrench, he found him flat against the wall at the head of the stairs. The big man's mackinaw had rents along the back; his face and neck were swollen and bruised.

Gun in hand, Shastri faced the door. It remained closed.

"Let's leave this place," he said. "We agreed we wouldn't take them on alone. Can you make it?"

Wrench was listening to the roar subside. A nod. With Shastri's help, he eased his flanks down each step. By the second landing he could stand. At times Shastri stared back up, poised with his weapon. No one followed. The stairwell above was shadowy, still. "I got impatient," Shastri told Wrench while they struggled to the lobby. He lifted Wrench's dead weight from his shoulder and held the big man against the wall, the palms of his hands on the massive chest. Wrench was laboring. Breathing was very hard, very painful.

"I decided to find you." Shastri talked rapidly to settle his own terror. Stephen Wrench's face was a disconcerting mixture of paleness and red blotches. "I guess they felt that two of us were too much to tangle with. Lucky the other Thug wasn't around."

Something like a smile. "You were right, Ram," Wrench gasped.

Once outside the building, Shastri guided Wrench down Hemenway. He was grateful the big man no longer needed support. Shastri's eyes rose to where he estimated the window was. Nothing, not even the rustle of curtains.

Slowly the two men made their way along the street. Wrench stumbled often, held his sides. Shastri searched for cabs but found none. They had neared Boylston when Wrench turned. The color in his face was even again, his breathing regular.

"It was like two different women, Ram: first Bala's wife and then, then that fucking bitch thing. Eyes like goddamn quicksilver. Powerful . . . so powerful. Breath like . . . like death."

"Hell of a job for a policeman, isn't it, Steve?"

"No job at all." Wrench fished for a handkerchief to wipe his face. "I can face any goddamn Thug in the world, Ram. But, jeez—that thing! We ought to report this to the local police, though. . . ."

"I don't think it'll do any good. Even if the pair are still there, the police will find only Chundra Bala's woman, not— whatever displaces her."

"Her name's Gauri Bala, his wife. Imagine being married to Mrs. Bala/Mrs. Hyde." They turned onto Boylston Street, heading toward Massachusetts Avenue. Wrench complained that his legs were getting rubbery. They found an entryway to an abandoned building and sat on the narrow stairway.

"Whew." Wrench wiped his face again. "Never felt so finished before I'd even started. And she, the bitch thing, knew about us. She expected us and waited. I'm sure of it. They saw through my act right away. Christ, Ram, how can we cope with something like that? It's always ahead of us. Waiting, lurking somewhere, waiting . . ."

He groped for his pipe. He found it, filled it; but he didn't light it. Instead, he stood again and looked through the window in the door, at the passersby on Boylston, and shuddered as if he saw more.

"This thing is out of our jurisdiction," he announced. "We need help—a certain kind of help to handle that fucking thing. Ever try prayer, Ram?"

This time his friend shuddered, but not from fear. The thought of prayer made Rama Shastri shudder. To him prayer meant that reason was at the end of its tether. It meant that he and

Stephen Wrench were defeated, too limited to fight this—as Wrench so well put it—bitch thing. There was no winning a battle like this. And he had craved so very much to hunt the Huzoor down, to destroy this new rise of Thuggee in the world.

For that he had left Ileana and Mother India. But now they were powerless—as if they were two lost old men in an empty entryway watching the rest of mankind pass by.

PART THREE

GARBHA

Development,
A Deepening

TWENTY-ONE

The flow of the Ganga beckoned . . . lured . . . summoned.

The sun, bloated with drought-season incandescence, low-ered to the horizon. It smeared the river with a garish saffron and red; a faded saffron rippled the shore, as a procession of sadhus shuffled to the Great Ghat, their whispering chants dim, unclear, perhaps soothing to the burning dead. Santha Wrench lost count of the cremation pyres, everywhere on the shoreline ghats, on the floating rafts. The Ganga was rising, and the rafts, tilted, dipped into the swell troughs, the pyre smoke trailing.

Santha kept her distance from them. She walked along slowly, parallel to the bank, re-counting again the progression of smaller ghats north and south—twenty, twenty-five, then thirty, then others, on and on, until their smoke traceries thinned, became diminutive black lines as in a pen-and-ink drawing. Santha was certain there was no place in India so ghat-congested. No spot in India, no such banks of the Ganga existed.

It was a dream . . . no, a dimensional place. It *was* a Ganga bank.

Santha Wrench turned back and approached the handful of stone stairs. They were so wide a marching army could have stood on them abreast. Over every square inch of the stone were carvings of figures too faded from erosion to decipher. Santha wondered what had caused the erosion, since she felt no wind. There were no odors, either, and for that she was greatly relieved. The dead burned and burned, it seemed, and still the cremation stink was blessedly missing.

While Santha took the long walk to the pyres, she noticed that this was solid ground and ahead was water. Santha was on ground, rapidly closing in on water, but she was also treading on space. Or, to be more precise, she was treading on time.

229

Santha groaned, exasperated. How in hell could a person walk on time?

It passed through her, cold, the trickling ice thoughts with a touch of suppressed laughter.

But, my dear, the dead do walk on time. Those that are beyond avidya walk on any time and any space. They do; they truly do, my child. Beyond avidya, the world illusion, they truly do.

Santha Wrench stopped. "Who are you?" she cried. "Who speaks to me? Who speaks in my mind?" She said the words in Bengali, the same language the voice had used, and was surprised.

Yet here it was fitting.

The billows of pyre smoke were shrouding her. It hurt neither her eyes nor nose nor throat; was only utter black or fuzzy swirls of twilight gray. Ahead, the procession of sadhus had parted, and they stood on each side, beating their dandas, or bamboo staffs, on the stone in unison. Was it a salute, a homage to her? Why? she puzzled.

Then the smoke draped back, and Santha approached the distinct mounds of burning wood, twigs, leaves. Bulb-rooted tuberoses, red marigolds, and white jasmine capped the pyre tops. The flowers made everything more like a celebration than a funeral. Santha's eyes centered on the semicharred body in the flames. And she screamed.

Uncle Ram! The profile was that of Rama Shastri.

Still screaming, Santha nevertheless looked at the next pyre. Santha saw then what she already expected: her father, the flames licking ferociously at his body. Weak, faint, Santha willed herself on. The third pyre held a smaller man she didn't recognize, and, farther on, close to the churning Ganga waters, was the corpse of an Indian youth. Santha quieted for an instant, filled her lungs with air, and surrendered with a long-drawn-out mourner's wail. It echoed across the waters, shattered against the rage of the fires, the frenzied lapping of the Ganga against the Great Ghat.

Grieve not, beloved daughter, the voice urged, seeping through the chill like a frosty breath; these dead will know heaven and be greatly rewarded. So it is with them who will die by the rumel.

A clinking and clatter of bracelets, the wings of mechanical birds colliding with each other. Santha recoiled from the harsh sting of a slap on her cheek. Slowly she lowered her hands from her eyes and stared at the woman before her.

The woman was familiar. Where, when, how had they met? The nose reflected the bloated sun, had a saffron rind.

"Who are you?" Santha asked, with unexpected calm. "Your eyes tell me already, I think, but I cannot look at them. Tell me with our lips."

"With my lips," repeated the other, "and with my voice that rustles like ashes on stone. I am She who has come for you. She who seeks a daughter, She who is Mother to all Deceivers." The woman used the word "Thug," and Santha understood. Yes, Thug—Deceiver.

Before Santha could protest, the woman grasped both her elbows and, holding Santha's arms bent and flush at her side, kissed her on the lips. Santha tried to struggle free but was in a vise. The woman's kiss was hard and like cold stone, but the longer the kiss held fast, the more the cold dissolved into a strange, passionless warmth. Serenity flowed through Santha, and the warmth seemed to melt through her own lips. Santha felt her entire lower body, her private self throb with ecstasy and pain simultaneously.

Santha began to moan. The nose ring pressed against her cheek and the corner of her mouth, but she no longer minded. The woman's mouth suddenly opened, and tiny teeth bit into Santha's lower lip. It bled, the blood mixing with Santha's saliva as her mouth, too, opened. The woman's tongue then touched hers and grew. Impossible that a tongue could elongate itself like that. It coiled and wrapped itself around Santha's tongue and squeezed and tugged until Santha thought hers would be wrenched from her. But again, despite the pain, the dizzying, pleasure-filled eruptions in her mind increased.

The woman's face darkened as she let Santha go. Shadow after shadow flitted over her, but the saffron light was still in the landscape. The shadows rippled, wavered with her words: "See who I truly am."

The woman raised her arms slightly, and her sari split without warning a few inches beneath her armpits. Santha's eyes watched the exposed flesh within the split begin to expand. Sounds followed: a fierce rending, the snapping of bone at the rib cage, the slosh of thick fluids. Blood and a sickly, bilious ichor poured from the cavities. It cascaded down the sari, pooled around the woman's sandals. Tongue lolling from one corner of the mouth to the other, the creature shrieked her joy.

That was when serenity left.

"Jesushelpme. Jesushelpme, help me," muttered Santha, falling back on her Episcopalian upbringing.

"You are not of Jesus!" the creature shrieked again. "You are mine. *Mine!*"

Knobs, ichor-coated knobs of flesh were forming. More snapping, more blood, more bilious seepage, and the knob elongated and ended at an elbow joint.

"Ganeshapleasehearme. Ganeshapleasehelp," persisted Santha.

"Ganesha!" jeered the other. "Ganesha! Ganesha cannot help you, my dear child. Summon Vishnu, even! Summon Siva! Summon whom you will!"

Now the woman's arms were raised above her head, the two stumps beneath them dangling. The cold, grating screech hammered across the shore, hollow, distant, as if scaling an endless pit.

"MARYSAVEME, PARVATIFREEME, SHAKTICOME-TOMYAID," screamed Santha.

The hold on her, the horror's spell snapped. Bounding past the pyres, she dove off the Great Ghat, plummeted into a hush that muffled the mocking shriek above. Desperately Santha swam through the intense murkiness. The river had tremendous viscosity, and swimming was difficult. She felt like a fish trapped in an oil slick.

Still underwater, Santha saw the dark patches of the cremation rafts, now over her head. As she passed one, an object suddenly fell from the raft's edge and began to drift down into her path. A charred foot entered her line of vision and, following that, the remains of a head. The empty sockets of the blackened skull stared back. Santha Wrench opened her mouth to scream, and the Ganga roared in....

"No!" Santha shouted at the bedroom wall. Then she gaped at the column of hand prints. A long, long time she gaped, until her mind collected every cubic centimeter of familiar and welcome stimuli. Yet she couldn't quite believe she was back. The Ganga River was still around, she was sure. It waited and churned and carried its floating funeral pyres somewhere nearby.

"No! No! No! FUCKINGGODDAMMIT NO!" she shouted again.

The phone was ringing.

Santha Wrench tried to catch the churning Ganga again, but this time it was gone. Truly gone.

"You're not real," Santha said aloud, with determination.

The phone rang and rang.

Santha Wrench rose from where she'd sat throughout this, on the bed, and looked at herself in the bureau mirror. Frowning at her reflection, she advised it, "You're quite a phenomenon, girl. Don't you forget it!"

But then everything about the strange woman returned. It was as if remembering were like a dike weakening, with countless breaks on its surface, and finally giving way with the arrested memory cascading in....

I BETTER TELL SOMEBODY!

Her lower lip was bruised. A small triangle of dried blood showed there, in the mirror. Santha opened her mouth, the scream rose again....

(NO!) Firmly, like the knuckles of a fist kneading her fear down.

(Tell no one, child.)

"Get out of my head!" Santha commanded the reflection.

(Obey.)

"GET OUT OF MY FUCKING HEAD!"

(OBEY!)

The reflection darkened. Santha stared at her skin. She was dressed only in a half slip.

The face in the mirror was black.

(OBEY!)

"YES, YES, I WILL! PLEASE STOP!"

(TELL NO ONE!)

"I WON'T! PLEASE. I PROMISE! PLEASE DON'T!"

The reflection cleared.

Santha Wrench examined her body—her face, her arms, her back, the exposed part of her legs and feet. She cupped each breast, examined the nipples, even. She slid out of her slip and panties and continued to explore. She breathed in, wiped the sweat from herself with the slip. Santha breathed in again. Nothing had changed.

The phone had stopped ringing.

Santha went to the window, pulled the curtains aside. The snowfall had ended. Santha recalled the pyres, shuddered as she saw them superimposed on the drifts. The afternoon sunlight filtered through the scene. Santha turned, fell back on the bed.

She should have listened to George, she thought. When he had driven her back from the Peabody, he had insisted that she rest at his place. That way she wouldn't have been alone.

But suddenly I couldn't talk about anything, she reminded herself. It was like being gagged. I couldn't even tell him about that creepy Elvira Moniz threatening to lock me in the safe this morning. I could only argue that I had to be alone, here. He finally gave in, though I know he hated himself for it.

Being Indian is very important. India is where everything began. Everything. But still I must tell no one. It seems sacrilegious to tell anyone. These events can't be hallucinations. They belong to me, are part of my secret life.

The phone rang again. Santha hesitated, then pulled the receiver to her ear. "Hello."

"George here."

Santha sat up again.

"Santha, you okay? I've been calling and calling."

"Yes. Yes, George. I was sleeping."

"I've been thinking—I could cancel our dinner date with Kurt Leinster if you don't feel up to it."

"Kurt?"

"Yes, Kurt. Don't you remember?"

"Of course. Still waking up, I guess."

"Do you want me to cancel?"

"No . . . no, George. I think the diversion would be helpful."

"You're certain?" He didn't sound pleased.

"Very certain. George, don't start pressing again. A few hours' diversion from . . . everything would be fine. Might be fun."

He was silent for a moment. "Think you can make it here by six?"

"Six? Yes, of course. Why do you ask?"

"Well, you sound so . . . so tired."

"I told you—I'm just coming out from under." Santha thought of the sepia murk of the dream Ganga, the slowly falling head . . . and shivered.

TWENTY-TWO

When Wrench and Shastri left the entryway on Boylston Street, they turned onto Massachusetts Avenue. Shastri suggested they eat lunch. Wrench, still unbalanced, reluctantly agreed.

Rama Shastri ordered a tenderloin with baked potato. Wrench settled for a salad and a bottle of Löwenbrau Dark, but most of the time he watched Rama eat. Conversation was minimal; both were oversaturated with the Thuggee subject. At times, though, feeling an especially sharp pain in his neck or shoulder blades, Wrench grunted, cursed "the bitch thing."

It wasn't until the meal's end that Stephen Wrench blurted out how much he missed Kamala. It was the most he'd said about her since Shastri had arrived in Boston. The little man nodded, and for once they reminisced. Neither could explain why they did, except that their need for pleasant, warm memories was strong. Even the pain that her loss evoked was somehow sweet. The normalcy of it all settled them.

Stephen Wrench was looking briefly at the handful of patrons when his eyes shadowed. "Sonovabitch has some fucking cheek," he suddenly barked. The rage in his voice made Shastri turn his head.

Chundra Bala and Bidhan were at the entrance.

"They're looking for us, Ram! How did they know . . . ?"

"She knows. Her astral body, or something like that, followed us."

Wrench slipped his Browning .38 from his coat pocket into his waistband.

Rama Shastri placed his hands on the table, interlocked his fingers, and willed them to be still as Chundra Bala came to the corner of the restaurant where they sat. Das's prone body on a temple floor flickered across Shastri's view like a movie scene caught in the projector. Over, over again . . . Das on the floor, Das dead, over again, Das calling Shastri's name, then prone. Das . . .

Bidhan took a chair from an empty table, and Bala sat. Bidhan stood at his right, his arms crossed over his chest.

The waitress came over, asked Bala if he wanted anything. No, the Thug replied. He wouldn't be here long.

"Give him tea," Wrench told her. "Anything for your friend?"

Bidhan didn't stir.

"No tea, please," Bala countered then.

"Tea," Wrench stressed, and, in the best British Raj tone he could summon, "Com'on, old man. You must have tea."

Bala tried a smile, but his eyes froze with hatred. He finally sighed. "All right," he said. "Tea."

When the waitress left, he said, "I have no fondness for these commercial teas served in most American restaurants."

"Really," Shastri said affably. "I quite agree."

Chundra Bala placed his elbows on the table. "I've been directed to you," he announced.

Shastri fiddled with a Sher Bidi. "Of course."

"Aren't you surprised that I'm here? Can you imagine how I found you?"

Wrench and Shastri were silent.

"You weren't tailed here," Bala told them. "Isn't that the American slang for it? 'Tailed'?" He giggled. "Droll word."

The waitress brought the tea. Bala stared at it.

"Drink it," Wrench said.

Bala left the tea alone. "You are a policeman," he told Wrench.

"My, aren't we all so very wise."

"I pray so. It is that very wisdom that I've been directed to appeal to. Since we already know each other, we can begin."

"What's your buddy's name? And you ought to drink your tea."

"Please stop this charade about the tea. My companion is Bidhan. He is very strong. He strengthened his arms by lifting the shafts of bullock carts in India. He refrains from speaking, since his English is very poor." He turned to Shastri. "Rama Shastri, you are very silent this afternoon."

When he received no answer, Bala continued, "You know of the Panjika? The astrological almanac? I trust you do. I trust, then, you will understand this meaning." Bala directed himself to Wrench. "Shani, the dreaded Saturn, the evil of evils, malevolent of malevolents, is astride his vulture. As his two serpents kiss, the time has come when Life and the Infinite have embraced. You two gentlemen are fortunate to be told this thing before all others, in order that you won't become victims of the plague that smothers the breath. The plague is inevitable. Nothing can stop it."

Rama Shastri steadied the flickering film. Das settled into a one-shot of him prone, dissolved, and Chundra Bala replaced him. The Thug wore a gray topcoat over an old gray flannel suit that looked a size too large. His tie was broad, a garish yellow with fading red stripes. Food stains were on the tie and the white shirt with its frayed collar.

Rama Shastri said in Hindi, "Where is she? Your wife?"

Chundra Bala gazed momentarily at Bidhan. The giant was dressed in a brown coat with huge brown wooden buttons. A checkered scarf was around his throat. Bidhan smiled slightly at his guru.

Bala wanted to know, "Why do you ask?"

"You are both but puppets of the woman," Shastri answered in a steady voice. "There is no Shani. But there is a malevolent vulture—your woman. We would prefer to speak with her at this time. We prefer the vulture to the rat that but scurries at her command."

The Thug flushed. In the same tongue he snarled, "I have seen that which would so shatter your heart with fear, Rama Shastri, that surely you would die in your tracks. I have seen this and lived!"

"Oh? Tell us of this, then."

"I was the one who went to the Cave of the Rishis with my great Lord. I! Not my wife. I saw and..." He slapped his chest. "It is recorded here. I am Chosen among the rest. I am present here among you, since I am the one who was with *Him* at the Roof of the World."

Shastri shook his head. "I can't believe that, Chundra Bala. Believing that is as false as believing in Shani, the dreaded Saturn. If you are so highly placed in the eyes of this great Lord you speak of, then why are you acting as but a mere messenger? I can't concede to your boast. Agreed, Steve?"

"Agreed," Wrench repeated in Hindi.

Bala rose in his chair but settled back again, his elbows thumping against the wood. His rage left his eyes as, in a whisper filled with cunning, he fought back. "This is more of the deceit that made you so famous in India."

"You recognize, then, a Deceiver?" Rama Shastri had used *toog* for deceiver. "Your boasting about the Roof of the World, the Cave of the Rishis, and being a guru among men: that is a fine deception, I admit. I recognize you as a great liar, Chundra Bala, but not a great guru. Gurus, great or small, do not lie."

Later, Rama Shastri concluded that Bala broke because of the presence of Bidhan. Shastri had purposefully taunted him in the language that Bidhan understood.

Chundra Bala hovered on his elbows, his face close to Shastri's.

"Remember," he warned, his words like drops of acid burning, smoking away Shastri's control, "remember the Temple of Satī months ago. When I led you and your spy—this Das, was it?—among the throngs that awaited my Lord. Recall how they obeyed me, how they parted at my command. Wasn't that the sign of a leader, a great teacher, a most high and trusted guru? Remember that morning, and let your mockery die, Rama Shastri. Heed the proof of that morning."

Rama Shastri needed no prompting. Das sprawled on the temple floor again as he reached.

Shastri grabbed Bala's garish yellow and red tie. With his other hand he slipped the knot back, flush against Bala's throat, and yanked the tie stem. Chundra Bala gurgled, and his chin fell forward, spilling the cup of tea. Shastri tightened the knot more and curled its ends around his fingers.

Wrench was sitting with one of his legs jutting into the aisle, in case he had to rise to his feet suddenly. But he hadn't been prepared for Shastri to make the first move. Stunned, he still got up in time to stop Bidhan from interfering. He placed himself partially behind the big Thug and put his .38 in the small of Bidhan's back.

"*Sanp!* [Snake!]" he said in Ramasi, recalling the guttural commands.

Rama Shastri was also muttering commands. He'd loosened the tie momentarily and told Bidhan, without taking his eyes off his victim, "Be still, or I'll change this tie into a rumel."

Bala's eyes were like lumps of white porcelain streaked with bloodshot. Spittle hung from his lower lip and trailed like spider's silk to the tablecloth. Rama Shastri was saying, "See, I do remember. I see Das, dead by your hand, even now. And note, too, how I have learned the ways of the Deceivers!" He then slipped the knot back again.

Wrench, whose broad back provided a sight barrier to the rest in the restaurant, began to worry. "That's enough, Ram," he warned. Chundra Bala's ruddiness had shifted with alarming speed to sickly blue. His cheeks darkened with strain, and sweat riveted from his forehead down onto the sides of his bulging neck. A bloodless ring of mottled white and red skin had formed around the silk.

"Ram, ferchrissakes, that's enough!" Wrench reached out to pull Shastri's hands from the knot. Chundra Bala had dropped his head. He'd worked madly to raise his hands, but Shastri had pulled him so close to the table that the Thug's hands were trapped beneath it. The table was bolted to the floor, and it was impossible to tip it over. The futile effort had exhausted his air supply.

Rama Shastri let go just before the waitress arrived, concerned about the strange noises she'd heard. Before she could inquire, Wrench pointed to Bala, who was holding his throat and gasping in rapid little screeches.

"He's having an asthma attack," Wrench told her.

Bidhan had lifted Chundra Bala to his feet. Bala kept shaking his head, trying to talk but surrendering to one fit of coughing after another. His look commanded Bidhan to do nothing.

The manager emerged. Wrench quickly ushered the two Thugs toward the exit. "He'll be all right," he said to the anxious manager as they passed him. At the door, Wrench advised, "Get your ass away from here fast," then replaced the gun in his waistband. Walking back to the table, he noted the many faces turned his way, wondering.

Stephen Wrench quickly paid the bill, leaving a large tip for the waitress, and he and Rama Shastri hurried out onto Massachusetts Avenue. "You had me worried for a minute," Wrench confessed to Shastri, his voice filled with admiration. "You put the shoe on the other foot. Bala never dreamed you'd play at Thuggee, too. Good work, old friend."

"Was it?" Shastri asked, turning sullen.

Wrench thought hard for a while. "Well, it was better than nothing."

"That's settling for less, Steve."

"Don't break the spell, Ram. My morale hasn't been too good after that encounter with . . ." Wrench concentrated on his pipe. Tobacco spilled from a leather pouch into the crusted bowl. "With her," he finally added.

"She wasn't there. She sent Bala instead, and that ox. She was demonstrating how easily they could find us if they needed to." Shastri ground each word that followed, filled with utter revulsion. "Chundra Bala was right. We weren't tailed. I'm certain, Steve, that no one followed us. I kept checking all the way."

Rama Shastri shook off the weariness that gripped him. "She knows too much, too easily, and it's got us both settling for less. Yes, it felt good to strangle him for a while. But I'm convinced we're being played with, Steve. And she is taking her own bloody time, playing with us until she decides it's the proper moment to pounce and send us along the heavenly road all Thug victims are supposed to go to."

They arrived at Pinckney Street in a blue funk. And at 6 P.M. Dan Terranova phoned.

TWENTY-THREE

Santha awoke at 4 P.M. in good spirits. She bounded from the bed, humming the "Village Green Preservation Society" song from one of her Kinks albums and ended up singing the words while she showered. She had decided to wear her best winter dress—the red one with the silk top. She would wear boots but carry her sexy flats.

Her tongue unconsciously wetting her bruised lip, Santha selected her jewelry. The pearl necklace, the solid gold rings, the zircon earrings—all her valuable Indian jewelry—she ignored. What was safe to wear in India certainly wasn't in Boston, her father had warned her years ago. She wore, instead, a multicolored bangri, or glass necklace. She wore two bracelets on her right wrist: one of silver alloy with British and Indian coins along its surface, none of them valuable, and one of coral with dangling mother-of-pearl curlicues. In India she'd worn four bracelets, but once in America, Kamala had insisted she use two. Four were "too Indian."

Wetting her lip again, Santha surveyed her jewelry. There were those wonderful gold earrings.

Before they came to America, Kamala had had them made for Santha. They were visiting Kamala's cousin, who taught both Greek and Bengali literature at Calcutta University, when her mother insisted they go to a small village along the surrounding watercourses. There, among the bamboo and vast swampland, they visited a sonar, or goldsmith, who was heralded throughout Bengal as the greatest of his kind. Using only crude tools and a miniature bellows, he fashioned the earrings from the gold Kamala gave him. They were long, ending at Santha's jawline. Paper-thin and heavily filigreed, each earring consisted of two separate strips hanging from a chain no longer than a quarter inch. Whenever she moved her head, the strips would meet and make a slight tinkling sound.

"I'll wear them," Santha decided. Two sturdy young men ought to be able to protect her from thieves this night.

Tall, black-bearded kesari. Tall, gray-haired Kurt Leinster.

Dressed, she checked the clock. Five-fifteen. Why not go to George's now? She took her white winter coat from the closet. And the hat, which was a white, fluffy crescent.

Santha suddenly decided that she had to tell her father and Uncle Ram about the attempted theft of the scroll fragment. They've got to know, she told herself firmly and went to the phone.

NO! The shock was tremendous. NO! Santha gasped and held her temples. Numbing cold shot from the back of her neck down her spine, and her hand hovered above the receiver as if paralyzed.

"I won't, I promise," she pleaded aloud. "Please stop. Please." The pain eased slowly. God, I'm possessed; I must be, she thought. Something's inside me; Something's living inside me. The pain left and was replaced by a euphoria so strong that Santha had difficulty believing that anything wrong had happened.

She looked at her watch and left.

Beacon Hill was alive with sidewalk shovelers. A woman and a man were hauling ski equipment into the back of a Volkswagen bus. She passed the Episcopal church she sometimes attended. It stood only across the street, but somehow the distance seemed much farther. The wind-chill factor made her wish for Calcutta before monsoon season; walk half a football field and everything, including toes, drips sweat. No, on second thought, not Calcutta.

As she neared Otis Place, the wind chill swept up from Storrow Drive and the river. Santha turned her back to it, struggling for air. No weather for a self-respecting . . .

Indian? Goddammit, Santha, you're Stephen Wrench's daughter, too! She rushed into the courtyard and rang George's bell.

He opened the door and held her tightly.

"Tea, George, please," Santha pleaded when he finally released her.

"English breakfast or Russian Caravan?"

"The Russian, and please hurry. And put a nice dollop of honey in." She took off her coat and settled on the sofa. "George?" she called.

From the kitchen: "Yes."

"Let's light a fire tonight, when we're alone again."

A minute later: "George, did you hear me?"

"Yeah. Sure, Santha." He reentered the living room and placed the tea tray on a low table next to Santha's elbow. He spoke with a mock British accent. "Tea is served, mum."

Santha sipped, sighed. "This part of Boston has to be the coldest place in the world."

"Yes, it is. I wish my words had frozen solid before Kurt heard my 'Yes, we'll go tonight.'" George worked at his tie. "It's too unbelievably cold to go anywhere, that's all. Staying home, you and me alone here, and a fire . . . That would've been the reasonable, the sensible thing to do." He looked at her. "Beautiful as ever."

"Thank you."

"How's your father? Still feeling better?"

"Uh-huh. He and Uncle Ram seem to be busy with something. Daddy's going to be all right from now on. Was Kurt supposed to have been here by now?"

George nodded. "Probably searching for the rarest of the rare—a Beacon Hill parking space. Don't worry; he'll show."

"Not worried. Hungry. Very."

She took some crackers and cheese he'd set out. She was relaxed, relieved she wasn't alone.

The doorbell rang at six-twelve.

"The bell," Santha called to George, who'd gone back into the kitchen.

"Let him in, Santha, could you?"

Opening the door, Santha was caught in an updraft of cold air that scattered her hair. Hands raised, she was attempting to control it when her eyes focused on Kurt Leinster, watching her, his expression rapt. Embarrassed, Santha blurted, "Please, come in."

He did, and Santha struggled with the door.

"Some wind," Kurt said with a smile. Santha nodded and offered her hand. He held it for an instant. Santha repeated, "Yes, some wind," looking at his eyes again. Her voice was even when she offered to take his coat.

"Oh no," interrupted George, emerging from the hall. "We should go. If we stay here, we'll never want to leave. Sorry, can't fix you a drink, Kurt. The warmth in here's too intoxicating. We'll never go out then."

"Intoxicating's a good word." Kurt turned to Santha. Then he said, "George always mixed a good drink. Does he still?"

"Yes," Santha said, but all she could think of was what she'd seen in the doorway. That look, so intense. She was George's, and Santha wanted Kurt to know that from the start. She gave him a frosty smile.

Since Kurt had parked as far away as Joy Street, they decided to take George's car.

"Where to, Kurt?"

"How about Grendel's Den?"

"Grendel's Den," Santha said reflexively . . . remembering.

"Would you prefer someplace else?"

"No, George. That's fine with me."

Would it happen again? she wondered, remembering the episode in the ladies' room.

* * *

Santha Wrench wasn't doing well. The more she tried to be pleasant, the worse it got. Finally, in resignation, she stopped trying and lapsed into silence.

She resented the amount of time George and Kurt spent on their old Harvard days. They had a right to reminisce, but not to make her feel ignored, left out. Santha wanted attention. She had never ever wanted it so much before. And if she couldn't get it any other way, she'd get it through silence, by just sitting and poking at her food and peering at them with that *loud* silence that had worked so well when she was little.

What's the matter, Santha? Daddy used to ask.

He'd been home only a short while from one of his mystery trips—it might've been only to another part of New Delhi, where they lived then, for all she knew—and been with Kamala a great deal of the time. But not with her.

What's the matter, dear?

He'd come home with many gifts for both of them, but the new chudders, the new dolls, the other playthings weren't enough.

Santha? Santha, are you listening, dear?

Suddenly, then, Daddy would smile with understanding and pick her up with those wondrously big hands and place her on his knees and whisper all sorts of "I missed you very much, little sweet" sayings in her ear and stroke her long, kinky mesh of hair and ask her whether she'd missed him, to which she'd nod, and tell her how pretty she was in her pale blue and white sari and how he would take her to the Old Delhi Jam House or to see the horse show outside Red Fort or the fountain in Connaught Circus or the International Dolls Museum on Bahadur Shah Zafar Marg.

And Santha would finally smile, secure that she'd not been forgotten, secure that she was loved. . . .

George had stared at her from time to time, grasped, she was certain, what was wrong; but, perhaps since he was obviously piqued at her attitude, he'd not reacted. But no matter. It was Kurt Leinster who nibbled.

"Are you bored, Santha? It's rude of George and me to rehash all that old-school-days nonsense, isn't it?"

Santha replied kindly, "You haven't seen each other for some time. It's to be expected."

Dammit, George, she thought then, stop watching me like a hawk; I won't be offensive anymore. Promise.

She smiled at both of them. "Absolutely charming," she said.

"What is?" Kurt asked.

"The evening," Santha replied quickly, startled at herself. She glanced around. "I'm definitely with the two best-looking men in the place."

Kurt raised his glass. "To the most attractive woman."

Santha eyed George and looked away.

"Where did you travel, Kurt?" she asked.

"Europe. Was in Paris for half a year. Then Italy, Sweden, Norway, Denmark, even Germany. I stayed near Elsinore Castle. Wanted to drink in some local Hamlet color. My new book is called *The Hamlet Papers*."

"In a sense, Kurt is a Renaissance man, Santha," George was saying. "He's dabbled in archaeology, too, haven't you, Kurt? Been at a dig or two. Then he fooled around in oils. Very Hieronymus Bosch, with his own special version of heaven and hell. Still have those, Kurt? They were certainly original."

"They're not especially good. And you know that, George. George is convinced that I can jump easily from one hoop to the other."

"Can't you?" George turned to Santha.

"My paintings aren't very good, Santha. That's the truth of it."

"Maybe you're too modest. Why don't you let others determine—"

"I already have. Nobody's moved by them. The truth is I'm a dilettante," Kurt confessed. "Restless, easily bored with whatever I undertake. I can't seem to commit myself to anything."

Santha said, "Maybe you just haven't found yourself yet."

Stunned, she heard George state, "Well, you've won Santha over, Kurt. She usually has little sympathy for people who can't figure out what they want."

The music had changed drastically. Sitar; Santha heard a sitar. "Well, there's a switch."

Now tabla drums. Finally voices, male, female, chanting. "Sonovabitch!"

"What's wrong, Santha?"

She evaded George's touch, was already out of her seat and crossing the room. The closer she got to the music's source, the clearer were the words:

Kali Yuga! Kali Yuga!
Kunkali! Kunkali!
Kali Yuga! Kali Yuga!
Kunkali! Kunkali!

The chant droned on and on.

"What is that?" she demanded from a leggy blonde who was the hostess.

"What?" The woman backed slightly. Santha had hurled the question at her.

"The music."

The woman hailed a passing waiter. "Duane, you put that on. Isn't that what they chant in the thing you belong to?"

"Yeah," he replied, turning to Santha. "You're from India, aren't you? I saw you sitting there and thought you'd like it."

"I don't. Turn it off. I insist."

"Why?"

"Duane," the woman ordered, "Lotte Lenya. Play Lotte Lenya."

"Do you know what the words mean?" asked Santha.

"Sure," Duane told her calmly. "The Kali Yuga is one of the Hindu Ages of Creation. First there was a Golden Age, and we're living now in the Kali Yuga, the Iron Age—a kind of Dark Age."

"Aren't you a smart fellow. And Kunkali? You know what that means?"

"Yes."

"Duane, the customer wants the damn thing stopped." The

woman sighed and went behind a shelf of potted plants. The chant broke off.

"What group is that?" Santha pressed.

"The Kali Akali."

"And you're a member?"

"That's right. What's wrong with that?"

"Everything," Santha cried and, noticing the stares from everybody, left. Lotte Lenya singing of Mack the Knife in German followed her to her seat.

"What happened?" George ventured after a moment.

"That chant," Santha growled. "They were chanting to Kunkali."

"Kunkali?" Kurt repeated. "I know who Kali is. But the rest . . ."

"Kunkali means Man-Eater, the worst aspect of the Goddess Kali, the aspect that is connected with the spilling of blood, with destruction. She's sometimes represented as quaffing drafts of blood from men and demons. I know it appears silly, but it startled . . . irritated me silly to hear that chant . . . here. Tonight."

"Why be ashamed of it?" Kurt offered. "You're part Indian, aren't you?"

Santha tensed. "Yes, I am."

"Then why be ashamed? I've never been to India, though I've often considered going. You know—rupees and annas, rajahs, and riding a howdah on an elephant."

Santha laughed. "Tourist mentality. I'm afraid that isn't India anymore. India has naye paise now—new money based on the decimal system. The rupee is now split into one hundred paise, though the poor people still use cowries, or shell coins. As for rajahs, there are very few left. Some are in exile, some have lost their titles, their lands and palaces. But you might find an occasional howdah placed atop some poor elephant for tourists with romantic fantasies."

"Ah, did you have to do that? It's like taking the jinn out of *The Arabian Nights*."

"We're off on a tangent," said George, who was strongly interested in Santha's recent anger.

"As for me," Kurt was saying, "I'm a devout atheist. Gods,

goddesses, or a supreme intelligence are as unreal to me as Winnie-the-Pooh or the Grinch. Nevertheless, I deeply respect conditioning. Kali's name and what she connotes must linger in your memory from childhood. Are you a Hindu?"

"No, I'm a Christian, an Episcopalian, like my father. My mother, Kamala, remained—or, rather, returned to Hinduism, you might say. She preferred meditation, the belief in a Path, to accepting Christian dogma. She believed that Christ had traveled to India in his formative years and was an accomplished guru, avatar, something like that. But she also believed in Rama Krishna and many of the other great Indian mystics. She thought they were equal to Christ."

"How long were you in India?" Kurt asked.

"I was in India until I was eleven, when Washington recalled my father to the States. He worked in D.C. awhile and is now a consultant to the FBI in certain kinds of cases, and we moved to Boston."

"Eleven years is more than long enough for impressions to stick with you."

"I'm an American, Kurt."

"Right . . . But your roots are over there. Do you ever miss it?"

Santha saw then that George was watching them both. She shook her head, thinking, He's jealous, I know it.

"I'm tired of this place," she announced. "Let's go somewhere else."

"Okay," Kurt agreed, but with disappointment in his voice.

"Where?" asked George.

"Anywhere. How about the Blue Parrot?" she suggested. While Kurt paid the bill, Santha squeezed George's hand. "Love you," she said softly.

"I love *you*."

Santha nodded, pleased. No more talk about India, she told herself. I know, she plotted, I'll get George to discuss his painting. I'll get George to take over the conversation. Maybe I'll even let them rap about those old Ivy League days again . . . as long as the subject's away from India.

George Buchan was moving toward the exit. Santha followed, while Kurt trailed behind her. Then the temptation to turn, to look at him, was too strong to resist. Santha did. She saw, "I need you," like hot, very hot fire dancing in the blue mist.

TWENTY-FOUR

The Yoga Center was a two-story building off Kenmore Square with a mural painted on the southwest side. Facing the parking lot, it was brightly lit by a miniature arc of lights that splayed on its bright pinks, golds, and blues. They signified other-worldliness and rapture. The picture showed a giant-sized Mai Yogini dressed in a dazzling roseate and blue robe, extending her arms lovingly to a group of disciples much smaller in scale. They, too, wore robes of pale blue with white trim. Behind Mai Yogini were streamers of gold. The streamers also poured from her hands onto the faces of the group, while they stared at her.

Rama Shastri squinted through the drizzle at the mural. Stephen Wrench and Lieutenant Terranova in turn looked from the painting to Shastri and back to the painting again, but Shastri walked on. Wrench shrugged and said to Terranova, "He's had a hard day."

Indeed, Shastri's mood verged on the surly. Perhaps he and Steve should have followed Bala from the steak house, some-how, Shastri thought. Perhaps they would have encountered Bala's woman again. Perhaps in the ensuing struggle they might have won.

But Rama Shastri didn't truly believe that. He, Indian's greatest kotwal, was playing but a child's shadow game upon a wall. Even to destroy Chundra Bala was an ineffective act: in Bala's thinking, a noble martyr's end. No, Shastri wanted the Thug to see the worst of things before his death. The end of his Meaning and Dream, of his Huzoor Master, of Thuggee, of . . .

Her?

Of Her, Mother Kali. Was it truly She?

And if so, just how and where could Mother Kali be defeated? What on earth could ever combat Her?

After Dan Terranova had called, he'd arrived at the Pinckney Street apartment, at Stephen Wrench's invitation, and suggested they go with him to the center. "There just might be some clue to what we're searching for," the detective had offered. "Mai Yogini's place attracts every Eastern-thought flaky around Boston. And tonight there's a special benefit. They just announced it on the radio: Nirmal Kapur, the rock star, will be performing. A one-man show with guitar, Indian instruments, and a synthesizer. That'll bring even more of the mind-bent out from their lairs."

Wrench had remarked that he'd seen Kapur perform once and thought it "interesting." So they had convinced Rama Shastri to join them, despite his doubts.

As the three men crossed the parking lot, a dark cloud heaved beyond the windswept drizzle spray.

As Terranova had predicted, the motley had come: first, Mai Yogini's faithful; then the rock music lovers and the special following that was Kapur's alone; and finally, those who hated the music but who'd heard that Kapur's guru-swami was there: the name of Hanuman cast its own spell.

A young cop took out his frustration on a group of picketers. "You're clogging up the road! Com'on, move on!" he bellowed at a tall, lean man in a crew cut and belted raincoat. Simon Ark, the leader of the group, stepped away from the young couple he'd been speaking to. In one hand he held a stack of blue-and-gold-covered books, each titled *The Redeemed Host.* Slung across his other shoulder was a strap attached to a portable cassette recorder. A taped voice blared a message at full volume, similar to the wording on the picket signs: THERE IS BUT ONE GOD AND HE IS JESUS CHRIST, THE REDEEMER. BEWARE THE ANTI-CHRIST FROM INDIA! MAI YOGINI IS THE WOMAN OF BABYLON AS PROPHESIED IN REVELATION.

Sahib Khan, across the way, asked Elvira Moniz, "Explain to me this occurrence."

"These Redeemed Hosts are unaccepted Christians," she said.

"Is a Christian not a Christian?"

"There are various groups. They disagree on dogma sometimes. These are considered to be fanatics by the many other Christians."

"And this Woman of Babylon?"

"She is a symbolic whore in the Book of Revelation of the Christian Bible."

"But it speaks of Mai Yogini as such," he snickered. "There is nothing symbolic about her whoredom, I wager."

Akmed and Ayub, the other two Muslim Thugs, laughed.

Sahib Khan, Akmed, and Ayub started to cross the road. When they reached the edge of the mob, Sahib noticed that Elvira was missing. He turned to see her talking with Simon Ark. When she was with them again, he asked, "What did you do, Yoni?"

"He gave me this booklet," Elvira replied, staring evenly into Sahib Khan's eyes. "It tells where their church is and when they have services."

He frowned. "You seek to join them?"

"I've joined nothing," she reassured them. But Elvira explained no further, and Sahib Khan stared at her with increasing distrust. By Kali's girdle, must she accompany them in this most sacred of tasks to be done tonight? She seeks to dominate, he concluded, and he was sick of the sight of her already. Her stretched olive skin over high cheekbones, her long, thick black braids slung over the shoulders of her threadbare coat, the dark smear of moustache above her upper lip—none of this appealed to Sahib Khan, who missed sorely the curvaceous young bride he'd left in Assam State months ago. Besides, this Yoni, this Elvira Moniz, had the stink of the unwashed. Even the other women of the Kali Akali complained of it.

Ayub grabbed Sahib Khan's burnous and tugged hard. "Rama Shastri! Ahead of us—see!"

Sahib Khan looked. By the burnished glow of Fatima's eyes,

by the brow of Allah's favorite jinn, by the perfumed gardens of the sacred houris, it was Rama Shastri!

"The Swami Hanuman first," interrupted Elvira. "The Swami was the chosen one for now."

Akmed wet his lips. "Perhaps the Goddess has given us two for one."

"Or more," Ayub agreed. "Rama Shastri has two others with him."

While their lives were being discussed, Shastri, Wrench, and Lieutenant Terranova were directed to their seats. Wishing to be placed near the stage, Terranova had finally revealed who he was to another policeman. The result was a trio of seats in the fourth row. The three men stared at the stage altar with its mural, a smaller facsimile of the wall outside.

Shastri then watched the assorted mix of people. Apparently the gathering was buoyed by the need to herd socially as well as to fill a spiritual gap. The din was deafening. Some of the more rowdy were shouting at each other across the room, while the better-behaved gathered in clusters and talked and talked.

When the houselights flickered their warning, the din settled, first into a low rumble, then to almost total silence. From the wings to the left, Mai Yogini appeared, and the audience drew in its breath. Beneath her blue and roseate robe, her body was contoured in near-transparent silk sheathing. Standing before the microphone, she raised her arms. Shastri looked around. They awaited her words eagerly, men and women both. He closed his eyes, seeking her secret with detachment. But he had to look at her again, since that was where the secret lay; the only place. The whole of her reminded Shastri of the soft, round, moist nestling places of a woman's body. Mai Yogini's power was of the womb.

Her voice broke through the resistance of the amplified mike.

"Greetings," Mai Yogini began, with her perfect diction. "This is a very special occasion. Nirmal Kapur, the composer and musician, has agreed to perform for our center. Since we desire to grant him all the time possible, we will do without our usual readings and have only our period of meditation."

She paused. Then casually: "And oh, yes—before we begin, permit me to announce that we have a very welcome visitor here: the Swami Hanuman."

The spotlight shifted from her into the second row. A small Indian in a blue turban was trapped in the beam. His face was expressionless. "Hanuman," Shastri repeated softly.

"Who is he, Ram?" Stephen Wrench asked.

"Hanuman!" Shastri repeated. "Swami Hanuman is here!"

Before Shastri could explain, Mai Yogini went to a marigold-bedecked dais, sat on a cushion, and stated that the meditation period would begin. The hall hushed. Eyes closed; faces became rapt, gradually; mouth lines lost their tension.

And Dan Terranova thought, as he lost himself in the hazy grayness of his closed lids, how beautiful this Mai Yogini was. He could still envision her pendant earrings sparkling from the arc lights and her dark, lustrous eyes. The kohl shadow around them promised maddening nights of drifting hours in a deep pool.

Hanuman attracted Shastri like a hypnotist's tool. Unable to see the little Swami after the houselights had dimmed, Shastri stared at the spot and thought. Again the Prime Movers were hard at it, redesigning, reshuffling the fates and stars. If the embodiment of absolute evil in Kali were present now within this myth called Life, then, too, the opposition must be around. And Shastri had, long ago in India, heard about the one who called himself Hanuman.

He then saw a silhouette rise and leave its aisle seat. Swami Hanuman was heading toward the back of the hall. Shastri whispered to Wrench, "I'll return shortly." He heard instead the traces of a snore. Shastri smiled, decided against awakening his friend, and eased himself from his seat and across the feet of the other meditators in the row.

In the rear of the hall, Shastri found there was standing room only. A wing of the building, directly head, was open to allow for the many who were content to drink in the atmosphere, so to speak, without viewing the stage. Mostly they were the music lovers, sitting or standing against the walls, awaiting the first strains of Nirmal's compositions. So they buzzed among themselves in heightened expectancy as the time drew near.

Shastri saw Hanuman pass between them, follow a corridor to its end, and, turning into another, disappear. He pushed against the wall of bodies in pursuit and entered the corridor.

Behind, Elvira Moniz watched and trailed. Where the corridor curved, she nearly collided with a policeman and then veered into an abrupt turning, with the pretense of heading for the ladies' room. But she passed that door and went on toward the dressing area.

Sahib Khan chuckled at her hesitation. He, Ayub, and Akmed had boldly passed the policeman and continued along Rama Shastri's route.

Restless, bored, Mai Yogini's chauffeur watched the Yogini from the wings, then exited to the parking lot for a smoke. Fredrico had lingered about eight minutes, his face raised to the drizzle like a man parched for water. The sight of the Yogini on the dais had been excruciating, haunting, and he couldn't understand how Nirmal had been able to forget her.

He had just gone into the building again, his chauffeur cap dripping, when he saw Elvira Moniz near Mai Yogini's dressing room and said, "Sorry. Nobody's allowed back here."

Smiling, Elvira replied, "I was looking for the ladies' room."

Fredrico caught the invitation in her eyes, ignored it, gave her directions. Humming inwardly with the life-quick fire that Gauri Bala had shared at the ashram, Elvira lingered. Her hands were hot and swollen with power.

Fredrico turned his head downwind. Elvira's hands rose, the rumel tightly gripped.

Rama Shastri reached the stairwell nearly at the instant that Fredrico died. The stairs led to the basement, and his mind spun with the question, Why had Swami Hanuman gone down there? He made the turn and descended. He paused before the basement door, looked through the thick window glass, saw a meshing of shadows. Shastri turned the knob. The door whished open. He walked into the dark, massive basement room. The door whished closed.

Through the ceiling came the reverberation of drums, the sustained *blaaaah* of an amplified guitar. The room was stuffy; heat steamed profusely from the surrounding pipes. Far to his left a boiler coughed and rumbled. The area was lighted by a single ceiling bulb, exposing part of a storage bin with the jutting legs and arms of furniture. The grayish outline of a stepladder stood at his side like a lonely sentinel at the area's fringe. Shastri passed it.

The dense cellar air became electrified.

Something snapped with shocking speed, whipped at his face. Simultaneously a foot kicked him in the ribs with tremendous force. Shastri fell, a silken web covering his throat for half a breath. He landed on his shoulder, wrenched the Walther .32 from his waistband, and fired. The *blam* rebounded from the walls and slapped his eardrums. But Shastri managed to hear a deep groan as he saw Ayub collapse in the gun's flash.

Shastri rose. He realized he had been followed through the cellar stride for stride. Yet he hadn't heard the stealthy cat's tread behind him. Not once. The hackles at the back of his neck tingled.

Apparently a pair of legs had kicked him free just as the now dead Thug had lowered his rumel. Fortunately, he'd recognized the feel of the silken scarf and fired.

But now the second assassin, the Arm Holder, no doubt poised to assist the Strangler, had been seized. Shastri saw Hanuman clinging to the ladder sides, his short legs, stiff and extended, some five feet from the ground, wrapped around the Arm Holder's throat. Tighter and tighter Hanuman squeezed with his small legs, while the Thug hammered at his calves and thighs. The strength and balance of the Swami never faltered. Once or twice the ladder wobbled precariously, only to settle again.

Rama Shastri watched Akmed's arms fall to his sides. As Hanuman released him, the unconscious Thug slumped to the floor.

Sahib Khan burst from the darkness, descended first to the

dead Ayub's side, then up again in a direct charge at Shastri. The Walther fired again but missed.

Tears streaming down his gaunt face at the thought that both his brothers were dead, Sahib Khan summoned the courage to dart between Rama Shastri and Swami Hanuman to pluck their rumels from the bodies. Then, with even wilder speed, he raced for the cellar door. Shastri fired again, heard the ricochets as the bullet careened off plaster and brick, and cursed the room's bad lighting. The door closed as he neared it. When he reached the stairwell, it was empty.

Upon returning, Shastri found Hanuman seated on the rungs of the ladder, watching Akmed vomit at his feet.

"Thank you," Shastri said.

Hanuman told him, "I would not have you take the noose that was originally intended for me this night."

Sahib Khan waited on the street corner, gasping from his run the three blocks to the rendezvous place. Tears of rage and pain blurred his vision, but at last he spotted Elvira Moniz. Her black braids bounced as she hurried to him. But she saw the kill lust in his smoldering glare, slowed, and kept her distance.

"They are dead, my Thug brothers," he rasped.

"Dead? Ayub? Akmed?"

"None other, thou dung stink! Thou filth of the pig!" he told her in Parsi.

"I'm sorry," Elvira replied. "I can't understand you. Speak in Ramasi, please."

"Where were you?" Sahib Khan bellowed. His rumel danced between his fingers.

Elvira backed again. "I killed one. The chauffeur of Mai Yogini."

"The chauffeur! . . . Foolish whore! The Yogini is one of us!"

"He wasn't!"

In Parsi again: "Thou stinkest of swine's piss. It seeps from thy pores."

"Who killed Ayub and Akmed?"

Sahib Khan spat. "Rama Shastri and the Monkey, both."

"How?"

"One with a bullet. The Monkey used his legs."

"His legs? How?"

"This was neither kismet nor karma," he barked. "Allah would've saved them had you been there."

Elvira suddenly raged. "I killed well! The Goddess transformed these hands and gave me a might even you have never known! I tell you, Kali is appeased. Now let us go."

Go, Sahib Khan thought. Would that they'd never come to this accursed land where women wielded the rumel, too. Would that this strange Huzoor had never been.

"It was Kali's will," Elvira pronounced.

Perhaps, thought the Thug. But I shall tell our Huzoor Lord, in case thou art wrong, thou wretched dung creature. Then, mayhap, Mother Kali will be appeased twice.

TWENTY-FIVE

Sitting among the hot ash and sulfuric stench
    of the Evil of the day thereof,
I've dreamed that my beloved was a witch
    filled with the licking spitting flames
And we made our love
    Writhing, writhing on the hot eternal magma
Like blackened naked devils at play in Hell.

Santha placed the book down on the quilt. No—the poem didn't work, she decided. Kurt Leinster was no significant poet. But those preoccupations, those constant references to fire in most of the poems. What caused them?

The little volume was called *Twelve Illusions*. A commonplace title. But Kurt had taken the book from his glove compartment and autographed it with the following remark: "To

Santha Wrench. The Thirteenth Illusion." What ever did he mean by that?

Santha Wrench put the book atop her bed table and nestled farther beneath the blankets. Outside, the rain, driven by a newly emergent wind, battered the windows. George Buchan, she told herself, was the real thing. He could really draw and paint; he had a sense of form, of technique. Kurt Leinster was a fraud who wrote ridiculous, sensationalistic images and fragments—actually, nonpoems.

She wondered what the big thing was about. Why, Kurt wasn't a Renaissance man, as George believed. He was only another dabbling dilettante, enthused one minute about poetry, then archaeology, then music, then oils, then novels, and so on and on. Dabble, dabble, dabble. Nothing fixed, no unswerving commitment. Nothing permanent.

She hadn't been able to refuse the book, though. They had returned to Beacon Hill early, and, when George had let Kurt off at his Porsche, Kurt had told them to wait a minute and had reappeared with the book.

When they were alone again, George had asked Santha if she'd had a good time.

"A little bit of Kurt goes a long way, George."

He had said nothing in return. Santha had sensed that he was pleased. Kurt had been too openly attracted to her for George to be otherwise.

George had then asked if she wanted to stay at Otis Place again. Santha had replied no.

"I wish you would, darling. I worry when you're alone."

She had insisted he take her to Lime Street.

Parked before her building: "Santha, I hate leaving you alone. . . . I worry. . . ."

"I'll be all right." Then she'd tried to soothe him. "I've been thinking. . . . Please contact that therapist tomorrow, George. Make an appointment for me as soon as possible."

It had worked. He had been convinced she was sincere. But had she been? Santha wasn't sure. She only knew that she was afraid that if she stayed at George's place, she might change again. She couldn't endure seeing that look of horror and repulsion on his face a second time.

But was she really telling the truth about the therapist? Santha turned on her side, reached to turn off her reading lamp. She was too tired to think anymore.

The phone rang. She sighed—that must be Daddy wondering why I didn't return the cylinder to him this evening.

"Hello."

"Santha, this is Kurt Leinster."

"Kurt?" she repeated. Then, angrily: "How did you get my phone number?"

"You're in the phone book."

"Do you know what time it is?"

"According to my Patek, eleven twenty-seven."

"Listen, I can't talk now. I have to be at work by nine in the morning."

"I'm sorry to bother you. I just wondered if you'd looked at my book yet."

"A little. But this isn't the time to discuss it. Now—"

"Santha, I have to say this. Please bear with me."

"Okay, say it, but afterward I'm going to hang up."

"I never had a more wonderful time."

"Fine. I'm glad for you. Now, good night."

"Santha, I think you're the most beautiful and interesting woman I ever met."

"I think you ought to stop right there, Kurt. Don't say any more."

"I had to say it, that's all."

"I'm going to hang up now, Kurt."

"I'm looking forward to seeing you again."

"Maybe someday. Good night, Kurt." Santha hung up.

She lay in the darkness thinking, The creep. Calling this late. I sensed something wrong with him from the beginning. Why must George be so lenient about creeps like that? Well, I suppose psychiatrists are used to all kinds.

Still, she found herself wondering about the poetry—"the Evil of the day thereof." Was Lucifer also preoccupied with that same lost fire?

Sleep was coming fast. Her mind was toying with strange concepts to while away the minutes before sleep. Just imagine, she thought, what it was like before the world had electric lights. When the very black night descended. A night without a moon.

Santha heard another ringing. At first she groped for the phone, then realized it was the doorbell. She rose, put on her robe, left the bedroom, and switched on the hall light. She swiftly crossed the semidarkness of the living room to the window. Peering out between the blinds, she saw her father and Rama Shastri.

Santha opened the door and let them in. She turned on a table lamp and faced them. They seemed harried, strained.

Nobody had said a word. Worried, Santha asked, "What is it, Daddy?"

Neither of the men sat. Wrench asked, "Have you got the cylinder, Santha?"

For a brief instant, she almost told the truth. "I forgot, Daddy. It slipped my mind. It was so stormy today that I was concerned about getting home without being caught in it. I just forgot about everything else." She smiled at them. "Would you like tea?"

"No. It's too late to stay. . . . Santha, you've got to return that cylinder by nightfall tomorrow. It's urgent. I can't stress enough how urgent."

"What's happened?"

"We've had a hard day," Shastri stated. He had been silent, thawing out from the cold, but now he seemed to come alive. "At first we intended to tell you as little as possible about our recent activities. But we've decided otherwise, since tonight."

"Then something did happen. And it was something pretty bad, wasn't it?"

Wrench nodded. "We went to a concert. I heard Nirmal Kapur perform again. He was at Mai Yogini's Yoga Center. Ever hear of the place?"

"Yes. Don't you remember how upset Mother was when she read about it? She said Mai Yogini ought to be deported to India for teaching such tripe."

Wrench wasn't listening. "A man was murdered there. Strangled, Santha. With a Thug rumel."

"Murdered? Why?"

"We don't know. But we do know it was Thuggee."

"Which means Thuggee is here in America," Shastri added.

Wrench cleared his throat. "Ram also had to kill a man. An Indian. A Thug, Santha, the genuine article. The police know that Ram did it. He used my gun. He was protecting his life, but I'll still have to pull strings like hell in Washington to get him out of this. My friend Dan Terranova of the Boston police is covering for Ram at the moment, but he won't be able to do that for long."

"You can't let Uncle Ram get deported, Daddy."

Shastri cut in. "Our first concern is your safety, Santha. The cylinder that I sent your father contains something the Thugs want. That fragment is so priceless to them that we've decided we can't possibly leave it in a place that close to your person. These fanatics will go to any length to get it back, you see."

Wrench stared keenly at his daughter. "Santha, I want you to promise me you'll be very careful from now on. Even after you return the cylinder to us."

Santha wet her lips. "You mean they might try to get at you through me. How careful are *you* going to be, Daddy? They've already tried to kill Uncle Ram."

"Don't worry about me, Santha."

"That's a totally inane statement, Daddy."

Wrench didn't respond.

"Daddy, you will be careful, too, won't you?"

"I will. I . . . Santha, there's something else."

Santha waited. A long wait. She thought he'd never speak.

"What do you think about the supernatural?" he asked suddenly. "I mean, do you think it exists? What about Christ, for example? Did He rise from the dead? You're an Episcopalian like me, Santha. The Episcopal Church believes in the Resurrection. You must've thought about it."

"Not for quite a while. But Mother and I discussed it. She believed in it. She said that there were Indian saints who had been resurrected, too."

"I'm glad she discussed it with you, Santha. She evolved something entirely of her own over the years. Something that wasn't really Christianity or Hinduism or Buddhism but, instead, a creed that included something from all three."

He groped for his pipe. "And your mother had a certain psychic sense about things. I remember instances . . . Like the time that I got shot up in Pakistan. You were too young to remember. At the very moment, your mother collapsed in a faint. She was at a garden party at your grandfather's house in Delhi, so there were many witnesses. When she came to, she told them that I'd been wounded."

"She never spoke of such gifts, Daddy."

"You may have inherited her talent. Tell me," he pressed, "have you sensed anything lately? A presence, good or evil? Why did you just do that?"

"Do what?"

"Tug at your neckline."

Santha's eyes turned to Shastri, appealing. But he, too, was staring at her.

"No reason. . . ." She gestured at the dark hall behind them. "Keep this up, and I'll be checking under my bed."

"This isn't a joke, Santha!"

"I know, Daddy. Don't be angry."

"You don't know. There is something . . . unusual. . . . I've seen it."

"Is it something evil—what you saw?"

Wrench bit hard on his pipe, took it from his mouth, and frowned at it. Then, "Yes, it's evil. Very evil. . . . Damn, but it's way over our heads, Santha, Ram's and mine. So, if you sense even the smallest thing, the barest sign of a . . . presence, a supernatural force . . . a power, please tell us right away. Do you understand me?"

"I think so. Yes, I do. . . ."

He looked at his watch. "You'd best get to bed, dear. But don't forget the cylinder tomorrow."

Alone again, Santha felt the taut strings pulling her will. She recalled that just when she had determined to tell her father and Shastri, she had grown numb, her will to speak gone. I am watched, she told herself, as I've been from the beginning of this dreadful thing, and unless it is found out, I'm doomed.

As if in reply, the wind grew steadily until it seemed it would explode. For a second, she thought the window glass would shatter. It is a Thing, she thought, climbing back into bed. Was it after her?

Tell George, she told herself. Tell him and stop the wind now, Santha urged, bunching her fists hard against her stomach. If you can't tell Daddy, tell George. Shit on this Thing. But she couldn't move. In time, Santha fell asleep.

TWENTY-SIX

Chundra Bala walked down the cinnabar carpet. He could hear the Huzoor raging on the dais and wondered why. Prone before the throne were Sahib Khan and Yoni-Elvira Moniz. Gauri and the rest of the Brotherhood looked on.

"Allah has forsaken us!" wailed Sahib Khan.

The Huzoor silenced him with a raised hand and stared at Gauri.

"The scroll must be whole," Gauri said. "We must recover the piece that Rama Shastri tore free. Kali Mother has discovered its hiding place. We must do our part and recover it."

The Huzoor listened but then pointed. "You, Sahib Khan, and you, Yoni, have failed, and it was your wills, not Kali Mother's, that made it so."

Elvira Moniz collapsed to her knees and burrowed her forehead into the floor. "My Lord, I am unworthy."

"Stupid hypocrite! Unworthy!" The Huzoor stood and spat on her head. "Where is your pride, daughter of Kunkali? I spit again on you. Until you rise once more as a proud wielder of the rumel, I will spit. Neither I nor my Mother will ever hearken to such Christ-like humility. We are not of his world. Or isn't that clear to you yet?"

"I did kill tonight," Elvira replied, in a muffled but firm voice.

"Yes, you killed. But not the devil you were supposed to kill. Not that monkey-faced meddler with Kali's aims. Oh no! Instead, you killed Mai Yogini's chauffeur! Why? Answer me!"

Elvira peered up at him. "He was there, my Lord. My hands grew strong. Fire pulsed through my fingers, and I was directed. I had to kill the man Fredrico, my Lord."

The Huzoor was silent.

"You were directed," he repeated at last. "Your hands swelled, grew hot? Fierce and hot and demanding that you wield the rumel?"

"My Lord, take my life freely if I lie."

The Huzoor paced. "Stand, Yoni," he finally commanded, in a more even tone. He turned to Duane Longstreet. "Go now to Mai Yogini's center. Explain to her that Yoni was directed to kill Fredrico. If she protests, tell her I have said it was so. If she protests too long, say that I have vowed by my Mother that I will repay the loss in full. It was destiny that Fredrico die tonight, but only because, in some cursed manner, another destiny was swerved from its course. Tell her that I will add to her wealth or give her more power in the Akali." He smiled thinly. "Even over Yoni, if the Yogini wishes. I will grant everything but the Yogini's freedom. Tell her that. Go now and, oh yes, you are to replace Fredrico temporarily."

Duane Longstreet scurried away.

Suddenly Chundra heard a groan. Gauri, he noted, was very pale and near-faint. "My Lord," he implored, "my wife!"

"Be seated," the Huzoor told Gauri kindly. He clapped his hands. One of the Akali women appeared. "Bring the Mother wine, quickly."

The Huzoor then turned to Sahib Khan. "Well?" he growled.

"I offer thee my life, too, O King of us all."

"Speak in Ramasi."

"Take my life, O Glorious Seed of Fatima."

The Huzoor laughed. It wasn't pleasant.

"Listen, brothers. Have you ever heard a craftier tongue? Flattery. Flattery. King of us all, Seed of Fatima. I ought to choke you with pigs' entrails, Sahib Khan."

The Muslim flushed angrily.

"And to think that Rama Shastri was there, too."

"Rama Shastri also!" blurted Chundra Bala.

"Yes, Shastri shot and killed Ayub. Correct, Sahib Khan?"

"Lord, I tell no lie. See Ayub's blood on my sleeve."

"And what happened to Akmed?"

"Hanuman choked him with his legs."

"Hear, Chundra. With his small legs this Hanuman choked Akmed. Have you ever heard of such a thing? Does it not shame every Thug since time immemorial? Indeed, this Hanuman has discovered a greater and more deadly rumel—his small legs. Are we not all ashamed, my brothers?"

A murmur from the Brotherhood, filled with pain, disgust.

The Huzoor towered, his long legs spread apart, the squatting Sahib Khan between them. He closed his knees until they neared the Thug's throat. "By Kali's girdle, I ought to try this new technique of the Swami's." He hovered, then pulled away.

Sahib Khan swallowed, ventured, "If the woman hadn't left us, perhaps . . . She was another rumel. Perhaps then we would've succeeded."

"And who controlled Yoni? Who was her guru tonight?"

"I was."

"I can control Yoni, Sahib Khan. Why can't you?"

"Because she respects and obeys you, my Lord. The same is not so when I give her a command."

The Huzoor lunged and gripped Sahib Khan's throat. The Thug's face reddened, his eyes expanded. The Huzoor let him go and flung him from the dais. Sahib Khan rolled, striving desperately to breathe.

"Then demand Yoni's respect, by God, or next time I will take thy life in the most painful manner I can imagine!" The Huzoor continued in Ramasi, since only the Brotherhood should understand. "It is because of thy great name, of the saintliness of thy ancestors, that I spare thee, Sahib Khan. Thou wert chiefly responsible for what happened tonight. Yes, two enemies might have died, and this worrisome time been ended. Fail again and, I warn thee, take thy own life quickly, or else I shall stuff thy manhood in thy mouth. Now it is over, so rise and join thy brothers. It is forgotten. Nay, say no more, lest I change my mind. My wrath is still strong."

When the Huzoor returned to his throne, Chundra Bala came forth. He spoke in low tones that only the Huzoor heard. "I advise now as one who traveled great heights with you and a holy man, months ago. I advise as the one your Mother manifested to while you suckled at Her breast. Take care of my Son, She commanded."

The Huzoor nodded.

"Then hear me now, my Lord. Our morale is low. My wife ails much from her ordeal; the men flick their yellow scarfs in the night hours in their frustration. Soon we must kill. And we must kill many, or else this strange land, this alien place, will consume our faith. Send us forth in service to the Goddess now. Hesitate no more. Seek to kill Rama Shastri and the Swami, true, but strengthen our Cause as well with many other deaths."

The Huzoor touched Chundra's shoulder and said warmly, "Wise and loyal Brother, noble-hearted Chundra, I hear you well." He produced a brochure from beneath his robes. "The woman Yoni has shown me this. It is a congregation. Pilgrims break bread with them and sing before the night fires, as it sometimes was in older days, when Thugs did join pilgrim ranks. You know the old stories. Then did they strike. Many in that manner did they kill."

"Aieeee," agreed Chundra Bala. "Spoken and planned like a true Deceiver."

"And it shall be done as well, I vow. We will maintain the old traditions. But three things must be done."

He rose and announced, "Brothers, we must see to the burials of Akmed and Ayub. We must take the bodies from the police."

Chundra Bala marveled. From the police! Yes, that would boost morale.

"My second plan is that one of us must infiltrate the ranks of our foes: the one who has become Kali's sustenance."

Chundra understood the wisdom of this, that it might work.

"But the foremost thing to be done is to make the scroll of Kali Mother whole again. For only then can we succeed," continued the Huzoor. "This before all deeds must we do."

Gauri faced them all then. "This the Mother told me must come to be. The scroll must be whole again because the scroll is the life of us all."

TWENTY-SEVEN

Captain Charles Adair walked with confident, ambling strides toward the interrogation room. He'd primed himself all morning for this. Ever since he'd read last night's report on the trouble at the Yoga Center, he'd known the time had come at last to settle his score with Rama Shastri and that big-mouth government man Wrench. Shastri had used Wrench's gun, which was registered to Big-Mouth. It couldn't be better. The last thing this country needed was smart-assed, brown-skinned cops from India taking over—especially one who had tried to strangle him, the little fucker!

He thought of the prisoner. Adair had walked over to the Tombs especially to see the Indian. The prisoner hadn't said a word, not even his name, since he'd been arrested, the report stated. And he was just as silent when Adair arrived. But at least Adair had a chance to explain to his jailers just what the killing was *really* about. Opium smuggling, that was it. Or hash, or maybe even heroin. Akmed had been dealing with Fredrico, and somewhere the greaser had double-crossed him. So the Indian snuffed Fredrico out. These Indians were good at that strangling shit. What else could you expect from a bunch of dung burners? The jailers had laughed at that one. Yeah, Adair had reiterated, he'd read that they burned cow shit for fuel in India. Imagine being invited over for supper with that shit stink everywhere in the kitchen. The Tombs' guards had laughed again.

And that attack on Swami Hanuman? The Swami claimed the Indians had been after him and not Shastri. Well, that figured in, too, if Adair could only prove it. Another phony mystic type, with a rock star disciple who'd once been an around-the-clock junkie. It was obvious as hell what that meant. The Swami was connected somehow. Maybe his place was used as a pickup spot for the junk. Christ, it was so clear, he was almost shocked that the narc boys hadn't caught onto it by now.

So that was more than enough to expose Wrench and Shastri for the fucking dummies they were. So much for that crazy stuff they'd told him about a Thug cult.

Captain Adair felt so elated he released a ripsnorter. The fart was loud, as fierce as he'd hoped it to be. Elinore Carter, one of the new patrol car team-ups, stopped in her tracks en route to Fingerprints and glared at Adair. He moved on, snick-ering.

In the interrogation room, Adair found Shastri, Wrench, and a funny-looking Indian in a turban, all in a huddle. Then Adair spotted Nirmal Kapur sitting on a chair tilted against the opposite wall. "Who the hell are you?" he demanded.

"I'm Nirmal Kapur—disciple and loyal friend to Swami Hanuman."

"Well, get your loyal ass outa here," growled Adair. "You were playing on the stage last night, and that clears you from any connection—at least, so far—with what happened in the basement. So get."

Nirmal shrugged at his Master and rose.

Adair walked slowly to the front of the room and threw the morning report onto a desk. From one of the drawers he pulled out a cassette recorder and sat down. Then he glowered at the three men. Rama Shastri was smoking a Sher Bidi, and the smoke wafted in a thin, wriggling line across the room. Stephen Wrench was blowing his nose, and the Swami seemed preoc-cupied with the window. Captain Adair turned to the window, saw nothing but the hint of sunshine filtering through from outside, and grunted. He shifted back to his original position, spoke softly into the recorder, giving the date, place, time of day, who he was, and what the interrogation was about. He raised the volume to its peak, placed the recorder a little away from him on the desk, and motioned that the men move their chairs closer. They did, surprisingly compliant, he thought. Well, they were resigned, it was coming. The bloody ax. They knew he was going to cut their goddamn balls off.

Adair cleared his throat. "Now, I want a detailed account of the entire fight in the cellar last night. I expect the entire story. Am I clear?"

Nods. Quiet affirmations.

Adair grinned evilly and, as he turned to Rama Shastri, said, "You first. What were you doing in the basement of the Mai Yogini Yoga Center?"

Rama Shastri told his story. When he mentioned that Dan Terranova had suggested they go to the center, Adair reddened. Then he decided, Here's where I get our local Smart-Ass, too. What business did Dan Terranova have including these two in his investigations? They were nothing but has-beens now, a pair of old farts. The word "fart" nearly pushed Adair into a fit of laughter. The look on Elinore Carter's face. Jeez, what a moment!

When Shastri finished, Adair turned to Hanuman. "Now you."

Hanuman began. Suddenly Adair interrupted: "Why did you go downstairs?"

"I knew that the Thugs were there to kill me."

"You did? Why? You're just some kind of teacher, aren't you?"

"Yes. But I am a great threat to them. I had already been attacked by Bhowani. . . . I'm sorry, I suppose you'd be more familiar with the name Kali than Bhowani."

Adair shut the recorder off. "Look, buddy. Let's stick to facts, shall we?"

"But that is a fact," Hanuman replied. "One night after another concert of Nirmal's, on Beacon Hill, Kali manifested in a raging inferno. She chose that form, you understand, and Nirmal and I, who were in an alley behind the concert hall, were nearly consumed in flames. That was when I was certain she had chosen America."

Adair stiffened. He turned the recoreder on. "Repeat that."

"I was at a concert on Beacon Hill. One of Nirmal's—"

"No. Not that. The very last sentence."

Hanuman paused to remember. "Oh yes. I said I was certain after the fire that Kali had chosen America."

Captain Adair stiffened again. "Chosen America? Why?"

"For the renewal of Thuggee."

"What's that mean? Exactly?"

"She—Kali, that is—would send her Thugs to America."

"What for?"

"To find new disciples. To find victims."

"What victims? Americans?"

"Mostly. Sometimes it might be a visitor or two to America. It would depend on who was available at the moment."

"But chiefly fellow Americans, you say."

"Yes."

"Tell me, Mr. Hanuman—by the way, that isn't your only name, is it?"

"My former name was Narayan Rana. It is still on my visa."

"I would hope so. And on your birth record in India, too. Is it?"

"It is. But the name is no longer important."

"Oh, I see. No longer important." Adair felt that to ask why would lead him into a quagmire. "Tell me, Swami—now, please answer this carefully: Would you say that these Thugs were . . . are sort of invading America?"

"Yes. In a manner of speaking."

"There's no other manner of speaking about an invasion of America, Swami!" Adair barked. Now he had something new, unexpected, more than the drug thing after all: a possible Indian plot to terrorize American society. No, it couldn't be just Indian. He asked, "Are all these Thugs Indians?"

"The ones from India, yes."

"No other nation?"

"Jesus save us!" exclaimed Stephen Wrench.

Adair pointed a warning finger. "I'm not talking to you!"

Wrench turned to Hanuman. "He means, Swami Hanuman, are there any Russians involved? Communists. KGB. Swami, humor him, will you? Tell him that Kali is the code name for the Kremlin's top agent."

Adair shut the recorder off again. "Listen, Wrench. You too, Shastri. All of you!" he shouted. "I've got you guys by the balls, and I'm going to squeeze plenty, see! You." He thrust a finger at Wrench. "Because you gave Shastri your gun to carry! And you"—this time at Rama Shastri—"because you killed a man with it. It's against the law to carry a gun without a license. And to kill someone with it is even worse."

"Even in self-defense?"

"That remains to be proved."

"It will be."

"Wrench, you've been sucked in by these Indians, that's what. There's drugs behind all this. Ever hear of the Golden Triangle? Well, these Thugs aren't Thugs at all but Golden Triangle people smuggling opium, hash, you name it, into the country. And I'm betting my bottom dollar they tried to waste the Swami here like they did Fredrico Gonzales because he's involved. And I'm going to prove it, Wrench."

Captain Adair towered over them, set to say more, when he saw that someone else had entered the room. He recognized the police commissioner's right hand, Mel Hughes. Hughes signaled to Adair and then went into the hall. Adair followed, his stomach grinding again. What the hell was Mel doing down here?

Once outside, Adair closed the door and waited.

"I'm getting worried about you, Charlie," Mel said, in a sad but friendly voice. "All that shouting and finger pointing. It's exhausting, isn't it?"

Adair started to answer. Hughes held up a hand. "Let me finish, Charlie. We want you to drop this thing right now. Please, Charlie—I'm not through. The commissioner got a phone call from Washington this morning. The whole mess has international implications, Charlie. International. Out of our jurisdiction. Seems this feller, Steve Wrench, has mighty big connections. And that Indian cop isn't exactly a slouch, either. He was top cop of the Far East in his day. Well, Washington's sending a man down. He's got such large chevrons that we can't honestly tell if he's FBI or CIA or something entirely new. But whatever he is, what this guy Horace Birch says goes. And he says we're to give those two birds in there all the help we can from now on. Not trouble, not flak. A helping hand, Charlie, understand?"

Captain Adair suddenly needed to fart again. If he only dared to. He managed to nod sourly.

"Look, why don't you take the rest of the day off, Charlie. You don't look too good. A lot of flu going around. This new strain's a doozy, they tell me. Hits you in the old exhaust pipe." Hughes turned, took a few steps, remembered something else, and added, "Oh yeah, one last thing. This Wrench guy requested that Lieutenant Terranova be assigned to him and Shastri. A sort of liaison man between him and us. Okay, Charlie?"

Adair stared, gave another nod. Then he farted.

Free of the burden of Captain Adair and his machinations, Wrench, Shastri, Hanuman, and Nirmal taxied to Pinckney Street. Dan Terranova was driving Mai Yogini—who had been interrogated in another room—to the Yoga Center and intended to join them later. When her lawyer had phoned headquarters that he was held up at court with another client, Mai Yogini turned to her new chauffeur to leave and immediately froze. Then she told Terranova that she couldn't adjust so quickly to someone else in the chauffeur's seat, so would Dan be so kind as to take her in his car? Dan Terranova was eagerly charitable. During the ride he had listened patiently to her volley of invectives against "that potato eater Adair" for his assault on her civil liberties and spiritual beliefs.

Dan Terranova, the policeman, learned little from the tirade but wondered much every time he saw the Yogini's limousine in the rearview mirror. What the hell was it about that new chauffeur that made the Yogini freeze? Difficult to believe that the runt had anything to do with Thuggee.

Meanwhile, in the taxi rushing to Wrench's apartment, Rama Shastri thought about Swami Hanuman. He had invited him to join them. There was hope at last, he felt.

Hanuman's reputation as India's greatest contemporary mystic was so widespread that Shastri doubted there was a seeking, thinking soul in the Far East who didn't recognize the name. Despite Shastri's ingrained reluctance to believe in gurus and saints, he had followed the Swami's career with great interest years ago. Born Narayan Rana, he was of the ever warlike Rajput people the Gurkhas. He developed a strong, sturdy body in his youth in the mountains of Nepal. But he was an oddity, nevertheless, with his simian features and short, squat frame that held a suggestion of deformity. His appearance and ability to climb smooth-as-slate pinnacles soon gave him the nickname Hanuman.

Later, in World War II, Narayan Rana was an asset. He had scaled the highest and most dangerous of promontories, scouting the Japanese advance and even moving with ease through their lines. That was when Rama Shastri first heard of "Little Big Jaws," as the British affectionately called him.

After the Second World War, a new side of Narayan Rana filled the written accounts that appeared on Shastri's desk. Rana had switched his loyalties to a militaristic faction dedicated to the freedom of India. This saddened Shastri, who believed that the long-yearned-for release from the damnable British Raj could be achieved peacefully; and he dreaded the thought of hunting down this heroic figure like a common fanatical insurrectionist.

Fortunately, this never had to occur, for it was at this point that Narayan Rana's life shifted from factual history to legend—at least, to the agnostic Rama Shastri. Hiding in a Nepalese village, since he was suspected of having stolen arms and munitions from a British arsenal at Agra, Narayan encountered a guru called Vishnarma. Deeply moved, Rana forgot about his dreams of a liberated India and followed the saint. For three years the two men roamed the Indian countryside and discussed Vishnarma's new teaching. Then, at Multan, near the Thal Desert, on a bright morning filled with wondrous promise,

Vishnarma was shot fatally during a skirmish between Pakistanis and Indian locals.

Narayan Rana was shattered. For five years he wandered grief-stricken from the death of his beloved guru. Unable to endure it any longer, Rana chose to wander into the Ganga one dawn and move on until the sacred waters enveloped him. Out he went into the Hooghly part of the Ganga next to the Howrah Bridge in Calcutta. Then—and hundreds of observers maintained they saw it—a blue-limned figure appeared just as Rana sank beneath the waters. The shimmering blue man dove and reemerged from the river bottom with Rana in his arms and brought him ashore.

"Master Vishnarma!" Rana cried when he awoke and prostrated himself at the other's feet. The hundreds of awestruck onlookers claim that the guru-god said then, "I have taught you, Narayan Rana, all there is to know of cosmic law. Rise and live and teach and serve me, Narayan Rana, who are now the embodiment of the great Hanuman."

This was the legend that Rama Shastri had been told. Often he'd wondered where the reborn Narayan Rana had gone. Certainly Hanuman hadn't been seen in India in decades.

As the taxi pulled up on Pinckney Street, Shastri felt the old conflict again. A new part of his nature sought the aid of Hanuman. He saw again the eyes and strength of the bitch-thing manifesting through Gauri Bala, as vividly as if it were happening now. But the old ways died hard indeed. He thought that maybe it was Hanuman's old self, the heroic Gurkha warrior, not the legendary mystic, that spurred his faith in the man. No matter; with Hanuman around, Shastri somehow believed there was hope now.

"Steve and I need help in this," Shastri said. He had just finished telling Hanuman everything he knew about the revival of Thuggee to date. Then he asked, "Do you know why they tried to eliminate you last night? I gather you haven't been hot on their trail the way Steve and I have."

"Yes, I do know," the Swami replied. They were in Stephen Wrench's living room. The flat, dim lighting from the windows sallowed everybody, and each mouth was a grim smudge, until they looked like a group of sad, pale clowns with an overapplication of lipstick. "Months ago, while meditating, I witnessed the reopening of the Dark Portals."

"Dark Portals," Shastri repeated. Why couldn't everything remain nice and simple?

Hanuman, reading him, sought to clarify. "Think in Modern Age analogues, if you must. A great Force of Resistance, quantitatively speaking, a universe of ohm resistance against the life-force circuit. Or, instead, think of a mysterious black hole in space, a possible sucking vortex of contraterrene matter. Yes, that will do. Anything that contradicts natural law, natural order.

"It has been released before. In commonplace terms, this polarity from beyond the Dark Portals is called evil. Sometimes it's represented in the abstract as a negative spirit, always very powerful. Sometimes it's personified, the devil, or, in this instance, the black Goddess Kali, Bhowani, Kunkali—use whatever name you choose. A Force of Resistance that permeates almost everything and anything. Very few persons can fight its overwhelming power. Almost no one has succeeded in defeating it totally."

"So we're stuck with the world, the flesh, and the devil, Swami. So what's new?"

"What is new is that this resistance is so tremendous, so anti-life in the purest sense, that it stagnated, nullified itself. The devil, all the Dark Gods died, or at least became ineffective. Mankind became its own demon. Now it can obliterate this globe with nuclear devastation. Indeed, if the devil were still alive and strong, such an event would defeat his very purpose for existence. Total devastation means there are no more souls to tempt, to lure into his domain. The playground is gone and so are the players therein.

"Cosmic evil has been in stasis. Mankind continues to do bad, since the results, the philosophies, the instincts of evil still linger—which is exactly the problem. A dark god or goddess would force man to expand his spirit, fight for his soul again."

Rama Shastri became impatient. He complained, "You're

stating that the cosmos has reopened the portals to allow Kali to step forth and maintain the balance between good and evil."

"Yes, Kali is trying to regain her position on the cosmic scale. Now, if the rumor about these sacred rishis' scrolls is true, kinetic supernatural evil has reentered the world with them."

Wrench cut in. "And the Thugs are after you because you know all this?"

Hanuman nodded. "This Force from beyond the Dark Portals I felt during meditation, emanating from the East, from Mother India, and I soon grasped that it had chosen a body—Gauri Bala's human body—to work through. Later, after a concert of Nirmal's on Beacon Hill, I was attacked by the Force and realized that I was involved in the conflict."

"If this great power was in India, how could it reach you over here?"

"It travels in a dimension alien to what we are accustomed to, where time and space as we know them to be do not exist."

Nirmal Kapur, who had been quiet throughout the discussion, finally joined in. "Baba, maybe the Thugs figure you can find out how to deal with them better than anyone else. Like Mr. Wrench and Mr. Shastri said, they're only cops, after all. But you, Baba, are more than a man."

"My son, your wisdom is still that of a child. I, too, am very much a man."

Rama Shastri went beyond his skepticism. "I think what Nirmal is trying to say, Swami, is that you are more familiar with the paranormal than most. I am forced to agree with him. Hence this appeal for help. Steve and I have seen this demon-woman, Gauri Bala, in action. Can you help us?"

"My Master, Vishnarma, can, perhaps. I say perhaps. I repeat. I can promise nothing." He smiled at Wrench and Shastri. "Don't be so alarmed, my friends. You say you have a part of their sacred scroll. That is an advantage already."

"My daughter, Santha, will be bringing it to us this evening," Wrench told him.

"Then I will wait here for it. We shall see what more I can discover once it is in my hands."

TWENTY-EIGHT

It was snowing again. Santha's office was quiet enough, she thought, without the snow muffling everything even more. She felt very enclosed, almost trapped, and if it hadn't been for the cylinder, she wouldn't have made the effort to get to the museum. But this morning she had awakened with the conviction that she had to return the scroll fragment to her father and Rama Shastri. That, at least, she could do.

She might be in danger, her father had said. For a moment last night, Santha had tried to tell them about herself, but the Something in her had prevented it. Well, if she couldn't speak about these things, Santha was convinced that she could still act. Somehow, she knew that Whatever controlled her wasn't that strong yet.

Santha left the window, returned to her desk, and reexamined the prints from the *Akbarnama*, the book commissioned by Akbar the Great in the seventeenth century. The print she studied now showed Akbar designing and constructing his new capital city, Sikri. The Mogul Emperor had never learned to read, so the illustration was especially vivid, filled with figures working at every stage of construction.

A phone call interrupted her.

"Peabody Museum, Miss Wrench speaking."

It was George Buchan. "I can't pick you up until an hour later than usual. An emergency session with a patient. Maybe you should take a cab in this weather."

"I don't mind waiting, sweet. Besides, we might get snow-bound here. We can always cuddle up together beneath that tapestry in the hall of the young Krishna seducing a woman. It might prove inspiring."

"Bringing you home to my warm fireplace is inspiration

enough. You're not planning to spend another uneventful night at Lime Street, are you?"

Santha paused. Should she take the chance, could she rely on herself anymore, after the other morning?

"By the way," George cut in, "I made that appointment with Dr. Kitteridge for four-thirty tomorrow afternoon."

"Dr. Kitteridge?"

"Yes, Dr. Annette Kitteridge, a colleague of mine. Don't you remember?"

"Of course. I just didn't expect that it would be so soon."

"Well, she and I felt the sooner the better. You'll like her, darling, believe me."

Maybe I will at that, Santha thought suddenly. Maybe talking to a woman will be easier. Her spirits rose.

"Don't mind me, George. By tomorrow I ought to be looking forward to seeing her. . . . And I will stay over tonight."

He sounded tremendously relieved. "Fine! Then expect me by six-thirty, thereabouts."

"Drive carefully, sweet. And, darling"—Santha almost caressed the phone—"it will be so nice by the fire tonight. I just know it will."

When she hung up, she thought, Damn, I forgot to tell him I had to stop off at Daddy's first. Then she decided, I'll have George drop me off at Pinckney Street, and after I give Daddy the cylinder, I can walk over to Otis Place. It's only a block away, after all.

Besides, she imagined, it'll make his warm fire all the more inviting. I can come in covered with snow and start peeling off my wet clothes immediately. That ought to set the tone for the evening. Santha smiled inwardly, completely relaxed with her imaginings.

The clock ticked five-thirty. Santha collected the dozen prints of the *Akbarnama*, rose from her chair, and brought them to the safe. She opened it, walked in, placed the prints on a shelf, and turned to the spot where the cylinder rested. She took it and headed for the doorway. For an instant the chilling memory of Elvira Moniz barring her way out from the safe came to mind, and she rushed across the threshold into the office.

Do you realize, Santha, she asked herself while settling at the desk again, that you never reported that bitch to the authorities? What in the world is wrong with you? That Elvira Moniz might just have followed through on her threat to lock you in the safe! George is right, she concluded; I need to talk to this Dr. Kitteridge.

Santha fingered the cylinder unconsciously; then, noticing, recognized that she hated to part with it. That ancient piece of scroll with its smooth bark surface and early Brahmi script haunted her. Santha cherished anything so ancient and was intensely fascinated by the mention of the Mother of Dark Wrath.

Kali. Yes, Kali, and that definitely established a link between the scroll and Thuggee. But what were the contents of the entire scroll? Was it a mantra, an invocation? Whatever the scroll was used for, Santha sensed that it was every bit as sacred and important to the Thugs as the Shroud of Turin was to Catholics.

Santha opened the cylinder, anxious to look upon the fragment one last time. Her hands shook as she reached for it.

It happened again. It had occurred only once before, the first time she had touched the parchment. The dank, cavernous place reappeared. The scene burst upon her as if it were a creature that had bounded into her presence. With the same abruptness, a black face rose even with hers, and Santha stared into eyes that seemed to reach into her and pull her spirit from her body. Then the scene dissolved, was replaced by the office. Santha gasped for air and collapsed at her desk, unconscious.

Her head was on the desk blotter. Santha knew that much, but it had taken a long time to filter through the numbness she felt. Her eyes were open, her vision blurred. Santha could see the green of the blotter, little else. Above her were sounds, voices. Maybe her boss, Dr. Kim, had come into the office and found her like this, Santha thought.

But as the words became distinct, neither were they in Dr.

Kim's voice nor was the language distinguishable. There was the fading memory of eyes like talons, and the pressure that held her head down lessened.

When the paralysis finally left, Santha raised her head.

"Ah, you're with us at last," Elvira Moniz said. "I have a message for you from my Lord. He says: Be prepared; your time is soon. Now that we have this"—Elvira held up the cylinder in one hand, the parchment in the other—"nothing can stop us. Soon, my Lord says, your time will come."

"Give that back!" Santha cried out.

"Hurry, Yoni! There may be another guard in the building," she heard then from the doorway, and Santha stared at Sahib Khan. He looked back at her briefly, then turned and surveyed the hall.

"Go and check," Elvira replied.

Sahib Khan muttered a few words in Ramasi and disappeared.

Elvira Moniz placed the parchment within the container. "I regret I can't stay longer," she told Santha. "Some day things will be different, and you will command me. But until then, for a little while, I must oppose you. When your time has come, though, you will forgive me, since you'll understand everything. Then I will serve you willingly. Keep that in mind."

Santha stood and said calmly, "Can't you tell me more?" She started to move away from the desk.

"Only that you're chosen. From the other side of the world. Gauri Bala prayed and meditated for a new Vessel to replace her. The eyes of Kali see far. What is an ocean or thousands of miles to Her? She saw you, chose you, and that is your destiny."

"Gauri Bala? Vessel? Kali? I'm confused. Can't you explain further?" Santha edged closer.

Sympathetically the woman replied, "I know it's been painful for you, frightening, even. But that will end, you'll see. I must go."

Elvira Moniz was near the door. Without warning, Santha threw herself at her. Her shoulder hit Elvira's arm, and the cylinder fell to the floor. Santha's hand flailed out and caught

Elvira's neck. With a moan, the woman stumbled to her knees. Santha began to search for the cylinder.

It had rolled beneath the desk. Santha groped, found it. She was about to stand again, when fingers dug into the calf of her left leg and tugged at her. Santha slid backward across the floor. Elvira let go of the leg and started to climb onto Santha's back. Santha rolled over, slid her foot between Elvira's legs, and kicked hard. Elvira screamed and released her grip on Santha. Then, clutching the cylinder, Santha rushed into the hall.

It was empty. Santha moved as soundlessly as possible to a closet at her left, opened it, and grabbed her coat, purse, and boots. Swiftly she dressed, her eyes on her office doorway.

She could hear Elvira Moniz still moaning. Now Santha took her keys from her purse and moved carefully toward the office. When she looked in, she saw Elvira finally scrambling to her knees. Elvira's face was grotesque with pain. Her eyes met Santha's, and she uttered a shriek that Santha knew Sahib Khan would hear. Santha closed the door and locked it. As she fled along the hall, Elvira's hammering seemed to trail her.

Nearing the main stairs, Santha glanced at the clock. Ten past six. By now everybody except Security would be out of the building because of the storm. She wondered why the guards hadn't shown up, with all this ruckus. Then she had the chilling thought that they'd been disposed of.

Santha stopped in the shadows before the stairwell and listened. She detected a barely audible creak from the stairs and slowly backed until she brushed against the doorknob to the room with the India exhibit. Santha turned the knob gradually and went into the vast, darkened interior. She left the door slightly open and stared at Sahib Khan as he reached the top of the stairs. In his hands was a sash or unwound turban—she couldn't tell which in the dim lighting from the landing below. For a second, Sahib Khan looked in her direction, then continued to the corridor leading back to her office.

Santha closed the door and searched for a place to hide. If she could remain here until six-thirty, when George would arrive, then maybe he would summon help when she didn't show up. That might mean the capture of these Thugs before they could get the scroll fragment.

Santha heard shouts from the hall and tensed. There was Elvira's voice, then maybe Sahib Khan's, then another man's, then another's. How many Thugs were in the building?

She moved quickly. She remembered where everything in the exhibit was placed and had no difficulty finding what she wanted in the darkness. Here were the glass cases of raja clothing: high-collared coats of brocade buttoned with diamonds, robes of hand-woven silk covered with silver and gold, turbans tasseled with pearls at the tips. Another case of Kuṣāna, pre-Guptan, and Guptan coins. Two statues of Buddhistic bodhisattvas, with their androgynous shapes; and finally a gigantic bas-relief of Kartikeya riding on a peacock.

Santha went behind it. There she found some workmen's tools, a bundle of rags, and a stepladder braced against the wall.

The door to the room opened. Elvira Moniz and Sahib Khan were arguing. Their voices echoed, making them seem very close, and Santha gasped. She held the cylinder against her bosom. They mustn't take it from her. She sensed that her father and Rama Shastri were in grave danger if the Thugs regained it.

"I tell you," Elvira was saying, "you must find the door that leads into the Botanical Museum. She may have gone there."

"Send Trande," Sahib Khan replied. "I feel she is nearby."

Another male voice spoke in Hindi. "Do not offend her, Sahib Khan. The Huzoor heeds her words more than yours."

A curse, and Santha heard footsteps walking back into the hall.

"Now, Trande, Ramanuja—search this place."

"Shall we put on the light?"

"No. Someone outside the museum might see it. I will search the hall again. Hurry, now!"

Santha was hot in her outdoor gear. No matter—she'd stay here forever if she had to. The two men were moving across the room, rapidly, with no regard for noise. They were under pressure to find her quickly. Maybe they know George is coming, she thought. But how could they know? They always seemed to know anything personal, private about her. Was she responsible? Was her link with the unknown Something responsible?

One of them stopped before the bas-relief. Santha could hear his breathing on the other side. She looked around desperately and saw the tilted ladder that reached nearly to the ceiling. Santha put her foot on the first rung and started to climb. She went up almost in slow motion. She waited at a height where she could see the top of the stone slab.

There was a slight noise below her. The Thug had discovered the space behind the relief. He moved about, his hands touching things as he felt his way in the dark. His hands reached the ladder, and she felt herself about to topple as it moved a few inches. But the Thug released his hold and a moment later left the spot.

The one called Trande said, "She's not in here. Let us leave." They recrossed the room, the door shut.

Santha climbed down the ladder and leaned against the wall. It would be only a short time now before George would arrive. Once he didn't find her at the Oxford Street entrance, he'd summon the campus police. Then she would be safe, once again in his arms.

Someone laughed.

It was a low laugh, taunting, and it left a breath that Santha felt on her cheek.

Santha ran from her hiding place. She reached the room center, heard the clink of anklets and bangles somewhere behind her. She shouted, "No!" despite herself.

The room door burst open. One of the Thugs was outlined in the faint stairway lighting. He moved toward her. Santha swerved, rushed to a display of Indian musical instruments on a stand. There were a sarangi, a tambura, cymbals, gongs, tablas, and two magnificent sitars. Santha put the cylinder on the stand, grabbed one of the sitars, and hurtled it at the Indian. Swinging in a wide arc, she smashed the sitar into the Thug's face. She dropped the instrument, pain from the impact shooting through her arms. The discord of broken strings rang in her ears.

Turning back again, Santha sped to the stand, snatched the cylinder, and raced past the fallen Thug into the hallway. She heard no more laughter, no more clinking of anklets, but, in her mind, the sound still echoed.

She bounded down the stairs. She must go out the front door, find George. She had to be free of the museum and the presence within it that had laughed in her ear and breathed on her neck.

Surprisingly, no Thug stopped her in the lobby. Santha pushed open the front door and ran into the stormy night.

Her eyes tried to see through the onslaught on snow. She didn't dare remain at the entrance. She moved on across the lawn to the walk beside Hoffman Lab. She stopped at Oxford Street, looked left and right for George's car. It wasn't there. The street was empty of traffic. Wind gusted the snow into her face; her cheeks stung, her eyes watered, misting her vision.

Santha turned back and stared at the Peabody. No one had emerged from the museum. She couldn't understand it. Were they letting her get away so easily? She huddled against another snow blast. The hood of her coat was layered in white, and her eyebrows were edged with crystals. She stamped the snow free from her boots where it had stuck when she crossed the lawn.

The street was terribly silent. It seemed to be waiting with her.

"Where are you, George?" Santha said aloud. "Christ, where are you!"

Her eyes fell to the cylinder in her gloved hands. Maybe I won, she thought; maybe I showed them. She felt almost proud and wondered that she had escaped at all. It occurred to her that perhaps the Thugs hadn't tried their damnedest to stop her. If she was as special to them as Elvira Moniz had stated, they would have balked at the kind of violence that could hurt or kill her. The thought increased her uneasiness. She had definitely been allowed to escape this far. Oh, come on, George darling, come on!

The crunch of footsteps in the snow. To her right, where Oxford Street went past Conant Hall, there were figures approaching. Two men, she was certain. One was tall, big, the other short. If they were Harvard students, she could ask them to stay with her until George arrived.

Santha put her hand above her eyes, shielding them from the storm, and strained to see the faces of the newcomers. "Hello, you there," she called. They didn't reply but came closer. Santha saw through a break in the blinding onslaught that they didn't look like students. The two men passed through the glow of a streetlamp, and she knew for certain that they were Indians and that the face of the taller one resembled Makunda, who had followed her to Otis Place the other night.

With a cry, she ran. The wind's force was so tremendous that a few times she had to fight for balance on the slippery walk. Santha elected to run through the low drifts bordering the sidewalk. Although that slowed her pace, she had better traction and was able to move without the fear of falling. Once, twice she tooked back and saw that the two Thugs were also running. She was passing the Mallinckrodt Building, nearing the turn into Kirkland Street.

Santha dared another look back. Her breath caught in her throat. Behind the running men were the welcome headlights of an approaching automobile. Santha cleared the drift and, reaching the middle of the road, waved her arms. The headlights blinked off, on again, and the car's engine roared as it accelerated. It was George, she thought; it had to be him! And he'd seen that she was being chased.

But now her two pursuers had darted into the road as well. One of them, Makunda, was closing in with his long strides. Santha turned and, lowering her head, spurted toward the Science Center on her right. Then she suddenly swerved. Three more Indians next to the center were blocking her way.

Santha spun about. She was nearly in Makunda's reach. His eyes were fierce with determination to catch her. Behind him George's Audi roared toward the other pursuer. The Thug leaped away and landed in a drift. The Audi came on now after Mak-

unda, but it would take only a stretch of the big man's arm
and . . .

Santha slipped out of Makunda's path and headed onto Kirkland. Makunda swerved, too, and forced Santha to run to the
sidewalk and into the galleried porch of Memorial Hall.

Breathing hard, bent over, Santha went on into the porch's
darkness. She could still hear the roar of the Audi, but that
was all. The pound of Makunda's heavy footsteps was gone.
Santha slowed, wondering what was happening behind her.
Were they attacking George?

She strained. She couldn't hear the Audi anymore, either.
"George," she called.

A swift motion at her side, the weighted clunk of many
bangles. Santha suddenly faced the woman of her dream. The
woman's face was in shadow, but the scant lighting from Harvard Yard outlined her long hair and the circle of her nose ring.

"Child of Kunkali," the woman whispered. Her hand raised
and something sharp dug into Santha's forehead. Santha Wrench
screamed in pain and dropped the cylinder.

She stood against the wall, her arms across her face. Footsteps,
someone running to her, George calling her name. His hands
seized her wrists, pulled her arms down. Santha felt blood
trickling along the bridge of her nose.

George had the flashlight from his glove compartment. The
light blinded her. "Santha, my poor darling!" he exclaimed,
staring. He moved closer to examine the wound.

"Not now!" Santha pushed him back. "Quick, George—
search the porch. Look for a cylinder, a mailing cylinder. Quick,
before they come back."

The light's beam seemed to dance over the porch floor. "Try
there," she directed.

"Who were those men, Santha? Why were they—"

"Hurry, before they come back! Before the woman . . . Now,
try there. And there!"

"There's nothing." He tugged at her coat. "Darling, I've
got to get you to the hospital."

"Where are they, George? Where is she? That horrible

woman." Santha began to shudder. "She took it. She must've picked it up when it fell."

George urged her on. His arm around her, he forced her to walk. As they neared Kirkland Street, Santha stopped. "Maybe they're still out there, George. Maybe she's waiting!"

George picked her up. "I don't think so," he told her. "After you ran in here, they scattered. Never saw people disappear so fast."

"The woman—did you see her, George? She attacked me!" Santha sobbed out the words.

"No, I didn't see her."

As they left the porch, he soothed, "See, dear, they're gone."

Still in his arms like a child, Santha stared along the street. "The woman slipped by you, George. But she's watching us somewhere. I sense her. I sense her in the shadows."

They arrived at the Audi. George lowered her to her seat and attached her seat belt.

When he climbed into the car, George took his medical bag from the backseat. He started to examine her again. "The blood's stopped flowing," he said, dabbing at her with a strip of gauze.

"Please, not here. Take me away from here. Now! Please!" she begged.

"I'll get you to Emergency at Stillman Infirmary. You'll need a tetanus shot. That wound was inflicted by something metallic, probably a signet ring. We'll have to talk to the police, too."

Santha, huddled in her seat, opened her eyes. "No. No police!"

"We have to. You were attacked, Santha."

"Give Emergency some other explanation. I fell on the sidewalk, split my forehead, anything like that. It's Daddy and Ram you must tell, George. Trust me. You must tell Daddy and Uncle Ram right away."

"Who were those men, Santha? In the beams of my headlights one of them looked like that Indian we saw at DeLuca's. Was it he?"

Santha uttered a low "Yes" and said no more.

TWENTY-NINE

Rama Shastri watched Stephen Wrench at the phone again. Wrench had tried to call the museum and Santha and George's apartments countless times. The clock said seven twenty-two.

Wrench slammed the phone down. "Santha should be home by now!" he growled. He paced. "I have one of those feelings, Ram. Something's happened!"

The others were eating. Nirmal Kapur had cooked up an improvised version of Indian green peppers stuffed with shrimp, served with Russian tea.

Shastri said nothing. The thought that Santha might be threatened by Thuggee made him nervous, too, but he fought the feeling. He must be as objective as possible, for Steve, for himself. He stared at Hanuman, convinced now that if anyone could grasp the more invisible, arcane motivations of the Thug cult, it was the Swami.

Hanuman asked Shastri in a low voice, "Has Santha any idea of what the parchment means?"

"I don't think so. We've certainly never told her. But she knows it's important and will follow through on bringing it here, even though she hasn't been quite herself lately."

Hanuman nodded. "How is that?"

"Steve says she's been disturbed because of the death of her mother."

"Acting strangely?"

"Her beau, who is a psychiatrist, has told Steve that she experienced a severe trauma, a—"

The phone interrupted him. Wrench grabbed the receiver. "Hello? Yes, George. . . . What! Is Santha all right? . . . Thank God, thank . . . Yes. Yes. Indians you say? Where the hell was Museum Security? Yes, I'll contact the police. We'll be right over."

Wrench put the receiver down. He was ashen, trembling. "They attacked Santha," he said, his great chest heaving. "She's at George's." He could barely get the words out. "The bastards marked her—on her forehead!" Wrench dialed. "Dan. Listen. My daughter was attacked tonight. She's still with us, thank God. It looks like our friends the Thugs again. At the Peabody Museum. Security guards? That's what I'd like to know. Get hold of the Cambridge police, will you? And get over there as quickly as you can and see what you can find out. I'll be at . . ." He gave George's address and phone number. "Yeah, call me one way or the other. I've got to"—his voice broke—"see my little girl. Fine. Thanks, Dan. Much appreciated."

Afterward, to Shastri: "George says they took something from Santha." Wrench pounded his fist into his other hand. "Goddamn!" he roared. "They knew where it was all the time!"

"Where is she, George?" Wrench asked when they arrived at Otis Place.

George placed a finger to his lips. "Santha's asleep upstairs. I gave her a sedative." His face was haggard. He looked at Hanuman and Nirmal Kapur wonderingly.

Tracking in snow, the group followed him into his office. Shastri introduced Hanuman and Shastri. Recognizing Nirmal, George said so. "We'll explain why they're present later," Shastri added.

George sat behind his desk. He shook his head. "Santha insisted I phone you, Steve, first thing. She didn't want me to contact the Cambridge police, for some reason. I don't understand."

"She did right," Wrench assured him. "They wouldn't know what to do. I've sent a man to them, representing Ram and me in this."

George sat behind his desk. "Her pursuers were Indian, Santha says. I saw one of them in the headlights of my car." He ran fingers through his hair. "She also says that it was an Indian woman who marked her."

"Sonovabitch!" said Wrench.

"The mark was on the forehead, slightly above and between

her eyebrows." George pointed, "Right here." His eyes scanned them. "Now, why in hell would anybody do that?" When there was no reply, he continued in a husky voice. "It's got me baffled, I confess. That and something else.... Santha was marked by a signet ring, I think. It bled for a while...." George scanned them again, looking suddenly helpless, lost.

"Well," urged Wrench.

"A short time ago, before I put her to bed, I checked the mark. It had been stitched and bandaged at the Stillman Infirmary. A small cut that needed only four stitches, you understand.... I checked it, as I said. I don't know why. A perfectly good job. I was worried, I suppose.... But, damn—it's medically impossible."

Now Shastri was impatient. "Tell us, George."

"There's no wound, no stitching anymore. Everything's gone except the mark, and that's very black and small, but distinct ... It's part of Santha, like a tattoo or a birthmark. How could it have healed that quickly? Where are the stitches?" George's rage grew as he narrated. "What the hell has happened to Santha, gentlemen? Can any one of you answer that for me?"

"It was a fingernail," Hanuman said calmly. "A fingernail made the mark. Let me finish, Doctor, before you reply. It wasn't a totally human fingernail, you see. This woman who accosted Santha is more than human sometimes. What she can do in that state is often beyond natural law."

George stood. "Swami, no offense meant: it's been a damn strange day, but not that crazy yet."

Shastri took command of the situation. "George, why don't you tell us what happened step by step, and then we can continue this debate later."

George told his story, adding what Santha had told him. "They were after an object she carried," he concluded. "A cylinder used in mailing."

Shastri explained, "Yes, it contained a section of a very ancient parchment."

"And Santha tried her best to keep it from them." Wrench was close to tears. "My brave little girl."

Hanuman announced, "Gentlemen, that the Thugs have recovered it is nothing short of disastrous."

"Thugs!" echoed George.

The phone rang. "For you," he said to Wrench after picking it up and listening for a moment.

"Yes, Dan," they heard Wrench say. "I see. They drugged the guards with chloroform and tied them up. Wanted to make it look like an ordinary burglary. Yes, let the Cambridge cops believe that. Christ, we don't want the truth to leak out. We'd have the media on our heads, then, and a local panic. Right. Okay. That's a fine suggestion. Thanks, Dan." He hung up, reported to the others. "No strangulations this time. A break-in, plain and simple. Dan Terranova is sending a patrol car here. They'll be parked in front as long as Santha's convalescing."

"Thugs," George repeated.

"Correct, George. You remember, we discussed them once."

Hanuman stood. "With your permission, Doctor, I would like to see your patient now."

George hesitated.

"Trust us, George," Shastri said. "The exigencies of this require that the Swami do it. Believe me, he won't hurt Santha in any way." George complied and they left the office.

Swami Hanuman started to walk upstairs.

Stephen Wrench was already behind the Indian. Shastri couldn't help admiring his friend.

He knew that Stephen Wrench accepted India and its people with a gut-level response to its uniqueness. If it was mysterious, even unfathomable at times, that was okay, too. Wrench's uncluttered instincts told him that this ugly little Indian with his wise, penetrating eyes just might be able to save his daughter.

Hanuman reached the bedroom and crossed the threshold. He went gradually, silently to Santha, moving with caution, as if walking through a minefield. He looked constantly about the room, concentrating especially on the ceiling. Wrench and Shastri surveyed the place after him, although they couldn't grasp why they had to be so alert.

The Swami bent and stared at the mark on Santha's forehead. He lowered the back of his hand to her cheek and kept it there for a few moments, his eyes closed. Then he gestured that the two men come closer. Hanuman pointed to the mark. They both stared at it.

"See," Hanuman whispered, "the shape resembles a pickax, the sacred symbol of Thuggee."

Hanuman's eyes veered to the stairwell leading to the town house levels above. "What's there?" he asked someone behind Wrench. Shastri turned, saw George Buchan's taut features. Behind him stood Nirmal.

"The guest room. And above that my studio. Then the roof."

"Studio?"

"I paint in my spare time."

"Ah, an artist." Hanuman tilted his head toward Santha.

"I just started to paint her. I wanted to do a lot of preliminary drawings first—to be sure I could capture everything I saw in her."

"Of course. What you saw in her. But of course. Please show me them, the drawings, the painting, everything." Then Hanuman warned, "No more the lovemaking here. For a while."

George Buchan was openly bewildered.

"Swami Hanuman understands what has happened to Santha better than any of us," Rama Shastri said.

"Look, man," Nirmal added, "the Swami tunes into vibes you and me can't hear. Believe it."

"Okay. Follow me." George went up. Stephen Wrench moved, but Hanuman touched his shoulder. "Stay below," he advised. "Stay with your lovely daughter. There is very much love in you for her, and such a person must stay near her at all times."

"You mean love will heal what troubles her?"

"Love helps. Only fire will heal, though. Isn't that the expression, to combat fire with fire?"

Wrench was as bewildered as George now, but he agreed.

Hanuman gestured that George go before him. On the next floor, Hanuman peered into the guest room. He studied the ceiling there. The hall window trembled, and Shastri went to it to see if another storm was brewing. He saw no rain, only a grey mist over Storrow Drive. But a wind tenaciously rattled things. Shastri watched a cast-iron balcony shake yet remain precariously aloft. The wind, livelier, stronger, pummeled that side of the house.

"Let us go on," Hanuman said.

George hesitated, when Shastri repeated, "Trust him." George nodded and replied hoarsely, "I'll do as you say."

The top floor had originally been constructed as a garret. Bookcases lined the walls of the Mount Vernon Street wing of the studio, even in the far corner beneath the sloping roof. The garret reverberated from the constant thudding of the wind.

George led them farther into the depths of the studio. He pulled the chain of an overhanging bulb when they neared his work area, and they passed under a wide skylight. The outside world was like a weighty gray mass pressing down on the skylight glass. They faced a few tables, a covered painting on an easel. One of the tables that ran along the side wall held a small, untidy display of jars filled with soaking paintbrushes, wiping rags, a much used palette or two, and a homemade wooden stand with every kind of pencil or pen. Against the wall a dozen or so oil paintings were stacked.

They were chiefly city scenes, especially of old Boston buildings with their oddly designed turreting, chimneys, and air vents. There was a picture of the Charles River on a sunny day. Sailing boats were plentiful, and a Harvard rowing crew, all watched by sun-bathing throngs along the Esplanade.

But Hanuman went straight to the center table as if directed and pored through the sketchbooks neatly stacked on the planed surface.

"Ah," he said, "these are Santha. Almost all of Santha."

"Yes," George told him nervously.

"Are they in chronological order?"

"Yes. The top ones are from months ago. The more recent are on the bottom."

"Strange they aren't on the top." Hanuman flipped through sketches of Santha eating, laughing, standing in various poses, sitting on a chair. "One would think the newest drawings would be on the top."

"What do you mean?"

"Please. I have no intention of disturbing you. Ah—see." Hanuman was holding the third sketchbook from the top. He displayed the sixth page. "Here it begins. And you have been so precise as to date each drawing. Three months ago, on the twenty-fourth." He held the sketch closer to the light so everyone could see. They all looked. "See the eyes." Hanuman flipped the pages, stopped again at the twelfth drawing, then the sixteenth. "You've drawn her many times."

"Sometimes ten quick sketches a day," agreed George. "Santha's a good subject. A fine, memorable face...."

"Yes, memorable." Hanuman skipped five or six books and took the one next to the last. "Now we shall..." He opened then to the middle, but the pages flipped rapidly back as if pushed by a strong wind.

"I see," Hanuman said. "You are all observing?" He tried again. The same thing happened.

"Hey," Nirmal cried. "It's cold in here. Like in that alley, Baba!"

Hanuman seized the last pad. He opened it flat on the table and held the sides down with every ounce of his strength. The table stirred, tried to rise, jump free beneath him.

"The table weighs at least one hundred pounds!" George gasped. "It took two big guys and me to carry it up here!"

The rest were too preoccupied with the pen-and-ink drawing before them to listen. It was of Santha, naked to her waist. The face was hers, all right, but Rama Shastri, who had known her longest, trembled at the something alien that was gradually replacing the soft Kamala likeness. Gone was the welcoming, whimsical smile that she'd adopted from her mother. The mouth was now loose, the lower lip slack with an impression of tremendous hunger. It was amazing how the ink had caught the exact sense. A few lines placed here, there, with the right slant and thickness. The slack lower lip seemed moist with a need ...almost rabid.

Nirmal broke the silence. "Man, who's she going to devour?"

Hanuman was sweating. He endeavored to turn to another page: a quick glimpse of a charcoal drawing, the eyes feral, the mouth with small teeth almost pointed. Hanuman released the book, wincing in pain. It slammed shut.

George was sweating, too. "I didn't realize . . . !"

"Yes. You were too close. Your consciousness couldn't accept it. And so you hid the new drawings beneath the older ones." Hanuman was regulating his breathing. It had been a terrible strain. "You are the consummate artist, my friend. You have captured the truth. The entire truth."

Rama Shastri stepped back. The agony was beyond his expectation. Were they too late to help Santha? He heard the wind shrieking through the framework, tearing at the joists. There was a thud on the roof.

"Now the painting." Hanuman reached for the cloth over the painting on the easel. The wind whistled across the skylight glass. A renewed series of thuds hammered above them.

"Who the hell's jumping up and down up there!" yelled George. Then he blushed. "Shit!" This is getting to me! There couldn't possibly be anyone up there. Christmas, what a wind!"

Hanuman pulled the cloth free.

"'Prisoner, tell me, who was it that wrought this unbreakable chain?'" quoted Nirmal Kapur.

"What is that from?" demanded George, gaping at his work.

"Tagore's *Gitanjali*," replied Nirmal. "This lady's in chains. Wow, is she!"

"She looks pretty damned unchained to me! She looks ready to leap free of the paint at us!" replied the painter. "But that's not Santha! What the hell was wrong with me?"

"Again, the consummate artist."

"That's crap! That's not Santha! I can't believe I painted it. Where the hell was I?"

"Perhaps you don't remember totally. Perhaps even Santha doesn't. But she did sit for it, didn't she, George?"

George stared at Hanuman, passed a sweaty hand over his face. He frowned at the roof. "Wish that wind'd stop. Can barely hear myself think. Christ almighty—yes, I painted her.

Santha was seated right in that chair. The other morning." He recoiled from the painting. "But I don't remember that!"

"What did it look like then?"

George Buchan's long bony fingers tangled in his beard. He closed his eyes, and his face got redder and redder. After a few moments, "Migosh, I can't say! I can't . . . I can't think!"

"Of course," Hanuman agreed with understanding. His eyes suddenly darted to the others. "Someone is missing. Where is Rama Shastri?" His voice rose. "Nirmal, find Rama Shastri! Bring him back here—quickly!"

Up there, Shastri thought, wishing he had a weapon; it's up there, gloating. He was in the hall before the stairs that led to the trap in the roof. Gloating over Santha, over Steve, over Kamala's ashes. Gloating over all of us living and those living in the memory of my spirit. Kamala's child. Not a Kunkali child. Rama Shastri released the hooks from the metal rings. The trapdoor lifted with his push. Then the wind took it. Shastri lost his grip, and the wood slammed against the roof leads.

Shastri pushed himself against the raging wind and raised his body until he was standing on the rooftop. He viewed the bleak Esplanade, the leaden Charles. Then he cried out and moved backward, shoved by an invisible, gargantuan hand. Wobbling on the slope edge, he started to slide down. Frantically he danced crazily over the sloping leads and, with a desperate lunge, seized a chimney corner. Below, to his left, the skylight extended like an opalesque scar across the black surface, eerie, dreamlike. A fog rose from the river side of the roof, as if from the very eaves. As it slivered across his vision, he saw brief glimpses of the river beyond, the reflection of a slowly emerging sun. But there wasn't any sunlight here!

It's happened again! he screamed in his mind. I've been lured up here!

There had been the maddening, thudding noise of heavy feet, pounding in glee or wrath, Shastri couldn't tell which. But something had been above them. Something watched, waited, knew, taunted on the roof. And he'd had to climb up and see what . . .

What taunted Kamala's child.

The fog had thickened and now had a stench like that of the many, many dead. Rama Shastri choked and dug his nails into the chimney brick until his fingers bled. Fool, he cursed himself, then listened to the echo: FOOL. And knew it wasn't his own mental voice. He heard his name meshing with the wind.

She had him now.

She was the fog or in the fog; around or above it. *She* was here! That was certain. *She* was in the drawings, the painting below. *She* was in Gauri Bala's eyes. *She* was, perhaps, even in Santha, too. Steve's baby. Kamala's child. Their Santha. His Santha. Rama Shastri began to weep.

"Rama Shastri!" A pair of very strong arms engulfed him. Warm, human breath, close to his ear. He raised his eyes and saw Hanuman's disciple. They moved away from the chimney. For a heartbeat or two, Shastri thought that he and Nirmal were about to be swept down the sloping leads to the gutter line and then finally over and . . . below.

But, hand in hand, they managed to reach the flat, level side and the open trap. The fog evaporated, left them. When Nirmal lowered the trapdoor, a streamer of sunlight nestled on the black, loose strands of his hair like a patch of fire.

"Whew, it stinks up there!" Nirmal said.

"The river fog," Shastri replied. He rubbed the tears from his cheeks. "Stings your eyes, too."

"Acceptance is difficult for you as a psychiatrist, my son." Hanuman touched George's shoulder sympathetically, once they gathered downstairs again. "But as an artist, you can understand what can be done with perspective and the redesigning, reshaping, of objects on canvas. Perhaps the dimension that Kali travels through is similar to that. And certainly I wasn't the only person in America affected during this period of time. Santha was, also. Santha, I believe, was another chosen body. Her experiences were the beginning of a possession, a reshaping of her psyche that has continued to this moment.

"We can tell Santha a transmitter, for though that is a trite and limited analogue, it is nevertheless true. She now bears the mark of Kunkali on her forehead. The Force of Resistance now works through her as it works through Gauri Bala." He turned to Rama Shastri. "Even while Santha sleeps. As you discovered on the roof."

"Santha did that?"

"No, Rama Shastri; Kunkali did it, through Santha."

"What the hell happened, Ram?" Wrench demanded.

"Please, I must continue. The new, revived Energy of the Dark Portals is flourishing, with Kali manifesting through the Bala woman and Santha, through the resurgence of Thuggee, through this Huzoor, who is the Keeper of the Rishi Scrolls. The scrolls are the key. They give to this Huzoor the leadership over all of Kali's people. We must find him, and we must get the scrolls, else . . ."

"Else what?" barked Wrench.

"Else we may not be able to save your beloved Santha."

The flat lighting glanced off the walls and furniture, gave the faces the cold, subdued luster of nickel. For a moment Rama Shastri started as he silently perused the men in the room. They looked expressionless, as if Hanuman's words had drained emotion from them.

Hanuman had seated himself. He resembled a grotesque, pug-nosed doll in a blue turban. For a moment it was difficult to take what he was saying seriously. But only for a moment. His soft, confident voice, the command in his eyes closed in on them. "We must all strengthen our wills now, because Kunkali attacks the will first. If we have a weakness in our defenses, she will find it. Each of us must check the other when necessary. We must keep the group intact. Alone, we are clay for her to manipulate as she desires. Together, we are a group will, with the strength to combat her."

"I pray so," Shastri admitted.

"Amen," came from Wrench.

THIRTY

Shastri, Wrench, Hanuman, and Nirmal were in a cab heading for Cambridge. Hanuman had requested that they go to his residence, where they could prepare their strategy. Wrench was hesitant to leave Santha. But the police guard had arrived, and George had assured him he would take good care of her. Now he was seated next to the cabbie. The other three were in the rear.

Nirmal asked Shastri, "The Huzoor. You've seen him? What does he look like?"

A few seconds later, Nirmal repeated the question; Rama Shastri hadn't replied.

Shastri's voice lacked expression. The temple cave was long ago at last, lost in those flat Indian shadows of the past somewhere. "A giant whose voice was like thunder. Otherwise, he's more like a phantom than real."

"But he can't be a phantom. He's got to be a man. I mean, like he's obviously some great guru, some sadhu who chose a Negative Path. But nevertheless a man. A Thug Lord is always a man, isn't he?"

"Yes. A man he is. I'm certain of that. But you see, the conditions were very unusual that morning. The tapers were thick with smoke. It made the lighting so dim in certain quarters that I couldn't see him as clearly as I wanted to. I suppose it was all staged that way. This Huzoor has a dramatic bent."

Still, when we meet—and we will—once more, I will know him, Shastri promised himself. Not merely because he is a giant among men, or because his voice remains in my memory like a tremor from the bowels of the earth. But because he is the power of Thuggee, and the evil of it will tell me that it is present. I believe that to be true, Das, since your swift, silent death speaks to me continuously all these months. I believe

300

that you must be avenged; that if there is a destiny of Rama Shastri in this, then justice must be done, and mine is the hand that must do it.

At Hanuman's place, they saw Molly Doyle and the fat woman in pedal pushers seated on the worse-for-wear couch, eating freshly made taffy from a bowl.

"Molly Doyle, Adelaide Jaworksi," Nirmal introduced, dripping pools at his feet. During the last hour, a torrential rain had replaced the snowstorm. It staccatoed against the doors and windows as if it resented being excluded from the room.

Molly was offering taffy, and Wrench responded, placed a dollop in his mouth, gave her a "hmmmmm" and a wink.

Nirmal ushered them on down the hallway, with its progression of doors. Shastri noted that the Swami was moving far ahead, eager to reach his quarters. When he and Wrench were about to follow Hanuman through an end door, Nirmal urged them along another corridor. "Baba's going to meditate," he explained.

They settled in a large, well-furnished room complete with a fireplace, armchairs, and bookcases along the walls. Nirmal asked if they'd like tea and some baklava he'd purchased from a place near Harvard Square. They agreed, and he disappeared. When Nirmal returned, Stephen Wrench was lost in his pipe.

Shastri asked, "Why did Hanuman go to Mai Yogini's center the other night?"

Nirmal explained, "Mai Yogini came to see me, weeping and wailing, and begged me to get Hanuman to make a showing at her splash. I know the lady real well. Used to bed with her when I was a cokey, before I cold-turkeyed and joined the Baba. So I asked the Baba if he'd come to the center, and to my great surprise, he agreed. Swami Hanuman knew he was on the Thug hit list, I'm positive. He's got a way of spotting things like that ahead of time."

"Yes," agreed Rama Shastri. "It must be that he went into the center cellar seeking his would-be strangler."

"Three of them, man! That worries me. It's foolhardy. The Baba is tough, but could he really handle three of them?"

"This Mai Yogini—you suspect her of being involved with the Thugs?"

"Absolutely. But not of her own chosing, I'm sure. It's not her style. Mai Yogini's all charlatan, a beautiful and graceful piece of mountebank, but much too cool for a killing. She was scared, plenty scared. I've never seen Mai Yogini like that. Never."

"Well, Ram—a possible lead?"

"Is there anything else, Nirmal?"

"Only what the Harvard Square grapevine tells me. They're all there, you know: the Eastern cult faddists, the Vedantists, Hari Krishnas, the Sikhs, the Zen-macro people. Anyway, you hear things. People talk freely to me because I'm Indian. I've heard lately of a new addition: the Kali Akali. And it has something for the female, too. The Kali Mahila Mandal, or women's society. Maybe the group's linked to our yellow-scarf kids, and maybe, too, Mai Yogini's been forced to join the Mahila Mandal—got me?"

"You believe forced?" urged Shastri.

"Yes, forced. The Yogini's no joiner. Not with her fat ego. That would take away from her smoke, being just another face with a bunch of women that way."

"Steve, if her heart's not in it, maybe we can apply enough pressure to get her to open up. If we can guarantee her protection . . ."

Shastri stopped. They heard scurrying in the corridor and a demanding voice, a man's, repeating Wrench's and Shastri's names over and over again. Nirmal went to the door, looked out.

"What's the rip-bob, Adelaide?"

"There's a man out there with a whacked-out girl. I think she's OD-ing. He wants to come back here. Says he's a detective. Molly won't let him. You know how she is about cops."

"Sounds like Dan," Wrench said. Hanuman's address had been left with George Buchan before they left, for Lieutenant Terranova, in case he showed or phoned.

"Be right back." Nirmal went toward the front room.

Wrench paced impatiently. Shastri was excited, too. This

new information about Mai Yogini had presented vistas of hope for both of them. A lead was a lead, and it might be just good enough to direct them to the hideaway of the Huzoor and his bunch.

Nirmal and Terranova came in, carrying a young woman between them.

"When I got here," Dan explained, "I found this young lady outside, drenched and moaning, on the steps. She's dazed, in a state of shock, I think." He paused both for breath and for effect. "But get this: she's blurted a few coherent sentences. 'They're going to strangle Bob tonight,' she said. 'We should never've taken the rumel.'"

"What is your name?" Stephen Wrench asked her, pronouncing the words slowly, clearly.

"Man, she's stoned!" Nirmal announced. The girl was sprawled in one of the armchairs, wrapped in blankets. She was shivering. Shastri, kneeling by her side, checked her arms for track marks, then raised her eyelids. The pupils weren't dilated. He said as much, adding, "Probably hypnotized."

"What's you name, dear?" Wrench repeated.

He had to bend his ear to her lips. "Deborah Klaus," Wrench told the others. He looked at them, checking whether the name was familiar. It wasn't.

Shastri carefully took both of her hands. The wrists were bandaged. "Deborah," he urged. "Tell us about Bob."

Her lips formed a soundless "Bob."

"Yes, Bob. What is going to happen to Bob? Tonight? Tell us about Bob, Deborah."

She stared at him blankly for a moment, then pulled her hand away and covered her mouth. "Ooooooh," she moaned. "Oh, Bob; migosh! Like with Abel!"

After a pause, an intake of breath, Wrench questioned, "Abel Fairley? The guy with the pamphlets?"

The volume of her voice had risen. "We shouldn't've done that!" A grimace. "That was so fuckin' stupid of Bob to do that!"

"Bob who?" persisted Shastri.

"Bob Fevre. He stole the rumel. The Huzoor—oh, Christ-almighty, the Huzoor was mad!"

"Of course he was," agreed Shastri. "Angry with Bob, angry with you, too, I wager."

"Yes. Yes. I ran away! They thought I was asleep, and I ran away! I escaped through the back door. The Mother wasn't there." Deborah shivered. "The Mother likes it!"

"Likes what?"

"Blood!" Deborah Klaus screamed.

Shastri held her hands tightly.

Terranova, who'd been silent up to this point, said, "We'd better get her to a doctor."

"Of course. Of course." Shastri was impatient. "Call a police doctor. That'll keep it under wraps." He waited until Nirmal directed Terranova to a room across the hall, to the telephone. Now, alone with Deborah and Wrench, Shastri lifted the girl's chin. "Deborah," Shastri insisted firmly, "tell us about Bob Fevre. Where is he? Why will they kill him?"

A return stare, and he let her go for a second, startled. He thought he caught a flash of familiar hatred, wrathful, kinetic hatred.

But Deborah calmed and swallowed hard. "Bob killed Abel." Another swallow. "I killed Abel. Bob said we should experiment with the rumel." She shouted without warning; "It was a fuckin' game!"

"He stole the rumel. And they want to punish him for it. Am I accurate?" So simple, Shastri thought while he spoke, the explanation of Abel Fairley's murder was so simple after all: Two warped children playing at Thuggee for kicks, the punk thing to do. Totally meaningless. But they had been found out. Deborah had been a prisoner. His eyes fell to the bandaged wrists. There had been blood. . . .

"Bob kept moving from pad to pad 'cause he knows they're after him. Tonight at nine-thirty!" Deborah was very lucid now. "Tonight they'll go to his new address in Arlington and—"

"Demand payment in full," Shastri cut in. "Where does he live, child?"

"At 216 Mundy Street. Fourth floor. Apartment 44. You've

got to stop them! I came here because I know that Swami Hanuman can save him! And me! Where is he?"

"He's here," Nirmal reassured her.

Wrench took over. "Tell us about the other place. Where did you escape from, dear?"

She nodded. "I escaped."

"From where?"

She closed her eyes, her forehead creased, sweat seeped down her temples, her shoulders heaved.

"Better ease off," Terranova suggested, as he entered the room. "And find some more blankets for her; she's shivering bad."

Wrench stood. "She knows where the Thug hideaway is, Dan, and we need that information," he barked. "My daughter's in the clutches of this thing, in case you've forgotten! If it's a question of priorities between Santha and the likes of her, I . . ."

Terranova pointed to the girl. "Can't you see she's unconscious now? What do you expect me to do?"

"Get Hanuman in here. She asked for Hanuman. There's that goddamn supernatural component again. We need him."

"Supernatural?" asked Terranova.

"There's a . . . a goddess, a demon. . . . Goddammit, this thing possesses women, Dan. It's unnatural, beyond the pale. . . ." He asked Nirmal, "Where's the Swami?"

"You're shitting me," Dan accused.

"Tell him, Ram. Help, will you, please?" Back to Nirmal: "Get Hanuman, will you? Look at her. She's slipping away. You heard her. She was about to tell us where the buggers are hiding."

"You're panicking, Mr. Wrench. The Swami warned we should check our fears, we—"

"Yeah, we should. But I was so close. This Deborah knows where they are! Can't you fetch the Swami?"

Nirmal sighed. "You try, then," he replied. He led Wrench and Shastri back down the corridor. They stopped before two massive doors. "The Swami had the ceiling to this room knocked down to get the effect he desired," Nirmal said. "He likes heights."

They entered a room, large enough that their strides echoed. It held no furniture, nor was it lighted. Haze from the windows on the southwest side exposed a series of ropes dangling from above. Wrench and Shastri craned their necks and stared, open-mouthed, at the figure nearly touching the lofty ceiling of the second floor. The second landing's windows limned the figure with the wet gray evening light outside.

"You see, he's still meditating," Nirmal told him.

Clinging to one of the six ropes by his toes, Hanuman, dressed only in a loincloth, extended in an almost horizontal line in midair, his arms crossed over his chest, his eyes closed. His features were rapt.

"When will he come down?" Wrench demanded.

"Who knows, man? I could shout my lungs out, start a bonfire under him, and it still wouldn't work." Nirmal grinned at his floating Master. "He's just not with us."

They returned to the library to find Deborah Klaus in a deeper trance than when they'd left.

Wrench started to pace. The door opened. He turned, expecting the police doctor. Hanuman walked into the room, completely dressed. Nirmal rose from his chair in surprise.

Hanuman nodded. Once informed about Deborah, he went to her, lifted her eyelids, sighed, sat opposite her in another armchair, and seemed abstracted.

He beckoned them out of the room. "She is a lure," the Swami said. "She has been hypnotized, placed into a trance wherein she can reveal only that which they desire her to tell. It is exigent that we find their hidden ashram, that we seize the rishi scrolls and thus nullify the Huzoor's power. They dread exactly this and thus have obliterated the memory of the ashram's whereabouts from her mind. We are being manipulated to go to this Bob Fevre's residence. This girl's concern for her co-partner in assassination is spurious. She was directed here."

Dan Terranova asked, "How can you be so sure?"

"Deceit pours forth from Thugs as certainly as the effluvium from dead things. You must learn never to read them literally. The Thug soul has great pride in its deceptions. Like a prestidigitator, the Thug would have you concentrate on the wrong hand. We are expected tonight, I assure you."

"Should we go, then?" From Wrench.

"Oh yes. They are seeking us, and we must be there. Better this way, aware that we are about to stare into the heart of darkness, than to be, someday, some hour, confronted like a group of somnambulists, unaware of what we are walking into. Indeed, there is a precipice ahead of us, but if we remain constant in our unity, we shall not step beyond the edge."

"Her eyes are dead," Wrench said, half to himself.

When the police doctor appeared with a nurse, he was immediately concerned. "There's barely a pulse!" he explained, about to give Deborah a shot of adrenaline. "Doctor, look!" the nurse said and pointed. Deborah was stirring, her face suddenly suffused with color, and the eyes flickered to life.

Wrench moved forward. "No more questions," the doctor insisted, pushing him back.

"Is my Santha going to be like her?" Wrench bellowed.

Calmly Hanuman suggested they eat and led them to the dining room. They ate a seafood potpourri of shrimp, mussels, stuffed quahog, and thin slices of finnan haddie. The vegetables were fresh-grown lentils, some Indian. Most of them ate without appetite, though. Instead, they discussed the supernatural aspect of the case for Dan Terranova's benefit. He listened intently.

"This bitch-thing, Kali, goes right for the jugular," Wrench added. "If you've got a weak spot, she'll find it. Look what she's done to me, to my poor Santha."

"What Steve means, Dan," Shastri continued, "is that if she can get to one of us, separate from the others, she will lure him to his doom through his most vulnerable area. So don't split off from us tonight, for any reason."

Terranova was very quiet. Finally he spoke up. "Yeah," he admitted, "I've got a vulnerable side to me. It was what made me decide to be a cop."

"Care to share it?" asked Wrench.

Terranova lit a cigarette and puffed on it awhile. "It was years ago, when I was in college. I knew a girl. We were going

to be married someday, we planned." He smiled, remembering.
"Betty Lassiter was the most beautiful and the smartest lady
in our senior class. Gawd, just looking at her, a man dreamed
on and on. Understand?"

"We've all been there," Wrench acknowledged.

"Well, she went away. Summer vacation in L.A. Her cousin
Eunice lived there. Weeks later, when Betty returned, she was
changed. She'd been introduced to drugs—LSD—by her cousin.
In fact, when I met her at the airport, she was on the stuff."
He was quiet again. Then, grimly: "Two weeks later, she jumped
off the roof of a ten-story building. The acid had convinced
her she could fly like a bird. After that, I forgot about my plans
to be an engineer and took my police exam instead. I wanted
to stamp out what had killed Betty—the maggot pushers on
the streets, the organized crime behind it. I never got over
Betty. Yep, that's my weak spot."

"Just stick with us, Dan, remember," Wrench said, breaking
the long silence that followed.

THIRTY-ONE

Mundy Street was one of the few neighborhoods in Arlington,
Massachusetts, with a row of brownstones. Constructed at the
turn of the century to meet a rise in the surrounding population,
they stood solidly on both sides of the street, a sepia barrier
against decades of New England climate. Mostly their upkeep
had been good, but Bob Fevre's building was an exception.
There was a long crack in one of the windows to the double
entrance doors, and there was no lock. Vandals had wrenched
it free long ago.

Dan Terranova, Stephen Wrench, Rama Shastri, Swami
Hanuman, and Nirmal Kapur stood before the dilapidated front
in the final throes of the downpour. The time was exactly ten-
fourteen, according to Shastri's chronometer. They were preoc-

cupied with two open windows on the fourth floor, where the drawn shades slapped in the night wind.

"Is that the Fevre dude's pad?" Nirmal asked.

"It's possible," Hanuman agreed. He wore his turban and an old yak-wool coat.

"Maybe he's a fresh air nut? Listen, do you hear it?"

"Chanting," Terranova said.

Wrench strained, heard the voice, and tried to shake it free like the rain. He could still see Deborah Klaus's flat, dead eyes, and he thought again, Will Santha get that way in time, too? Distraught, he slapped his hat against his thigh, trying to release the moisture in the fur. The rain continued, drumming on the parked automobiles, slapping brick, pouring off roof gutters and down drains. Snow, dislodged, thudded from heights. Slush was everywhere.

"Let us go upstairs," Hanuman directed. He turned to Nirmal. "My son, you must be a watchdog at this entrance. But make an effort, please, to be as invisible as Vishnu's breath."

Terranova took a gun from his topcoat pocket. "Can you handle one of these?"

Nirmal took a stance, moved his arms into esoteric patterns. "Forget it. T'ai chi."

"Only two classes," Hanuman revealed, with a smile. "But I've trained him well. He heeds the wind, this one."

Terranova wondered what the hell the wind would do for Nirmal in a fracas, but said nothing.

Apartment 44 was minus a nameplate. From behind the door came the low, monotonous drone of the chant. For a moment they listened; then Terranova pounded on the door and called out Bob Fevre's name. Exasperated, Terranova suggested at last, "Maybe we ought to break it down."

"Do not draw attention to us," warned Hanuman. "We must avoid publicity. The more people involved, the greater the danger of losing the trail. Then these Kunkali followers will hide and it will be most difficult to trace them again."

Terranova renewed his efforts. The chanting never wavered.

"Maybe he's already dead. Maybe that voice is from a recording."

"Let us find out."

Hanuman walked down the short hall and stopped before a window leading to a fire escape. "Mr. Terranova. Your arms are long. Can you lift me to that sill?"

Dan paled. He looked at Wrench for help. Wrench nodded. "He climbs like a monkey."

Hanuman continued. "That window has to be part of Bob Fevre's apartment, probably a kitchen or bathroom. If it's unlocked, I can squeeze through and enter."

Terranova stepped onto the fire escape. "Now lift me," he heard, and placing his hands under Hanuman's armpits, Terranova obeyed. It was easy, like lifting a small child. At Hanuman's bidding, he raised the Swami over the edge of the railing. For a second he saw the sodden back alley four stories below. Holy Christ, he thought; suppose I slip?

The window was a foot or so higher than the fire escape. Terranova stretched as much as possible, and the Swami's fingers gripped the ledge. "More," he urged, and the policeman's hands slid down Hanuman's body to his ankles. This gave the Swami the necessary lift, and he managed to press against the glass and push slowly. With barely a sound, the window opened. The chanting, a man's low drone, filtered out into the alley. "Now release me," Hanuman whispered. Terranova did, and the little Indian hung precariously for an instant, his hands clinging to the window's lip.

The Swami's body did the rest.

Gradually his body rose, pulled by the sheer force of his hands and wrists at first, then by the rest of his arms, his shoulders in the end bearing the brunt of the rising. Finally, with the ease of a master contortionist, his abdomen and bent legs leveled with the sill. Wide-eyed, Terranova watched Hanuman's toes grip the stone ledge, then raise again and ease into the apartment. Finally, only his head, shoulders, and bracing elbows showed; then they, too, disappeared.

"Amazing!" Terranova uttered, and his foot struck something. He bent and picked up Hanuman's shoes. The Swami had slipped out of them before his climb. Terranova took them back into the hallway and stared at them. They were a small boy's size.

Hanuman, meanwhile, had discovered he was in the bathroom. He closed the window silently. But the cold seeped from the room beyond, flicking the upturned corner of a Mick Jagger poster on the wall. The thick scent of sandalwood incense carried with the breeze. He went to the door.

The entrance hall outside was unlit. Hanuman walked swiftly but noiselessly toward the living room, toward the chanting. He craned his neck around a hall corner and saw a young man seated lotus style in the center of an Indian rug. On each corner of the rug was a tall candle held in place by melted wax in a saucer. The sandalwood burned in a container before him. Facing the open windows, the young man chanted, praising Kunkali, supplicating Her aid, imploring that She protect and avenge him. The chant was a mix of Indian words and English, which were "Have mercy on me," "Protect me," "Slay my enemies," all ending in "O Kunkali." Similar to a Catholic litany and, like one, repeated over and over. Hanuman smiled grimly at Bob Fevre's improvised ceremony. Then only the grimness remained, as he heard another cry.

The sound came from the night above somewhere. It came as before, drifting in with the wind's pulse, a drawn-out note, part bird, part animal, part something female. For the past hour, weaving between the praises and imprecations of his litany, Bob Fevre had held his breath and listened and heard and known. Suddenly he had known that he'd won at long last: that She had been pleased with his constant vigil, his penance, his plea for forgiveness, mercy, protection, even guidance.

Bob Fevre was gaunt, much more so than the night he and Deborah Klaus garroted Abel Fairley. Ever since, he had slept little, eaten little, and hoped not all all, doomed by the stars, doomed by the Huzoor's command, doomed by the cruel, arctic whim of a goddess he barely realized.

She was still a blur in his mind, a manifestation through the strange Indian woman, Gauri Bala, one night at the ashram.

There had been eyes, floating dark vises that squeezed his soul, and a voice from the ice-rimed bowels of hell.

Yet still he had defied the demon Goddess, stolen the rumel.

They would kill him. They would find him and make him one of their victims. It was their nature, their credo, their religion.

Lately, though—was it two days ago, one day?—he'd had an inspiration. It was morning, and he'd awakened in a sweat, since in his dreams the eyes had returned; the lips like curling blood had spoken, "Seek me."

And so he had, with fasting, prayer, the chanting of his homemade litanies. Perhaps he could court Her favor, change Her mind, convince Her to hold back Her ultimate vengeance. Perhaps She would adopt him, make him very special, teach him to serve, to be Her slave, do Her bidding faithfully and ever after . . .

An hour ago he had heard the reply.

And he had been chanting feverishly since. Dressed in only his briefs, he opened the windows to hear the sound clearer. It was somewhere out there, above, high: calling, summoning, beckoning.

Three times Bob Fevre heard the sound.

Save me. Save me. His lean body drenched with sweat, despite the blasts of cold sir, he begged on.

It came. Once. Twice. Thrice. Long trailing sound. Alien blissful call. The call of Kali. The summons of the Dark Mother. Kali . . . Kunkali . . . I, Bob Fevre, your repentant child, a babe . . . I come . . .

Bob Fevre rose, rushed to the window, and stuck his head out.

Hanuman leaped across the room. "No! No!" he screamed.

In the hallway, the others heard Hanuman's cry. Dan Terranova and Wrench took turns hurtling at the door. It gave with a tremendous rending, and Wrench sprang through the gap, gun in hand. He rushed to the window and suddenly shouted, "Holy Christ!"

Rama Shastri joined him. He held the Walther .32 that

Terranova had restored to him from Police Headquarters. Shastri gaped, transfixed by the sight outside the window.

High above, extending from the roof, two powerful hands held the legs of Jadu, the Thug. Jadu, in turn, hanging upside down, held a rumel tightly around Bob Fevre's neck. The youth hung in Jadu's iron grip, his neck broken.

Hanuman had bounded to Fevre, grabbed his legs, and been dragged over the sill, too. And that was what Wrench, Shastri, and Terranova saw: a dangling rope of human bodies held in the viselike hands of Bidhan on the roof.

The moment Hanuman landed in midair, he heard the harsh snap of Bob Fevre's neck. Quickly, before Jadu could release his grip and send the corpse and Hanuman to the street below, the Swami climbed up Fevre's body until his fingers dug into the shoulders, and he was face to face with the horror-filled dead eyes and open mouth and distended tongue. Another swift lunge, and Hanuman's fingers clamped around Jadu's arms above the elbows. Now his safety was assured. Bidhan, who was straining to lift his brother back to the roof, would have to take Hanuman along with him.

Sweat began to trickle along Jadu's brow. He pulled the scarf free, and the corpse fell, bounced off a hydrant and the grid of a Ford, and landed in a pool of rainwater in the gutter.

Renewed faith surged through Jadu's hands. He blinked against the sting of the rain in his eyes and started to arc his rumel for Hanuman's neck. Praise Bhowani, this was the monkey Swami himself, a fitting victim for his newly inherited status of Strangler! But again Hanuman's speed bested the rumel thrust.

Above them, Bidhan growled in frustration. Still gripping Jadu's biceps, the little Swami raised himself until the soles of his naked feet kneaded into the Thug's face. Jadu screamed as the force broke his nose. His hand loosened on the rumel, and it flapped wildly in the wind, about to be blown away. With a sweep, Hanuman grabbed it, raised himself farther, and landed his soles again, this time between Jadu's extended legs. Then, seizing Bidhan's wrist with one hand, he flicked the rumel at the big Thug's head, jutting from the roof edge. Bidhan released Jadu's left leg and pawed at the snaking scarf.

Jadu had bellowed with all the pain his stomped-on testicles darted to his brain. He had flung his body wildly away from the building, seeking to upset Hanuman's balance. But the Swami had leaped again, suddenly, and Jadu now hung by the grace of Bidhan's hold on his right ankle.

Bidhan's left wrist was held by the Swami, and the strain on his entire left side was tortuous. The Thug was lying on his stomach, which restricted his mobility. Hanuman never loosed his grip for a second. His force on Bidhan's wrist seemed to astonish the giant, and Hanuman's persistent snapping of the scarf close to his right ear was maddening, distracting.

Bidhan tried to reassure his brother. Through the filmy rain spray, he could see Jadu's blood-streaked face whenever it was free of Hanuman's pounding. Again and again, Hanuman used Jadu's head as a stepping stone.

Bidhan pushed himself onto his knees. He sought to dislodge Hanuman with one final, massive blow from his free hand. But the Swami scrambled with him, first clawing and climbing up his torso, then clamping himself on Bidhan's back. Determined, Bidhan rose ever farther, pulling his exhausted brother toward the roof lip. He could feel Hanuman's scarf looping over him, but he counted on the thickness of his neck to hamper its effect. His main concern was to drag his brother to safety.

Hanuman jerked the rumel, Bidhan's head flung back, jarred his shoulders, and the abruptness of the motion forced the fingers of his right hand to slide down to Jadu's shoe.

"Save me, my brother!" Jadu screamed.

Bidhan moved his lips to speak, as the rumel bit into his neck again. Crazed, he flexed his back muscles, twisted to shake Hanuman from his body. The rumel tightened one last time. Bidhan choked, stood fully to relieve the rumel's pressure, and Hanuman leaped off his back, chopping at Bidhan's right elbow as he tumbled to the roof.

The rumel slithered harmlessly with Hanuman's motion, and Bidhan croaked a loud "Jadu!" The area below his right elbow was now numb, and he knew suddenly that his brother was gone. Bidhan froze as Jadu's scream seized the moment, then broke off with a final, rain-smothered thud.

Bidhan whirled. His long strides brought him up to Hanuman, who was just springing to his feet. Here was the cursed monkey man responsible! Bidhan's right arm lashed out. It met Hanuman in the chest, hurling him toward an unused chimney. Hanuman swiftly doubled his body and rolled it from its course as he flew. His head missed the chimney corner by inches. Landing in a belly flop across the slippery gravel, he lay still.

When the men in Bob Fevre's apartment had seen the human rope outside the building, they had bounded to the stairs leading to the roof door. It was locked, and Wrench had fired his Browning once, twice, kicked the door open. He paused cautiously, peered around the door at the reach of the gravel-covered roof.

Except for chimneys and jutting air vents from the gaslight days, the area was flat. On either side, it blended with the other flat roofs of the block of brownstones.

The three of them were standing before a small, peaked cupola that housed the roof exit. Wrench heard a scream from behind the cupola somewhere and started to move around its corner. Terranova followed him. Shastri was the last to emerge into the night. He heard a soft snicking sound but turned too late. A rumel dropped over his head. Perched atop the cupola peak was a Thug, his taut, wet jawline glistening.

Simultaneously Wrench, moving in the cupola's shadows, lifted his eyes and saw the silhouetted curve of the Thug's shoulders on the peak. He turned, pushed Terranova from his path, reached one of the lowered arms of the Strangler, and pulled him down.

The Thug was stunned. Stretched atop the cupola roof, his bent legs pressed against the sloping sides, bracing his weight, he had thought himself invisible.

With one blow, Wrench rendered the man unconscious. He dragged the body to the open door and threw it down the stairs. Wrench kicked the door shut, but just as he spun to check on Shastri, the night exploded.

Wrench heard the Ramasi *sanp*! cry, the kill command of the Thug. Two men leaped the divider from the next roof and came at him, while two more sprang for Terranova and Shastri. One fastened himself on Wrench's back. The other sought to grapple with him from the front as Arm Holder. Wrench kicked. The Thug before him fell away, holding his groin. Wrench was left with the Strangler, who slung his scarf. As Wrench saw the rumel's blur encircling, he raised his gun and shattered the Thug's cheekbone with its butt end. The Thug lost his perch, fell against the cupola, and eased down the clapboard wall to his haunches. Wrench kicked hard and broke the Thug's jaw.

Terranova was grappling with a non-Indian, a chela, whose hands were up to Terranova's nose. Terranova had dropped his gun to seize the Thug's wrists. They wrestled for a moment, when Terranova became aware that the wrists were unnaturally cold. They throbbed in rapid, rhythmic surges and then began to glow and to swell. Panic overwhelmed him. He pulled the young Thug around so that his back was to the cupola wall. He slammed the Thug's head against it again and again, until a dark, wet circle formed where his skull met the surface. Yet the hands, ever rising with the rumel, glowed more, grew more.

At last Terranova heard a sickening *splat*, and the wrists lost their power. The coldness disappeared, the Thug's lids lowered, the rumel loop collapsed. Terranova pushed the youth away and turned from the streaking wall to spit out a mouthful of vomit.

It was Trande Gautam, the Arcotee, who descended on Rama Shastri, who was still recovering. He cried out *"Sanp!"* and darted with rumel arced. Shastri looked up, his vision blurred, and sensed the threat more than saw it. His fingers scooped at the gravel at his knees, and, cupping what pebbles he could, shoveled the lot into Gautam's face. As the Thug tried to sidestep the spray, Shastri struck at Gautam's shins with his Walther. With a howl, Trande Gautam backed. By the time he regained his composure, Rama Shastri was standing, holding the .32, and Terranova was free from his attacker. The Arcotee, seeing that he was alone and outnumbered, ran into the darkness.

"I'll get him!" said Terranova, bounding onto the next roof.

Wrench started after him, then stopped. He had to find the Swami first. Without Hanuman, Santha had no chance. Wrench began his search, his mind imploring: Save her. Hanuman. God, must save her. Please, dear God, help . . . My baby, my . . .

A chimney. High. A block of dark against the lambent city glow. The rain did things to the lighting, a coating of diffused scintillation, limning borders, roof edges. . . . Growling, gargantuan, a figure stepped from the chimney shadows and met him in full stride.

Bidhan growled again like a rabid creature as his great arms pinioned Wrench in a bear hug. The hold was fierce, comprised of all of Bidhan's recent rage and pain. He flexed, bunching his muscles and shoulders in a bone-crushing effort.

Stephen Wrench tried frantically to remember his wrestling technique. He gulped in all the air he could hold, and then, as he released it, his chest caved in for a brief second, creating a finger's breadth of space between the two opponents. Wrench used it to pull the trigger of his Browning .38, aiming for Bidhan's foot.

But the giant moved, and the bullet richocheted from the roof to the chimney and into the night.

Berserk, the Thug pressed harder. Agony seared through Wrench, hot wires pulled through his bones and tissue. He strained and struggled, gulping in more air. Again, after the breath release, the excruciating pressure loosened. Wrench fired. Another miss. But this time Bidhan cursed in alarm.

Rama Shastri had heard the noise of Bidhan's attack ahead and raced for the spot. The flash of Wrench's gun outlined the two interlocked figures. Shastri leveled his Walther. A brush of air next to his sleeve, a sharp blow on his lower arm, and the Walther clattered onto the gravel. Shastri turned to face his assailant.

There were two of them, two crouched assassins, edging forward gradually, calmly. Beyond the layers of soaked gravel and roof shingle, where the shadows wedged like gashes of pitch. His gun was probably back in those dark depths with them. He could hear them now, shuffling over the small stones . . . nearer, nearer.

It was brighter now, with moving funnels of glow patterning across the sky. And there was clamor below: sirens, the crackling, static voices of police radios. They'd been alerted, somehow.

But still the shuffling closed in on him.

Meanwhile, not too far away, Wrench filled his lungs again. The sinewy bands tightened, the pressure bunched the fabric of his coat into his arm, and that, in turn, into his ribs and that . . . God, the bastard was strong! Bidhan's eyes bored their hate. . . . Wrench's chest expanded to its fullest. He worked his numbing fingers around the Browning's trigger. He emptied his lungs.

He managed to raise the gun's barrel. A fraction more . . . Wrench fired. With a cutting sting, the bullet had grazed Bidhan's thigh. Stunned with pain, he let Wrench go and ran behind the chimney. About to pursue, Wrench heard his name!

Rama Shastri had spotted Wrench again in the Walther's flash and called for help. The two Thugs pursuing him were in the ring of light now, their strange, pulsating doughy hands extended, the rumels twined in the swollen fingers. Shastri stared at the hands, paled. In the diffused lighting, they seemed like fungoid creatures growing separate from the rest of the bodies, supernatural hands.

Wrench, numb, aching in every limb, registered Shastri's danger, but knew he could not react in time!

"Ram, catch!" Wrench shouted and threw the Browning. He pitched it underhand, softball style, the best his numbed arm could do. The gun rose, arced the near-twenty feet. Still it was too far off to the left, heading for Mundy Street. Rama Shastri lunged, and the weapon slapped into his palm. He whirled at the crush of gravel behind him and fired, holding the grip firmly with both hands.

Part of a Thug chela's temple splattered into the night air. Shastri whirled again, aimed, fired, and the other chela grabbed his rib cage but continued to move, to fling himself on. Shastri sidestepped the charge, pushed the passing shoulder, and the

Thug hurtled from the roof to the street below. Screams commingled with the police sirens as the body crashed against the front of a patrol car.

Dan Terranova had slipped as he crossed the divider between the roofs. There was no gravel here. Light reflecting from the street streamered the tarry surface. Terranova raised himself on one knee and anxiously surveyed the area. Except for the weird outlines of the air vent with its duncecap shape, a pipe with an elbow jointing, and a chimney cluttered with television aerials, the roof looked empty. The only noise was the sploshing of rain onto the puddles where the roof buckled into small hollows.

He pulled himself upright, his stomach still churning from his struggle with the Thug chela. The rain hammered his cheeks, chin, neck. He was facing the nor'easter's thrust. Passing a small, sloping skylight, he heard a mix of new sounds.

The butt of his .38 wavered as he pointed it here, there, facing the pockets of darkness ahead. Terranova suddenly heard gun shots behind, back there on the other roof. He ought to return—to protect Wrench and Shastri.

Then sirens! The police. Those crazy bastards will shoot first and ask questions later. He had to be there to calm them down.

But from nearby came a different sound. Metallic noises! Coins? Clinking? Falling on top of each other? Who, what in all the hells of the damned would be fiddling with coins up here? Terranova's heart jumped, like a dead, leaden weight in his chest. It hurt, it pounded so hard. A signal. It could be a signal. One of the Thugs had kept shouting something. Terranova tried to mouth the word. Unpronounceable. A magic word that made the strangler's hands grow? Fuckin' eerie, unnatural.

Then he saw her, stationary by the roof gutter.

A woman? Wrench, Shastri, Hanuman—they'd all warned about a woman. And Wrench's daughter. There was a woman who'd attacked her!

She was dressed in a long coat and wore an even longer

dress beneath it. Silhouetted against the sweep of the patrol car beacons that brightened this entire end of the street block, her back was to him. Terranova neared, paused when the figure moved.

Terranova thought at first that she was dancing. Her legs splayed, the arms raised, bent, stretched, arced, pointed. The smooth flow spoke to him, the fingers danced and said more, the clunking bracelets stilled his panic, and he stood ramrod-straight.

The woman's sari dropped from the lower half of her face, and now there were words, rapid, hoarse sounds filtering to him somehow. They replaced the rain staccato, the sound of the vehicles below.

(And Betty Lassiter told him, "I have to jump, Dan. I have to fly. It can be done, believe me." She was drenched in her nightgown, and her naked toes curled over the gutter lip. Her windswept hair flapped, fluttered as if she were a winged thing, and her voice beckoned softly across the short gap between them. "I love you, Dan," she purred at him. "Love you, and I'm sorry I have to leave you. But I can fly, Dan. You've got to believe me.")

Dan Terranova howled in despair and threw himself at the slender outline to stop her dive. His shoes squished in the overflow from the gutters, and he toppled. "Betty! Betty!" he wept, as he slid on his stomach to the roof boundary.

His tears meshed with the rain on his face, and he couldn't see. "Oh, Betty, I've failed you!" he wept.

("How can you fail the dead?" it said mockingly in his brain.)

From the street, a police loudspeaker amplified a man's voice: "You, up there. You, up there. Come down. We have you surrounded."

Running footsteps nearing, anklets clunking by his ear, and he saw sandaled feet and, lifting his eyes again, the woman in the long coat. She looked down briefly, sneered, "Weak, weak man-thing," and ran.

Rising, Terranova saw the woman's form disappear behind the skylight, then somebody much bigger, definitely a man, running opposite him, near the other edge. With each stride the man bellowed in pain. Terranova raised his gun. "Hold it!" But now the newcomer was behind the skylight, too. Terranova moved to pursue.

Something grabbed his arm.

Terranova cocked his .38. A familiar voice broke through his blurred vision.

"Lieutenant, it is myself. Swami Hanuman."

"My God, Swami! I almost blew you away!"

"Do not go any farther. I beg you."

"They're behind that!" Terranova pointed at the skylight. "A woman and big man limping. My God—the woman, she cast a spell on me!"

"Remain here. Mr. Wrench, Rama Shastri—they are coming. Listen. Wait for them."

"Hey—don't you go, if I can't!"

Hanuman backed into the darkness. He reached the side of the skylight before Terranova finished. With his palm he wiped the blood that trickled from his temple. The terrible dizziness that he had felt when he'd awakened from Bidhan's blow was gone. For a while he'd remembered nothing, but consciousness had returned, slowly, steadily. Somewhere to his right there was a reverberating shot, and when he looked, the wounded Bidhan was heading for the skylight. Hanuman went after him, but the effort was costly. A few times he had to stop and wait, lest he encounter his foe too soon. The Swami wasn't yet ready for another battle.

He listened to the creaking on the skylight's southwest side. Certain that it was a door that led from the small enclosure into the building, he glided along the wall. He found it, a small door partially open and moving in the wind.

Peering inside, he found a short stairwell and another door. Hanuman slipped down to it. Its lock was broken, and a second later, the little man stepped into a dimly lit hall.

He listened, heard, finally, the whisper of a noise, and compressed his lips thoughtfully. From his trouser pocket he took the dead Jadu's rumel. Now, he thought, come to me, O lice of the Dark Mother. Come, and pretend that you are a guru of Life and Death.

Trande Gautam was alone in the building. Gauri, Bidhan, the rest had made their escape with ease, but Gauri, her stare flashing with Kali's fire, had taken Gautam's wrist with such force that he still trembled at the memory. "The monkey is coming. Stay."

Trande Gautam now watched the shadow elongate on the wall before him. See, Hanuman, he gloated, your very own shadow betrays you. May Bhowani peel the flesh from you soon. May your skull clack against the others on Her girdle.

It has to be, Gautam told himself. All else had failed, as before, and it was he who was the leader tonight—except when the Mother, through Gauri Bala, intervened. Gautam shuddered, remembered her cold, unyielding grip.

Why couldn't it be as with the saintly Thugs of old, he wondered? In times past, Thug bands had needed no Goddess present. They left Her in the heavens where such creatures belong. In those days the Thug Masters were enough. They led efficiently and wisely, and, sometimes, up to fifty victims were dispatched in one raid. Then they had much booty.

It was this land, this America. It was this new blood, the new chelas, who were especially trained in that Godawful, unnatural fashion....

Hush, mind, Trande Gautam told himself; concentrate on the shadow. Make amends for our losses tonight. One Swami Hanuman dead by the rumel's kiss is worth ten thousand thousand of these spiritless Americans, who do not live side by side with their gods.

The shadow continued to elongate. Gautam bit into his lip, wishing he could do the same to his breath. It sounded much too loud to his ears. He held the silk taut.

Unexpectedly, the shadow shortened, then was gone. Gautam cursed all the monkeys in creation. The shadow had sped close to the upper border of the wall, and Hanuman landed facing the corner curve where Gautam was hiding. Their eyes locked. Hanuman gestured with his hands, and Gautam bit his lip again, broke skin, and spat out blood. Hanuman was wielding a rumel, too!

Pain, deep shattering pain. Gautam felt betrayed. How could Kali Mother ever allow this? Gautam corrected himself. Hanuman was just playing with him. Yet an uneasiness lingered— that the Swami knew how to use the yellow scarf.

Gautam feinted to the right. Hanuman moved. Now left. Hanuman moved again. Once more right, and the weighted end of the rumel carried it to Hanuman's neck. Gautam blinked. The Swami was gone. Hanuman had lifted over Gautam's head, hit the wall with the soles of his feet, and bounced somewhere behind the Thug.

Gautam spun about frantically. His rumel dangled loosely, too loosely, and he nearly dropped it. Gautam regained control of the scarf, set himself to strike, when suddenly his breathing constricted. Gautam gurgled, clawed at the coil tightening against his throat, and doubled simultaneously from the impact of the Swami landing on his back.

He heaved his broad shoulders, bunched his back muscles, leaped to shake Hanuman off, kicked with his heels, but Hanuman was too high. Gautam's eyes bulged, white specks in his ashen face. He felt himself blacking out and made a violent lunge for the wall. A low groan in his ear, and, elated, the Arcotee wrenched free. It had worked. Hanuman, slammed against the wall, had lost his hold.

Gautam hovered in the center of the hallway, breathing in short, rasping intakes of air. Sounds farther along the shadows, and the Thug saw Rama Shastri and two other men emerge from the roof. He hoped they would try to intervene and thus hurt Hanuman's concentration. They didn't, though, but remained where they were.

Gautam inhaled deeply, shuffled, tried a feint, and then attacked. Again and again he hurled the weighted scarf end. Again and again Hanuman disappeared from the spot, sometimes springing off the walls with his awesome agility. Minutes passed, and Gautam started to show fatigue. His rumel thrust slowed, the calves of his legs became heavy. He became aware that Hanuman was maneuvering him toward the stairway. Far below, four flights down, there were voices. He was trapped.

Whatever the outcome of this struggle with Hanuman, he knew his chances of escape were nonexistent.

Yet Trande Gautam continued until he stood before the stairwell, panting, dripping with sweat. He could just about raise his arms. The Thug's look was feral as he stared at the four men on the landing. Then, straightening himself, Gautam attached his rumel to his waistband, seized the railing, and cartwheeled into the well. As he fell to his death, Gautam cried, "Kali! Kali!"

THIRTY-TWO

At 11:10 P.M., paramedic Eric Lindstrom checked the girl asleep on the couch. He picked up Deborah Klaus's wrist to take her pulse. Hell, her hand was ice-cold. He put her hand down and laid his palm on her forehead. Strange, that wasn't as cold. Pretty normal. Must be circulation. Eric made a note of it.

He scrutinized the room. Temperature seemed okay in here. As the doctor was leaving, he had explained that the place was a yoga center or something like that. Indians lived here. Real live Indians from India.

Eric bent forward to take the pulse and brushed aside the drape that somehow had dropped over the couch end. How the hell did that happen? He rose, pushed the drape aside, and reached for the cord that tied it back. It wasn't there. Eric looked at the opposite drape, saw it had a cord, and shook his head. He hadn't noticed especially, but he could have sworn both drapes had been tied when he came into the room.

Eric Lindstrom frowned. This girl's a police case. I ought to be careful, he thought.

He stared at Deborah Klaus. Her hands were beneath the blankets. She'd moved since he'd turned. The cold hand that

he'd held to take her pulse wasn't out on the covers anymore.
Cripes, that was a cold hand. Eric bent to investigate further.
The doctor had left the girl in Eric's care until he returned, and
he'd better make sure that everything was . . .

As Eric lowered the blankets, Deborah opened her eyes.

Outside, in the hall, Adelaide Jaworski paced. She was
restless because of all the excitement today and knew she
shouldn't be. She was smoking cigarettes again, too. The Swami
didn't want her to. He believed in her, believed that some of
her visions had been authentic, not just hallucinations. Swami
Hanuman knew she had spent most of her life in mental insti-
tutions, but he loved misfits. He claimed that God usually
preferred the unwanted, society's outsiders. She, Molly Doyle,
Nirmal were little else but lost, abandoned people before they
met the Swami. He had saved them from—

Adelaide heard a crash from behind the door where Deborah
Klaus slept. Adelaide hurried to the room and burst in. She
screamed for Molly when she saw Deborah breaking the neck
of Eric Lindstrom with the missing drapery cord. Then, instinc-
tively, Adelaide leaped at the girl to try to rescue Eric.

She fell back as her cheek was raked, and, before Adelaide
could regain her balance, Deborah gripped her shoulders and
flung her across the room. Then Deborah came toward her with
the cord, her eyes different and dark and seeming to float ahead
of her. The voice Adelaide heard was also new, and it rasped
along her nerve ends. And the hands, the growing, writhing
hands, neared. . . .

The creature—Adelaide no longer thought of her as Deborah—reached. The cord swung, looped, and suddenly jerked
back. The creature's shriek reverberated against the walls. She
smashed into furniture, toppled lamps. A large kitchen knife
was imbedded in her back. Molly Doyle stood nearby, pale
and trembling, watching the creature careen here and there.
When she had heard Adelaide's screams, she'd dashed into the
kitchen and grabbed the weapon. Entering the room, she'd
stabbed and . . .

Both women started to scream at once. Adelaide rushed to

Molly, and they held each other, still screaming at the nightmare before them.

Steam, fetid odors, spurted from the crazed thing. Blood trickled down the body in tributaries as the flesh cracked. The face was now a cross-hatching of minute crevices. The hair was burning from the scalp outward. The creature raged at them with its eyes. Its blackened lips snarled soundlessly. It lay in its death throes, sprawled on the floor before the window that had broken its fall.

As it died, somewhere deep within the shell, the last flickering of Deborah Klaus burned out.

Hours later, Chundra Bala stood on the cinnabar carpet and stared at the rich purple arras behind the Huzoor's throne. He moved a step or two toward the arras, then quickly returned to his original place. The murmur, the low, indistinct talking drifting into the room like faint incense, was driving him crazy.

Sweat lined his brow. Was he actually jealous? If so, he deserved the worst from his infallible Lord. It was so unexpected, so maddening. Chundra had never realized that his love for Gauri could grow like this, blossom anew after all these years of marriage. Chundra had no right to love this way. Gauri was Chosen. She was his wife, yes, but only when she wasn't serving his Lord.

Yet there were those murmurings again—the ones that occurred whenever Gauri and the Huzoor went behind the arras.

Chundra Bala went to the tapestry, covering his face with his hands, ashamed. He hadn't the strength to resist this time.

"But, Mother," the Huzoor grieved, "I have failed."

"Hush, my son," soothed the voice, not an inhuman rasp of a voice but Gauri's own, soothing, warm, and loving.

Chundra bent closer to the tapestry folds. He had to hear every word. Gauri had filled his heart until there was no void there. He had become jealous, possessive, Kali forgive him.

"Failed," the Huzoor repeated. "Tonight we lost Trande Gautam, Jadu, others. When will the stars realign in our favor, as it is prophesied? When is Shani to be astride his vulture?"

"Hush, child. Shani is astride his bird."

"Then what god usurps my moment, Mother?" wept the Huzoor. "Why do this monkey Swami and his men win in their struggles with us? I am Chosen, I have the missing fragment of Kali's scroll. I am the Lord of Thuggee, and yet we cannot kill mere men. Has the power of the scroll been lessened? Why must Hanuman, Rama Shastri, this man Stephen Wrench— why must they cast shadows on my Path?"

"Hush. There is great change ahead. There is the woman, Santha. Once she is with us, they can win no longer. There are also the Redeemed Hosts. Their hour is fast approaching. Tomorrow night there will be many dead, many skulls for Bhowani's cave."

"O my Mother!"

Chundra heard kissing sounds. He touched his rumel and darted to the place where the arras parted. He peered into the chamber beyond, his temples throbbing in his frenzy.

Gauri was on an ottoman, a thick piling of brightly colored cushions propped against it, holding the Huzoor, who was sprawled with his head in her lap. He was kissing her fingers. She stroked his hair, looking serenely before her. Chundra backed, afraid she'd seen him.

"She's mothering him," he told himself. "As is fitting for the vessel of Kali Mother, his only mother. Now stop this foul and treacherous business, Chundra, and leave them alone."

But he remained, nevertheless, as he heard the Huzoor say, "This woman is indeed hope for us. Makunda has seen her, talked with her. Ramanuja of the poetic heart has seen her. I have seen her. And you, blessed Gauri, have touched her. She is very beautiful."

"Yes, very beautiful, my son. Chosen for a Thug Lord. Once Santha is with you, all will change. A new vessel will mean more power.

"It is the Will and Power of Kali that grants us success, my son. Not ourselves, not even our skill with the sacred rumel. Consider the rumel. We tie two knots in it, am I correct in this?"

"You are."

"One knot is fixed. That, my son, is Kali, ever fixed, to

remind us that death awaits all in the end. But in its center is the other knot, the slipknot. And that is us, my son, Her servants. We do the killing, help the soul to its fateful and ultimate reward in the heavens. The fixed knot, the slipknot. Thuggee cannot exist without either. But the fixed knot is the controlling one. Do you understand?"

Chundra Bala heard a muffled "Yes" and more kissing. He wiped his brow. He rocked on his toes. And peeked one more time.

His breath caught. Gauri had lowered her sari, exposing her shoulders and breasts. One of her hands held the Huzoor's head between her breasts. The other stroked his hair. "My son," Gauri told him, "suckle." Obediently, he took the breast she offered. "Suckle well," she continued, "and sleep and forget. Tomorrow night, the bele, the killing ground, will be droll indeed. Kali Mother's laughter will ring everywhere."

Chundra Bala stared while his Lord mouthed the nipple. He forced himself away and almost slipped from the dais. "She mothers him, nothing more," he scolded himself, "as is fitting for the son of Kali."

But despite the explanation his intellect provided, Chundra trembled in his grief. And for the first time since he'd known the Huzoor, Chundra Bala hated him.

PART FOUR

NIRVA- HANA

Conclusion Or Catastrophe

THIRTY-THREE

Dan Terranova's fears about the police proved valid. They were extremely worked up. One group came in via the skylight, firing into the small stairwell first. Their other assault was from below, after Trande Gautam's body hit the landing, and the residents in the hallway flew into Mundy Street screaming. That squad arrived commando-style and peppered the stairs above. Rama Shastri was pushed away from the spray of bullets just in time by Terranova, and for a while the only safety left was to hug the floorboards. When it ended, a bristly sergeant demanded they surrender. Terranova shouted back his name and that he was a Boston policeman.

The police approached slowly. When they reached the prone men, they pulled them to their feet and had them face the wall, their hands flat on the surface, their feet wide apart. Then they were searched, their weapons confiscated, along with their identification. Convinced at last about Terranova, the sergeant demanded an explanation.

Terranova told a story about a gang of Far Eastern hit men and stopped at that point. "I can't reveal the rest, Sergeant," he stressed, "since it's government stuff. Top secret." He pointed to Wrench, Shastri, and the Swami. "These men are working for Interpol on this, and that's the most I can add. Sorry."

"Oh yeah?" barked the sergeant. "And what about this kid? We found him outside. He said he was guarding the house. Is he on your side, too?" The police pushed Nirmal Kapur forward.

"That he is, Sergeant."

The policeman studied them. "Oddest bunch of heroes I've ever seen." He glared at Terranova. "Funny that you're the only one with a police ID on him. I guess I'm going to need more convincing than you've provided. Since there's three dead guys on the roof, and three down in the street, one of which fell on top of a patrol car and went through the windshield. Plus the body downstairs. That's enough to keep you cooling your heels at the station until you prove otherwise."

"Will Mel Hughes of the Commissioner's Office in Boston be enough for you?"

Wrench checked his watch. "Or Horace Birch of Special Branch in Washington? He'll arrive in Boston in a few hours."

The sergeant swallowed and said in a mellower tone, "Yeah. Try someone like that on us, and we'll see."

Later, at the precinct, Terranova contacted Hughes, who was in bed. Hughes was concerned about the press: seven dead from a battle on Arlington rooftops was big news. "Get the hell out of there fast," he said, "and put Steve Wrench on." To Wrench, Hughes pressed, "I expect Horace Birch to cover this with the press tomorrow. Tell him that. It's out of our hands now. Seven dead? What is this—another world war?"

Afterward Wrench told the officiating heads of the precinct, "Our Washington liaison, Horace Birch, will issue a statement to the press by tomorrow afternoon. Can you get us out of here? By the back door, maybe?"

"The mayor ain't gonna like it," came the reply. "He's heading over here. Maybe the whole town council with 'im."

"Well, you can't hold us now." Wrench decided to throw Birch's name into their laps again. He was certain none of them knew who Birch was, but they'd never admit it. "Horace Birch will speak with the mayor, anybody necessary, when he arrives. Just bring Dan's car to meet us at one of the unwatched exits. This is international, gentlemen. Top secret. Okay?"

Wrench's tone implied that Horace Birch was closer to the President than even the Cabinet. Some guessed he was CIA, some figured FBI, some didn't know what to think, except that it was Washington-connected and big.

It was arranged as Stephen Wrench requested. Now, in Terranova's car, they sat brooding, feeling the results of their intense combat. Terranova broke the silence. "That was some fancy climbing, Swami. Amazing. What's your secret?"

"I don't understand, Mr. Terranova. There are no secrets."

A sigh. "I mean, sir . . . none of the rest of us could do it."

"Why not? The laws that determine the success of my climbing are similar for every one of you. It is in the level of observation."

"Now it's my turn not to understand. What level of observation?"

"It is much like acupuncture. Chinese doctors see pressure points in the human body that empirical medicine ignores. There are such points in the landscape, also. Everything is observation."

"If I translate that correctly, Swami, you're saying that you see a different reality than we do, and you act upon its laws, not the proven laws of nature that science as we know it calls facts. Well then, how does one ever acquire this insight of yours? This level of observation? I mean, how could any one of us become familiar with these hidden points in the landscape, as you put it?"

"Easy," quipped Nirmal, who was used to Hanuman's offhand extrapolations. "Just reach samadhi, nirvana, something like that. Anyone can do it, anytime. Just like snapping a finger."

Everyone laughed but the Swami. *Yes, my son; it is the snap of a finger, exactly that immediate,* he thought, but kept the wisdom to himself.

They reached Hanuman's place at 2:10 A.M. They saw the blinking patrol car lights from more than a block away. "Sonovabitch!" cursed Dan Terranova, thinking he'd have to call Mel Hughes again.

Which proved true. "What?" Hughes was losing his usual smooth veneer. "The Cambridge police think two of this Swami Hanuman's disciples burned the witness up? Why would they do that?"

"They didn't. The dummies can't explain it, so they're grabbing straws. But it's pretty strange, sir. Our own doctor thinks the witness, Deborah Klaus, might've swallowed a combustive. Like lye but much more powerful. He'll determine more after the autopsy. She burned up from the inside out and . . . it's uncanny . . . weird as hell!"

"Dan, people just don't burn from spontaneous combustion. You think these disciples are innocent?"

"Of course. Deborah Klaus attacked them, too, sir. After she strangled our paramedic."

"This is getting out control, Dan."

"I agree, sir."

"Well, put whoever's in charge on the line. I'll apply pressure about the federal angle. This thing's for the federals. Let them take on the stink. That Birch feller better pull through tomorrow, though. Somebody's got to clean up the mess. Confidentially, Dan . . ."

"Yes, sir?"

"Washington spoke over the phone like Birch was God Almighty Himself. Rumors I picked up from my own D.C. contacts say he keeps a low profile. Been at his job since War Number Two. OSS in the beginning, probably, or G-2, or whatever it was in the Far East. Been in charge since then, from FDR to the present. That's as strong a pull out there as Hoover had." There was a long pause.

"Maybe we shouldn't rock the boat, after all," Mel Hughes finally decided. "Why pull the plug if Birch has clout like that? He was Steve Wrench's boss all that time, so that means that Wrench was really something in those days."

"Oh, he is now, too, Mr. Hughes. And Rama Shastri is also extremely efficient. They know their enemy. Much more than we ever could, sir."

Another pause. In finale, "I'll speak to the commissioner. If this Horace Birch is God Almighty, it'll look good with Washington if we keep cooperating. Can't tell when we'll need a favor in return. But nine dead! What a night!"

Terranova asked. "Do you want to talk to the Cambridge police now, Mr. Hughes?"

"Yup, put them on, Dan."

Terranova handed the phone to a captain of detectives, then went across the room to where the smell from the consumed body of Deborah Klaus wasn't so bad. The windows were wide open, and the loose drape was flapping wildly. It *was* big, he

THE RISHI

335

seen tonight.

Rama Shastri met him in the hallway and announced, "We
have to hurry back to George Buchan's. Steve's just phoned
there. Santha's been having nightmares; she even awoke so
disturbed that she threw a hairbrush through the window."

They headed for the living room. Molly's and Adelaide's
sobs preceded them. They found Hanuman seated between the
two women, who were holding him in their panic. Wrench was
pacing. Nirmal leaned against the wall, lost in his own musings.

Terranova listened to Hanuman comforting. "Rest, my children," he was saying. "The horror is done." At least for now,
the lieutenant agreed.

At 4:55 A.M. Dan Terranova dropped off Rama Shastri and
Wrench at George Buchan's. George looked even more harried
than they did.

"She awoke in the early evening," George began, "and
insisted she wanted some fresh clothes, a few books, and things
from her apartment. She was all right. Quiet, warm, almost
exuberant."

George hesitated. "But I soon discovered something was
very wrong with her. Santha couldn't understand why she has
a police guard, why she's being watched here. So I reminded
her about the Thugs, everything."

"How could she forget?" demanded Wrench.

"She's repressed it. Try as I did to get her to remember the
Indian woman who struck her, she couldn't. Then she asked
me to go to the Lime Street apartment and fetch the clothes
and things she wanted. I refused, of course."

"Good man," snapped Wrench.

"Even with the police car parked on Mount Vernon Street
right before the entranceway into the courtyard, we're not entirely
safe. There's only one policeman on duty, you know. Anyway,
Santha seemed to accept my refusal all right. She started to
read this month's *Smithsonian* magazine. After that we watched
television. About twelve o'clock she announced that she was
going to bed."

"Didn't she talk about anything during this time?"

"She chatted a little about the *Smithsonian* article on Thracian art treasures, made some funny, witty remarks when she critiqued Kurt Leinster's book of poems. He's an old friend of mine. We were dining with him the other night, and he gave her the book. Poor Kurt, he'll wish he hadn't. Santha's critique was devastating," George smiled.

"She even ate well, Steve. Earlier, she had an avocado and later, about ten-thirty, we shared a tossed salad with crab meat that I had made."

"So her concentration was pretty good?" asked Shastri.

"Uh-huh. There was nothing irregular, believe me. No strange looks, odd remarks or actions. Nothing. She just seemed a bit tired still."

From Wrench: "She didn't have any fear, any worry for herself?"

"No. If anything was peculiar, it was that. Santha doesn't seem to realize the danger she's in." George was silent for a moment. "She didn't before she went to bed, that is."

"What happened then?"

George Buchan went to the cupboard, took a fifth of Teacher's Highland Cream, and poured himself a drink. "Join me," he urged. They agreed.

"We should've had this earlier," Wrench said.

George surveyed their bruised faces. "Yes, I can see it's been some night for everybody." He sat again. "Here's the rest," he offered quickly. "It shook the shit out of me, Steve, Mr. Shastri. I slept here on the divan. About one-thirty I heard a lot of shouting. It took me a minute to realize that it came from Santha's room. I rushed up the stairs right away. I could hear the words before I reached the threshold. Santha was shouting at somebody. I rushed in, ready to grapple with whoever it was.

"But, goddamn, Steve, there wasn't anyone there but Santha. She was sitting up in bed, her eyes wide open, shouting across the room. First she'd turn her head to one corner, then the other, and shout like hell. Something fierce, believe me. She was in a rage."

After a moment Wrench asked, "Could you tell who she was yelling at? Did she call them by name?"

George nodded. "One of them, sir." He wet his lips.

"Who, George?"

"Your wife, sir."

Wrench's hackles stood on end. "My wife?" he whispered. "Kamala?"

"Yes, sir. Santha was shouting at her for not saving her. She kept saying, 'You're my goddamn mother, and it's your job to protect me!'"

"Santha said, 'Goddamn mother'?"

"She wasn't herself, Steve. She said, 'You're my real mother, and the only mother I want!' Then she'd point to the other side of the room and ask, 'Why is she here, too? She's not my real mother. Why don't you get the fuck out of here!'" George flushed. "Santha doesn't use that word. It's not her style."

Shastri cut in. "Santha was telling her mother, Kamala, to protect her from some other woman who was in the room, too? The other woman claimed to be her mother instead of Kamala?"

"That's it. So far as I could make out, that was it. It went on like that for about five minutes. Back and forth, with Santha accusing her real-life mother of not being involved enough to free her from the clutches of the other one. Then Santha would turn to that corner—where the mystery mother was standing, in Santha's imagination—and scream things like, 'You're very, very ugly, do you know that! You think you're beautiful, but you're so ugly and evil no one could possibly love you!' Then, in the end, Santha jumped half out of the bed, waving her fists. 'No! No! I won't do it! I hate you! I hate everything about you!'"

Wrench said, "This was to the other. Not Kamala?"

"That's it. She went on, 'You won't make me! I won't do that! Ever! I don't care who you are!' Finally she appealed to Kamala, 'You'll save me, won't you! Stop her! You're my only mother! Ever! Always!'"

Wrench cleared his throat. He fumbled for his pipe.

"Then it was all over, suddenly, and I said, 'Santha, it's me, George.' Hell, she just stared—right through me. That was when I knew she was in a trance or asleep in some way. I just stood there and watched her settle back slowly and close her eyes, her face serene, undisturbed, as if nothing had happened. It was damn unnerving."

"To say the least," Wrench murmured sympathetically.

"What about the broken window?"

"That was about an hour later, Mr. Shastri. I stayed in the room in case she needed me. I had just dozed off when I heard this loud crash. Santha was out of bed, drenched with sweat. She'd thrown her hairbrush through the window. Her face was all twisted, and when she saw me, she just collapsed. I caught her in my arms and could hear her babbling in my ear. The same stuff again and again."

"Which was?"

George took a deep breath. "Okay—here it is: 'He wants to take me, George. I'm sorry. I don't know if I can resist him. He's strong, George. He's terribly strong.' I asked, 'Who, Santha? Who?' And she replied, 'He's in the Death Wind, George. He rides the Death Wind like a god.' Santha spoke this softly in my ear as if she was barely emerging from a stupor. Then I sedated her and brought her to the guest room to get her out of the draft."

"And that was it?" Wrench stood, his mouth set.

"Yes."

Wrench left the room and walked up the stairs to the guest room.

He was standing before Santha, asleep on the bed. Her eyelids twitched slightly, but she didn't awake. Hearing a footstep, he turned. Shastri was at his side.

"'Death Wind,'" Wrench repeated. "'He rides the Death Wind.' The Huzoor intends to mate with my little girl, Ram."

"The Huzoor has a dramatic bent. I discovered that in the Temple of Satī. He's whittling away at our emotional defenses again with this 'dream' of Santha's."

Hoarsely: "Then you don't think that was Kamala she saw?"

Shastri touched Wrench's shoulder. "No, my old friend, I don't. With all that we've seen the Huzoor and the Kali vessel, Gauri Bala, do in the past, we can believe they could create an apparition of dear Kamala—especially if it will disrupt any internal balance we might have."

"It's an evil and dirty way to fight, Ram."

"What more can one expect of a Deceiver? Com'on, Steve. She's quiet for now. Let's get some rest."

Wrench stared at his daughter again. "Goddamn evil and dirty way of fighting," he said and left the room.

THIRTY-FOUR

Neither Wrench nor Shastri had a desire to sleep at the apartment on Pinckney Street; they wanted to stay near Santha. They decided on the study. Wrench would use the couch, Shastri the big leather armchair.

Wrench stared at the grime on his topcoat. "We'll pick up a fresh change of clothes tomorrow."

"Now, how about telling me what happened to both of you tonight?" George asked.

Shastri nodded, but Wrench begged off. "We'll tell you everything tomorrow. Right now we're desperately in need of shut-eye."

However, Rama Shastri couldn't sleep. He ached down to his toes, and although he'd had plenty of time to dry out at the precinct house, he still felt soaked to the bone. Wrench, too, must be aching badly, since he groaned whenever he turned over. Shastri finally rose, went into the bathroom, and took a long, hot shower. It eased the pain in his joints.

When he emerged, he heard footsteps on the stairs. Looking up, he saw Santha descending. A moment later he was in the living room with her.

"Uncle Ram!" she cried, touching his bruised neck. "What's happened to you?"

He decided to be direct. "We encountered Thugs, Santha. One nearly succeeded at his job, that's all."

" 'That's all'!" She lowered her voice. "And Daddy?"

"Asleep in the study. He's fine."

She took his hand. "Thank God you're both all right."

Santha was wearing a white nightgown with a satiny luster. Her long hair covered most of the décolletage, but when she moved, the cleavage of her breasts was exposed. He looked away.

"I awoke in another room," she suddenly said, running her hand across her temple.

"You broke the window in George's bedroom. Don't you remember?"

"I did! Why? Why would I do that?"

He tried to probe if this was the "real" Santha. He couldn't tell. It was like sounding the depth of murky waters.

"Santha, where can we talk in private?"

"There's the dining room."

They went there. Seated at the magnificent table in the shadow of the highboy, Shastri found an ashtray and lit a Sher Bidi.

"These experiences you've been having were harrowing, weren't they?" he began, upset already with his choice of words. No matter, he was pressed for time.

Santha gestured in annoyance. "I'm so sick of thinking about me, Uncle Ram. Tell me about yourself. Do you realize this is the first opportunity we've had to talk alone since you arrived?"

Shastri frowned, then decided to play along. "Well, there isn't much to say," he replied, "except that here I am."

She reached out to him and squeezed his fingers. "And I'm so pleased. So very pleased. My special Uncle Ram. Tell me, did you have to leave anybody? Back there in India, I mean?" Santha winked.

Rama Shastri paused. Now what? He waited.

"Oh, come on, Uncle Ram," she said, with a knowing air. "Whatever happened to that mistress of yours?" She giggled. "Didn't think I knew, did you? My father didn't tell me, of course."

"Who did?" he asked softly.

"Mother."

The drapes were closed over the window, and he wished he could see her face better. "She did?" He rose.

"Yes. One day she and I were discussing you, and she confided in me." Shastri pulled the drapes slightly. He faced her squarely and almost gasped. For an instant—Kamala!

He sat down again.

"Tell me about her. It'll be our secret. We won't tell Daddy."

So he did, hoping to establish a trust in her. He talked of Ileana, the pleasant memories of her, her skill at fan-tan, the languages he'd taught her, how she looked, and the way she dressed.

"And you miss her, of course?"

"Lately I haven't thought of her too often. I've been preoccupied with this Thuggee thing. Santha, now about that—"

"Did she have a private name for you? You know, a nickname that lovers like to give each other? Did she?"

"Santha . . ."

"I call George 'Kesari,' for example."

"Kesari," he repeated. How wonderfully young-woman-in-love that was. Kesari. But still, how elusive you are.

Shastri stopped playing ball. "George says that you dreamed of your mother last night."

"I did?" she asked, in a hollow tone.

"Yes, and another woman."

Even more hollow. "I did?"

"You did," he stressed.

She was smiling every second. "Aren't you hungry, Uncle Ram? I am. Simply starving. Com'on, and I'll cook you the best breakfast you've ever had." She moved her chair with a screech.

Shastri held her wrist. He held it down flush with the table so she couldn't rise. "Santha, listen attentively. This Thuggee threat is serious. And you're one of their targets."

"You mean," she mocked, "they want to"—with her free hand, Santha gestured as if she were holding a noose and tilted her head, tongue dangling—"little me?"

Shastri slapped her. He did it before he understood what

he'd done. For a moment he stood trembling with rage. He waited, expecting her to make a scene or leave the room.

Instead Santha finally blurted, "Uncle Ram, I'm frightened. I'm feeling, thinking, seeing things I can't explain. George tried to straighten it out for me last night. I know you can do it better, and I'll listen to you. I honestly will. But I'm so terrified, Uncle Ram, that I'd prefer it in small doses. Can you understand that?"

"Certainly, dear."

She leaned forward, and the window lighting swept the shadows from her face. Her eyes pooled black and lusterless, as if she were momentarily lost in a vast dark place. Shastri wished he could enter that black gulf, no matter how alien. God, he wanted to save her! And Steve. And—yes—and dear Kamala.

"My child," he nearly sobbed, filled with love so painful that the room blurred.

"Please, Uncle Ram. I will speak with you about it. But I want George and Daddy out of the house before I do. Please . . . It will be easier that way."

Shastri nodded to those imploring eyes. They were warm again, moist.

In the living room, Shastri discovered that Wrench and George were both up. Apparently he and Santha had awakened George, who was so on edge he couldn't sleep beyond the drop of a pin. In contrast, Wrench's few hours had revived him. At the moment he sipped black coffee while talking on the telephone to Horace Birch. The government man had taken a suite at the Sheraton-Boston. Wrench saw his daughter and lowered his voice. He was giving Birch an account of last night's events. He waved at Santha when she passed him to give George a kiss on the cheek. He lowered the receiver, said to Shastri, "We meet Horace at twelve at his hotel."

Santha bent, kissed him on the cheek, too. "Morning, Daddy."

Wrench gestured at her nightgown. "Put on a robe, dear, will you?"

Santha's reaction was a searing look. She turned abruptly and ascended the stairs.

Shastri said, "Why don't both of you go out for breakfast? That'll give you an opportunity to give George a rundown on last night."

"I like it fine here," Wrench replied defiantly.

"George," Shastri appealed, "please direct the man to a good eatery, will you? Steve, Santha and I have things to discuss."

"I see." Wrench stood. "I suppose I'm blocking the flow of traffic."

"Santha and I were just having a tête-à-tête in the dining room."

"Nothing like a little bit of avuncular understanding."

"I just might learn something important. Now, hurry off."

Less than five minutes after they left, Santha returned. He was certain she'd waited, listening, upstairs. She hadn't put on a wrap, either. Santha glided toward the kitchen, chiming pleasantly, "George said he'd saved a steak for me. How about it with eggs, Uncle Ram?" Her eyes were mischievous. "A prime cut of sacred cow." Then Santha giggled.

The giggle made him yearn for India. Women giggled much more freely there, it seemed. He sat at the kitchen table, drinking tea in scalding gulps. He kept remembering Kamala and wondering why, since Santha no longer reminded him of her. Kamala would never've been dressed in nightclothes before him. Yet Kamala's memory dominated everything.

It was all the talk in the dining room about my love life, Shastri concluded. I'm getting lonely, missing a woman's presence when I stir at dawn. That was about his awakening time when he was at the kotwalee. Once in a while, Ileana had been awake, too, and they'd make love.

Santha placed a grapefruit on the table. Shastri ate quietly for a while. The small strip of steak was already cooking on the stove. Santha sliced an onion, a hot pepper, and then added a slight touch of garlic salt to the meat's juices. She was humming a tune, something contemporary, something for the young. He liked the modernity, he admitted, the casualness, the unabashed looseness.

"Why me?" she asked suddenly.

"Why?" he said, rather than say nothing. He didn't understand what she meant, however.

"Why did they pick me?" she continued, never once looking at him but at the steak instead. "Things have been happening, you see. I wander into places, Uncle Ram. The landscape resembles India, but I'm certain it's only a facsimile. As I wander, I know I'm special to them."

"To whom? A man? A woman, Santha?"

"Only a woman, so far. But I know that there's a man somewhere. I can smell him as if he's drifting in on the wind."

Shastri was startled. "That sounds almost romantic, my dear." He was frowning.

"It does, doesn't it?" Santha broke an egg in the pan. Then she stopped, poised, addressing the wall. She wouldn't look at him. "That's silly of me. There's really no *him*. I think it's . . . the call of India."

"The call of India?"

Santha didn't reply. Shastri scooped out the grapefruit and stared at her satiny back. Her gown sheathed her flanks tightly; the curves of her backside were clearly delineated. Shastri swallowed dryly.

She served the steak and egg, chatting while she brought herself cinnamon toast and more tea. "It's exciting, cooking for you. I don't know why." Santha sat opposite him and bit into a piece of toast. "I suppose it means that I have a larger family than I did a week ago."

"I'm flattered. Tell me, are these experiences of yours what you mean by 'the call of India'?"

"Yes, I think they are, Uncle Ram. I have felt a summoning, something calling me, for months now."

Her voice had lowered considerably, her words seemed weighted with awe.

Shastri cut into the steak. "Do you miss India?"

"Why not, Uncle Ram? Women are becoming more liberated there every day. Besides, lately, I miss the old, the very ancient things. You know—the roots of India. Saris, champa flowers, Bombay duck, the sound of tablas, bullocks in the fields, fakirs on their beds of nails. Yet that still isn't it. I'm not thinking of the little things. I've been recalling the great epic poems, the massive sculpture, the Kathakali, the dance-drama. Mother and I used to attend the performances. I saw the story of Poothana performed."

"I'm afraid my knowledge of the myths is limited, my dear."

"Poothana was a demoness. One day she disguised herself as a pretty maiden and tried to kill baby Krishna with"—Santha giggled—"her poisoned teats. Isn't that delightful!" This time she laughed heartily.

"Did Krishna survive?"

"Of course, silly. He always does. He wouldn't let go of her breasts, and she transformed back to an ugly demoness, and he continued to suck her life away."

"Amazing."

"I've missed so much of India, lately. The culture. Traditions. Old customs."

"Santha, this preoccupation with ancient India—do you think you're being shaped in some way?" Shastri's eyes fell on the scar, the mark on her forehead. It looked darker than it had yesterday.

"Shaped? You mean, influenced, manipulated? Why? Is it wrong to appreciate my Indian roots?"

"Of course not. But you admit that someone or something had been seeking you out. You were shouting just last night to a woman who claimed to be your new mother. Perhaps a demoness like Poothana. A false mother."

"A demoness! You, Uncle Ram? Are you saying you believe in a demoness?" Santha studied his face.

"Yes. You see, I've met such a . . . creature. Something not human. She's in command of this new wave of Thugs, along with their new, Messianic guru. The Huzoor, that is."

Santha pushed her toast away. She looked sick.

"What did she look like?"

Rama Shastri told her.

"Oh my God—you've described her exactly. Then she's actually alive!"

"George tried to tell you that, didn't he?"

"I was barely concentrating. She's alive?"

"You're shivering. You need a wrap, Santha, a robe."

"George claims that I said a woman attacked me. Was that the one, do you suppose?"

"I'm certain. Her name is Gauri Bala. She's flesh and blood, all right. But when the spirit enters her . . . Do you follow me?"

"Yes, I think I do. It is all so strange and yet so logical. Somehow the human heart unites then with the true Heart of Darkness."

"You're well acquainted with it, aren't you, Santha?"

"I must be. Yes, I've seen her, the woman, in the 'events,' Uncle Ram. I don't remember her the other night, though, even if I did tell George that she hit me."

Shastri wrenched his eyes away from the forehead mark, the miniature pickax.

"Perhaps if we discuss these 'events' of yours in detail, we might diffuse some of the influence. But you should cover yourself first. You're shivering terribly."

"Why me? Am I more susceptible to their evil? Am I more evil than others?"

"I doubt it. You're receptive, that's all. Like a medium. You were easy prey because of a psychic condition."

"Mother was that way, too."

"I never knew that side of her. Why don't you get your robe? Or perhaps I could fetch it for you. . . ."

"Wait! I have to know. . . . Can I be . . . helped?"

"There is Swami Hanuman."

"Yes, I've heard of him. Hanuman, the Monkey."

"Yes. He and his disciple, Nirmal Kapur, have already been very helpful."

"The rock star! A wonderful musician and composer. We attended one of his concerts. . . . Oh, I remember now—a delightful little man with simian features and a turban was there!"

"That's Hanuman, I'll fetch your robe, Santha."

"In George's room. Draped over the chair."

"I'll hurry, dear."

Shastri rushed up the stairs. He entered the bedroom, feeling the draft immediately from the broken window. George had covered the hole with bits of canvas board.

Shastri thought he heard a bell. He found the robe, took it, and went back down. At the foot of the stairs, Santha waited with a tall, gray-haired young man. "Uncle Ram," Santha introduced, "this is George's old friend, Kurt Leinster."

THIRTY-FIVE

The morning sun was warm. It nibbled at what was left of the snowdrifts and watered down the slush flow in the street gutters. Gauri Bala looked through the Volks bus's rear window, smiled at the sun flash off the windshield of the car trailing behind. How stupidly obvious they were, Gauri thought. Did they really believe they were invisible? It was hot inside the bus, and she'd taken her coat off. Sweat lined her brow and that of Sahib Khan. Only Ramanuja seemed cool, but as he steadied the cot holding the corpse of Ayub, she noticed his sleeves were sweat-soaked.

The sun-filled weather was an omen. The day was to be one of much death-giving. By midnight the morale of the Kali Akali Ashram would be high. All that had been endured by her would suddenly acquire meaning and direction. Then tomorrow, some time tomorrow, she would finally be free, replaced by the Huzoor's new consort. She and Chundra could return to India. Even the women of the Bala household would be a welcome sight after this country! Even her mother.

And India, of course. The sunlight blazoned through the bus's window and ignited her nose ring. Noticing, Gauri smiled again. Indian sunlight did that always. Indian sunlight was Gauri's constant companion, so close, so intimate. She thought of the wondrous poem by Vidyakara which told of the cat that licked at a sunray caught in a bowl, thinking it was milk.

Gauri thought, too, of Santha Wrench, grateful that she was

no longer jealous of her. She would greatly miss the Huzoor, though. To be his Mother incarnate on Earth had made her indeed blessed among women. Gauri's fingers passed lightly over her breasts. Lately they were always ripe, swollen with their strange nutrient.

Gauri had gone to the morgue with Sahib Khan to claim Ayub's body. They had stated they were his only friends in America, provided papers with proof of their identities. No other questions had been asked. The other dead—Jadu, Trande Gautam, and, of course, the acolytes—they couldn't claim, and so their victorious moment was incomplete. But the Huzoor had foreseen that the police would allow them to take Ayub, and that the police would follow them to locate the ashram. How the Huzoor knew these things Gauri could only estimate from her own experience. Sometimes Mother Kali saw the future so clearly.

But only certain happenings. There were enemy gods who misted Kali's vision, limited the range of her prophecies.

Gauri sighed. It was wrong that the deities had to live with mystery, too. Were she the breath of Brahma, she would have created things far, far better. Gauri Bala then sat stunned that she had had such a thought. It was indeed time she be replaced, if she questioned the will of Creation this way.

How Gauri yearned for release. True, the Huzoor tried everything to help make the burden tolerable. She was never quite drained now. The blood of animals had appeased the goddess's hunger for a while. And today, this Day of the Death Wind, the Goddess was to be satiated as She hadn't been for a long, long time.

Gauri Bala watched the unmarked police car behind them, mused, And this morning comes the beginning.

THIRTY-SIX

"I realize it's pretty early in the day," Kurt Leinster said, "but since I had business in this part of town, I decided to catch you and George before you made too many plans."

"George isn't here now," Santha replied.

"Well, maybe you can talk him into the Shakespeare Company's *Macbeth* tonight. I've got free passes. They've modernized the production some, and it ought to be fun."

Santha looked coyly at Rama Shastri. "Think the prisoner will be allowed out on probation?"

Before Shastri could answer, Kurt echoed, "Prisoner?"

"Have you had breakfast?"

"Yes, I have."

"Then stay awhile for tea." She took Kurt's hand.

Shastri stepped forward with her robe. She wasn't shivering anymore, but he slipped it over her shoulders nevertheless.

She steered Kurt toward the couch. Shastri observed there was a forced warmth to her now. Damn this intruder. Who was he, anyway? Santha acted as if he was someone very meaningful. Shastri felt like a man snubbed. I've been cheated, he raged with frustration. I was so very close, probably closer to her than anybody had been for many months. Well, nothing to be done. He must wait.

But he felt there wasn't enough time. He neared the couch. Maybe Kurt Leinster wouldn't stay long.

Leinster went on talking about *Macbeth*. "They're using very modern effects at times, even chopper sounds during the early battlefield scene, to remind the audience of Vietnam. What do you think?"

"That something wicked . . . Oh, nothing!" Santha passed her palm over her scar. "I'm afraid I've been marred since you

349

last saw me. That's why I'm virtually a prisoner here. Did you see the police guard outside?"

"Yes. I was wondering why he was there."

"They claim . . ." She gestured to Shastri. "Uncle Ram, my father, George . . . they claim an Indian woman struck me. It left the strangest mark. See." Santha bent closer to Kurt and laughed harshly. "A witch did it! By the prickling of my . . . forehead, I suppose."

"It's barely noticeable, Santha."

"You think so! It healed immediately. I shall have to have some plastic surgery done in the future, though." She rose. "I'll fetch the tea." Uneasy: "I'm not as pretty as I was, am I, Kurt?"

"Believe me, that's not true!" He said it with such fervor that Shastri thought, My, my.

Santha went into the kitchen. "You must get to know each other, you two," she called to them. "Kurt is very talented, Uncle Ram—an artist, a poet and novelist, an archaeologist. Have I listed everything, Kurt?"

Shastri was attentive.

"He even plays the psaltery, don't you, Kurt?"

"Yes. Yes, I do."

"Writes poems. Oh, I finished your book last night, by the way."

"I'm prepared for my execution."

Santha approached with the tea tray. "It was a challenge. Even disturbing. You see, it can't be that bad, if it stirs the emotions."

Kurt winced. "Yes, with disgust. I know I'm not a good poet. It's all right, Santha. I'm not sensitive about it."

"Really, I liked the poems, Kurt. I wouldn't lie."

Rama Shastri was doubly attentive.

"Well, I only published the book to pick up my spirits. I was going through a deep depression." He turned to Shastri. "I've always had to fight depressions, ever since I can remember. The book was a temporary placebo. I was conning myself that I'd finally achieved something."

"Could I read the book, too? Would you mind?" asked Shastri.

"Be my guest. If it's all right with Santha."

"Better Uncle Ram than Daddy, Kurt. Daddy hates modern verse." A giggle. "He never got past 'Danny Deever.' The book's in the bedroom, Uncle Ram. The one with the air conditioning." Somberly she explained, "I broke a window last night."

Kurt Leinster stared at her.

"I awoke upset, I guess. Anyway, I'm not angry now." She smiled at Shastri, prepared to change the topic. "Uncle Ram is India's greatest policeman, Kurt. He's had a brilliant career. He's tracked down everything from the Japanese in World War II to Thugs."

"Thugs? Are there still Thugs in India, Mr. Shastri?"

"Yes." Shastri decided to follow Santha's lead, even though she was motivated by forces he couldn't understand at the moment. "Thuggee still exists."

"I've read a bit about it. The subject is fascinating."

"Is it?"

"To a layman like myself, yes. The Hashashin assassins of the Old Man of the Mountain, Jack the Ripper, Thuggee, Bluebeard, the original Black Hand—it's all fascinating. My hidden bloodthirsty self is aroused by the subjects, I guess."

"Have you ever been to India, Mr. Leinster?"

"Kurt, please. No, I haven't. Which is surprising, considering how interested I am in ancient cultures. But Santha tells me that India is losing its exoticism. No more rajahs riding atop elephants in howdahs. I suppose even the Indian rope trick is passé now."

"Kurt, I didn't mean to ruin India for you. Sometimes I really talk too much."

Kurt smiled. "I must admit I find the fact that Thuggee has survived into the twentieth century so intriguing, I'd like to buy an Air India ticket right away."

"Kurt, that's bizarre!" scolded Santha. "Can't you think of better things to go there for?"

"I guess it did sound a little odd."

"Not odd, Kurt. Twisted."

Shastri was standing at Kurt's right during the silence that followed. Kurt tilted his head at an angle that allowed only Santha to see him fully. She backed, easing her body away from him, her eyes reflecting his reaction to her words. Shastri tensed; why, she's frightened!

"That wasn't very nice of me!" Santha apologized and reached for Kurt's hand. Exuding warmth suddenly, with an abruptness that appalled Shastri, she then urged, "Let's talk of other things, Kurt dear. Please."

He smiled. "Of course."

Santha was thoughtful for a second. "Uncle Ram. Could you excuse us? I'd like to speak with Kurt alone." Her voice was hoarse.

"All right, Santha. I'll go upstairs and read Kurt's poems."

Shastri reached the staircase and glanced back. She was watching him, her lips moving. He wondered what she was saying. Damned if she wasn't attracted to Kurt Leinster, so much so that she dreaded Kurt's anger, his rejection.

Santha said, in a low voice, "Wait until he goes upstairs. Then I'll explain, Kurt . . . There, we can talk freely now." She touched his hand again. "I hated being rude to Uncle Ram. I'm a victim of cabin fever. I've got to get out of here soon!"

"What's wrong?"

"They're forcing me to stay here, and under police protection, besides. George, my father, Uncle Ram—their idea. It's about the Thuggee thing that Uncle Ram mentioned. He claims that Thuggee has . . . well, migrated to America. Imagine that!"

Kurt was poker-faced.

"Lost your tongue?"

"You just put me down for my interest in the subject, remember?"

"I said I was sorry. But listen—if it's true, if Thuggee is around, I have a lead to them. Maybe."

"You do?"

"Yes. And I'm appealing to you to help me, Kurt. Please, I have to get out of here."

Kurt stared at the ceiling.

Impatient, Santha shifted, doubling her legs under her. Then she fiddled with the hem of her robe.

"You want me," he began slowly, "to help you escape."

Santha giggled. "Yes. That's it. Escape from my Daddy and Uncle Ram, and George, of course."

"Of course," he repeated, turning to her. It was said so abruptly, so coldly that Santha started.

"It'd only be for a while, Kurt," she stammered, "I promise. I just need to be free for a few hours, that's all. Besides, I'd be helping Daddy and the others by tracking down my bloody lead, don't you see?"

"Tell me the lead first."

"You won't tell?"

Kurt sighed. "No, I won't tell, Santha."

"Remember the other night? When they played that recording at the restaurant? Remember how it upset me?"

"Yes. The Kali chant."

"Kunkali, to be precise. Well, one of the employees there belongs to a cult, a commune, an ashram—I don't know what exactly—that is called the Kali Akali. He told me he was a member."

"And you figure this Kali Akali is connected to the Thugs?"

"They chanted to Kunkali. The worst of the Goddess's aspects, Kurt."

"Okay. But why not just tell Mr. Shastri or your father or the police for that matter?"

"No! Damn you, Kurt; you play everything so goddamn safe! I want to check it out for myself!"

Again that coldness. "You've never liked me before. Come on, don't deny it. I'm no fool. You've made that very clear. Why are you using me now?"

Santha's robe felt taut around her breasts. His eyes were hard and his voice harder. She flushed and caught her breath. Her mouth felt dry, almost brittle. She shifted on the couch again and spread her knees apart.

Kurt's eyes lowered. She knew he could see into the space between the knees now, see her thighs. Transfixed, he seemed to glow. His eyes were now a darker blue, and, as they lifted to hers, they were no longer serene. My God, she thought; what am I about to do? I've never, ever done anything like this before. My God.

"I don't mean to use you, Kurt," Santha blurted then. Tears streamed down her face. "It's not what I'm doing. Honest, Kurt, it's not. You've got to believe me!"

"I want to," he whispered, and his eyes dropped again.

Santha couldn't say any more. Her mouth, her tongue seemed filled with hot dust. Her mind said things, though. Her mind raced and talked on and on, like a speeding monsoon wind.

My God, this thing! This hot, hot moment that's making me all body, mindless and all body . . . !

Santha Wrench spread her knees farther. Her eyes talked on, while he stared: See how much I understand you now. Accept your great need, that great, fearsome, childlike hunger. And see, indeed, how welcome-moist I am for you, sweetie. A special, dark, pubic forest, moist with my very own rose-petal lips . . .

As if seized by a rictus, Santha pulled her legs from the couch and dropped her feet to the floor. She stared at the apartment wall, shocked with herself.

Kurt Leinster said, "I'll help you, Santha, I will. Here's what to do. We'll keep in touch by phone, and when you know the time is right, just call me. I promise—I'll come then to take you away."

Santha sighed. The apartment walls seemed to echo his soft tones: ". . . take you away . . . away."

THIRTY-SEVEN

Carmichael said, "We should've used other trailing cars, Captain. I bet they've spotted us."

Adair grunted, "Let 'em see us. We'll just stick with them like a tick on a bitch's belly. Sooner or later they gotta take Junior home."

"You mean to a funeral parlor?" asked Jacobs.

"Naw, they burn their dead."

"Them's Hindoos, Captain. This stiff was a Muslim."

Adair hadn't considered that. "Well, what the hell do Muslims do with their dead, anyway?"

No one knew.

"I've got an idea," Francosi offered, who was at the wheel. "Let's call in and ask. HQ can find out for us."

"Like hell," Adair growled. "This thing is ours. That was the agreement. We take care of it ourselves, and we get the credit. You guys want to show your worth, don'tcha?"

"I'm not sure." Carmichael lit a Salem. "As much as I agree that the feds are a bunch of assholes, I don't like moving in on their claim. This Indian thing's theirs, and I say, good luck to them and the Red Sox. Shit, lookit the rumor from Arlington about what went on last night. Guys being thrown off rooftops and all kinds of weird crap like that."

Adair shifted his bulk in the front seat, glared back at Carmichael. "Why did you volunteer for this, then? I told you guys not to come along unless you really wanted to. I arranged it with the morgue people to give me a call right away if anyone came to claim the Thug's body. I wanted to beat that sucker Terranova at his own game, and I thought you guys were with me. Shit, here's Terranova sucking up to the feds and the Commissioner's Office and that Hindoo cop. He's making us all look like we're a bunch of fucking dummies."

Carmichael shrugged.

"What's that mean? This was strictly a volunteer effort, Earl. You want out, you can leave now."

Francosi slowed the car.

"Move on, Nick," Carmichael said.

They were silent for a few blocks.

"Jeez, they gonna throw the stiff into the harbor?" asked Jacobs suddenly. "This is the wharf district."

"It's funny," agreed Adair.

The Volkswagen bus turned a corner between two warehouses.

"I know that turn," Francosi said. "It's a dead end, with Boston Harbor for the end."

"I guess Muslims drown their dead," concluded Jacobs.

They neared the corner.

"Maybe we ought to call in for a backup."

"Is this to be ours or ain't it?"

"It's just that calling for backup's the usual procedure."

"This isn't usual, Nick. Even the fucking suspects ain't usual. These Indians are big stuff. Hell, they've got a drug link all the way to Southeast Asia. And you know how the Commies like to infiltrate us with drugs. I explained that to all of you one day, don't you remember? Ferchrissakes, why do I always have to repeat things!"

Adair gave the order to turn the corner. Ahead, flashing shiny in the sunshine, was the Volkswagen bus. It was parked, its bumper almost touching the pier lip. In the shadows, halfway down the warehouse wall at their left, was a long, sleek limousine. It faced the pier entrance. Nick Francosi slowed the car again.

"I don't like this." He looked eagerly at the radio.

"Keep it off," ordered Adair. "As far as HQ is concerned, we're not out on the road today. Now stop here."

He stepped onto the asphalt. Carmichael and Jacobs joined him. Francosi exited last and was about to walk forward when Adair directed, "Stay here, Nick. If you see us in trouble, then, and only then, do you call for backup. Okay?"

Francosi nodded.

They started to walk. "This isn't getting us to their hideout," Carmichael said softly. Adair frowned until his eyebrows seemed to touch. No, it wasn't, he admitted, but something told him he'd better see what was happening here. Something told him deep, like a voice in his head or in his ear, like a whispering voice in the breeze, urging, "Go see. Go see!"

The Volkswagen bus had its rear doors open. A woman was getting out, with two men. "There's the driver, too," Adair reminded the other detectives.

"Maybe they're gonna transfer the body to the limo." It was Saul Jacobs. But the limousine doors were closed. They were suddenly passing it. Adair took his gun out and edged to the limousine. He looked through the windows, went back to his men. "Empty."

"Lookit that nose ring, Captain!" whispered Jacobs.

"Is something wrong, sirs?" Gauri asked, staring at their guns.

Adair stepped forward. His eyes darted from the woman to the tall, long-faced, swarthy man next to her elbow. His hold tightened on his gun's grip. The third Indian was a few paces behind the tall one.

Back at the patrol car, Francosi strained to see what was happening with the group at the bus, but the sun glare hurt visibility. He could just about make out that something was shining in the woman's face. What the hell was it? Francosi walked forward a little, then checked himself and hurried back. He quickly explored his surroundings. Just when he was closing in on the car, he thought someone was looking at him. Where? Who, and from where? The warehouse to his right had a doorway with two stone steps. Maybe he ought to see if it was unlocked. Maybe one of those Thug guys was behind it.

Detective Lieutenant Nick Francosi jerked backward as the door suddenly opened, like a live thing responding to his thoughts. He sighed with relief as two young women stepped out. One was dressed in a leather jacket, and the other wore a short imitation-fur coat that was a scruffy gray. Their Levi's were tight around their long, thin thighs, and they clacked on the asphalt in spiked heels.

"Okay, girls, clear out. We're conducting police business here." The leather-jacket girl nodded, plucking at the kerchief tied around her waist. Francosi concentrated on the Volks bus again.

The captain was now talking to the Indian woman and the two men. Adair was holding out his identification. Francosi could hear the words: "Just checking on what you're doing here. We've had a lot of warehouse robberies lately." Francosi figured that what Adair was really thinking was that this was a drug pickup. The limo was maybe carrying packets of heroin, and the Thugs were planning to transfer the goods to the bus. Hide it on the corpse.

The driver of the bus had left the cab and was heading toward them. A big sonovabitch, thought the detective, wishing he were there. Carmichael, meanwhile, looked inside the back. Francosi wondered why the bus was parked so close to the pier end. Might think they'd have parked closer to the limo for the transfer.

He tensed. What was that? He thought he saw something. Francosi moved forward a few strides, then shielded his eyes from the sun with the side of his free hand and gaped. A pair of human heads were bobbing above that very boundary wall! Goddamn, but there were men hanging off the pier, and now they were lifting themselves up and over onto the asphalt! Adair, the rest, were peering into the bus's interior, their backs turned to the newcomers!

Francosi braced himself to shout a warning. He heard a clacking, spun, and strong, lumpy fingers clamped over his mouth. His eyes fixed on what he'd thought was a kerchief, pressing on his Adam's apple.

The first inkling Captain Charlie Adair had of an attack was that suddenly his knees buckled. Makunda, who had silently crossed the five yards from the pier edge to the back of the bus, hit him from behind with all the ease and skill of a football lineman. Jacobs, too, was buckled at the knees, while Carmichael, who rushed forward, was seized at the shoulders by Bidhan and thrown into the bus's interior. Then the giant, limping from his healing flesh wound, scrambled in after the policeman.

In a handful of seconds, Adair's universe collapsed. He saw Jacobs succumb to the rumel of Sahib Khan, while Ramanuja held the detective's thrashing arms. From the bus came the echoing *blamms* of Carmichael's feet, as he desperately tried to break free. Repeatedly, for a short time, his heels hammered at the metal floor, only to stop suddenly. Adair had no doubt that Francosi was already a victim, too. The timing, the precision of the attack left him with a torpid "Hail, Mary" that he could barely utter. Later, though, he was to credit the uttering of this same prayer as "the spark of the miracle that saved me."

One of the young chelas was acting as Arm Holder. Dripping from his partial immersion in Boston Harbor, when he had hung by his fingertips from the pier wall, his flanks squinched in the cold wetness as he tried to grip Adair from behind. Adair fired without thinking, a behind-the-back shot that carried with it the legendary luck of the Irish. The bullet punctured the chela's rib cage. Adair rolled toward the harbor side, but not before another chela had struck his wrist with a karate chop. The Colt Detective Special clattered on the pier.

On his knees, Charlie Adair saw the faces of death rushing at him. He rose, kicked from a semicrouch, felt his shoe impact with someone's shin. Then, terror propelling his leg muscles, he outdistanced the circle of reaching hands. Quickly scanning the harbor, Adair saw one alternative and took it. As he leaped off the pier to the murky waters below, his "Hail, Mary" ended with "now and at the hour of our . . ." The splash of contact blotted out the sound of the final word.

THIRTY-EIGHT

Rama Shastri studied the drawings again. The leering gargoyles, cherubs, angels, hunched scruffy cats, forked-tongued lizards, the animal bodies with heads of men and women. The huge naked woman, her features strained and contorted as she sat astride a free-floating earth, an elfin child on her shoulder, clinging to her ropy tresses. . . . They all leered.

Often a particular drawing would have little or nothing to do with the poem on the adjacent page. The figures were frequently non sequiturs, representing other transient imaginings. Something rushed, fleeting, was suggested in the thick, abrupt pen strokes. Kurt Leinster was a man running, then.

The drawings captured that perfectly. He was good, an artist of promise.

But the poems were an atrocity. Kurt Leinster must've been depressed indeed to have felt they were worth publishing. Rama Shastri closed the book for the fifth time.

Keep out of it, he warned himself.

He was becoming too possessive about Santha. Like Steve. Taking the Uncle Ram role much too seriously. Why couldn't an artist have every sort of demon in him? Shastri, the policeman turned analyst of the creative maelstrom in Kurt Leinster? It didn't make sense. Keep out of it.

He heard the door close below. Going into the hall, he watched Santha climb the stairs and enter the guest room. Her head was lowered.

Leave it alone, Rama.

When Stephen Wrench and George Buchan returned, however, he told them of Kurt Leinster's visit.

"It was very untimely," he explained. "Santha was beginning to recognize that she was under the control of something invisible and malevolent these many months when the doorbell rang.

360

Your friend Kurt, George, has tickets for *Macbeth* tonight. I don't think you and Santha should go."

"Why not? It might do her good. She can't stay cooped up in the house forever. Don't worry; we could all go and greater ensure her safety."

Shastri gave him the book of poems. "Have you looked at this?"

"No. Kurt gave it to Santha the other night, and she insisted on reading it first."

"The poems are terrible, George. You can ignore them, except for their content. Gothic creatures, you know—mythological demons and such. But terrible poems. Unreadable, almost."

"So?"

"But the artwork is masterful. Reminded me of Goya at first. Artistic caricatures. Look for yourself."

George whistled. "Wow—Goya or Heinrich Kley! I didn't think Kurt had it in him. They're good all right."

"Yes, and like your own work upstairs, the better it is, the more it can't resist exposing the truth. Look closely at the faces of his creatures, and tell me what you feel about Kurt."

"He's laughing up his sleeve, the sonovagun," George said finally.

"Naïvely put. I'm sorry to be so blunt, George, but Kurt is doing far more than just laughing. Show it to Steve."

In time, Wrench gave his opinion. "It's disturbed. He's angry as hell at everything, everybody. These critters gloat as though they're going to put something over on the rest of the world, the first chance they get."

"Precisely."

"Well, of course they look that way," George protested. "They're demons, hobgoblins. Even the cherubs and angels are tainted with diabolical mischief. That just happens to be the tone of the book, isn't it? They're illusions, dark illusions. So Kurt drew these from all that churning mess that's supposed to be in the id. So what?"

"Well, isn't there a similarity between what we see in your depictions of Santha upstairs and these drawings? The same gloating menace, the feel of total atavism? This new Thug movement does have non-Indian recruits."

George laughed outright. "Kurt Leinster! A Thug?"

"He did express a knowledge of Thuggee," pressed Shastri, concealing his irritation. "He said the fact that it had revived held his interest greatly. In fact, he was absolutely delighted."

"Well now, Ram," Steve interrupted, "in the beginning, we weren't exactly depressed about the idea, either. We reacted like a pair of overly imaginative boy scouts. Maybe Kurt's the same way."

"That's right!" George cut in. "Kurt may be excited about Thugs, but I guarantee you that if he ever met one, he'd run damn fast for the hills."

"Granted that you're correct, George, do you think that it's healthy for Santha to be with him? She is very disturbed herself at the moment."

"I maintain that taking her to see a play is damn good sense. It would be therapeutic for her to do something she normally would do."

"You, Steve?"

Wrench asked George, "You're positive about this pal of yours?"

"As certain as you are of Mr. Shastri. Kurt's confused, and maybe when he did these drawings he was disturbed for a time, but if that's the extent of it, he's okay with me. This isn't a dipsomaniac or a freaked-out druggie we're talking about, Steve. Kurt Leinster has managed to keep his head straight through a miserable childhood and many years of loneliness. He's all right. Odd, an eccentric, an anomaly, but all right."

"Then a night at the theater gets my vote, too." Wrench tapped Shastri's shoulder affectionately. "Hey, don't take it so hard. Basically, that was sound police work. A cop ought to suspect almost everybody."

Rama Shastri withdrew into his thoughts.

But it wasn't until he was having lunch at Horace Birch's hotel later that day that he forgot the matter. Horace Birch was the kind of man who compelled attention. Tall, Lincolnesque-lean, and WASPish, he surveyed Wrench and Shastri with slate-grey eyes that never wavered. They were all eating chicken, and a moment of sorrow gripped Shastri as he remembered that the last time he'd eaten chicken had been at Ved Addy's home. He could still hear Ileana's prickling laughter. He mentally switched to Ileana in the garden and felt better. The last time he'd held a woman in his arms. God, he missed the comfort.

Birch checked his watch. "Let's get up to date on this Arlington business. I've managed to mollify the police authorities and local politicos sufficiently." He pulled a cigar from a case and proceeded to cut off its end. "But there's been a leak to the press. Nothing too worrisome. So far they think the Thugs are part of the Golden Triangle bunch."

"They and a certain captain," said Wrench, thinking of Adair.

"Who's that?"

Wrench told Birch.

"It's troublemakers like him that we have to worry about. The would-be local heroes. They won't cotton to what you lads are doing at all. That's why I'm planning to stay around Boston for as long as you need me here to clean up after you. A little bit of governmental elbow grease, you understand."

He puffed on the cigar, smiled contentedly. "Also, don't be surprised if the other big boys try to muscle in now. I mean the CIA or the FBI. Our hands are going to be damn full. Yes sir, as full of everybody else's officious shit as you can find.

"We have no recourse but to let them in on some of it. A little bit here, a little there. But I want you to know that I'll back you as much as I can."

Rama Shastri pushed his plate aside and hunched over the tablecloth. "Thugs like secrecy, Mr. Birch. The very philosophy of the Deceiver demands it. The moment their existence in the area becomes too advertised, they will move on. That would prove disastrous. It would be difficult indeed to trail them again.

"You see, the unusual incident of the death of Abel Fairley, of the rumel stolen by two of the cult members, gave us the scent here in the Boston vicinity. In itself it was uncommon good fortune for us. But if they decide to pack up and leave for another city or country or even continent"—Shastri raised his hands in a gesture of despair—"well..."

"What Ram is saying, Horace, is the bastards are as elusive as a whore's virginity. We know some of them are Indians, and that ought to make 'em stick out among the population, but we still can't find them. Then there's this leader of theirs, who never shows his face, and the sacred scrolls that are the raison d'être behind the entire Thug revival."

"Sacred scrolls? You haven't briefed me on them yet."

"Don't worry, I will," Wrench replied, wondering how in hell he'd do exactly that.

Rama Shastri lit a Sher Bidi. "Lately I've had a growing conviction that a Thug migration is already in the planning stage. They've already been exposed too much for their own comfort. Also, their morale must be low. They've been bested every time, in India at the Temple of Satī and here. They must do something that will have impact and meaning to themselves, quickly. What they must achieve is the establishment of a bele."

"What's that?"

"A secret burial ground for the honored Thug victims. Honored, you understand, by immediate admittance into paradise. A bele is a very sacred place, and often new victims are lured to its vicinity in order to enlarge the cemetery. There were countless beles throughout all of India, north and south, in Sleeman's day. He once discovered one that had over a hundred dead in it. Yes, I believe they will try to establish a great bele in the Boston vicinity soon. Then they can move on to another location with a feeling of accomplishment."

"You mean they're looking for a gathering of people to kill all at once?"

"That, Mr. Birch, was a Thug specialty. Thugs would often befriend traveling caravans in order to join them. Then, at the proper time, usually while they were singing before the campfire, they would do their duty, as they saw it. This new breed of Thug, however, isn't so concerned with the ritual skill and timing involved in breaking the neck.

"From what I've gathered from the attacks on ourselves, they are content with simply death-dealing strangulation. Sometimes a Thug tries to kill a victim by himself, even without the aid of an Arm Holder. This implies that they're more reckless of their own welfare and more driven. More fanatical. They still use the yellow scarf, but I see no reason why, in time, to ensure greater success, they might not use cords or, like the Mooltanee Thugs, ropes."

"And you predict they will seek a group of victims soon? And, if successful, bury them secretly afterward?"

"Exactly."

"That means forty, fifty, or more American citizens could suddenly disappear from the face of the earth without a trace!"

"That happened in India for over five hundred years, Mr. Birch. Philosophically, the Thugs have no other recourse, you see. They must have a great bele. They must fill it with many corpses. They must do it very soon. And the most horrible thing about it all is that we have no apparent clues as to where, when, how, and to whom it will be done. In short, a tragedy of no small proportion is imminent—" Rama Shastri stopped talking. He was staring at the entrance.

"Dan Terranova's here," he announced.

Terranova, spotting them, came to their table.

He sat in an empty seat. "George Buchan told me where you were." He was flushed, and he took a minute to wipe his brow. "Charlie Adair's just fouled up everything," he panted. "Seems the body of the Thug from Mai Yogini's cellar was claimed at the morgue. Adair had the morgue staked out and went after the Thugs with three specially chosen men. For the glory. He had no backup whatsoever. The Thugs lured them into a cul-de-sac and killed the three guys. Adair escaped by jumping into the harbor. Christ, he's been blabbing all over Headquarters. Got the whole department shook, from the commissioner down to the traffic cops."

Wrench bit into his pipestem. "And in daylight, to boot!" he growled. "The enemy grows bolder."

"And even bolder than that," stressed Shastri, still preoccupied with his dreadful conviction.

THIRTY-NINE

When Wrench and Shastri left Horace Birch, they returned to George Buchan's to find Kurt Leinster there. The *Macbeth* performance was to begin at eight-thirty. Shastri waved to Dan Terranova, who'd driven them to Otis Place and was now leaving. But Shastri remained at the window afterward, staring at the court below and at intervals observing Kurt Leinster in the pane's reflection. The three young people—George, Santha, and Kurt—seemed encapsulated by the ring of lamplight near the couch. Stephen Wrench was somewhere, lost in an armchair, and only a whiff of pipe smoke showed now and then, reaching from the shadows in a fingering blue haze to where the trio sat.

Relax, Steve, Rama Shastri thought; it's their night. But if ostracized was what Wrench actually felt, Shastri sympathized with him. Santha made the sensation painfully acute by basking in the attention of Buchan and Leinster. She was playing the dilettante, Shastri thought, and he could barely stand it. She'd itemized every stage play she'd seen for the last ten years, with a critique of each, and it all preyed on Shastri's ears as if the words were an assault by thousands of tiny mites. His mood was much too serious, too edged with gloomy presentiments for such free-falling gush.

Then again, he kept seeing Kurt Leinster's nasty little angels and demons peeking from the ill-defined drapes and objects throughout the room. Huddled somewhere in the splash of darkness. Huddled and jeering. Rama Shastri pulled the chain of a table lamp at Wrench's elbow. The big man grunted, startled from his reverie. Sorry, Steve, old friend, but we need more light.

Shastri decided to phone Hanuman's residence. Nirmal Kapur answered and told him that the Swami was meditating. Shastri

366

lingered at the receiver, relieved to break his mood. "Swami says that we've no choice but to wait for things to run their course," Nirmal told him.

"I can see that," Shastri replied bitterly.

"How's Mr. Wrench's daughter?"

"Very cheerful. She and George and a friend are going to the theater." Rama Shastri ventured more information.

Nirmal was interested. "Yeah, old blood-and-guts *Macbeth*. Heard they jived it up some." Nirmal paused. "Hey, I've been going bonkers here, what with Molly and Adelaide still moanin' to beat the band. *Macbeth* might be just the thing to soothe me. Why don't I come along?"

"Well, we could always use an extra hand watching Santha."

"That's what I mean. How about it?"

Immediately afterward, Shastri notified the others. He was very curious about their reactions.

George was impassive. He obviously didn't mind in the least. Kurt Leinster smiled, the same disarming smile he'd given Stephen Wrench when he was introduced earlier. Either the man was a superb actor or he was as totally open as he appeared. It was difficult to tell.

Santha said, "Wonderful! But do you think there'll be enough tickets on sale?"

"We'll take that chance. Steve and I will go in Nirmal Kapur's car."

She was more accepting now. "Then he must come here afterward! I'll get his autograph at last."

Rama Shastri placed a Sher Bidi between his lips and reached for an ashtray on the coffee table. As he bent, his profile very close to Kurt Leinster, he said softly, *"Tama-khu Kha-lo!"* (Smoke-tobacco!), the death call of Thuggee.

Leinster's left hand raised slightly, the fingers trembling. Rama Shastri breathed in deeply as he straightened himself. There had been a response, although not sufficiently conclusive.

He heard then, "What did you say, Mr. Shastri?"

The detective looked into the clear eyes. They were unflinching, fixed on Shastri, with a slight curve to the pale, bloodless lips that could be a hint of mockery. Again it was too elusive.

"I'm sorry. I was thinking aloud."

"It sounded like an Indian language. I'm afraid I'm not acquainted with any of them."

"It's Hindi for tobacco," Shastri lied, nodding at his cigarette. "I was about to light up."

The theater had more than enough tickets for the play. Wrench and Shastri shortly discovered that being with Nirmal Kapur in public had its price. He was soon surrounded by rock fans, mostly students. Santha was chagrined. She'd had him to herself for a moment until the invasion occurred. By the time Nirmal freed himself, the play was about to begin.

The theater itself proved small, and although it wasn't quite in the round, it was as close to that as could be. Wrench, Shastri, and Nirmal were seated in the upper tiers, which they found to be overly warm. Santha, George, and Kurt were seated below, nearly onto the set, and once, before the curtain rose, Santha turned in her seat and waved to them. Wrench eagerly waved back, and as Shastri watched his friend's profile transform to simple joy at Santha's gesture, he swallowed hard.

The night progressed. The modernization of *Macbeth* proved the least offensive. But the acting, Shastri thought, was abominable. The leading man's mumbles barely carried to the back-row seats. Shastri was relieved when the curtain fell at intermission.

It was then that he noted something that held his interest. Kurt Leinster and Santha were in deep conversation while George was away buying refreshments. The two pulled apart quickly as Shastri neared.

"Oh, Uncle Ram," she said, "it's so wonderful to be out and about again." She took his arm. "The production's nothing to write home about. But isn't Lady Macbeth a sexy little package? My Uncle Ram's a notorious roué, you know, Kurt."

Rama Shastri patted her hand. "That's enough, Santha. Be a good girl."

"Good? No one remembers a good girl, Uncle Ram. Look

how interesting Lady Macbeth is. She goes on and on, plotting, changing events, with her bloody dagger before her."

"Yes," Kurt cut in, "but it's too bad that she repents and goes mad afterward. She's a strong, forceful creature in the beginning of the play, predatory in her lust for power."

"You admire her, then?" Shastri asked casually.

"Of course I do. Don't we all admire those who are willing to do the bloody deed? Most of us may live like sheep, but it doesn't mean we don't wish it otherwise. Be honest with me, Mr. Shastri. You've been a policeman most of your life. Haven't you ever wondered what it would be like to be a thief or even a murderer?"

Wrench appeared then, with Nirmal. He handed a cup of coffee to Shastri.

"Yes, I have," Shastri admitted. "But only for a moment."

"And why just for a moment? Because, like myself, like everyone here, we've all been conditioned to be sheep. There is no other reason, really."

Wrench, who'd caught the gist of the conversation by now, commented, "I believe, Kurt, that some people are just naturally nonviolent, naturally peace-loving."

"They they're born sheep. Sheep by nature, by evolution."

"So?"

"Well, suppose one is born to be as ferocious as, say, a wolverine. Then what does such a human being do?"

Wrench: "You talking of the bad-seed theory?"

"I mean a genuine non-sheep by birth, by the heritage of one's genes and chromosomes. I mean a human creature who must destroy, must kill, must prey on others. Without qualms of conscience. Without even a reason to do so, except that it's the natural state for that person. Why do we have to assume that all human beings are born human? We have no scientific proof that it's so, you know."

George interrupted. "You're speaking of a psychopath."

"Perhaps . . ." The bell rang for the next act. "Damn! I guess the rest of this discussion will have to wait." And they returned to their seats.

Shastri reviewed everything Kurt Leinster had said. Over

and over. Why? Certainly there wasn't any reason to suspect the man. Even if Leinster should ultimately prove to be as disturbed as his drawings were, why connect him with Thuggee? It was just that Shastri had learned to trust even his most irregular hunches as providing the possible germ of an emerging truth. And uneasy, yes, unsettling hunches about Kurt had increased with each moment of exposure to his presence.

En route to George's after the play, Shastri questioned Wrench. "What's your gut feeling about Leinster, Steve? As you say, your visceral reactions?"

"His mind is full of all kinds of shit about everything."

"That's pretty visceral, Mr. Wrench." Nirmal grinned behind the wheel of his car. George and Santha were in Leinster's Porsche.

Shastri was disappointed. "Isn't there anything else, Steve?"

"Sure. He's too confused and indecisive about things."

"He didn't sound that way when he was telling us his theory."

"All those sophists have some pet theory about the worst in mankind. It's their way of getting back, because they themselves are so goddamn ineffective. You've met their breed in India, Ram. Studied apathy."

"But suppose, Steve . . . suppose Kurt Leinster isn't like that in the least? Suppose his convictions are really very strong? Suppose he's actually a forceful man?"

"I watched him fawning over Santha. My daughter has him wrapped around her finger—and she doesn't even care about him."

I wouldn't be so certain of that, Steve, Shastri thought, but he didn't say so.

"Those drawings of his—" he began.

Nirmal Kapur interrupted. "Want my opinion, Mr. Shastri?"

"Yes, I would, Nirmal."

"He reminds me of a word that Swami Hanuman uses all the time: asrave. It means mental intoxication. Filled with ideas that make the mind drunk. It prevents it from attaining enlightenment. Kurt Leinster's mentally drunk, and I think he's very tanha, besides. Alone, a solitary. Combine asrave and tanha and you end up with a pretty mixed-up somebody. I know—I was there myself."

Shastri probed. "One could be those things and not be weak necessarily."

"Yeah, I know. A megalomaniac. You might be right, Mr. Shastri."

When they arrived at Otis Place, they discovered that only George and Santha were in the living room. George explained that Kurt had had to leave early, on personal business. Rama Shastri noted the lost look on Santha's face. Nirmal Kapur was the last to enter, with his knapsack and a guitar. He smiled at Santha. "How about a sing-along?"

She stared at him.

"A sing-along?" he repeated, holding up the guitar.

"Oh!" Santha pulled free of her preoccupations. "I'm sorry, Nirmal, but I'm not up to it." She turned to the others. "I'm going to turn in. I can barely keep awake."

George touched her. "Are you feeling all right?"

"Don't!" she scowled, backing off. "I'm just fine. Can't you stop treating me like some patient in an asylum?"

"That's pretty unfair!" growled George.

"I'm going to bed. Good night, everyone."

Santha blew them all a kiss and went upstairs.

"She was okay until Kurt decided to leave," George complained, heading for the liquor cabinet.

Rama Shastri took the bottle from him. "Settle for tea, George. We'll be needing a sturdy fellow like you soon—and with a clear head."

"I think she's suddenly attracted to him," George continued. "I think that's the real reason Kurt went off so early. He didn't want to screw up our friendship." George put his face in his hands. "Damn, but she played up to Kurt all evening. It was as if I didn't exist."

Nirmal soothed. "Never happen, man. Not that sweet little deicer. She's just strung out right now, that's all."

Deicer? Wrench almost laughed aloud. He hadn't heard that aeronautical slang for a pretty girl since those days when fighter pilots were making strafing trips to the Burma Road in '44.

Where the hell did Nirmal get such a grab bag of American-isms? He winked at Shastri, yawned. "I think Santha is in good hands, Ram. What say we sleep at my place tonight?"

Shastri agreed. Once at the Pinckney Street apartment, he asked Wrench, "Do you suppose George might be right, Steve? That Santha's attitude toward him might be changing?"

Wrench stopped unbuttoning his shirt. "Ram, if there's any-thing I'm certain about regarding Santha, it's that she's not fickle. Perhaps she was being flirtatious with Leinster tonight. So what? I don't think it's more than that. I'd like to believe my daughter has some taste in men."

"Suppose she has no choice in the matter? Suppose some-thing changes her, makes her react against her nature? George has seen her do exactly that in the past, remember." Shastri decided to continue, even if it did hurt his friend. It had to be said. "And since Santha has been marked by the Bala woman, it's probably worse."

Stephen Wrench slumped, on the verge of tears. "God!" he muttered, "I forgot about the mark." He looked up. "But this is ridiculous—a little mark on the forehead couldn't possibly . . . Or could it?"

"Hanuman has told us otherwise, Steve. We'll discuss it further with him tomorrow. Meanwhile, let's rest, old man."

But sleep didn't come easily. The two men tossed for some time. Finally Shastri heard Wrench snoring, just before he himself began to doze. An hour passed, two. The phone rang.

"Yes?" Stephen Wrench said.

"They've found what seems to be a Thug burial ground in Lincoln, Massachusetts," Horace Birch began.

FORTY

Simon Ark lowered his razor blade, went to the bathroom door, and shouted down the hall, "Jacob. You forgot to close the back door again!" He tightened his robe against the draft. "Jacob!" He tried again. "Jaaaaaaa-cob!"

"I'm throwing out the garbage," came the surly reply.

He shivered, pleaded, "Alma, will you remind Jacob about that door!"

Simon barely heard her yes. Alma had nurtured that soft voice of charity and understanding ever since that Sunday morn when Jesus had entered their hearts. He wished Jesus would teach her that to assert herself was fine, necessary, when the cause was a righteous one.

The back door, which was in the kitchen, finally slammed. Chloe appeared in the hall in her new white dress with its taffeta trim. Her shiny black shoes squeaked as she ran to him. "I closed it, Daddy."

"Aw, hon," Simon chortled, "I'd give you a big hug and a squeeze for that, except I'm full of lather."

"That's okay, Daddy. I don't mind."

"'I don't mind,'" mimicked Christine, who looked exactly alike in every way, plumb to the polished shoes with their black straps across the tiny, white-hosed feet. Sometimes he had to pause to determine one twin from the other. But then Christine would mock Chloe in her green-eyed way, and the problem was solved. There was a crafty, wild thing that showed briefly in Christine's eyes, a premonition of when she'd be full grown and have to be watched. Simon Ark cut himself, applied the styptic pencil. No! he warned himself; Christine had a bit of the devil in her, that was all there was to it. The devil with a small *d*. He mustn't read the hand of Satan in his children whenever they showed a moment of humanness.

Christine would never be the way Alma was years ago, when all too often she would disappear from home and return later, after days of drinking and every kind of sinfulness with men. Not now that the Word of God had entered his heart and Alma's. Not since the Lord had granted him the Redeemed Host to nurture and lead, in His wisdom.

Simon went into the bedroom, selected a starched white shirt, and snuggled into its fresh, clean smell. Alma prepared his shirts. He adjusted his black knitted tie. How old was the thing? Before 1960, at least. He loved knitted ties, as he did white shirts laundered extremely well, with stiff, starched collars. Amen.

The front door opened and he heard his eldest child, Elizabeth, enter with the Browder girl. Funny how the two had taken so well to each other. The Browders had only recently joined the congregation, and Penny Browder had resisted for a time. Elizabeth's warmth and patience, her continued attempts at friendship bore fruit, however, and now the two girls attended services together.

The church. His very own church. Here in Lincoln, Massachusetts, of all places, God had seen fit to grant Simon the abandoned church whose denomination had formerly been First Baptist. Simon hummed the hymn he'd composed for tonight's occasion.

In the dining room, he found his family and pretty Penny Browder waiting to eat their small meal before they crossed the thirty yards from the house to the church. He spotted Penny blushing under Jacob's steady gaze. Simon sat and proceeded to say grace. Raising his head, he noticed that Jacob was still staring at Penny. Simon frowned.

"Did you join us in grace, Jacob?"

"Yes, sir."

The tone was surly again. Lately Jacob had been restless. Jacob was five years old when Alma stopped drinking and fornicating, Simon reminded himself. Some of that sinfulness might have lingered in the child.

"They're already here," Elizabeth said suddenly.

"Who are?" Simon asked, still wondering about Jacob.

"Those people. The guests," Elizabeth replied. "Penny and I saw them. They came in four or five cars. They're standing before the church."

"Before the church!" Simon Ark realized whom she meant, at last, and rose. Going to the window, he stared at the group waiting at the church steps. Christ Jesus, Miss Moniz had spoken truthfully. He counted thirty . . . thirty-five. . . . Christ Jesus! Simon returned to his seat, dipped a spoon into his barley soup.

"Some are really Indians." Elizabeth again. "Just think, Daddy. They've come to hear you preach the Word! Isn't it simply thrilling?"

"Yes. Yes." Thrilling? Was it that? How would the rest of the congregation take to them? Well, they'd have to adjust. The Word of God was for all who were willing to listen. He said as much.

Alma remarked, "Lizzie says that some of the women are wearing those colorful saris."

"Maybe they'll give you the pattern," he joked. But he was uneasy. Dear Father, he prayed inwardly, help me to say the right thing, to breathe Your love and grace on them. "We mustn't be too impressed," he told his family. "I read that when the Reverend Billy Graham went to India he had a full house, but few true converts. You see, it's an Indian custom to listen with an open mind to anybody's new ideas about God."

"Why not?" From Jacob.

"There are many, many false teachings, son, you know that. Satan is a liar and a deceiver. He teaches falsely, truths that aren't that at all."

"Is God that uptight about everything? Does He really care if everything is exactly by the book?"

Simon Ark lifted the Bible at his elbow. "By this Book, yes, Jacob!"

Alma adjusted her glasses. She was about to say something, then bit her lip. Her husband was tense this evening, she reminded herself. This was a new experience in his ministry. The guests tonight were the true heathen, those who probably knew as much about Christ Jesus as she knew about Brahma.

She'd always thought that was only the name of a bull, until Simon told her otherwise the other day.

"There's an Indian woman with a ring in her nose. And it attaches to her hair!" Elizabeth said with a giggle. The twins, who'd been unusually quiet, giggled in turn. Chloe squinched her nose, crossed her eyes, and tried to imagine a ring in it.

Jacob quipped, "Well, at least they don't look all alike, like we do."

"You're just being contrary," Elizabeth fought back. Penny smiled at Jacob's wink, however.

"Well, we all look as if Christ Jesus put us on a rubber stamp."

"What would you prefer, Jacob?" Alma asked. "That your father minister in long hair and beads? No, thank you. This country's had too many of those long-haired false Christs for my liking."

Simon Ark was silent, scowling at his son.

"Now let's stop this haranguing," he said finally, once he was calm. "This woman, Elvira Moniz, approached me, as you know, the very night we were picketing the Mai Yogini Yoga Center. She said that she knew many Indians and their followers from this cult she belongs to who were seeking a new, sound teaching. Now, when the Lord manifests that way, saying 'Here are the needy,' am I to deny them sustenance? Think on that."

They did, and, with a malicious glint in his eye, Jacob broke the silence. "Maybe it's another test, Dad. Like the time those students from the Harvard Divinity School came to hear you and disrupted your sermon. What was it one of them claimed? That John of Patmos of Revelation lived hundreds of years before Christ and not afterward, as supposed? That Revelation has absolutely no connection with Christ's message?"

Alma's voice rose. "Jacob, you know that isn't true. The student made it up to upset the service."

Simon Ark stood. In a low voice he stated, "Think whatever you will, son. I am about my Father's business." He tucked the Bible under his arm and took his coat from the hall closet. Then he returned and glared across the table at both Jacob and Penny. He began, "You remember what hell is like, don't you,

Jacob?" He quoted: "'A place where sinners and unbelievers drink of the wine of God's wrath.' Revelation 14:10." He paused, gloating in the joy of his assault. "A place where 'the smoke of their torment ascendeth up for ever and ever.' Revelation 14:11." Then Simon Ark left.

A few moments later his family followed. Simon was already at the church door, welcoming the guests. Alma studied them. They weren't all Indians. Some were white folk, mostly young people.

To Alma's surprise, when she met the woman with the nose ring, she was strangely moved by her serene smile. Despite herself, Alma clung to the woman's hand longer than usual, overflowing with unexpected charity for the calm, passive creature, especially when the woman placed her fingertips together in that church-steeple way these people had of greeting one another.

The rest of the congregation was arriving: at least six dozen folk, according to Alma's census. The crowd grew thicker at the door. Jacob, holding Penny's arm in the mob, tugged her away. Like wraiths, they sneaked behind the church wall and then scurried for the surrounding woods.

In his pulpit, Simon Ark, dressed in his plain gray suit, heavily starched white shirt, and black knitted tie (his church allowed none of those ministry frills—no robes, no stoles), stared at the evening's gathering. Projecting his rich, commanding voice to the upturned faces, he began by referring to their visitors at "this blessed hour." The church regulars murmured approval and smiled. The children just stared in wonder at the saris and turbans, and at all the jewelry that the Indian woman in the second row was wearing.

Simon Ark said the opening prayer, stressing his need to introduce correctly the Word of Christ Jesus to those among them that night who had come to hear from a faraway land. "May their hearts be lifted, O Lord," he cried out, "as the hearts of Your Redeemed Host have been!"

Simon scrutinized each face below him. The newcomers were sitting in alternate rows, he noticed. In the first row, Simon's family, the Browders, the Perellis with their five boys.

Then the Indians in the second row. Their faces were smiling at him! The woman with the nose ring, who was in the center, was actually looking at him with love. He was actually getting to them! Oh, grant, O Lord, that they can hear and see! Simon could feel the love emanating, even at this distance, from that woman. What was her name? He'd have to remember her name when he held her hand again at the door when they left. He mentally groped as he paused, silent, bent over his Bible. Mrs. Bala—that was the name. Mrs. Bala.

Spurred on, Simon Ark told Christ's meaning as he saw it. The only way to salvation was through Christ Jesus. The law of the Living Christ would destroy the law of sin and death that was created by Satan. And who was Satan? He was deceit, false teachings, sickness, and death. He was often a god under other names in other lands. He was often hiding. Yes, beware, one and all, for Satan is often in high places, wearing the masks of priests and leaders of every kind, in order that he might play the counterfeiter. "For Satan is nothing but 'the god of this world,' Second Corinthians 4:4, and . . ."

Simon Ark went blank. His eyes had flashed to his wife when he finally saw that Jacob was missing. His son always sat next to Alma, and now, as he looked at Elizabeth, he saw, too, that Penny wasn't with her.

In self-pity, he wailed inwardly: Oh no, Lord; test me not like this! Let not my Jacob be mine Absalom! The rest of Simon's sermon lapsed into incoherence. Realizing he'd lost his zeal, he ended it, and announced that they were to sing from the mimeographed sheet placed in each hymnal: the words to "Law of Christ, Oh, So True," which he'd fitted to the tune of "Rock of Ages."

The singing began. The regulars of the congregation swung their heads back, vocalizing loudly in a demonstration of unity and their joy in Christ for the benefit of their guests. The bass section—that was the Perelli youths—was especially strong. It lifted Simon from his depression slightly. He looked hopefully to Mrs. Bala's beatific face and accepting smile. It was still there. Simon Ark sighed; perhaps he hadn't failed in his ministry, after all. Perhaps Jacob and Penny could be restored, in time. . . .

Then he froze. What was the murmur coming from the second and fourth rows? From the guests?

It was a whisper, but the uniformity of it was chilling.

Kunkali. Kunkali. Kunkali.

A stir in the second row. The Indian in the turban, with the hawkish nose, moved, his eyes ablaze.

Sahib Khan lowered his rumel, and Alma Ark was the first to die. All evening the Thug had waited and endured this babbling of the pig-eaters, and now at last it was over. But this plan of Yoni's was wrong, against Thuggee tradition.

Women and children. Sahib Khan had counted many of them present. And it was known that whenever women and children were killed, Thuggee luck changed for the worse. Yet here it was happening. He'd strangled his first woman victim, and now he was disposing of the second. And here there were little ones. No, he, Sahib Khan, would not touch them. Who, then, would?

Simon Ark saw Alma bend backward over the pew when Sahib Khan tugged her to him. Eyes bulging, mouth open, her head eased back into the Thug's lap, and now all Simon could see were her kicking legs. Simultaneously it registered that the same thing was happening everywhere. There were gasps and screams and strange cracking noises. The strong Perelli boys were already slumped forward, their heads listless, looking weighted.

Then his daughter, Elizabeth, went over the pew. Her legs shot up, kicking and thrashing, and abruptly stiffened, two bony stalks hosed in sheer beige. Simon Ark started to vomit.

The acolytes, who were in the fourth row, led by Elvira Moniz, had chanted Kunkali's name until their hands re-formed and swelled, appearing ripe enough to explode. At the moment that Sahib Khan struck, so did they, and the monstrous hands twisted and looped rumels smoothly around unsuspecting necks.

The other members of the congregation, those who weren't in the first or third rows, scurried for the door.

But waiting there were Makunda and Bidhan, the biggest

of the Thugs. They'd locked the door and barred the way until the Stranglers up front could move in their direction. When a few of the victims fought back, some of the Tugs dropped their rumels to serve as Arm Holders. The supernatural strength of the killers provided by Kali's glow hurried the event to a swift finale.

The glow flickered everywhere, suffused the room. It was as if the walls, the floor, the ceiling were afire, that the very air had incinerated. Faces flushed as the roseate death light leaped from one Thug to another, bounded into Thug, blazed in their brains with one command: Kill! Kill!

Sahib Khan headed for Simon Ark, who, crazed, was staring at the whirl of firelight across the ceiling. He couldn't look anywhere else. His mind had spewed forth the scene before him. The writhing, kicking legs and arms; the eyes bulging from their sockets as the rumels shut out oxygen; the gasps, gurgles, screams; the dying, the dead, the loved ones and friends—all this had become non-existent.

A LAKE OF FIRE (REVELATIONS 20:10-15). A PLACE OF TORMENT (LUKE 16:22-24). THE FIRE IS NOT QUENCHED! (MARK 9:43-48). A PLACE OF WEEPING, WAILING, AND GNASHING OF TEETH! (MATTHEW 8:12). Bible quotations and their references, all concerning hell, raced through Simon's mind like the churning blood light.

As he hovered near the pulpit, his madman's stare still fixed on the ceiling, Sahib Khan lowered his scarf.

With the struggling done, the Muslim turned to Gauri Bala. She had watched and moved among them, the glow casting a nimbus over her face. She was its source, and whenever she saw one of the Akali who needed its fire, she raised her arms, and it darted from her fingertips, encircled the Thug at work.

Sahib Khan shuddered as he said to her, "What of these?"

Elvira Moniz had ushered the children into a corner. There were nine of them, including the two babies. Some had tried to break free and help their loved ones, but Elvira and another woman acolyte had held them back.

"You murdered Daddy and Mommy and El'z'beth," wailed Chloe.

Christine just kept spitting at Elvira, who was nearest to her.

"They are witnesses," Elvira replied.

Gauri Bala walked before the children. "You're an evil witch!" screamed the eldest, a seven-year-old girl. "You're the devil! I can see the devil in you!" And she tried to shelter the babies, with the assistance of a young boy, who was six and striving very hard to be brave.

"Save the girls," rasped Gauri, her hands twisting like claws and growing into enormous shadows on the flickering walls. "I need the girls!"

"The girls. Yes, of course," repeated Elvira.

But not one Thug moved to kill the rest.

"I want only the girls to live!" shrieked Gauri Bala, filled with the wrath and nature of Kunkali.

And with that she seized one of the babies from the young girl's arms and smashed its head against the wall. Oh, this is very unlucky, thought Sahib Khan; very unlucky.

Elvira Moniz reached for the other baby. Makunda, sick from the sight of brains and blood dripping down the church wall, pushed Elvira aside and held the child close. In a minute the baby was suffocated. Then, with speed and dexterity, he killed the three remaining boys.

"There," he said. "Better it was done mercifully."

Still he would not place his eyes on Gauri or Elvira. Makunda didn't like to kill children. He had left two young sons in India. He hoped they wouldn't be as easy to kill as these were.

"Good," cackled Gauri, her words thick. "Now we have more vessels to serve Kunkali. And they are young enough to prepare for many years of service."

Jacob Ark led Penny Browder into the vegetable garden supply shed. Jacob had brought a pair of pillows to the place a few days earlier. He was proud. He'd planned this well.

He had eased Penny's panties down to her knees and was stroking the wonderful girl-mystery between her legs when he thought he heard screams. But he continued. Later, when he'd come much too soon and was looking at Penny, disappointed and ashamed of himself, he heard footsteps passing the shed. He rushed to a chink in the wall.

After a while Penny asked, "Is it your father or my folks come looking for us?"

He didn't answer. The bristles at the back of his neck were up. He could see only the outlines of figures, but he was certain that they were carrying bodies. One figure passed near the shed wall, and Jacob suddenly felt sick.

"What's wrong?" Penny asked, when he finally turned away.

Jacob covered her mouth. "Shhh," he stressed, while tears trailed down his cheeks. "They'll kill us if they hear you." He didn't tell her any more then. He was afraid she'd struggle free and scream if he told her that he'd seen her mother's corpse being dragged into the woods. Jacob had recognized the silhouette of a turbaned head. He knew that the Indians had done the killing. He was sure that they'd killed his family, too. His eyes fell to his naked penis, also lifeless now. It's the punishment, God's wrath, that Dad always warned us about, he concluded.

FORTY-ONE

A raw-eyed Horace Birch met Wrench, Shastri, and George Buchan at the burial site. When Wrench had phoned George to inquire about Santha's condition before they left, George had insisted he go along. He had to do all he could to end the horror for Santha, he said. Impressed, Wrench agreed. Then George hung up and told Nirmal, who had been sleeping on the living room couch, that he was leaving. Nirmal promised, "No sweat. I'll stay awake until you come back. If Santha gets restless, I'll play her a tune or two. That should calm her down."

Wrench introduced George to Birch, and the four of them crossed to the police cordon. The place was beyond a thirty-yard boundary of trees and scrub brush that fringed the Redeemed Host property. Observing the patrol cars, the morgue vans, and the officials scurrying within the church, Wrench shivered. "Of all places to massacre human beings in," he said, gritting his teeth.

Rama Shastri nodded. "There seems to be a message to it—Straight from the Huzoor himself. Contempt, open disrespect for the beliefs of others."

"Some sweetheart."

"I doubt it was religious prejudice," Shastri went on, as they headed for the wood. "I feel that the Huzoor is speaking to us by doing it this way. There's something perverse, petulant about it. We've defied him successfully, and he's out to embarrass us for it."

At the site, Dan Terranova joined them. He blinked at the flashes as the police photographers hovered over the long dirt mound and took pictures. "So far we've kept the press away. But I doubt that'll be for long."

Birch added, "Gentlemen, I've spent half the night calming down the Boston police commissioner because of those three murdered detectives yesterday. But I can't perform miracles. How many bodies so far?"

"Twenty-five. But there's lots more." Terranova's eyeglasses were spotted with morning dew. "Everybody's here. The Lincoln officials, the state police, the Arlington constabulary, the Boston police commissioner and his gang, detectives from all three cities."

"Just what we need."

"Right, Steve. When the thing got on the police wire, everybody who was connected showed up. I wouldn't be surprised if the governor arrived. This is considered a state of emergency. Here's Mel Hughes coming over."

"Well," began Hughes, rocking back on his heels. "What do the experts suggest we do now?"

"Come off it, Mel. This wasn't their fault."

"Mr. Birch, with all due respect, we really can't allow this sort of thing in Massachusetts. You'll hear from the commissioner. Oh yes."

Rama Shastri moved away. They were in a ribbon of treeless ground some sixty yards from the woods. The opposite side sloped, a hillside, apparently, since Shastri could see the tops of leafless trees beyond. On both sides, left and right, the woodland curved, shaping the cleared area into an incomplete oval. He looked at the high grass at his feet, wavering from the breeze. The perfect spot for a Thug burial ground, he thought, if they'd not been seen.

Nearing the grave, he watched policemen pulling away brush from the mound. A lot of brush had been used, since the trench holding the bodies was at least twenty yards in length. The trench was shallow and just wide enough to hold the dead side by side. A twig snapped. Shastri turned. Wrench and George were behind him.

Horace Birch came forward, surrounded by a group of well-dressed men. He introduced only one of them. "Steve, this is Winslow Parker. FBI." Birch bit off the end of a cigar, placed his hands in his pockets, and almost cursed in frustration. He didn't light the cigar.

Shastri was concentrating on a young boy being led gently by a man he recognized as the police doctor who'd taken care of Deborah Klaus. They were moving along the grave edge, and the boy stooped and examined each corpse as it was uncovered by the diggers. The agony, the torture, in his eyes was clear in the strong glare of the scattered arc lights. The portable generators running the lights coughed often and gave a ripping sound that added to the din of at least forty men and the constant squawking of walkie-talkies. Somewhere and nearing was a police helicopter, probably searching the countryside for the killers. A waste of manpower and energy, Rama Shastri knew.

He heard the boy cry out, "Dad! Dad, I'm sorry!" The boy's weeping carried into the night, and for a moment the diggers stopped their work. Their eyes, usually veiled with policemen's detachment, looked hollow and bleak with incomprehension. This was too much even for them.

The FBI man, Winslow Parker, neared Shastri. "Careful, now," Birch warned Parker softly. But Parker was respectful.

He'd heard of India's Rama Shastri. He said. "Mr. Shastri, maybe you can clarify some things for us."

Shastri nodded, staring at the dead, upturned faces in the narrow ditch. The shock was etched in their grotesque, wide-eyed stares, the open mouths and swollen tongues.

There was a scream, suddenly. "Mom! Elizabeth!" and a scramble as the boy tried to throw himself into the grave. Brave boy, Shastri pondered. If only he could have been braver still. Horace Birch had said that the boy had crawled from the shed and followed the Thugs with their victims into the woods. He'd watched them bury the dead and then somehow had managed, despite his overwhelming grief, to go back to the girl he was with and drag her out to the highway and stop a patrol car. But when the police arrived, the Thugs were already gone. The boy had watched as the band sat on the mound and ate and laughed gaily for a short spell. If he'd been able to fetch the police then, while they performed their ritual of feasting over the dead, they might have been trapped. But the boy hadn't dared move until Kunkali's children had started to leave.

Pity.

The boy was still screaming about his parents and sister and God and sinning. They were taking him from the site.

"He's going to be under psychiatric care for a long time," said Parker. "The girl's in worse shape. Shock. She can't even talk."

Rama Shastri fumbled for a Sher Bidi.

"Mr. Shastri, we need any help you can offer."

"Yes, of course."

A crowd was gathering. Faces. Big, hefty men, mostly. Officials, a commissioner, captains, lieutenants, sergeants. They hovered around to listen, to hear and try to understand what exactly they were dealing with.

Parker pointed. "Why are the corpses hacked to pieces? They were already strangled. Wasn't that enough?" The FBI man's voice was hoarse. It grated through the crisp morning, already beginning to gray with the false dawn.

It was a good, rational question. Rama Shastri replied, "To

hasten decomposition. Also, in order that the escaping body gases from so many dead might not break open the earth."

"Say, I want to know something," someone cried at Shastri's feet. An elderly man in a mackinaw scrambled out of the grave. "I'm Stevens from the Medical Examiner's Office." The man offered his hand, wheezing from his climb. "I've been told this was all done by Thugs, am I right?"

"That's correct."

Stevens shook his grizzled head. "Couldn't be. Impossible." He stared into the grave. "Not unless the killers had the strength of King Kong. Thugs use nothing but a scarf, am I correct again?"

"Yes. They use a silken scarf, weighted at one end, and it is then whipped around the victim's neck and pulled. Very tightly." Shastri noted a man standing apart from the others. He was familiar.

"Well, it's pretty damn amazing, then. Mister, there's up to forty-two bodies, not counting a few kids. And every neck is broken clean through! Broken! Every one! Now, the kids and the thin old ladies and some of the others like that I can understand. But there's a bunch of size-sixteen-and-a-halfs and -seventeens in there and, to boot, an old gal with a neck like a rhino's. Necks don't break easy, pal. And if they did the killing fast as hell, which I figure they had to, they couldn't've had the time to hold the big ones down at the right angle and apply the amount of force it would take.

"Christmas, you've got the sternomastoid muscle, the omo-hyoid muscle, the scalenus anterior muscle, to name a few obstacles to breaking the neck. That's besides a lot of fatty area with some of the big sizes, nevva mind all the plasma and glands and big arteries like the carotid. Christ, there's a couple of young brothers in there—the Perellis, the Ark kid said— who could play defense for the New England Patriots. You mean to tell me that all these goddamn Thugs got hands like Gargantua?"

Exactly, when they change from their normal size and enlarge, thought Rama Shastri, but he said nothing. Who would believe it?

Stevens continued, "Course, I can't fully say before the autopsies, but the breaks look clean as hell to me. Every one! Are you sure these Thugs didn't train a bunch of orangutans to help them along?"

At the opposite end of the long trench a voice shouted, "Babies! Two babies!"

"Babies!" came the echo around Shastri.

Dan Terranova was with the diggers who found the two small bundles. As he went down the stretch of grave, he saw Charlie Adair standing alone, a disconcerting smile of triumph on his face. Terranova passed him without a word. He found a photographer with a Polaroid and said, "Mac, I want photos of the worst hack jobs you can find. For myself, understand." When the babies were lifted to the surface, he added, "These especially." Once the photographs were developed, he pocketed them and left the area.

Captain Charlie Adair watched him go. Then, no longer able to control himself, he rushed up to Shastri, who'd been observing him.

"Babies, didja hear that?" yelled Adair, his face ruddy as fire in the lamplight. "Babies! Who asked people like you to come here anyway? Coming here and killing our kids!"

"Easy, Charlie," warned Mel Hughes.

"I am not responsible," replied Shastri, and he turned on his heel.

"Not responsible!" raged Adair at Shastri's back. "Sure you are! Lookit that swill hole of a country you come from! Comin' here to murder our kids, you black-faced sonova!"

Stephen Wrench's right fist shot out. Adair doubled, holding his stomach. Wrench's fist arced then and smashed against Adair's jaw.

"Oh, Steve." Shastri stared down at the supine captain of detectives. "Now you've done it."

They stared at each other. Mel Hughes finally said, "You can't do that, Mr. Wrench. I'm sorry." He motioned to two patrolmen, who stepped forward to Wrench's side.

Wrench smiled thinly. "So let him sue me."

"It'll be more than that, I'm afraid. He's a police officer."

As Adair rose, Wrench said to him, "Next I'll break your jaw so totally you'll never yap again."

Horace Birch was whispering in the police commissioner's ear. Mel Hughes looked nervously their way. "Is it all right, sir?"

The commissioner nodded to Birch, then replied, "Mel, why don't you go check up on the press? I can smell them approaching, can't you?" He squinched his nose and sniffed. "It's the big stink they always make."

Laughter.

Hughes, in a piqued tone: "Of course, if you—"

"Mr. Birch here has just reminded me that he could easily leak out the story of Captain Adair's disgusting racial slur. Now, that, added to what has happened early yesterday and tonight, would just please those smutheads fine, wouldn't it? So move on, Mel, while I handle this."

Hughes hesitated. The commissioner frowned, and Hughes hurried on.

"Now, Captain Adair," the commissioner said, "I expect you'll want to press charges against Mr. Wrench for his assault. That's your prerogative, according to law. You might even sue, as Mr. Wrench suggested. It would be helpful, with your patrolman's salary."

"Patrolman's salary!" repeated Adair, through bloodied lips.

"Who can tell? Of course, that might not be necessary. You've given Boston's Finest years of dedicated service. That might weigh in your favor during the hearing concerning yesterday's tragedy and tonight's shameful performance. In fact, the force might look the other way, if you can learn to control your rage and"—the final words were a command, coldly given—"leave things alone."

Breathing heavily, Adair stared at the commissioner. What would his wife think if he was demoted to patrolman? He shuddered.

"Yes, sir," he told the commissioner. "I'll do that."

When Charlie Adair was gone, Birch wiped his brow and turned to Parker of the FBI. "Go on with your questions, Winslow."

FORTY-TWO

Santha Wrench woke up. She'd been so tired, she'd gone to sleep with her clothing on. But now she was consumed with resentment. More and more she felt like a prisoner, a trapped animal, even.

They say I am being watched for my own protection, but they're destroying me, she thought, and before Santha could stop the fierce onrush of rage, it crowded her consciousness. I am caged and I shouldn't be. It is very, very wicked to cage a living, breathing thing. Any creature, lions, tigers, bears. Lions and tigers and . . . In Delhi, Bombay, Varanasi, Calcutta, Hyderabad, Mysore, the millions throng beneath a hot, saffron sun. Teeming life noises and sweats and defies the gate, the wall, the bars.

Santha touched the new mark on her forehead. I am abundant life, came the breath of words in hr mind. I am filled with the nature of things, unrestricted, unfettered by time or space or place. Or man.

Santha thought of Kurt Leinster. To run away with him, if only for a little while. He'd been so handsome, so self-assured tonight. The world had seemed a vibrant, dynamic place when he'd pulled her aside during the play's intermission and told her so fervently that she could leave here so easily, if she but wished it enough. . . .

She'd felt unfettered then.

(The Wheel of the Juggernaut moves on. One can ride the wheel and watch the many dead and dying below. There is a high place where one can look even into the saffron sun and withstand its fierce fire. There is perpetual shadow in this Right Perch. The shadow soothes and cools and veils all living things upon the earth, veils with the balm of its comforting haze. Come, climb to the Right Perch. Come.)

But where? Santha asked.

(Rest, child. Sleep. The free unfettered things are once again upon the earth. They shall be parched no longer beneath the sun's hot pulse. Let the millions be and ride the Wheel instead. There is a perch upon the Wheel without a cage. Sleep and dream on that. Sleep, child.)

Santha Wrench paused, a quizzical expression on her face, as if she'd lost something and couldn't remember what. Then she closed her eyes.

When she awoke again, Santha had a vague memory of overlooking the pinnacles of mosques and temples covered with carved filigree. There had been a vast plain, too, with familiar tufted trees and snow-layered mountains, but all that was much less clear.

Santha blinked. She'd left the light in the room on when she fell asleep, but now it seemed much dimmer. A gray film permeated everything. She rose and walked through the grayness into the hall, which was dark. Santha flicked the hall switch. The grayness had followed her. Was she going blind? Santha decided to go downstairs to tell whoever was awake. Gradually she descended, trying desperately to curb the panic that was suddenly rising in her.

Nirmal Kapur squinted, then stared at the night light again. The bulb must've weakened, he concluded. He stepped closer to the circle of gray light and checked his watch. Unable to see the watch face clearly, he pulled the chain to one of the table lamps. He squinted again. The table lamp seemed to be as dim as the night light. Must be a brownout on this side of Beacon Hill, he decided.

He sat on the couch, exhausted. For some inexplicable reason, he'd been thinking of his mother again. Like the old days, the druggie years.

Nirmal wondered why his mother's death bothered him now so much. After all, there had been countless Indian women who'd died in exactly the very same way. Also, he'd never known her. She'd died immediately after he'd been delivered. He knew only what his father had told him.

The irony was that Nirmal's elder brothers and sisters had

been delivered correctly. In a hospital. Why had he been so cursed to have been denied a proper birth? Maybe then his mother would've lived.

And his father had scoffed openly, to everyone, about the ignorance and barbarism of the old ways. Which was why his wife had always received the best of care at the hospital during her pregnancies. Gian Kapur was a successful Bombay merchant, educated, a man who had taken the best that the British Raj offered and put it to use. There was no shame in that. Progress, scientific truth, reality demanded that a present-day Indian accept that which made his household safer, healthier.

For many years, however, that household had been split. The matter of Gian's wife going to the hospital for her deliveries piqued Gian's mother. On and on she raved, that in her day only a shed and a good dhai, or midwife, were necessary to deliver a baby.

And Gian also had an unmarried sister, who, like the mother, was tradition-bound. She added her potent religiosity to the mother's verbal assaults, saying that it was unfitting that a good woman place herself in the hands of the hospital staff, most of whom were Christian converts. It would demonstrate to the children that an Indian must be dependent upon nonbelievers. In the end, these children would keep away from the temples and sacrificial ghats. They'd respect nothing that had always been.

This argument finally convinced Nirmal's mother. She approached her husband with her new conviction that a dhai be summoned to assist her this time. Gian said no, firmly. But then his mother went to her son and, after a haranguing that lasted an entire afternoon and part of an evening, drove him to a loud "Yes! Yes! Yes! But leave me in peace!" It sufficed.

So when her time came, Nirmal's mother was ushered to a shed some sixty yards away from the main building. There the dhai placed her on the same unclean rags that were used by earlier women during their deliveries.

And the old methods began. The dhai covered every air hole, in the ancient belief that fresh air was bad. Lighting a smoky kerosene lamp, she then tossed four-smelling powders into a coal pot to ward off the evil eye.

By now Gian had had second thoughts about his decision. He ran from the house and headed toward the shed. His wife's screams met him halfway there. Barging in, he discovered the dhai walking up and down upon her patient's body, to speed on the delivery. His wife then, ashamed since he was present, begged him to leave. Gian exited and hovered by the shed.

Later, he learned what else the dhai had done. She had shoved against the woman's thighs with her naked, dung-crusted feet and literally pulled out Nirmal, along with the hollyhock roots, rags filled with quince seeds, and earth mixed with cloves, butter, and marigold that she'd thrust into the birth canal earlier. In her filthy palm the hag showed Gian the rusty nail that she'd used to cut the umbilical cord. When he raged at her after his wife's death, the dhai replied, "I am not to blame for the will of God. Be gracious enough to offer thanks that the child lived. And a healthy boy, too!"

Nirmal Kapur cringed at his imaginings. His mother writhing in the shed . . . For the first time in many months, he wished . . .

Nirmal lowered his hands from his face. "Baba Hanuman, help me," he prayed.

He was immediately distracted by a giggle. It angered him, and he turned to look over his shoulder. Through the gray haze he saw Santha speaking into the hall phone. He thought he heard "I'll be ready. Don't worry." Santha hung up.

Nirmal watched her cross the room. For an instant he was stirred by her beauty. His thoughts raced back to Bombay and a certain nautch girl who danced like a goddess of the wind. Her hair had been the same, a trailing, blue-black cloud. Santha's eyes were even darker in the haze, and for the first time since he'd met her, Nirmal felt uneasy. She looked so soft, pliable, dusky, full of ripe moistness. Nirmal shifted his haunches, restless. He wished the brownout would end.

Santha said, "Funny. I was so tired that I fell asleep with my clothes on. And now I'm as wide awake as can be."

"Me too." Nirmal was reticent, wondering about her phone call.

"Are we having a brownout? I thought I was going blind, until I came downstairs. Then the fear left me. . . . Where's George?"

"He went out with your father and Mr. Shastri."

"Oh . . ." She moved about the room. "It's so hard to see things." She sensed Nirmal's eyes fixed on her. It made her feel vicious, mad as hell. This watching. This prying. Always watching. Passing the fireplace, her fingers groped toward the poker in the stand. Christ! Santha grasped her hand, held it across her breasts. The hand wanted to do things.

"I'll be there right away," Kurt had said. Once downstairs, somehow she'd known that Nirmal was alone. How could she have possibly known? Santha edged away from the fireplace. It frightened her suddenly.

"Thuggee," Santha said, more to herself. "It's hard to believe that it's true."

"So true," Nirmal replied.

He'll be here, Santha panicked. Kurt will come! Oh, God, why did I call him? How can I get out of this? Santha lifted a glass paperweight from the coffee table. She stared at the imitation snow falling onto the miniature village within the globe. Silly, funny little weight.

"You brought your guitar." Santha motioned to the instrument against the wall. "Maybe if you play something, we'll feel better. Lift our spirits in this damn haze." She brushed her blouse sleeve. "Makes me feel like I need a bath!"

Nirmal reached, picked up the guitar. He fiddled with a few chords. "Here's something I learned in Nova Goa. A little bit of Portuguese sentiment."

"Oh, that's very romantic," she told him, walking back and forth, listening, balancing the paperweight in her palm. Yes, she thought, you can see the tropical moon in that music. There's water and there's a beach, and the breakers are splashing in the moonlight. There are lovers and yearning and the lovers can see black flecks of hunger in each other's eyes and . . . He'll be here any minute! Santha went to the window. The curtains were drawn. How could she see the flash of Kurt's headlights? She arced back across the room behind the couch.

The guitar strains rippled over the breakers, smashing against great moon-dripped rocks. Santha's hand lifted. The paperweight descended. Nirmal's nails scraped down the frets. Santha looked at his temple and the snaking trail of blood.

What have I done? What have I . . . ? Santha Wrench crouched down beside the crumpled Nirmal. Then she rose and went to the window again. She raised the shade. Headlights blinked off, on, off again at the Brimmer Street exit to the court outside. Santha turned, looked down at Nirmal once more, blinked again at the gray haze, and rushed up the stairs. A moment later, she was running down them, wearing her coat, scarf, and gloves. Outside, her lips repeated over and over, "Got to hurry. Got to hurry. Got to hurry." Santha ran to Mount Vernon Street. The policeman seated behind the wheel of his patrol car saw her coming and opened the door to meet her.

"Miss Wrench, anything wrong?"

"Officer, please come in. Nirmal Kapur—the person who's been staying with me—I think he fell and hit his head! Please help me!"

"Yes, of course." He looked for an instant at his car radio, decided to report the incident later, and followed Santha. She opened the door. "In there," she pointed. The policeman rushed by her.

As he entered the living room, Santha moved silently out the door again. She didn't close it. Once on the walk, Santha spun about and raced for Kurt's car. On Brimmer Street, she jumped into the seat and slammed the car door just as the policeman followed after her, shouting, "Stop! Miss Wrench!"

Kurt pressed hard on the accelerator, and they were heading toward Storrow Drive.

Santha Wrench kept her eyes on the Cambridge shoreline. Its lights streaked the Charles River a clear red. The gray haze was gone. She wondered where it disappeared to.

"He didn't get my license plate. Congrats, perfect timing," Kurt said.

She couldn't look at him. Huddling in her coat, Santha started to cry. They were deep, hacking sobs.

"What's wrong, Santha?" he asked.

"I just remembered. Nirmal didn't fall and hit his head! I struck him with a paperweight! Oh, Jesus, Kurt, I think I killed him!"

His hand touched her arm. Then he took it away and she still felt the pressure.

"You didn't kill him." The tone was strong.

"I didn't?"

"Of course not."

"But why couldn't I remember what I did? Kurt, I'm in trouble! I think I'm losing my mind."

"You're going to be fine, Santha."

He touched her again. She breathed; lowered the window slightly, breathed, studied the night. "It's very late outside," she mused absently. "Very late. What are we going to do now?"

"You said you had a plan to help your father and his friend."

"Yes. But it's too late . . . now. Where can we go? Oh, why am I doing this? Why?"

"Do you want me to take you back?"

"No! . . . Not after what I went through to get out. . . . Oh, God, Kurt, I killed Nirmal."

"Stop that. Nirmal's okay."

"How can you be sure?"

"I just feel it, that's all."

"Feel? . . . Isn't it strange, these feelings? I somehow knew that George and the others were gone when I called you."

"Where did they go?"

"Something about the Thuggee business, I suppose."

They turned onto Massachusetts Avenue.

"Where are you taking me?"

"There's a Howard Johnson's up the river. On the Cambridge side. We could get a coffee before they close. It'll give us time to figure out what to do next."

Why doesn't he mention his apartment, she asked herself. Why doesn't he take me there? Is it because he doesn't want to be alone with me? Is he afraid if we're alone together . . . ?

Santha was quiet until they crossed the bridge. Then she saw him looking through the rearview mirror. Santha looked back.

"Are we being followed? It must be the police! Poor Nirmal!"

Kurt took a left turn. After a while: "We had this big sedan on our tail for a time. But it's gone on. Up the avenue." He laughed. "I guess I'm all worked up, too. Come on, we'll feel better once we have our coffee."

But that proved to have limited results. Santha barely touched her cinnamon toast, and the coffee was the worst she'd ever had. Kurt Leinster, the ever observant host, ordered tea for her. Sipping it, Santha idly scanned his lean face and mentally traced his mouth lines with an imaginary finger. If I were in bed with you now, that's what I'd do, Kurt, she promised herself. After all, wasn't that the real reason for her escape tonight?

Santha's eyes fell from Kurt to the parking lot outside.

Then, tense: "Kurt, is that the big sedan you meant?"

He shifted in his seat and looked. "Could be." He laughed that crisp laugh of his. "Oh, com'on, Santha. If it is, it's only a coincidence."

"Kurt, let's leave."

"You're shivering. Are you cold?"

"Kurt, I . . . I want to go. Take me away. Take me to your place."

"Sure," he said.

"Do it right away, Kurt! If we don't get away from here fast . . ." Her eyes fixed on the sedan's windows. The curtains were drawn. Why did people drive around at night in a big black car like that with the curtains drawn? It was like moving around in a crypt.

"Take me to your home, Kurt," she continued. "Lock me in with you. Kiss me, then, and hold me for a long time. Then make love to me. Please."

He pressed her hand.

"Forever," he whispered.

"Then take us away from here!"

Without another word, Kurt rose and paid the bill. Santha stood and waited, and he returned and slipped her coat over her shoulders.

Santha Wrench took his arm as they headed for his car. On the way they passed the sedan. Her eyes scanned the windshield, saw there wasn't anyone in the front seat. She straightened and laughed and playfully tugged him to his car.

"Can't wait, eh?" Kurt asked.

"I'm not telling," she replied.

Once seated, Kurt kissed her, a long, lingering embrace that settled her back into the seat, secure again, warm again.

"Well, here goes," Kurt said, his hand on the car key.

Santha sniffed, rubbed her nose, sniffed at the attar scent. "Kurt!" she tried to say, but an odiferous cloth suddenly covered her mouth and nostrils. At her side, something else flickered, and Kurt Leinster's profile convulsed into a grotesque, nightmare face with bulging eyes and a gaping, open mouth. The last thing Santha saw before she blacked out was the powerful brown fingers tightening the yellow silken noose around his neck.

FORTY-THREE

In the parking lot outside the Mai Yogini Yoga Center sat Lieutenant Dan Terranova, staring at the mural. He was about to break the law, and he wasn't quite prepared for it—yet. To spur himself, he took the photos of the Thug victims from his pocket. Quickly he shuffled through them until he got to the one of the baby with the crushed skull. It did what it was supposed to do. Terranova got out of the car.

He stood before the glass doors of the center and pressed the bell imbedded in the wood border to his right. Probably that creepy chauffeur, Duane Longstreet, will answer, Dan thought. He'd seen Mai Yogini's limousine parked on the other side of the center, near the back entrance. Terranova rang the bell again.

He heard a sash open and saw a head crane out, three windows away. "Let me in," Terranova said.

"Go away. It's too early," Longstreet told him and shut the window.

Dan Terranova pressed the bell again, leaned on it for a long time. No one came.

Terranova cursed and walked along the center's wall. Before the third window, he took a handful of pebbles and flipped them against the glass. Finally Longstreet lifted a shade, pressed his nose against the pane, and shouted, "Get lost!"

"Open the fucking door!" Terranova repeated. Duane Longstreet showed his middle finger and lowered the shade.

Terranova scruffed his shoes, flipped more pebbles for a while, and then went back to the front door and continued to press the bell.

He stared through the pane into the entry. There was another glass door leading into an alcove cluttered with aspidistra and yellow marigolds, he remembered, surrounding a receptionist's desk. Terranova thought he saw a figure moving in the alcove's murkiness. Then, suddenly, the ceiling fluorescents went on, and Mai Yogini, wrapped in a translucent something that seemed a cross between a kimono and a sari, peered out.

"Claudine," Terranova said, "I've got to see you!"

"Later, Lieutenant. I must meditate. Every morning, with the rising sun, I meditate."

"Let me in or I'll break in anyway."

She frowned. She had the alcove door open, and he could see clearly now that there was a long, white slip beneath the sheer cerise nightdress. "Just what are you seeking at this hour, Lieutenant?"

"It's strictly business. Now open up. I'm not playing games. I want to talk with you."

"Have you a warrant, Mr. Policeman?"

"No, I don't. And if that concerns you, call the police. I won't mind having them here."

"Really, Lieutenant Terranova? Are you certain?"

Dan Terranova kicked the glass door.

"What are you doing? Are you mad! You'll break the glass!"

"Then let me in."

Mai Yogini threw up her hands in despair, came into the small entry, and pulled back the locks on the front door. When the two of them were in the alcove, she said, "You have five minutes. No longer. Now, what is so important that it can't possibly wait?"

"These!" He held out the photographs.

Mai Yogini didn't take them. Instead, she studied his eyes.

"Look at them!"

Her hand raised. It was shaking.

"Here!" He forced her fingers onto the paper. The glossy side was in her palm. "Turn them over!"

"What kind of . . . pictures are they?" she managed to ask.

That made him angrier. "Look!" he almost shouted.

Slowly Mai Yogini turned them over. Midway, scanning them, her eyes glazed.

Terranova saw it coming. His arm reached out. Seconds later, he was carrying her through the alcove to the stairway which led to her quarters above.

"Longstreet!" he yelled. "Come help me!"

He called Duane Longstreet a half-dozen more times as he climbed to the second landing. Mai Yogini was still in a deep faint. "Little sonovabitch," Terranova said, and, finding her apartment door partially open, kicked it. He entered the living room and placed her on a sofa. He then hurried into a bathroom, found a facecloth, wet it, and went back to her. He dabbed at her forehead, lips, and wrists.

Mai Yogini moaned.

Terranova rose, filled a glass with water, and, raising her head gently, watched as she sipped and stared at him with her wide, expressive eyes. Tears glistened on the smooth olive complexion.

"There is brandy in the cabinet," she said. "Please."

The cabinet was an antique and lacquered. He opened it and found the brandy container and a small glass with a raised fleur-de-lis design on its surface. He poured a sizable amount into the glass and brought it to her.

"You're not a Thug, but you're connected to them," Terranova told her gruffly. "You're my short cut to stopping them fast."

She drank heavily then, gasped, and held on to his arm. "Someone's here!"

"Sure. You and me."

"Don't be stupid, Dan! We're not alone."

Terranova pulled his hand away, brushing her breast. He rose, rubbing the knuckles that had met her body. He circled the room, opened the three high cabinets against the wall, then a huge, carved chest, and stared at a piling of expensive chudders. He noticed, finally, that the door was still ajar, and closed it.

"Nobody's here."

"Look in the other rooms."

He did, this time gun in hand. In the bathroom, Terranova had his first unnerving experience. He had parted the curtain to the shower, when, turning again toward the door, he thought he saw something flicker by. Terranova rushed into the hall and from there to the dressing room and bedroom. He searched all of the closets, pushing the clothing aside and looking behind it, since the closets were unusually large. He looked under a settee and then under the bed. He pushed back the billowing drapes in the bedroom. Heading for the hall, he caught the flicker again in the hall shadows.

"I think it's only the sunlight playing off the walls," Terranova reassured her, when he returned. But he didn't really believe that.

Mai Yogini was still lying down. Her eyes were calmer.

"Sit here," she directed, patting the sofa. Terranova did. "I do feel better," she went on, "and you're right."

"You'll help us, then?"

A nod.

"Take off your glasses," she said.

"Why?"

"I want to kiss you. You're a man, Dan Terranova. Not one of the whimpering, neurotic males who come to me every day seeking a path to confidence through God. You don't need God very often. I can tell that."

"Is that good?"

"Very. Let me kiss you."

"Uh-uh. Stick to business. You know where the Thugs are. Thuggee, remember?" Her eyes watered again. "That won't help. No more tears, Claudine. I want facts. Where they are, how many, who their Leader is. Now!"

"I'm frightened, Dan."

"I know you are."

"I've never killed anyone. I'm bad, often. But not a killer."

"Okay, I believe you. But you did set up Swami Hanuman the other night, didn't you?"

Mai Yogini's eyes searched for a way out. But the apartment door was ajar again, and she saw Duane Longstreet slide in.

"Yes, I did," she admitted. "Oh, Dan, they made me!" Her hands gripped Terranova, pulled him down. He tried to break free, but her lips pressed against his, and she felt the tension in his body loosen.

Hateful, she thought; hateful, to do it this way.

But *She* had been in the room all along. The Mother had flitted, a wraith, a warning in Mai Yogini's peripheral vision.

Duane Longstreet was edging behind them. Terranova lifted his head, and she pulled him down to her lips again. His palms moved along her thighs. It made her breathe deeply. Dan Terranova felt and smelled good. So hard and manly and good. Such a waste of splendid manhood.

Mai Yogini's head tilted as Terranova started to kiss her neck. Her eyes fell to the glass-topped table before the sofa. In the reflection, she saw Longstreet's puffy fingers descend with the rumel.

Terranova became taut, he jerked back, and his knee rammed against her pelvis. The pain was excruciating. Mai Yogini cried out and tried to push Terranova's body away. The knee straightened, but he was still pressed against her. The rumel was flush with his flesh, she saw, and Longstreet's pull was so violent that a ring of blood was forming along the silk. The detective's eyeballs were rising higher, higher. His mouth was open, and, claw as he did behind himself for Longstreet, he couldn't reach the Thug acolyte. Longstreet's knee was bent into the small of Terranova's back.

Mai Yogini managed to pull Terranova's gun from its holster, and she tried to angle it to shoot him in the stomach. Somehow she felt that, at least, would end his torture. But Terranova lurched forward again, and her arm doubled across her chest.

Frantically lunging with one leg, she struck Longstreet's shin with her foot. He toppled forward, loosening the rumel for a brief second. Terranova raised his body a little, and the Yogini's hand slid free.

But the force of Terranova's effort smashed her wrist and the gun onto the glass-topped table instead. The glass shattered, and the gun slipped from her bleeding fingers to the floor.

She groaned, seeing Longstreet arch his back to regain his taut grip on the noose. Mai Yogini seized a shard of the glass and thrust it at Longstreet's carotid with all the strength her adrenaline supplied.

The rumel dropped. Blood splattered against Terranova's cheek. He shoved Longstreet from him and stared. The chauffeur was wild, slamming into walls, furniture, while trying to stop the geyser of blood spurting from his neck. Though he had managed to pull the shard of glass free, the pierced artery was emptying his life's blood.

Dan Terranova was still holding his throat and coughing hoarsely when Duane Longstreet finally collapsed before the lacquered cabinet. Mai Yogini rushed from the room. Dan found her in the bedroom, her back against the wall, shaking.

He hit her hard. "You set me up to be killed!"

She blurted, "But I saved your life."

"You've just killed one of them. They'll never let you get away with it—you know that. You'd better tell me where the bastards hide out when they're not breaking windpipes."

Mai Yogini started to shake again. But she checked herself. Dabbing at the streak of blood trailing from the side of her mouth, she surveyed the room. Perhaps the Kali spirit had left with Duane Longstreet's dying throes. Anyway, Dan was right. She had no choice.

FORTY-FOUR

George Buchan's Audi pulled into Otis Place with a screech of tires that alerted the dozen policemen in the court. Wrench, the first to leap from the car, asked one of the detectives, "Any sign of her yet?"

"Mr. Wrench, we've sent a description of your daughter throughout the country and then some. But nothing at all."

Wrench pounded the car.

Earlier, at the burial site, Jacob Ark had been able to continue identifying the bodies. He'd suddenly announced that his two younger sisters, who were twins, and possibly two more young girls were missing. Shastri had been attempting to explain the Thugs' reason for the kidnapping to the authorities when the alarm came over the police radio that Santha had attacked Nirmal Kapur and fled from Otis Place with the assistance of a stranger in an automobile. George's drive back to Beacon Hill had broken all the speed laws.

Inside the house, Wrench found Nirmal lying down with a bandaged head. A male nurse was taking his blood pressure. Wrench grunted, fell into an armchair, and said kindly, "You all right, kid?"

"Except that I let you down, Mr. Wrench."

"It's not your fault, son. My baby's gone crazy. She could've damaged you badly."

"She only wanted to lay me low a little. But, man, my head hurts."

Rama Shastri saw Hanuman's turban. "Where is the Swami?"

"I phoned him as soon as I could. He's upstairs, testing the vibes, I guess."

"The police say there was a car waiting."

"That's the way it was, sir," the patrolman who had been on duty cut in. He told his story, ending, "I'm sorry. I should've

403

been more careful. And to make things worse, I didn't get a make on the car or its plates."

"Your bosses should've put two of you on duty, not just one." Wrench was bitter. "But they didn't take this very seriously then." He thought of the dead in Lincoln. "They sure do now."

A detective who'd been waiting patiently cleared his throat. He glanced at his notebook and began, "I'm Sergeant Abbot, sir. About Miz Wrench . . ."

"What about her?"

"Since Mr. Nirmal refuses to press charges, she's not on our arrest list. Nevertheless, it's obvious that your daughter is a very sick woman. Can we assume that she might be violent? Even armed?"

"Assume whatever you want about her mental state. But my Santha armed? Never!"

"Would any of you have any idea who drove the getaway car?" the sergeant asked, printing *p o s s i b l y   a r m e d* in his notebook.

Rama Shastri looked at George Buchan, who was sitting alone in the far corner.

"Any ideas? Suggestions?" asked the detective again. "Did she have any friend who might help her run away? A boyfriend, maybe . . . a lover?"

Wrench frowned, found his pipe.

"Kurt Leinster," whispered George.

The detective turned. "Excuse me, sir, I didn't hear you. And could you please state your name and why you're here?"

"George Buchan. This is my home." George passed a hand through his hair. "Kurt Leinster," he repeated hoarsely.

"Spell that."

George did.

"Mr. Leinster's address and phone number?"

George gave them.

"What kind of car does he drive? Do you know his plate number?"

"Of course I don't!" barked George. He described Kurt's car.

"We'll get this out right away. Anyone else?"

"Can't think of anybody."

"It seems reasonable that she left with someone she trusted."

Everyone agreed, but they couldn't think of anyone else.

"Why do you think Leinster is the one?" the detective asked George.

"Santha . . . likes him. . . . Enough."

Abbot scribbled some more. Then he left, the patrolman following.

"Why do you think it's Kurt Leinster, George?" Wrench ended the silence that ensued once the police were gone.

"Who else could it be?"

"Well, Santha does have other friends."

"None who'd do a thing like that. Besides, she had the opportunity to arrange it with him. Remember, he was with us last night. None of her other friends have been around Santha for weeks. Yeah, she had the chance to con Kurt into doing a crazy thing like that. God knows what she told him."

"I'm sorry, George." Wrench's tone was soft. "I'm very sorry for what Santha's doing to you. I truly mean that."

Shastri decided to express his ideas. "Perhaps Santha wasn't responsible, George, Steve. And I don't mean that she's suffering from mental illness. At least, not in the same way we usually think of it. Let's not forget how Kali affected my thinking in the past. And Dan Terranova's, too. Why, he almost—" Shastri stopped.

Hanuman had entered the room, his finger before his lips. Hanuman gestured that they all listen. They did and heard it.

Susurrating, it came from upstairs. Unintelligible words, rasping sounds. Floorboards began to creak. A tread, slow, powerful, as if to a beat, dancing while it walked. With it, the metallic clunking of an Indian woman in motion. But along with it, an unfamiliar, hollow sound that made everyone in the room bolt upright.

It was coming down from the attic. From the room with the chilling portrait of Santha.

Hanuman spat into his palms, then faced Stephen Wrench. He placed the palms over the big man's eyes. Stunned, Wrench reached for a handkerchief to wipe them but gaped instead. Reaching to the ceiling, no more than half a foot above them, was a translucent gray bar that went across the room, into the hall, and up the stairs.

Hanuman was busily moistening the eyes of the rest.

The strides, the clunking, the strange hollow echoes were getting louder.

Then, like a mechanical non sequitur, the phone rang.

The Swami whispered in Rama Shastri's ear, "Answer it. Be brief in your replies. Afterward, do not speak until I tell you to."

Shastri nodded and went into the hall. Sweat poured into his eyes as he watched the gray bar leading up the stairs. He placed a clammy hand on the receiver.

"Yes."

"Who is this? This is Dan Terranova."

"Shastri."

"Good. I've learned from Mai Yogini where the Thug ashram is. Here's the address!"

Shastri wrote it down, tore off the sheet, and shoved it into his pocket.

"We'll meet you there," he said. "Can't talk longer." He hung up. Whatever was coming was close to the second landing. Rama Shastri went quickly into the living room. There the rest waited, every pair of eyes fixed on the staircase. Its end was visible from where they stood, half immersed in the gray; then the bar ran obliquely into the living room.

The temperature had dropped. George, who was closest to the doorway, began to rub his arms and tried desperately to stop his teeth from chattering. Yet his gaze remained fixed on the final steps. Slowly, louder came the rhythmic strides. George saw a naked foot covered with anklets jut out, step upon the boundary of the gray plane. Still the stairs creaked as if they bore the weight. Then he saw the bent knee, the thigh, the girdle, the abdomen, and they were very black. Not human black. George thought of tar. He thought of a heavily greased axle, full of a black sheen. The figure was shaped like a human, but there was a sense of machinery to the body, of something robotic.

The figure reached the oblique angle and turned in its rhythmic, jerking motions toward the living room. George backed; he could barely breathe in the sweep of arctic air that pushed at him from the hall. Frost hung from his hair, his brows, the top of his nose. It rimed the furniture.

George thought they were all about to freeze to death. Looking at Wrench and Shastri, he saw them rubbing and stomping, too. But Hanuman was missing, and George searched for him beyond the couch. He saw only Nirmal lying back, his blankets up to his eyes. Where had the Swami gone?

"*Bivo viswaneth*," George heard and, turning back, saw Hanuman heading toward the figure. "*Pahi. Pahi.*" Over and over, Hanuman appealed to the Lord of the Universe, Vishwanath, to protect them. The figure paused, its left leg raised, about to complete a stride. Then came a loud susurration, like a miasma. It thickened the air, soured it for an instant, and they felt nauseous. Then the arctic cold left, but not the terror.

The intruder continued its weird dance and walk, scaling the vast, gray angle until it was above their heads. Walking, swimming, wading, dancing, she gradually came to them through the murk. Her four arms jerked and bent and arced sinuously, in cadence to the strange, discordant music of her appurtenances. In one hand she held the dripping sword that had decapitated the demon, Raktavīja; in another, a rumel noose; in a lower arm, the sacred pickax; while the fourth was free, and it gestured, pointed at each man below her.

"Don't look at her face," warned the Swami, but his warning was too late. Up to this point her features had been unclear, lost in the gray haze. They now started to form, become human, and her dance lost its abrupt, mechanical starts and pauses. Everything, the features, the limbs, flowed suddenly, with a wild, sensual pulse. Even the horror of her girdle of thonking skulls was lost beside the humanity of the face.

Wrench cried out, then the others in succession, except Hanuman. Stephen Wrench saw Kamala, then Santha looking down at him; Shastri, the brooding face of Ileana; George,

Santha, mouthing her pet name for him, kesari; and Nirmal, the face he'd seen only in photographs—his mother. The goddess knelt, her eyes speaking with a thousand pain-filled memories. She returned to each man all the sorrow and yearning and love his being craved. She spoke without words, and they wept and cried out to her.

But Hanuman saw the demonic eyes, the pointed fanglike teeth, drooling with her blood-craving, the lolling tongue flickering, flickering.

Having lured the others spiritually, Kunkali, the Man-Eater, squatted. Her vulva opened and spoke in a different language. Sex, blatant, compelling beyond reason, clawed at them, tugged at vital needs. The black pubic hairs smothered, promised a sweet oblivion; the glistening vulva lips kissed softly at the four paralyzed men.

Swami Hanuman raced from one to the other, covering their eyes again with spittle. When next they looked, the gray tunnel of space and the apparition were gone. Placing a finger before his mouth again, Hanuman silently directed that they leave the building.

FORTY-FIVE

Santha Wrench didn't want to wake up. Something beyond her terrible headache urged her on, though; spoke with words that were blurred, almost unintelligible. The voice seemed to come from Santha's left, very close, as if lips were pressed against her ear. The voice commanded, insisted that she open her eyes.

When Santha did, she saw that she was lying on her back in a rectangular space with side curtains and a canopy above her. At intervals, light wavered and filtered between the curtains onto her face. That made her aware of motion, that her boxlike bed was being transported somewhere.

The voice droned and soothed. Her headache would disappear soon, it promised, and the weakness in her limbs would dissipate. Santha waited. Gradually she began to feel better, and she lifted her hands to the curtain and held it back. Then, at a surge of demands from the voice that she look outside, Santha managed to raise herself on her elbow and crane her neck over the edge of the compartment.

Santha faced a bleak, rocky terrain. The arid yellow soil erupted beneath the gigantic wheels of a two-decked cart similar to the type used by farmers in the Punjab. The air was hazed by the billowings of dust, and sometimes she could barely see; but Santha did note that she was in the upper deck and that the curtains of the deck below her were fastened. She thought, Perhaps it's occupied.

But here the voice interrupted her curiosity. It became louder, forcing Santha to duck her head inside and to lie on her back again. Once she settled, the voice returned to its more soothing, intimate tone, and, fleetingly, Santha felt concern that she was being manipulated. By whom? By what? The voice was so blurred and so meshed with her consciousness that Santha couldn't tell whether it was male or female.

Now she was being told to raise her eyes to the canopy. Its surface was bright orange with grain running through it, as with wood. Then, as Santha stared, she saw Brahmi script. Her mind, which had cleared considerably, recognized it, and with that came the memory of the scroll fragment. And the language on the inner side of the canopy was Vedic Sanskrit! As Santha studied the lower lines of the script, she noted that they were identical to those she had seen on the piece of parchment.

It was as if the entire scroll had been attached to the canopy's surface for her to read.

And Santha could do that now—could read the Vedic Sanskrit as easily as she could read English. Neither the language nor the early script confounded her, as before. And as her eyes read the ancient signs with their many serifs, her lips began to speak the sounds aloud. The other voice, the one in her ear, read the Scroll of the Wrathful Mother in unison.

As Santha went on, her clarity increased, as did her understanding. Images trickled, then flicked past her vision, and she both sensed and visualized dark secrets, long hidden within unfathomable depths. Santha felt the ripple of an evil so timeless that it transcended itself, thrived in its own universe, abided by its own laws.

She recognized, felt its power, as the words glowed on the canopy's surface with each uttered syllable. Her voice rose in pitch as she neared the final lines of the Scroll. The tonic accent was sweeping her along. There was no doubt that the Scroll could summon, evoke.

And . . .

Something was coming, emerging.

Santha Wrench stopped. She could read no more. The voice of the ever present prompter became angry. It threatened, its demands seemed to tear at her consciousness, shred some of her resistance. Still her will fought back, wouldn't succumb. . . .

The voice suddenly left her.

Stunned, Santha waited in the hush. The writing on the canopy disappeared, the orange color of the deck's ceiling dulled. Then she felt the cart lurch to a halt.

Again she waited. An unreasoning fear welled in her. The curtains parted, and hands pulled her from the upper deck. She was being held high over the heads of women whose faces were but impressions. Santha's eyes blinked in the brightness of a hammering sun. She turned her head away, looked below her. From the lower deck, turbaned men were lowering a limp figure. Santha saw the pale features of Kurt Leinster. Full memory crashed in. Santha screamed.

The hands quickly covered her mouth. Her bulging eyes focused on a courtyard where women were weaving. Santha was lowered gently now. Fingers worked at her clothes. Within an instant, Santha was naked. Carried by the women who held her arms, her legs, she could see her body extended before her line of vision. Other women's hands were darting in between those that held her, pouring aromatic oils onto her breasts, her flat abdomen, and her flanks. These hands massaged, working the oil into her skin. There was much chattering. Women everywhere.

They had taken her to the courtyard. The sunlight was dying, shadows converging on everything. Santha was placed on a white and gold fabric. The women's hands wrapping it around her. The cloth was cool to her body, calming.

Santha Wrench blacked out and just as abruptly came to. In a different place . . .

Voices again, everywhere, around her. Speaking low, this time, but women's voices, nevertheless. Long, supple fingers were daubing at her face.

There were scents: sandalwood, champa or temple flowers, the aromatic rootstock of the turmeric plant, and, from a distance, lentils cooking and what she'd decided was fish curry. There was rustling of cloth and the noise of metallic jewelry and the softer click of beads.

And there was the whispering, sometimes in Hindi, sometimes English, sometimes in a language that sounded Indian that Santha didn't recognize.

Still Santha was determined to keep her eyes closed.

Her hands moved gradually across her body, and she started. She was wearing silk. It was a sari, she recognized; they'd dressed her in a sari.

Then Kurt Leinster's face crowded everything else out, and Santha moaned, recalling the look in his tortured eyes as the noose, held by a pair of strong, masculine hands, extended from the backseat of Kurt's car. They'd been waiting for Kurt and Santha there. They'd scurried from their black sedan and broken into Kurt's car and waited. Santha Wrench thought she would die from the tremendous pain that welled in her.

A man's deep bass voice reverberated through the room. Santha opened her eyes to look for him. More of that strange, Indian-like tongue. Was this the Ramasi of the Thugs she'd heard of? Fighting the renewed hammering in her head, she bolted upright. She tried to scream, "You killed him, you bloody bastard!" But her words were a murmur. She could barely hear herself.

The man had apparently left, since he wasn't there. Santha

saw Elvira Moniz, in a sari, carrying a thalis or Indian tray. On the tray was a silver food bowl and banana leaves. "Eat," Elvira offered, speaking in English. She took a utensil, scooped the fish curry from the bowl, and placed it on the leaf.

Santha tried to hit the tray from the woman's hands, but she was still too weak from the choloroform and fell back. The throb returned.

She heard another woman's voice command, "Yoni, leave us."

Turning her head, Santha looked. The other woman was sitting crosslegged on an ottoman, surrounded by mounds of brightly colored pillows. The woman looked at Santha kindly, a touch of a smile on her lips. Santha recognized her. She'd seen her often enough: in her psychic dream events, in the gallery of Memorial Hall. The face of the woman that night had been muffled, but Santha knew that this was the one.

"Child," the woman said, raising a hand as if bestowing a blessing, "what is done is done."

"You've killed Kurt! Filthy, murdering scum!" Santha fell back, weeping. After a while she raised herself again and wiped at her tears with her sari. It was a beautiful garment, mostly white, with gold trim, made of the finest material. "Why am I dressed this way?"

The woman was watching. Her calm settled Santha a little, but she struggled with the weakness. She mustn't be lulled into passivity.

The event in the abandoned house in the courtyard, the event on the Ganga—this woman had been there, so her calmness hid an evil beyond comparison. This much Santha knew for certain. Yet it was relaxing to look upon her.

Santha Wrench straightened her shoulders and made her voice even. "Who are you?"

"I am Gauri Bala, Supreme Vessel of Kunkali."

They were speaking in Hindi, and Santha stammered somewhat, since she hadn't used it very much lately. "Kunkali! How can anyone serve something like her?"

"Look into yourself, child. You have served Her, too."

After a pause. "Yes, I can believe that. Doing someone else's bidding . . . Ever since my mother died. Why?"

"Ah, you are perceptive as well as receptive. So well chosen to follow in my Path. We are as sisters."

"Sisters!"

"Yes, sisters. Or mother and child. Kunkali Mother's reach is long. She reached and touched you here from our Mother Land, once you were receptive. You have many gifts, child."

"Don't call me that. I don't like it."

"Child? But you are. And one that should never be long without a mother. Come, rise. Our Lord awaits us."

In English: "Yes. I'd like to meet this Lord. I'd like to claw his freaking eyes out for what he did to Kurt."

"It was Makunda who did the deed."

"Yes, I remember. Makunda, who uses attar," Santha replied.

Gauri nodded. "Life is but a thought, my dear. It lasts only as long as the Thinker chooses to perpetuate it. Then Brahma forgets, until we are remembered again by him. Kurt Leinster will be remembered in paradise, for he was indeed fortunate, among many. The victim of the rumel is released immediately from the Karmic Wheel. It is the boon he is granted for the price of his life. Grieve instead for those without a Path or a boon."

Santha Wrench rose. Her legs were rubbery, but she managed to stand. The room was large and dimly lit. Before her was a huge, gilded mirror. She strained in the dimness to see her reflection. Her eyes were thick with kohl, and the scar on her forehead was colored with vermilion, as with a tikka mark.

"Ramanuja, one of our Thugs, described you to be as comely as Sati Herself," Gauri Bala whispered. The woman held her close, her ghee-scented hair pungent. "Fitting, indeed, for our Lord." Santha broke free, uneasy.

She was led from the room into an even darker corridor. Another room was open to her left. Four women in saris, all non-Indian, were busy in a kitchen. The stove was electric, but the kitchenware consisted of handleless saucepans, cooking bowls with two handles, a huge rice pot weighing possibly over thirty pounds, a bin of ashes and sand on a counter for scouring the utensils, and, on the shelves, more Indian trays and another katoris, the silver serving bowl. Bengali fish curry, spices, seasame oil smells wafted down the hall with them.

They passed a closed door, and Santha heard a young girl crying.

"What are they doing to her!" she asked, reaching for the knob.

Gauri grabbed her wrist. "Do not concern yourself." The grip hurt Santha, and she was pushed farther along.

They entered a room at the corridor's end. Huge dark draperies covered its entire length. Gauri Bala squatted on a pile of garish pillows in the floor's center and motioned to Santha to do the same. Santha did, her stomach churning. Despite her fear, an overwhelming curiosity concerning the Leader of these Thugs overcame her. Her palms were clammy. She could barely wipe them on the pillows. Her weakness lingered. Still, unconsciously, she adopted the lotus position, like Gauri Bala.

The draperies parted.

Santha Wrench forced herself to look up at the towering figure. He wore a long robe of deep purple and a high white turban. Most of his massive body was in shadow, and the flickering light on his features told her little except that they seemed inhuman. The skin, the cheekbones had a peculiar sheen, while the long, matted hair jutting from the turban reminded her of the mane or tail of a horse. The face appeared to be molded and chiseled from something other than flesh and bone. He was like a wild mountain god, a fierce hirsute thing meant for jagged peaks and forgotten caves. His cheekbones bulged darkly, and his glowing eyes above the wide beard made her cringe.

I'm Stephen Wrench's daughter, she mentally stressed. My mother was Kamala Wrench and she feared nothing, neither in life nor in death.

Gauri spoke first. "My Lord, the Chosen Daughter of Kunkali is with us."

"It is as She decreed." His voice, the same Santha had heard earlier, reverberated, so deep, she thought the very walls would shake.

Daughter of Kunkali!

He continued, "As Gauri Bala has served us so well, you, in turn, will be the new Vessel. Kali Mother will come to you, and from your lips Her wisdom will be heard."

"New Vessel? What does that mean?"

"Kunkali is with you always. I, the Chosen Son of the Dark Mother, speak for Her when I bid you heed Her Will."

Santha lost control. "Why did you kill Kurt Leinster?"

The Huzoor stopped.

Trembling, mindless with rage, she asked again, "Why? You rotten Thug scum! Why did you kill him?"

"Kali Mother must have sacrifices."

"I don't believe in Kali Mother! I don't believe in any of that nonsense!" Santha's vision reeled. She fought desperately not to faint.

"Your beliefs do not matter," she heard, like a distant echo.

Still she persisted, gasping the words: "This is no illiterate Indian peasant girl you're talking to now." Santha struggled, her speech thick. "I don't believe in her, I'm telling you. You've controlled me once, but never again! I'll fight you with all the will I have in me!"

"Daughter of Kunkali, the man was unworthy of you."

"I wanted him!" Santha tore at her hair. "He was . . . something I wanted to . . . touch . . ." She fell to the pillows, exhausted. "Touch . . . and hold. God! God, why did you kill him?"

The Huzoor's booming resonance continued, but she barely heard. "Be glad in your heart, little one, for you are blessed among many. I, too, was lost and had a great sorrow long ago. I searched for a place, the Meaning that would nourish me. In a village on the road to Lucknow, I heard the call of Devi. True, it was Her aspect Kunkali that called; and I, too, shuddered with fear and paused, but my reason grasped then the true meaning of all creation. One must listen and hear the call, and when it beckons, one must go willingly. A place is waiting for he who will dance unquestioningly to the rhythm of creation, and so I was destined to lead a new generation of Thuggee.

"In the village that day, a sadhu, eyeless, yet full of sight, and Chundra Bala, my first Thug among the ranks, went with me, high to the Cow's Mouth itself, where stands the Gangotri Glacier. There, in a vast cavern within the bowels of an escarpment, I encountered the sacred rishis of old. Four they were, and they transformed from aged sages to very young gods and gave to me the four scrolls granting the sacred rights to my dominion over all Thuggee on this earth. Ah, the wonders I did see that day!"

Santha started. The voice had changed, slightly. It was lower, and she listened intently, wonderingly.

"If only you'd been there, Santha Wrench, you would have proclaimed far and wide: this man has no choice but to fulfill his destiny. You would never have scoffed then. And later, once I'd met my true Mother. Yes, I've met Her, Santha, and been in Her arms and known Her sweet, dark power. Later, only Chundra and I descended the mountain, filled with a new light and a new hope."

Santha raised herself slowly and staggered straight to the speaking figure, shocked by the familiarity of the voice. Her trembling fingers stretched, touched the Huzoor's robe. He backed; then, as if in afterthought, remained still. Santha's head tilted up and studied the strange face.

They stared at each other, so close now that she could feel his breath as he bent his head to her face. Santha's hand raised to his cheek, and he grabbed her wrist. Then he let her go, with a shrug of resignation. "Do it," he challenged softly.

Santha's nails raked the cheek and felt it crumble from the pressure. A viscous paste, lumps of cockleshell lime and ground rice, fell onto her sari. Putty used as a makeup base followed. Santha clawed more, this time at the false hair made of dyed grass fiber. A section of the beard ripped free from the left side of his jaw. Her fingers were discolored from various stains.

Only the cold, observing eyes remained untouched. Santha saw the green and velvet-black stains on the lids, the red eyes. His own hand stretched his right lower eyelid, and she noted the cundapoova, a vegetable seed, placed there to achieve the bloodshot effect.

The Huzoor explained, "I learned this art from the Kathakali performers of Cheruthuruthy." His manner was so offhand, deliberately casual, that she sprang back, repelled.

"You're gaping, Santha." He reached for her hand. Santha backed farther. "Only a minute ago you were totally heartbroken over me. Now, don't prove disappointing and play the irate, misused female. Keep looking at me like that, and you'll spoil everything."

Between gritted teeth, Santha asked, "And how would I ever do that, Kurt Leinster?"

"Well . . ." His hand touched her shoulder. Santha remained where she was this time. "You must understand that it was fixed before we were even born. Certainly you can grasp that. It's a gift, look at it that way. Until it happened, I was a misfit. I even went near insane for a while, during the time that I wrote that terrible poetry. Then I groped. A futile effort. I went to San Francisco and joined a Satanic cult. They promised me an actual, living God, and I went along, grabbing at their straws. Can you believe it?"

Santha sighed, a wisp of a smile. "Barely."

Staring at her intently. "You do understand, don't you?"

"I think so, Kurt."

He kissed her lips lightly. "But I had to keep searching. I was directed to India at last. The moment I arrived there, I was home. It all made sense at once. It was a revelation— God, the supernatural, was a part of evolution, and I was chosen to lead the next step forward."

She gently pulled away. "And how was that, Kurt? How?"

"When I was given the rishis' scrolls, made Lord of Thuggee, I knew that I'd brought something into creation that was greater than all the technological power in the world. I had brought life out of the twentieth-century swamp. No electric shock or nuclear arsenal could change its direction, its destiny, once unleashed. I'd brought God into life again."

"God?"

"According to some Indic thinking, yes. The Dark Path, where whatever part of God you serve doesn't matter. That's why the great Thugs are considered to be saints. Santha, by

now it should be very clear to you. I'm a true avatar. A real
hero."

"Why did you play dead?"

"You'd been controlled for months. Most of your thoughts
and emotions weren't your own. Everything that you did, your
attack on Nirmal Kapur, your escape were all part of that
control. Only your feelings for me hadn't been tampered with.
I knew that I loved you totally, Santha. Totally. But I needed
to be certain that you felt as strongly about me. So I directed
Makunda to stage a fake strangling. I had to be certain. Can
you accept that?"

"That's very impressive, Kurt. Very. And you had me fooled.
One hundred percent fooled."

"Thug means Deceiver, remember," Kurt Leinster replied.

"Indeed you are one." Santha came closer. "That makes you
very, very special."

Kurt relaxed and reached for her again.

Santha Wrench tried to hit him. Kurt sidestepped, lost his
balance, and fell to the floor.

"I'm a Deceiver, too, Kurt," Santha announced. She'd been
still too weak to strike a blow. But he'd slipped, and, now,
lying there, he looked very ridiculous.

No sooner had Kurt Leinster fallen than Gauri's voice behind
the drapes gave a command. The room brightened, and Santha
Wrench found herself encircled by four of the Akali women
and two Indian men. One of the women unloosened her sash
and shuffled forward.

"Take her downstairs, Yoni," Leinster told the woman with
the sash. "Let the Mother determine her fate."

While they ushered Santha to an open door leading to a
balcony, Gauri Bala touched the Huzoor. "Lord," she implored,
"this isn't the proper way. Lock her up, alone in a dark room,
for a time. Change her slowly, gradually, and with stealth and
cunning mold her to our thinking. This way, she will never
truly be yours."

"What am I to do?" he barked. "Didn't you see the eyes of
my brothers? She has humiliated me! They have witnessed it,

the unpardonable! I may agree with your wisdom, but I can't abide by it. She must be punished immediately."

"But, my son, I fear greatly that I am without sustenance at this hour. The Goddess was very strong at the church. You were told how completely She manifested in me. You were told what She did to the babe. I grieve that She used my hands to shatter its small head against the church wall. For centuries, Thuggee has successfully held back Kali's bloodlust. Now it is different. Now She does whatever She wills!"

Leinster's tone was sympathetic. "Would that it were otherwise. I share your grief. I love Her, Gauri, hunger for Her as I've craved no other woman. But, unlike my brothers, I'm not an Indian. Remember that for months I had to appear to most of them"—he pointed to his made-up face—"like this, with lifts in my boots for greater stature, until they gradually accepted me. If I weaken at this moment and do not punish Santha in some manner, they will say, 'Ah, this is to be expected from one whose line is not rooted in his Thug forefathers, like us. This man,' they will think, 'is but another weak Occidental who enlists other Westerners and women to the ranks of Thuggee.' No, I must act as is befitting a Huzoor among them. I must be strong in this."

He left her. Gauri Bala trailed behind, her thoughts reflected by the gloomy, barren room when she flicked off the light. Aiiiee, more than the shadows, she felt, gazing at them now. The night is with us. The terrible, onrushing night. The very Night.

Resigned, shoulders back, Gauri stepped onto the balcony.

"This place used to be owned by a richly endowed Theosophical Society here in Cambridge," the Huzoor was explaining to Santha, as if nothing had happened. He spoke English. "It was appropriate that we took it over." Santha looked below at the dais, the pews, the cinnabar carpet, the cinnabar-draped throne, the braziers with their snakings of incense, and she trembled. Then she saw the statue of Kali and, try as she would, her sense of victory over Kurt Leinster dissolved, so completely that for a second the Akali women had to hold her up.

In the past, during her "events," Santha had always known,

somehow, that they were unreal, that she was moving about in a dream state from which she would ultimately escape, no matter what happened within its confines. This time, however, the sensation, the deep, inner conviction that it would disappear and be replaced by something warm and familiar, was gone.

Santha was led along the balcony to the winding stairs that covered the north wall. The floorboards creaked, and, staring at the railing, she saw that it was old, wobbly. For a moment she thought of hurtling herself against it, that she'd smash it, fall, and break her neck below. The hands that gripped her held her tight and secure, though. She felt like a child being led in a procession toward an unwelcome initiation. Santha had once seen a child bride in India being directed to her wedding in the same manner. The bride's eyes were filled with terror and misery, and her parents had dragged her along.

Why do I think of myself as a bride? Santha questioned and then blurted, "My God, it's starting again. It's into my head again!" Someone laughed harshly.

Santha struggled all the way down the rickety steps. When they finally reached the ground level, Bidhan, who had been waiting at the foot of the staircase, took her in his arms at Leinster's command and carried her to the dais.

He lowered her to a pillow on the floor and stood before her, arms folded over his chest.

Gauri Bala emerged from the group and sat on another pillow opposite Santha. Kurt Leinster went to his throne.

Acutely aware of his quiet, persistent stare, Santha Wrench refused to meet his eyes. She noticed that only a handful of the Indian men and Gauri Bala remained in the dais area. The rest sat in the pews. Yoni-Elvira Moniz, as head of the women's Akali, took her usual position against the south wall.

"Now," began Kurt Leinster. His voice was a deep rumble again. "Now, brothers and sisters, children of Kunkali Mother, I have gathered you here that you may judge this woman who has assaulted me. Were she not chosen to be our most Supreme Vessel, a true daughter of the pickax and the rumel, I would have commanded your sister, Yoni, to end her days immediately."

Kurt Leinster was immersed in his destiny once more. Hadn't he been the one to do what the most religious in their cloisters desired most? Hadn't he been touched by an aspect of God? Hadn't he climbed the Mountains of the Moon, been to Shangri-La, scaled Olympus, and been nurtured by Divinity? Wasn't he that Special One, Kali's adopted son? No one on Earth was more chosen or gifted than he. He was the one who had returned from the Caves of the Aged Rishis with their scrolls. No man could judge him. Only the stars could, and they'd already realigned themselves in his favor.

"I have commanded you here to request of you that you determine the fate of this woman," he continued. "Is it fitting that we leave her to the wrath and justice of Mother Kali?"

Santha Wrench eyed the ebony and gold statue. The brazier flames moved along the limbs, carved to represent motion. The bent leg was raised to descend in her unearthly dance, suggesting the renewed thud and beat of the tablas, the stirring of cymbals, the clatter of those haunting bracelets and anklets. The statue's gold eyes seemed filled with accusation. Santha tried to concentrate on Leinster instead. He had discarded his beard and matted hair. She still could barely believe it was he beneath that grotesque face.

"I must add that Santha has never witnessed that which we have been granted through our beloved sister, Gauri Bala. Were she to see, perhaps then Santha would believe and obey much more willingly the Call of Kunkali."

There was a murmur of assent.

What's he talking about? Santha asked. Jesussaveme, what the hell does he mean?

Voices in unison cried out, "Let her see, let her hear Our Mother! Kunkali! Kunkali! Kunkali!"

Kurt Leinster rose. "Kunkali, whom we serve! Let us raise our sacred rumels." He seized a pickax from the base of the statue. "Here I raise, too, the sacred pickax of Thuggee! Mother Kali, Mother of Life and Death, we appeal to You. Come to us!"

"Come to us, O Kunkali!" they repeated.

"Have we not done as You commanded of us? Have we not

wielded the sacred rumel and granted You victims to appease
Your hunger? Have we not been Your children in spirit and
mind and body? Have we not killed, and will we not kill more
and more for You, our Dark Mother?"

"Kill for Kunkali! Kill for the will of Kunkali! Kill! Kill!
Kill! Summon Her, Huzoor of Thuggee," cried out Makunda,
and the others repeated and repeated his words.

They spoke in Hindi instead of Ramasi that morning. Kurt
Leinster had purposely used Hindi so Santha Wrench could
understand every word. The brazier flames and incense wavered and licked and limned his tall figure before the statue.

Santha Wrench kept turning her head from Kurt Leinster to
the group, to the flames, to the wisps of incense, to Gauri Bala.

The sound of the litany became a roar, the billowing onrush
of waters. She could almost see that timeless Ganga of her
"event" overflowing its banks. She plucked at her sari, stared
down at it, and wondered why she wore no jewelry. Why wasn't
she wearing bracelets, anklets, earrings? It didn't look right.
It didn't look Indian. She should be wearing as much jewelry
as possible. Santha's eyes fell to Gauri's serene, meditative
gaze. Gauri must be hearing the Ganga, too. Maybe Shiva and
Shakti, his wife, were making love, and Gauri could hear them.
Maybe their love sounds came to her on the timeless wind.
Santha sighed. Gauri was so very Indian.

Then Santha tossed her head again, her long spray of dark
hair passing before her eyes and blocking off Gauri's stare. It
broke the hold of the spell, and Santha tried to rise. But she
had barely started when Gauri Bala proceeded to glow.

Kali's light was transmitted to the essences of those around
Her, and so it leaped at Santha in a blinding current, and she
fell back onto her haunches.

Gauri's dark stare continued. Her mouth loosened with a
terrible slackness. Her jaw appeared a mechanical, unhinged
thing. From the thick, swelling lips a black tongue seeped and
crawled down below the chin, dangling like a serpent.

Santha screamed, raised her palms to her face to blot out
the horror. Then her eyes wrenched free and turned pleadingly
to the faces surrounding her. "No, please stop her! Please!"

Santha begged. She implored Kurt Leinster most of all, but, impassive, he bent forward on his throne and watched. Again Santha pleaded with the others. She turned to Chundra Bala nearby. "Please, don't let them do this to me!"

But the current of dancing light was too compelling. Gradually Santha eased her face again toward Gauri, while the brightness danced over her cheekbones, her nose, her mouth. It entered every cavity it could find, flowed into her nostrils, her ears, between her parted lips. Santha felt it spill into her, hot fiery darts that rebounded off her palate and down, down her throat and then deep into her visceral region. She couldn't scream anymore. Breathing was almost impossible. Within her the fire grew. Santha convulsed, kicked her feet out.

As the darts of flame rose and reentered her mouth, spittle spurted from its corners, and then froth that soaked her neck and sari. Santha's hands raised, tried to push the energy away, but her fingers twisted clawlike. Santha stared at them with widened eyes that could no longer blink or close. Without warning, the fire rushed into her brain.

Then the terror died, replaced by a giddiness that was intoxicating. A sense of weightlessness, of lack of gravity . . . Santha felt ready to levitate, to fly. The entire room was brighter, as energy crackled from her eyes and fingertips. Leaping to her feet, Santha, transformed, raised her head to the ceiling and shrieked her welcome to demonic madness.

Then the dance of Kunkali began. Santha's legs spread apart. Her naked toes splayed. The left leg rose, held stationary, while her wrists, hands, and neck flickered left and right, forward and back to inaudible strains of music. The hovering foot lowered. Santha's neck expanded, her face puffed out and swelled. Like a long, heavy petal, her tongue slithered over her cracked lips. Then she lowered her head, raised it quickly. Her black hair fanned.

The Kunkali in Santha Wrench suddenly unleashed her radiation back at Gauri Bala. Unwittingly the squatting Gauri drank in the intense force until it suffused her features.

Then Gauri Bala cried out to the heavens, but no one heeded. Chundra, transfixed by what had happened to Santha, didn't stir until Santha tossed her head at his wife for the third time. By then it was too late.

Kunkali-Santha now was cackling gleefully as she gyrated around the smoldering body at her feet. Chundra, suddenly aware of what had happened, moved and reached for Gauri's shoulders. But as he touched her, he screamed, stared wildly at his burned fingers. Still he persisted, lifted Gauri, trying to smother the smoke seeping from her pores.

As the others watched, too horrified to react, Chundra pulled Gauri quickly behind the drapes.

"My husband," he heard. The words were thick, and the stench of burned flesh overwhelming. His hands now alive with pain, Chundra dragged Gauri to the stairs that led to the back of the ashram.

"Husband," he heard again, "we are betrayed."

The thick sounds were barely decipherable. Chundra Bala lifted his wife over his shoulders and, as he started to burn even more, raced down the stairs with her. From above he could hear a great commotion.

He freed a hand and groped for the bolt that held the garage door fast. He cried out in crazed agony but finally succeeded in moving the bolt, leaving bits of his fingers on the metal. Gauri was still smoldering. Her sari was falling from her in burning strips, and the flesh beneath was beginning to char. Chundra Bala kicked at the garage door, and it flew open. Chundra raced inside.

He already knew what he must do, for Gauri was right. They'd been betrayed. And Rama Shastri, Hanuman, their followers were not the enemy in this new day of the Thug.

No, it was the Goddess Herself. She and Her cursed changeable nature and this dog of a Huzoor, who wasn't even born one of them. There was no meaning anymore, no predestined cause, no stars to chart the way in the heavens. Kunkali just devoured and devoured, like any predatory beast. Worse, She was like the lammergeier, the bearded vulture who had squatted and stared at him before the hut of the eyeless sadhu. She had no more value than a creature that picked at the bones of the dead.

Chundra Bala laid Gauri gently against the garage wall behind the Huzoor's sedan. He studied her peeling face, saw the smoke trickling from her open mouth. The stench was worse than ever, but he refused to turn away from her. Gauri was his wife.

And she still had life in her, her eyes were conscious. "Beloved," he told her, "I am with you." Her eyelids seemed to move in response.

Chundra rose, fought back tears, and scurried to a small side door. Behind it was a sizable piling of firewood. He searched the garage for the three cans of gasoline he knew were stored there as fuel for the sedan. Chundra Bala opened a can and poured the contents on the firewood.

He turned. The garage door had slammed. Makunda came to him, Elvira Moniz behind him. Makunda looked briefly at Gauri, then said to Chundra, "The alarm has sounded. We are being raided." Then he stared at the open woodshed door. "What are you doing, my old friend?"

"Gauri must have a proper funeral," Chundra replied impatiently.

"This place is unsuitable," Makunda told him in a soft voice. "I understand your great grief. But if you light a funeral pyre here, you endanger us all. Come and help your brothers."

"My brother," Chundra Bala whispered sadly and placed his hand on the Thug's shoulder. Then, before his lifetime friend could stop him, Chundra pulled a dagger from his sash and imbedded it in Makunda's stomach. As quickly, before Elvira Moniz could protest, Chundra picked up a gas can, splashed its contents on her, and threw a lit match in her direction. While she screamed and ran frenziedly, a figure shrouded in flame, Chundra picked up his wife and went back to the woodshed.

At the door, he looked at her and saw that she was dead. Her body was still burning from within, however, and he hurried, lest she become ash before the pyre could do its work. "You are due a noble funeral, my beloved," he told her. And he placed her atop the firewood.

"I am with you. I am with you," he cried out as if she could hear, while he emptied the final can. "Beloved Gauri, has there ever been an Indian husband who has done this before?" Chundra Bala climbed the mound of wood and sat beside his wife for a moment before he lit the match.

FORTY-SIX

George Buchan squinted in the morning sun flash off his windshield. He crossed the bridge into Cambridge and, looking at M.I.T., said, "I wonder how they'd explain what we just went through."

"Believe it, man, they couldn't," replied Nirmal, who was seated next to him.

"Astral body or astral projection—that isn't an apt description." It was Hanuman. "We need a modern thaumaturgical vocabulary. It is enough to say that Kunkali is capable of bilocation."

Wrench turned to Shastri. "You suggested that from the beginning, Ram."

Oh yes, thought Shastri; I was right there with the immediate answer. It took long enough for me to fathom it, however. Maybe if I'd been less a cynic, I would've grasped the difference in this case from the real beginning. Back there in the kotwal, when Das tried to warn me. Then perhaps he'd be alive today. Perhaps, too, Santha would be safe in bed with George this morning, asleep from hours of lovemaking.

They were heading to the Thug ashram. Shastri had given them the address he'd received from Dan Terranova before the Kali apparition had come down George's staircase.

"Step on it, George," Wrench barked. "If we don't get there before the cops do, they'll screw everything up, for certain."

Hanuman said, "They will be cautious. They know that the Thugs have four little girls captive." He added, "Your daughter is also there."

"How can you be sure?"

"Kunkali's followers have taken her. The goddess wouldn't have shown herself so boldly a while ago otherwise. She has what she wants now."

Wrench groaned.

Hanuman assured him, "Kunkali's reflexes, her ability to think have been tampered with, Mr. Wrench."

The big man stared in disbelief at the figure seated between him and Shastri. The Swami's gaze never faltered as he returned the look, and his eyes were like crystal.

"Kunkali is now like them." Hanuman pointed to a pair of winos seated in an entranceway at the rim of Central Square.

"She's drunk? Brother, she sure seemed to know what she was doing at the house!" From George.

"Yes, her projection was in control. But her matrix, the self that we must fear the most, has been tampered with. It will not react reasonably to whatever the astral projection will report to her. The matrix is drunk, so to speak, discombobulated, incapable of total self-possession. This self at the center of Kunkali's being is the source of all her powers."

The Swami became silent. Of the rest, the two Indians were the closest to understanding what had happened. During his meditations, the Swami had experienced whatever gave him this insight.

Hanuman relived those meditations now as the car turned down a side street and nearly met an oil truck head on. Someone cursed, but Hanuman remained unruffled. He thought, And now—what was it Stephen Wrench called her?—now, Bitch-Thing, the time has come at last when we shall see who is the greater, you or Vishnu. Vishnu of the many incarnations—Matsya the Fish, Kūrma the Tortoise, Varāha the Boar, Parasurāma Rama with the Ax, and also the Prince of the Ayodā. Hanuman thought of his Master, the same Vishnarma, who had helped him while he dangled in meditative stasis from his ropes.

During the trance, Vishnarma had led Hanuman's astral body into the garden of Kunkali the Sleeper. Always there was the astral Dreamer, the Sleeper who seldom wakens, the spirit-essence of a god or goddess that must dream of the countless realities, of the what-is.

They had faced the Wall of Shadow before the garden, and his Master, pointing, had commanded him to climb and had given Hanuman blue gloves and sandals made of the flesh of Vishnu, since that which was of Kunkali must never be touched directly. "Find a tree in the garden," Vishnara had directed, "that resembles the kadamba. It, too, bears fuzzball flowers, except that these are made of dark congealed blood with a liquid pitch dripping from the pistil and stamens. The pitch is the human quick of those who have died through her machinations. Every night the creatures who dwell with her in the garden feed one fuzzball flower to her. You must pick three and empty the contents into her mouth and her ears, and, finally, brush the pitch over her eyes. Don't be fearful of her demon guardians. Touch them with your protected hands and they will wither and die. But move with haste, since, if they make too much noise while you are there, she will awaken."

Hanuman had quickly scaled the wall. The climb was difficult, since the shadow was soft, and it quivered as he moved up its surface. Then he had waited for a moment on its top and scanned the saffron and black flora for the correct tree. When he finally spotted it, Hanuman dropped softly to the ground.

The murk was thick. Gnarled, stunted trees with coiling black branches interlocked in an ominous canopy before him. Whispers were everywhere, flutterings, and deep sighs. A lizard scurried across his path and raced up a trunk.

Past the trees, Hanuman entered a stretch of bright saffron grass. Ahead was the tree he was seeking.

He reached it and started to pick the fuzzball flowers, but when he turned to search for the sleeping goddess, he found himself surrounded by five demon creatures: a lammergeier with a woman's breasts and legs and thighs; then a dark, shrouded, faceless thing that was shredding from an invisible wind and re-forming; two black skeletons with bright reddish outlines that shimmered and emitted a suffocating miasma; and last, a Shape Changer; at the moment, it resembled his Master, but the eyes were malevolent.

Hanuman walked forward, leaving one hand free. Four of the demons backed away from his blue outstretched fingers and ran into a tangled wood. But the Shape Changer rushed forward, arms outstretched, as if to embrace him. His fingertips touched it slightly, and the demon folded in on itself and fell to the ground in a withered, ashen mound.

The Swami followed a path along the Shadow Wall. It was strewn with gray leaves with projecting barbs along their edges and a brittle crust that crackled beneath his sandals. Every so often a half-dozen leaves would rise and head for his face, pushed along by an unexpected updraft. Hanuman protected his face with his free arm while worrying lest he drop the fuzzball flowers or spill the precious syrupy pitch inside them.

Now he noticed that the strange leaves themselves were whispering. As he neared the Bower of Skulls, where Vishnarma had told him Kunkali slept, the leaves became very excited. They headed for him again but kept at ground level this time, parted to let him pass, and then formed a high pillar behind him. They topped each other, until they were at least ten feet high and six feet in width. Hanuman watched the pillar form, peering nervously over his shoulder. "Show them no fear, and they will let you be," his Master's voice directed calmly in his mind, and the little Swami obeyed.

The pillar continued to trail behind him, and when he looked at it again, he saw that it now had the semblance of a face. Its mouth yawned, a maw with a vortex in its center. The tattered leaf things spun about in the maelstrom, forming concentric circles. For an instant, Hanuman felt a terrible dread, and his legs began to move backward, for he thought he'd be sucked into the orifice. But Vishnarma demanded, "Calm yourself," and Hanuman smothered his panic.

During the entire walk to the bower, the pillar followed him, but in the end, it veered off into the Shadow Wall, where it crumbled, its thousands of leaf entities drifting back onto the garden path.

Swami Hanuman tiptoed under the creepers sheltering Kunkali's bed. Grinning skulls hung from the ropy vines, held by narrow stems, as if they'd grown there from buds. Hanuman pushed his way into the well of night, and, there at his feet, he saw the sleeping goddess. Energy sputtered up and down her limbs in flashes. The light delineated her ebony features and naked body. Her eyes were, as always, open, golden ellipses with red, bloodshot traceries. By her heavy breathing and mumbling and the gnashings of her fangs, he knew she was dreaming. She stirred and tossed fitfully at intervals, as fly-like life buzzed around her head. Sometimes her lolling tongue lashed out, caught an insect, and rolled it in between her lips.

As Hanuman crept to her side, his head brushed a clattering object, and he started. Looking up, he saw her girdle of skulls dangling from a vine loop. She was snoring now. The noise was very hollow, as if her nasal passage were a massive cavern. It seemed to stir the skulls above to clatter more. Hanuman stared at the long, sleek figure. The pendulous breasts heaved with her deep sleep.

Quickly he lowered the first flower and let the pitch drip into her ears and her mouth. Her lips smacked with delight at the taste. He brushed her eyes with the soaked fuzzball. Then he did the same with the other two flowers. When the three flowers were emptied of their human quick, he threw them away. He had no sooner risen, however, than a clacking din sounded around him.

The skulls on Kunkali's girdle were lowering and raising their jaws, speaking in their dead way. The skulls on the creepers followed suit. "Run!" shouted Vishnarma in his brain, and Hanuman obeyed.

His instincts directed him along a trail between an array of bushes trimmed into shapes that only a deranged gardener could have designed. The shapes hurt his eyes, his very consciousness. Still he ran, concentrating on the shadowy climb ahead that led to the trail exit. Reaching it, he saw a bone-white tree that branched out over the Shadow Wall. The tree slanted close to the ground, and Hanuman ran up its trunk until the tree straightened, and he had to climb. Behind him, the night was shattered by a wild shrieking, and he could see a black mist roiling toward him. "Hurry!" Vishnarma urged from the other side of the wall.

Swami Hanuman reached a branch that was so thick he could race along its surface. He followed it until he was under a branch that extended outside the garden. Then he leaped, caught the limb, swung like his monkey namesake atop it, and crawled to its end. As he peered down, he saw the roiling blackness reach the branch he'd just left.

Hanuman dropped beyond the Shadow Wall into his Master's arms. As they fled, the cloud hovered at the wall lip, crackling energy in its fury.

"Now you have an advantage over the awesome powers of Kunkali," Vishnarma told him. "The life quick from the fuzz-ball flowers will affect her judgment for a time. Her thinking will be severely altered. She will ignore what is important and become attracted solely to her appetites. Kunkali will be unable to think and plan. But this state will last only a short time. You must act with speed, my son."

With speed, Hanuman agreed, as George Buchan braked the car before the police cordon.

FORTY-SEVEN

Dan Terranova was hoarse from arguing with the authorities. Again and again he'd assisted Horace Birch in convincing them that they ought not to move in immediately, that the lives of four girls in the ashram could be at stake.

Birch had willingly used Mai Yogini, too. He promised her total immunity from prosecution, and she made a valiant effort to explain to the others that there were "things beyond life" in the large house on the far left. The result was blank stares and grins, until Charlie Adair suddenly arrived with Hughes and the Boston commissioner. What Adair then added from his experience on the wharf, about the hands "as big as catchers' mitts" and the speed with which the Thugs had dispatched three Boston detectives, made them pause. FBI man Parker theorized that possibly the Thugs injected themselves with something that enlarged the hands and gave them more strength.

Again, as at the Lincoln burial site, more than the local police were present. Boston had contributed the closest thing it had to a SWAT team, and some of the metropolitan district commission and state police had also contributed. Fortunately, Terranova had contacted Horace Birch first. Together they'd held the veritable army in check at the corner of Grey Park East, the short, affluent Cambridge street a quarter-mile from Harvard Square. At the street's end, on the left-hand side, was the Thug ashram.

The rest of the area was cleared for the safety of the hostages. At one home a dairy truck pulled up, and the inhabitants were secretly ushered out. At another the residents were sneaked into the back of a diaper service van. And at the house opposite the ashram, a policewoman dressed in civilian clothes entered, then left with a pair of eightyish sisters who'd already been very concerned about "the goings-on" across the way.

Birch checked his watch. Where the hell were Steve Wrench and his crowd? Reading him, Captain Charlie Adair volunteered, "Dan and me understand these scumbags, Mr. Birch. Why don't the two of us sneak into the place, free the kids, and then you can give with the tear gas."

Birch held up the house diagram that had been provided by the Cambridge City Hall. "And just how do you propose to do that, Captain? There's land almost the size of a lot surrounding the place. Even the men who've had tactical-style training would have a hell of a hard time approaching undetected in daylight."

"What about that garage and shed in the rear?" Adair pointed.

"Man, it's daylight, I said! They could see you easy enough from the upper floors, if you tried the roof of either building." Birch studied Adair from head to toe. "And you aren't exactly a little guy, either."

"I ain't in worse shape than your man Wrench."

Horace Birch grinned. "Not the way I saw it back in Lincoln."

Adair grunted. "Okay, I deserved it. I was out of line. I'd

like to make up for it a little. Christ, I saw three of my boys killed by 'em. 'Sides, I like kids. Got a bunch of daughters myself."

"Thanks anyway, Captain," Birch said with compassion. "But I'm afraid we need another plan."

The commissioner came over with a look of "What's he mucking up now?"

"The captain was just offering suggestions," Birch covered. Adair walked toward one of the squad cars, wiping the sweatband on his hat.

That was when George Buchan's car screeched to a halt beyond the cordon.

"What took you so long?" Birch demanded. He threw a cigar stub into the gutter.

"We had trouble." Wrench looked down the street. "Which one is it?"

Horace Birch saw that Wrench's mouth was twitching. "The last one on the left."

"Do you need an army like this? Tell them at least to turn off their radios. It'll be a miracle if they don't know we're here."

Birch nodded. "Couldn't be helped."

"My Santha's in there," Wrench muttered.

Terranova joined them. "Sir," he told Birch, "this is Swami Hanuman. He can get in the place, if anyone can."

Birch could sense Parker's eyes on him, filled with challenge. The FBI man had his own ideas about what to do and was itching to get his own scenario in motion. But these weren't terrorists, goddammit.

Besides, he had heard about the Swami's climbing skill from Wrench. Birch turned to the odd little man in the blue turban. "I want your honest opinion. Do you think we're too late?"

"No," Hanuman replied simply. "But we must begin now."

Birch blinked at the Swami. "Okay," he agreed. "Then it's all yours." He glowered at Parker with an unspoken "And don't you try to interfere."

Swami Hanuman went to Wrench and Shastri, huddled with them for a few seconds. Then he took off his turban, gave it to them, and left. He walked slowly down the street beneath the thick shelter of the elms and maples that lined the walk.

Dan Terranova was saying, "The Yogini told me that the name's Kurt Leinster. She says he's the Huzoor."

Rama Shastri shook his head. "It can't be. I saw the Huzoor in the Temple of Satī. He was a giant, bearded, with a voice that rumbled like thunder. I'm not surprised that Leinster is connected with them, but he can't possibly be the Huzoor." He went to Terranova's car, where Mai Yogini was sitting, bent over the opened window, and spoke to her in low tones.

"Hey, where's the little guy gone to?" someone asked.

"Hughes, get one of the boys on a roof to see if they can spot him," ordered the commissioner.

Later: "They see him. He's crawling through the grass to the house. The grass is pretty high there, sir."

"Who is he, anyway?" asked Parker aggressively. "He wasn't with you in Lincoln last night."

Wrench lit his pipe, his raw eyes concentrating on the pipe bowl as if it were the only thing worth noting. In fact, he was very aware of the FBI man, aware that he, like the rest of them, was exhausted from lack of sleep, his frustrations close to the surface. Wrench weighed his words; he wanted to impress the federal man. "His name is Swami Hanuman. Years ago he used to earn his keep crawling in and out of the Jap lines in Burma. Best man the Indians had."

"He certainly was." Horace Birch was enjoying this. He turned to Parker. "We even used to get reports about him Stateside. A born killer. If there'd been a bounty on Japanese lives, he'd be the richest man in India."

"It's hard to believe—"

"Well, believe it, Parker," roared Birch. "There's a message, loud and clear, in it, if anyone wants to learn a thing or two. We need fellows like Hanuman who understand this Thuggee problem better than we ever will. You've seen what they're like firsthand. You've even tried to interrogate the one Thug prisoner we've got. He just sits there, grins at us, and keeps repeating his prize mantras."

"There's no reason to get so worked up, Horace. I—"

"Horace is it now? Listen, Parker, you've been standing here eyeing me as if I'm a fucking idiot all morning, and that's enough to limit you to a 'Mr. Birch' permanently. If you don't approve of how I'm running things, then take a walk. But take your boys along with you. I don't need them, if you still want to barge into that house without concern for the lives of those little girls!"

Parker opened his mouth, closed it, and headed for his car. He beckoned to his men, who joined him. But they didn't pull away.

Horace Birch breathed in the morning air. "Goddamn mosquito. Too many commanders on the battlefield always hurt the strategy."

Wrench let the pipe smoke linger in his mouth, and he savored it. And so much for keeping the peace, he thought.

Hanuman was against the house. There was a drainpipe at the border of the side wall. Hanuman could climb it to the boxed-in enclosure of the back porch. From there he might find a means of entry.

He went to the pipe, felt it, concluded it would hold him. He shinnied up the drain. He had stretched to reach the porch when he heard voices from the window at his right. He turned and peered into the room. He saw four little girls. One of them was lying on a cot, crying, while another, wearing a similar white frock, was seated by her side, stroking her hair. A younger girl was huddled in the corner next to the window. She was in the arms of the seven-year-old who had called Gauri Bala a witch in the Redeemed Host church.

Hanuman tapped on the window.

The eldest looked out at him. Hanuman smiled at her and signaled for her to open the window.

She did, but only slightly.

Hanuman said, "The police have sent me." He remembered the one and only Western show he'd ever watched on American television. He added, "I am a good Indian."

"How do we know for sure?"

"Would I be here outside the window if I were like the others?"

That convinced Christine Ark, who told the bigger girl, "Let him in, Jenny."

Once inside, Hanuman went to the door and listened. He tried the knob. The door was locked. Hanuman turned to the girls. He squinched his nose. Christine giggled. Chloe looked at her sister, then at Hanuman, wiped her eyes, and giggled, too. "I am a friendly funny-looking Indian," Hanuman told them, understanding why they laughed. "Continue to smile instead of weeping, children. I will help you escape."

He went to the closet, took one of the hangers that held their coats, and removed the wire. Placing a finger to his lips, Hanuman warned, "We must be very brave and very quiet." Each one nodded. Christine giggled again. Hanuman told her patiently, "Please—even laughter will reveal us to them. Behave, and I promise to make many more funny faces for you when we are free." Christine slapped her palm against her mouth.

Hanuman fiddled with the wire and, once it was straight enough, placed it in the lock. A moment later the lock clicked. Hanuman paused, listened again, and then opened the door slightly. The corridor outside was empty, but he could hear a voice nearby, muffled but nevertheless not too distant. Hanuman whispered to the girls that he would return.

The Swami crept along the corridor wall, stopping before a door on the way and pressing his ear against the paneling. Assured there was no one behind the door, he continued. A dozen feet farther, he eased up level with a door on his right. He could hear voices shouting a chant. Carefully, slowly, he turned the knob and peeked out at the balcony above the dais room. Then, after a surveillance of the balcony's reach, he glided to its railing.

Below, a drop of at least twenty feet, Kurt Leinster was speaking to his followers. Santha Wrench was seated on a pillow before Gauri Bala. Hanuman returned to the door, closed it, and darted back to the children.

"We must find the porch now, little ones, and we must be very silent. Like tiny mice." He could see by their smiles that they liked his simile. They moved in single file, Hanuman in the lead. They were passing the entrance to the balcony when

Chloe made a face to sneeze. Christine quickly pressed a finger under Chloe's nose. The sneeze died.

There were three more doors ahead, two on the left and one at the end of the hall. Hanuman checked the two side doors for sound and motioned the children on until they were before the last one. Again he listened awhile and turned and winked at them. The porch was empty. Hanuman opened the door and ushered them into the daylight.

It was still late winter and cold enough that the girls began to shiver. Hanuman directed Jenny to climb over the banister and drop to the garage roof a few feet below. Then he picked up Chloe, who was rubbing her eyes from the sun glare and, bending over the banister, lowered her into Jenny's arms. When he had the two others safely down, he descended. The roof was flat, and they were able to cross it with ease. It ended at a picket fence bordering another yard. The tactical force, spotting them with their binoculars from a surrounding roof, notified the men below, and a handful were now waiting beyond the fence to assist.

As soon as the girls were in police custody, Hanuman had the men relay the message that he'd seen Santha Wrench alive and that he wanted her father, George, and Rama Shastri to join him.

A Cambridge police chief complained, "What the hell are we here for?"

Rama Shastri took Horace Birch's arm and led him where they wouldn't be overheard. "With the Swami's guidance, we have a reasonable chance to free Santha. Otherwise, the moment the police attack full force, the Thugs will either escape with her or . . ."

"Or make her a Thug victim."

"Yes, and that can be done so swiftly that no tactical force man could prevent it. I beg you, sir, to hold them back a while longer."

Birch agreed but warned Shastri to be careful. Wrench, Shastri, and George Buchan took a back route to the yard behind the garage. Nirmal Kapur watched them go, depressed that, because of his head injury, he could not follow the Swami.

In the yard, Hanuman quickly explained his plan. He was counting on his secret knowledge of Kunkali's current state. They climbed the fence and started to head for the ashram.

They were in front of the ashram porch when they heard the shrieking from within the building.

"Holy Christ, what are they doing in there!" Wrench cried, breaking out into a sweat.

"I don't think that was Santha, Steve," Shastri replied. "It was too inhuman."

Hanuman ordered Wrench into action. He hoisted Hanuman until he could reach the porch edge. Then he hoisted Shastri and George. George, in turn, lowered his arms, grabbed Wrench's wrists, and pulled him to the banister, where the big man could get a grip. Wrench managed to get onto the porch, and Hanuman opened the door to the corridor.

More shrieking met them, and this time it was very human. George and Shastri held Wrench back. Hanuman whispered, "Remember, we can only win, Mr. Wrench, if we maintain control." Drenched with perspiration, Wrench nodded.

Gauri Bala's scream from Kunkali's attack reverberated throughout the street. The toughest of the policemen felt their skin crawl. Officials stormed around Birch, demanding action. Parker and his FBI men rushed from their cars to add their outrage.

"I've never heard anything so piteous in my life" came from the Commissioner. "Birch, we can't let this go on."

The government man looked at Nirmal Kapur for help. Birch knew that he was somehow linked to the Swami. "What do you think?" he asked.

"Not until the Baba gives the okay."

"Who is this Indian kid, anyway?" the Cambridge police chief demanded.

"He's a rock star, sir," replied one of his men. "I've seen his face on posters all over Harvard Square."

"A rock star! Since when is my department run by a goddamn rock star!"

"I'm one of Swami Hanuman's disciples," explained Nirmal.

The chief flustered, then raged at Horace Birch. "Look here. I don't care if you pull in my entire department on a federal rap afterward, we're going in."

Dan Terranova wedged between them. "Lieutenant Terranova here, sir. Boston police. With all due respect, I think Mr. Birch is right. I've tangled with this Thug bunch and know how dangerous they are. They've a hostage in there, and I think she'd be dead before the tear gas even began to work."

"Those screams may mean she already is."

"I know. I know, sir," Terranova soothed. "But just in case she isn't, I'd like to suggest that I take a couple of your men with me and reconnoiter the place for a few minutes. Maybe we'd end up with a clear picture of exactly what's going on."

The chief pursed his lips. "Okay, but make it fast. Sooner or later the media'll be squeezing in and demanding to know why we're just standing here playing with ourselves."

Birch thought, The media. He was already very worried about their probes on the Arlington fracas and the Lincoln burial site. There were certain kinds of pressure that Washington couldn't ignore. He said hoarsely, "Go ahead, Lieutenant Terranova."

Dan Terranova set off with two of the best men from the tactical force. They kept to the tree shadows on the street. Nearing the house, they went toward the high bushes boxing in the walkway. They ran stooped over, to prevent anyone seeing them from the windows. It was far from foolproof, but the best they could do.

"I'll go first," said one of them. "I've got baby here." He patted his automatic rifle.

They were crossing the grass patch before the front porch when the man cursed. "I've tripped over something!"

Terranova barely saw the wire before the ground caved in to reveal a pit at least ten feet deep crowded with massive boulders. He heard the first tactical cop land, and suddenly Terranova was dangling above him.

But only for a moment. He was swung backward in a short

arc and slammed against the pit's sides. The muscles of his right arm stretched until he thought they'd dislocate. The second tactical cop was holding on to his wrist and forearm. He'd grabbed Terranova just as he toppled, and now he was trying to brake himself by digging his heels into the ground. But he had started to slide, too. "Oh, Gawd, Lieutenant!" he cried. "I'm gonna join you!"

Terranova collided with the pit side again. As he began the return swing away, blood poured from his temple across his cheek and eyes. He shoved his free arm upward and tried to get a handhold, but the pit's side was smooth, tamped evenly with spades.

He felt his body lower, slightly. The tactical cop was being pulled nearer the pit's edge. Just then Dan heard brush crackling and the heavy thump of someone running. Then another hand, thick and strong, worked down his arm beyond the elbow and pulled Terranova clear of the pit.

He looked at his rescuer. Sweet Jesus, it was Charlie Adair.

The captain was breathing heavily. "Hi, Smart-Ass," he said.

"Jeez." The tactical man looked down at his partner. "Smithy's skull's caved in." He cleared his throat, added, "What a fucking hole! Look at those boulders. Must be the way they trap dangerous animals in India!"

Dan asked, "Birch send you here, Captain?"

Adair wiped his brow, then spit. "I sneaked away from the cordon when I saw him send you out."

"Thanks, sir. If you hadn't come along, I'd be like Smithy."

"I just wanted to make certain you wouldn't fuck things up." He glared at the wire. "And sure as shit, you did. You tripped the alarm." Breathing normally again, he moved on.

"What about poor Smithy?" It was the tactical man.

"You go report it to the jerk-offs back there, feller," Adair muttered. He disappeared into the bushes. Terranova got on his feet. "I dropped my gun, give me the special," he told the cop. He was in a rush to prevent Adair from going into the place without him.

"Should I go report like he said, Lieutenant?"

Terranova glanced at the crumpled body below. "Yeah," he agreed. "You better do that."

FORTY-EIGHT

Inside the ashram, Hanuman scanned the balcony. Except for an ancient, mirrorless sideboard, it was empty. He motioned, and they all lowered to crawl to the balcony rail. The first to look below, Hanuman whispered back to them, "Santha is still alive."

The rest just breathed deeply.

George then joined the Swami, his eyes on the dais. Santha was in the final throes of a convulsion. She was on her back, her legs kicking out slowly. Foam trickled down the sides of her mouth. Then her body relaxed and she was still. There seemed to be a glow around her that was gradually disappearing.

George Buchan's hand held the gun Terranova had slipped to him before they left. His eyes focused on Kurt Leinster, seated on his throne. George uttered a low growl and raised the weapon shakily. "Easy, son," Wrench warned, grabbing his wrist.

"It was Leinster all the time," Shastri whispered, half to himself. Then, to the others: "See, he still wears the remnants of makeup. Probably, in the Temple of Satī, only the inner circle of the Thug band knew his true identity, that he wasn't an Indian."

Hanuman nodded. "Yes. An American was picked by Kali. Only an American could lead them here, where they'd be even more invisible."

A bell rang, high on the north wall.

Kurt Leinster leaped up. His mind had been immersed in his awe that Santha had absorbed the spirit of Kunkali so completely. Tragic as Gauri Bala's death was, he now saw the wisdom in her destruction. Santha was a far greater receptacle and should rule from now on among the women. She would become his consort; they would be children of the same Mother. Together they would create a new race. Life was now like the epic poems he'd desired to write, in which gods and men communed with each other again.

But then the alarm bell had rung.

"A raid," Makunda had said. "Why didn't Kunkali warn us?"

His Huzoor could not answer.

Makunda had made a wry face and left in disgust. Elvira Moniz, reading the Thug's look, had followed, to ensure that Makunda wouldn't betray her Lord.

Now an acolyte raced to the foot of the dais. He'd been looking out of the front window. "Police, my Huzoor!" he cried. "Two of them fell in the pit."

Leinster strode forward and regained command. "Bring the children! We will need hostages!"

Sahib Khan and three women headed for the stairs.

"Quick, Steve," Shastri whispered. He saw then that Wrench and George were gone. Hanuman was heading for the balcony's end, where the drapes hung down to the throne area.

Where was Steve? Shastri heard the screech of wood, but before he could look, Sahib Khan appeared at the top of the stairs. The Thug's voice rang out, "Rama Shastri!" and the three female acolytes behind him froze.

Below, the Thug gurus grouped their disciples and rushed the stairs. Shastri's name sent the Indians into a fever of hatred. A reckless craze gripped them that he must pay for their panic. Leinster, still on the dais, bellowed at them to return, but their rage drove them up the stairs instead.

Shastri aimed his Walther .32, but Sahib Khan approached him with a defiant, twisted grin, his rumel swinging.

You fanatical fool, Shastri thought, ready to press the trigger. You, at least, will go down. But a rumble and vibration in the floorboards distracted him.

"Out of the way, Ram," Stephen Wrench shouted. Shastri sidestepped, and the sideboard moved past him. Wrench and George were behind it, pushing it with all their might. One of its compartments opened, and two huge canisters filled with aromatic oil rolled out. Sahib Khan gripped the railing and flipped himself to the floor below.

The rest of the Thugs, though, weren't so fast. Some turned, only to collide with those behind, while the ones on the topmost stairs received the brunt of the canisters and the sideboard. Its momentum carried it off the balcony, and it hurtled down the stairs with half of the Thug force beneath it.

"A perfect strike, Steve!" said George exuberantly.

Rama Shastri looked to see how Hanuman was faring. The Swami had leaped from the balcony to the drapes and was sliding down to the dais. Kurt Leinster was below him, bent over. Shastri stood at the balcony railing and saw an opened compartment in the statue's base. Leinster was extracting something from its depths. "Steve—the rishis' scrolls!" Shastri cried out. Leinster was cradling the rolls of parchment in his arms.

Wrench and Shastri were moving to cover Hanuman from the balcony when, in the building's rear, the woodshed, a cubicle of flame from Chundra Bala's pyre, spread its inferno to the sedan.

The gas tank exploded and, with it, the garage. The house wavered on its foundations, and the south wall began to crumble slowly. Wrench grabbed Shastri's arm and yanked him from the railing and onto the staircase, just as the balcony split down its middle. They tumbled to the main level, surrounded by falling wood, plaster, even bricks from the chimney. Rama Shastri was buried in the rubble; Wrench escaped with only a bruised shoulder where the edge of a beam struck him.

But George, his gun lost, went down with the balcony planks as they parted. His hands flailed out and caught what remained of the railing. It dangled above the pews and, hand over hand, he descended, holding on to the rungs, his eyes on Santha's body. She was still unharmed, he saw, but some of the Thugs were grouping directly below him. He dangled precariously for a moment, not daring to drop to the ground.

The entire ceiling began to groan and creak, and, with a tremendous rending noise, its top poured into the ashram throne room. The Thugs scattered. George Buchan let go of his hold and landed safely on a pew bench. Then he lay prone and covered the back of his head with his hands until the downpour stopped.

When he rose, clouds of dust billowed everywhere, but through them he saw that Wrench was on his feet. The big man still retained his Browning .38, and he fired once, twice, into the dust. Someone screamed.

Wrench shouted, "Are you out from under yet, Ram?"

"Almost, Steve," came the reply, and there was the sound of bricks being kicked about.

George clambered over the pews. He had to get to Santha. He reached the aisle and saw Hanuman on his knees. The Swami had been thrown out of the dais area by the blast and was trying to right himself. A figure hurtled from the cloudiness, arms outstretched in a rumel thrust. George shouted a warning to Hanuman, grabbed a beam that jutted from a pew, and swung. The beam met Ramanuja in the face, and his nose flattened and spurted blood. George swung again, and the Thug was hurled back into the murk.

"The scrolls," Hanuman blurted, still groggy. "Get the scrolls. The Huzoor is nothing without them!"

The Huzoor, George Buchan thought. He had difficulty thinking of Kurt that way. This was Kurt Leinster, the son-ovabitch who had kidnapped Santha, maybe hurt her beyond repair. He ran for the dais.

Wrench spotted him, bellowed as he turned, and fired again at an approaching Thug. A groan, a thud, then, "Com'on, you buggers!" Wrench waited. Then he heard them shuffling, dim outlines closing in. He still couldn't see all of them.

Shastri was hard at work nearby, flinging the rubble off his chest. Wrench didn't dare leave him, lest Thugs rush his fallen comrade.

Wrench pulled the trigger twice more, but the flashes showed him nothing. He had missed. Wrench peered into the settling dust, determined to make every bullet count, when someone tackled him from the rear. His face was slammed against the floor, skin tore from his cheek. Knees dug into his sides as Sahib Khan straddled him, yanked his head back, and started to tighten the scarf.

Footsteps, heavy, thundered to his side. A blast burned behind Wrench's right ear and deadened all sound, but he felt air flow into his lungs again. The smell of cordite was thick, stifling. Wrench pushed Sahib Khan from his back and gaped at the bullet hole in the Thug's temple. Above him a broad, thick-featured face was speaking. Then sound returned in a rush, and Wrench heard Charlie Adair say, "You owe me one."

"Like hell I do!" Wrench roared, but Adair was helping Shastri. Dan Terranova, the side of his head a bloody streak, suddenly appeared and joined in the effort to pull the Indian free.

As soon as Shastri was safe, Terranova headed for the black smoke pall ahead. He was convinced the Leader of the Thug band would be behind that. He had to see the man who had commanded the deaths of so many, the man responsible for the mass grave at Lincoln. The policeman's special in his hand seemed to urge him on. It was as though he were an avenger, had been spared in the past just so that he could stop this special Thug. Hadn't he been on the brink of death three times and survived?

Wrench searched for his daughter among the rest of the ashram people. They had backed to the north wall and were huddled together. The dust had settled in this part of the room, and Wrench could see that they were frightened, even slumped in defeat. Outside, police and fire engine sirens were closing in. There was noise at the entrance.

"Santha!" Wrench called out in agony. "Santha!"

George Buchan's mind was echoing her name. Ahead, the dais area was congested with smoke. The draperies were burning, the ceiling above him was like a radiating coal. He flung himself through the churning maw.

A sheet of fire missed his face by inches. Hot coal from a

flung brazier hit his hair and clothes. He fell, slapping at the burning areas and yelping with pain. He rolled onto his back and saw Bidhan step toward him. But Bidhan stopped at a sound behind him. The Thug turned, and the same brazier whapped across his neck and shoulders. Bidhan's thick fingers gripped the metal stem and pulled. Bidhan blinked as he discovered Hanuman at its end. Forgetting George, the Thug grabbed for the Swami.

Rama Shastri, racing for the dais, came upon Bidhan just as the giant was about to close his fingers on Hanuman's neck. When Bidhan saw the foremost Thuggee enemy within his range, he quickly seized Shastri's shoulder.

Rama let himself be pulled closer and shoved the Walther .32 into Bidhan's face. The Walther's muzzle exploded.

George gasped, "Look!"

Covered with Bidhan's flesh, blood, and bits of brain, Rama Shastri still managed to follow George's direction.

Leinster was before them, his arms raised. He called shrilly, "Kunkali, my Mother, save me! Kunkali, come to my aid!"

The smoke darkened. Leinster disappeared from view. Hanuman and Shastri backed, choking. But George leaped past the barrier.

He found himself in a circle of light, free of the blaze around it. Four gigantic black arms extended out of a column of white mist before Leinster. Sparks of light crackled through the swirling milkiness. Leinster was placing the rishis' scrolls into the clutching fingers of hands at least a foot wide.

Kurt Leinster turned, saw George, and bent for Santha. George screamed, "No-o-o!" and left the ground in a flying tackle.

Leinster gripped the sacred pickax. George hit Leinster's knees and both of them struck the floor. Leinster grunted, raised the pickax. George clawed at the fingers gripping the handle. He rolled his weight onto Leinster, and the pickax slammed against the ground. But Leinster maintained his grip.

Behind them, Terranova blinked his smarting eyes. He was half-blinded from his passage through the smoke. When he saw the struggling figures on the floor, he gripped the special with both hands. "Hold it!" he shouted. "Police!"

Terranova aimed the gun's muzzle at the face staring up at him. It was as white as the swirling murkiness, and it seemed to disassemble and come together again—except for the unflinching red, raw eyes. Eyes filled with rage, pain, bloodlust.

Kurt Leinster's past with Kali had left its sign. "Get on your feet!" Dan Terranova bellowed with revulsion and hatred.

Leinster pushed George away as he stood up. George leaped to his feet, prepared for more trouble, but Leinster was still, his head tilted to the side, the pickax in his hands.

"Drop the ax," Terranova commanded.

Leinster's eyes swept to Santha. "She's mine," he challenged George. "She's mine now."

"Shoot him, Lieutenant. Shoot him," George said. He stared longingly at the gun.

"Drop the ax," Dan repeated and took a step forward.

Leinster looked through him.

He's waiting for something, Terranova suddenly knew.

SOMEONE, he heard then, a rasping current of sound that froze his marrow. The circle of light became colder, brighter. Terranova spun despite himself, facing the awesome arms, black, sinuous, reaching for Leinster. SOMEONE, It repeated, and the blast of it sent George reeling back. Terranova balanced against the force. Leinster, he saw, was heading for the embracing arms.

George shouted from somewhere, "Dan, get away from them!" Then the place shuddered, tilted. Dan Terranova lost his footing. His special fired into the floorboards, once, twice. Terranova struggled to rise again. A face loomed above him, and the detective lifted his arm to ward off the blow he saw coming. Leinster's pickax raked Terranova's shoulder, lowered, and went in just below the collarbone. For a second the two men faced each other. Terranova felt himself being lifted, standing on his tiptoes. His life breath was lost somewhere in his chest. The room, Leinster, his own name, meshed into a meaningless blur.

Leinster pressed the point of the pickax in farther. Terranova slumped, and his weight pulled the weapon down. Leinster placed his foot on the body, wrenching the ax free.

Leinster turned in time to see George Buchan carrying Santha into the smoke. He heard Stephen Wrench calling her name, close now. They were all converging—Shastri, Hanuman, the police. Yet he hesitated.

COME, She commanded.

Leinster saw the faces of his enemies rushing into the circle of light. He threw himself into the embracing lower arms of Kunkali. Swiftly, with such speed that the rest barely saw it, She lifted him into the white column. The column ascended into itself. Leinster and the Goddess were gone.

FORTY-NINE

The ambulance sped through the Cambridge streets. Police cars, sirens wailing, went before them, clearing the way. Within, Stephen Wrench stared at his unconscious daughter. Following, Horace Birch drove George Buchan, Hanuman, Shastri, and Nirmal Kapur. They were silent as they thought of the morgue wagon behind them with Dan Terranova's body.

Captain Charles Adair sat next to it and wiped the sweatband of his hat. Then he pulled the sheet down and stared awhile at Dan's profile. He spoke aloud. "Smart-Ass, you sonovabitch, why did you have to get yourself killed? Christalmighty, no one expected you had to be so much of a cop. You could've had it sweet, boy, with your brains and good looks. Department head some year, sitting behind a big desk, waiting to have your sweet puss photographed by the newsies. Hell, but you had to screw it up by dying on duty." He coughed. "Aw, but I'll miss your smart-ass ways," he blurted. Then he quickly raised the sheet again. "G'wan, but I'm sick of the sight of ya."

* * *

Kurt Leinster watched. He thought maybe he was above them, but sometimes it seemed that he was right on their level. The place he was in was dark and very cold, and only when one of the fluttering things with leering, almost human faces went by with their tongues of fire was he able to see the cavern clearly.

The landscape hurt his eyes. Nothing was connected as it should be. The angles shifted, even dissolved; the only constant thing was the tremendous cold.

Mother, he called, I see her now.

Yes, She replied, and he thought he detected a hint of laughter.

Mother, he asked, why are we here? Why am I alone? Why did I lose her?

Do not think of the world, my son. Nor of her. Meditate instead and be glad of heart that we are together.

Kurt Leinster sighed. He tried to walk, but his legs refused to move.

See what you have done? he heard then.

Kurt looked below and saw Dan Terranova in the morgue wagon beneath the sheet. Yes, he thought; I did that.

But we didn't succeed, Mother. We were driven away. We had to flee. What is the meaning of all this?

He is dead, my son.

But the others aren't. George Buchan lives. Santha is not with me. I am alone here, Mother.

Things moved in the blackness. Another flying, leering face with a sparkling, forked tongue, and the landscape this time was composed of fungoid-like mounds with webbing between them. Kurt Leinster wondered what crawled on that webbing.

The cold continued. He wished he could walk. Just a step. One step.

Kurt tried to concentrate below or above or beside or wherever it was.

Santha Wrench's eyes were opening. "Baby," her father said.

"Daddy. Daddy," she repeated and started to cry.

* * *

This is who I should've killed. Directed the rumel at him first instead of even George or the others, Kurt thought. Daddy. He hated the word, the sound.

His Mother spoke then. Her words touched him like arctic fingers. We have the rishis' scrolls. They are still ours.

But why are we here, then? Why must we wait? Or are we waiting? Will I ever see Santha again, Mother? I shouldn't be alone here like this.

The ambulance had reached the hospital. "Where is George?" Santha asked suddenly. "Is George all right?"

"George is fine," Wrench told her.

"Are you certain?"

"Of course, Santha."

She reached out. He took her hand.

"George is all right," he repeated.

Santha raised her head. "You wouldn't lie?"

"That's enough," said the medic. "I better give her a shot."

"You wouldn't . . . ?"

Wrench grasped her hand. "I wouldn't. You'll see George soon."

"Poor Kesari." Santha Wrench wept. "I left him for Kurt. He's the Thug Lord, Daddy."

"I know, dear. Now rest."

The medic moved forward and injected his needle.

I don't understand, Mother, Kurt said. Why is Santha not with me? I love her. She should be with me. George is a fool. He has no vision. There is no destiny to him.

He waited. There was no reply. A winged thing landed before him on the ledge at his knees. Its tongue lashed left and right, and the cavern was lit up again. From the stalactites, scaly women were hanging. Their long tresses trailed, the hair ropy and blood-red.

Why do we stay here? Kurt asked. What are those dreadful women doing there?

Hibernating, She replied.

* * *

At the hospital, Wrench touched Hanuman's shoulders. "Will Santha every be really well again?"

The Swami replied, "Your love for Santha is very great." He nodded at George and Shastri. "The three of you are her recovery, her strength."

Wrench nodded. "Oh, please let his words be true," he prayed.

Mother, Kurt Leinster questioned, why don't You answer me? Is all this to remain a mystery? Why can't I walk? Why am I here? Why have I lost Santha Wrench?

He heard a distant laugh, hoarse, grating, faraway.

Kurt thought of the ledge at his knees. No, it was at his stomach now. Strange. Kurt waited for a flying thing to pass by again. When one did, he looked at the ledge in the light and saw that it was a gray, translucent block and that he was immersed within it.

Kurt called out. Mother, why am I trapped this way? What is this?

The cold was even more intense. Kurt vaguely remembered reading about someone being eternally a prisoner in a block of ice. It was from a poem, wasn't it? Satan, wasn't it? Why couldn't he remember? Mother, Kurt Leinster appealed, Mother . . .

So faraway now, a whisper of laughter.

What is happening to me? The ledge was up to his chest. Wings fluttered, and a foul, man-faced hybrid flickered bright streamers of tongue light before Kurt's eyes.

Please tell me, Mother. Please . . . What is happening to me?

It came so low. An arctic, neurological vibration, more than a voice: Hibernation. Hibernation. Hibernation.

The creature flew away. Everything was black. Everything was still. The ledge was up to his chin. The flying thing never returned. Before Kurt Leinster forgot all he'd ever known, the final vibration came: Sleep, my child, sleep.

EPILOGUE

The roof was the perfect place to be. Stephen Wrench looked down at the Hatch Shell area on the Esplanade. People were already coming in with folding chairs and blankets, and by 3 or 4 P.M. the whole lawn would be congested with them. Sitting down there with that mob was not for him, he concluded. He'd remain where he was, listen to the outdoor concert from the roof of his building.

Besides, today was a special one. Friends who'd meant so very much to him and Santha these past months were present. What more could he desire? He shook his drink and listened for the tinkle.

Nirmal Kapur plucked at his sitar. Wrench sat upright in his chair. Not again, he prayed. When Wrench had invited Hanuman and Nirmal for tea, Santha had insisted the musician bring the sitar along. Wrench, who'd endured a near-lifetime of the instrument, felt that Nirmal's half-hour of the droning variations on variations had sufficed.

The rest were all drinking tea and eating the cookies and brownies Santha had baked. Except Hanuman. He had his own kind of sweet tooth. At first Santha had considered making Indian pastry instead, but then decided against it. Too much Indian business at once still left her uneasy. Understandable, considering the nightmares that happened now and then.

That, and short periods of depression. It could've been much, much worse, Wrench told himself. Santha could be permanently "out of contact," as the specialists put it, or dead, even. Wrench shook his head as if someone had spoken to him: No, not dead. That creep Leinster had wanted Santha to be very much alive. For himself, the goddamn maggot.

There were also things that Santha didn't remember, and perhaps that was just as well. Something had happened to her

452

just before her rescue, and it was undoubtedly a happening that only someone with a foot in both worlds, like Hanuman, could understand or deal with. That was okay, too. Stephen Wrench had a feeling that probing any further would be similar to looking into the face of Medusa. Better to leave things alone.

Yet, at times, he knew they all wondered, was it really over?

Nirmal was talking about a rock opera. He wanted to compose one, in time. Something that encompassed East and West, that bridged both worlds through music. It was his usual chatter. He was seated on a blanket with the Swami. Hanuman had refused the refreshments, and, after much questioning, Santha had discovered the man's secret weakness. Yes, she told him, they had some of that in the freezer. He squatted now, spooning the last of the maple walnut.

Wrench heard George Buchan's low murmurs, next to Santha's lawn chair. Wrench grabbed for his pipe. He was sure he heard the peal of wedding bells months ahead.

Santha reassured George that she was okay, fine. She was in a lavender summer dress and matching flats. As she sprawled in the lawn chair, her hair glinted in the sunlight. "What are you looking at, Uncle Ram?" she asked.

Rama Shastri, who stood at the roof's edge, lowered his binoculars. Beyond him was the Charles, filled with boats, their white, blue, and yellow sails arching against the breeze. "The boating, Santha," he replied.

She giggled. "He's fibbing," she told George softly. "He's been watching the girls on the Esplanade for the last half-hour."

Wrench rose. He moved awkwardly in his summer shorts. He reminded himself he needed to change his life-style. Maybe he and Ram could take up jogging. Shastri didn't need it, but Wrench thought it might be lonely jogging along the Esplanade by himself. He joined his friend.

Rama Shastri had been very quiet lately, and Wrench understood that now that the Thug adventure was over, there was time to think and yearn. To miss India. To miss that woman, Ileana what's-her-name, he left back there.

Shastri broke the silence. "Be alert, my friend. Santha wished Hanuman here today. She'll bring up the matter soon."

Wrench almost inhaled his pipeful and choked. Shastri had warned him of the same thing earlier.

He looked at the group. Santha, George, and Nirmal were laughing at something. He said, "Look, she's smiling. She's just having fun, Ram."

"Santha hasn't discussed the matter with us once, Steve. I understand she talked to the doctors a little. But never with us together. And we were the ones present when it happened. Doesn't that concern you? It's as if she's frightened that one of us might give an opinion she doesn't want to hear. Especially Hanuman. If anyone could truly answer her questions, it would be he."

Just then, "Kurt" carried to them. Santha had started at last, as if on cue. They both neared.

Santha swallowed hard. She continued, "What was he, Swami Hanuman? He seemed a lost boy, and then at . . . at their ashram, he was so . . ." She couldn't finish.

In the hush that followed, Stephen Wrench saw George turn pale.

"Perhaps he was both persons," Hanuman suggested.

"But . . . how could that be? And could I have been so over-whelmed, so changeable, too? . . . Am I an evil person like him? Please tell me the truth. . . ." Tears came.

"Please, Santha," George pleaded.

"I have to know. I must understand this."

Hanuman stood. His turban was like a colorful bird perched on his head. "What is it you seek? A conviction of absolute goodness about yourself? To ask if Santha is evil is to request a guarantee of the outcome to your soul's lifelong struggle. A thousand gurus cannot answer you. How do you expect me to, then? You have survived to this very moment. You are the Santha of old, and perhaps more, because of your conflict. That speaks very well for Santha Wrench. But only to this moment."

Then Nirmal added his thoughts. "It's like a beat in music, Santha. It stirs you, excites you maybe, but you don't have to stick to it forever. You can always change the beat, play a different tune. Kurt Leinster only heard the same music. That was what he played, that was what he danced to. And it was all bad, all discord. That's not you, lady. One look at you, and a guy hears a lot of different sounds. He looks at you and thinks of a nautch dancer moving to the tabla drums, or, other times, it's a tenor sax talking about how you're sweet and lovely."

Santha beamed. "I could kiss you for that, Nirmal," she said, and, taking his hand, she drew him near and did.

Hanuman concluded, "Again the disciple outshines the Master."

Later the Swami and Nirmal left for other commitments, and Wrench went downstairs with them. Outside the building, he thanked Nirmal for saving the day. He shook both their hands and watched them until they reached Charles Street. Then he went back in.

Pausing in the lobby, he breathed deeply. Santha would remember Nirmal's words, he was sure. It was the kind of simple response the young woman needed. Santha Wrench inspired good, healthy feelings, romantic thoughts, music even.

On the roof again, he found Santha in deep conversation with George and Shastri.

"Santha has an announcement to make," George said.

She smiled broadly. "I've decided to go back to work, Daddy. Soon. I feel I can handle it now." She stood. "Swami Hanuman is right. At this moment everything speaks well for me." She extended her hand to George as the concert began. "I feel like dancing, kesari," she urged.

The pair waltzed along the roof. Passing Stephen Wrench and Rama Shastri, Santha waved to them. "Let's go around again," she told George and laughed. It was Kamala's laugh. Wrench looked at Shastri and knew that his old friend was thinking of Kamala, too.

GLOSSARY

achkan	man's tunic-like coat
akali	a political organization, often militant
akshara	sacred syllable
Arjuna	hero of the epic poem *Mahabharata*
Arun	Surya's charioteer, who is legless; symbol of dawn
asanas	postures used in yoga meditation
ashram	monastic abode
asrave	mental intoxication
attar	a perfume made from rose petals
avatar	a god descending into the world in human form
avidya	world illusion
baba	old man
babu	clerk
bayadere	dancing girl
bhakti	a person or life of service to God and mankind
Bharata Natyam	one of four classical dancing styles; temple dancing of Southern India
Bhowani	a name for Kali
Brahma	chief god of the Hindu trinity
charpoy	bed with ropes on sides
chela	disciple, pupil
chudders	sheets, bolts of cloth
dacoits	robbers
danda	bamboo staff
dassis	streetwalker
deva	good spirit
Devi	a name for Kali

Dharma	sacred laws, the path that a man follows according to his nature and station in life
dhai	midwife
dhoti	draped cloth worn by men
Fatima	daughter of Mohammed the Prophet; also, a name for Kali among Muslim Thugs
Ganesha	the elephant god
ghat	wharf; used for bathing, funeral pyres, and sacrifices to gods
ghee	clarified butter
Gita or Bhagavad Gita	book of verse wisdom
godown	warehouse
goor sugar	coarse sugar
Gurkha	member of race dominant in Nepal
guru	spiritual teacher, master
Huzoor	Lord
Kali	goddess of destruction
Kali Mahila Mandal	women's group
Kali Yuga	the present Age of the four basic Ages of the Hindu calendar; a Dark Age
karma	destiny brought about by one's acts
kaula	a form of tantra (Tantric Buddhism)
kesari	lion
kotwal	a police magistrate
kotwalee	police station
Kunkali	a name for Kali; the Man-Eater
lammergeiers	bearded vultures
mantra	a chant, spell, or prayer
maya	illusion
mudra	a gesture of ritual and religious significance
muri	parched rice
namaskar	greeting
nautch	a type of Indian dancing

nautch girl	dancing girl
Panjika	Hindu astrological almanac
Raj	rule
Raktavīja	demon who battled Kali
Ramasi	the secret language of Thuggee
rishi	seer, usually the most ancient; believed to be present at the Dawn of Time
rumel	the scarf or cord used by Thugs to strangle victims with
sadhu	holy man
sadvi	holy woman
samadhi	the state of pure consciousness
saptak	in music, equivalent to Western octave
sari	woman's draped garment
Shani	Saturn
shruti	enlightenment
Sikh	a follower of Sikhism, a religious movement
somosas	pastry-covered spiced vegetables
sonar	goldsmith
Surya	the sun god
suttee	practice of wives burning themselves alive on husband's funeral pyre
tantra	a type of esoteric, erotic yoga teaching
Thug death calls in Ramasi:	
Tamakhu Kha-lo!	Smoke-tobacco!
Sanp!	Snake!
iikka mark	a cosmetic mark on the forehead
Vedas	the earliest Indian scriptures
Vishnu	the second god of the Hindu trinity
Yoni	the female sexual organs

About the Author

LEO GIROUX, JR., has traveled in India and spent years as a student of the country. He lives in Medford, Massachusetts, with his wife.